ADVANCE PRAISE FOR *BONEYARD*

"*boneyard* is a restless dream of a book, one that lifts away from the dreaming writer only to turn and look back at him, regard him, and make his dream its subject . . . Skeptical of the dreamer, the book carps like a neglected lover, casting doubt on the author's honesty and motives. This house of mirrors is also a house of cards, which the author brings gleefully crashing down upon himself with baroquely entwined story-lines reminiscent of the best work of Bo Huston or James Purdy."

—Matthew Stadler

"*boneyard* does for the Amish diaspora what Junot Diaz did for Dominicans with *The Brief Wondrous Life of Oscar Wao*."

—Scott Heim

"*boneyard* is a horrifically alluring monster under the bed. It will draw you in on a bone-deep level; overawe you. Existentially profound and emotionally dangerous, this is a text that will make you surrender to the extremes of the unnameable pleasure at some bottommost outpost of experience from where the human drama can be viewed in an array of its most criminal loveliness and most personal violence. Read this and know how fiction can be a discovery."

—Lonely Christopher

"About a third of the way into this book, there's this stuff about Rosalie Lombardo, an early 20th century girl whose dead body has been kept almost perfectly preserved. People have been staring at her shiny, pretty, doll-like corpse in ways one never could—or should—in real life, imaging things they never would admit. *boneyard* is about how we stare at people, especially children, wanting to freeze them into figures we can possess, reform, make into what we want. It's also about how we present our selves to others, shiftily and slyly, that is, lyingly, as creatures we think they'll want and about our culture's obsession with victimhood. Intelligent cultural critique wrapped in a twisty, turny, funny, damning fairy tale that happened neither long ago nor far away but every day and here."

—Rebecca Brown

PRAISE FOR STEPHEN BEACHY

The Whistling Song

"An admirable, highly original tale . . . [by] an exuberant and nervy writer who is in awe of the open road and all of its beauty, irony, and menace."
—Meg Wolitzer, New York Times Book Review

"*The Whistling Song* has that energy and abandon of all great first novels. At the same time, the story never gets lost in its long bursts of honest, palpitating language. This book's wild force reminded me of the first time I saw John Malkovich on stage in *True West*."
— Jim Carroll

"A hypnotic, unshakable, painfully funny vision of America by a word-drunk writer."
—Kirkus Reviews

"Stephen Beachy's America—so fast and freewheeling and dangerous, so full of intoxicated language and pretty lies—clangs in my head like a fire truck."
—Bob Shacochis

Distortion

"Beachy's triumph of prose, hypnotic and lyrical, bathes his characters in the revealing light of a photographer's eye . . . An artistic and literary achievement."
—Jay Quinn

Some Phantom/No Time Flat

"Henry Miller said that the moment you have an original thought, you cease to be an American. These 'fissures in the architecture of the Dreamtime' are great unAmerican novellas."
—Thorn Kief Hillsbery

"This is some of the most interesting and exciting writing I've read in a long time. Not since Halldór Laxness, a completely unrelated author, have I been so simply surprised by the glamour and skill and darkness of another writer's art. Not so much a great book as a great reading experience. You forget how you got there, which is the best. Writer to writer I thank Stephen Beachy. This is how we *live*."
—**Eileen Myles**

"Bold, addictive, and hauntingly beautiful, Stephen Beachy continues his dissection of the American landscape and character through these two finely crafted and thematically linked novellas charged with memory, mystery, desire, violence, and the destiny deprived itinerants who lived and imagined them."
—**R. Zamora Linmark**

"Stephen Beachy has created a disturbing text that reaches from a darkness below our cities' streets, where children, desire, cruelty, and dissociation meet in a shadow land that readers will sadly recognize as contemporary North America. Suspense builds toward surprising, metaphysical conclusions. The work is creepy, desolate, and rich. Do not read before bedtime."
—**Stacey Levine**

"Stephen Beachy is a visionary. In these twin novellas, he explores madness and crime with the nocturnal lyricism of empty time and space. Beachy's dear criminals reach an exquisite isolation and so does his reader, a non place where categories collapse, like freedom and confinement, chaos and lucidity, the angelic and demonic. A harsh dream, and we will never wake."
—**Robert Glück**

boneyard

STEPHEN BEACHY

Verse Chorus Press

Published by Verse Chorus Press
PO Box 14806, Portland, Oregon 97293. www.versechorus.com

Portions of this book first appeared in *Chicago Review*, *Blithe House Quarterly*, *Shade*, and the anthology *Madder Love: Queer Men and the Precincts of Surrealism*.

Stephen Beachy would like to thank Steve Connell, Katherine Spielmann, Brian Pera, Jonathan Hammer, Tim Beachy, Lester Beachy, Lorraine Beachy, and Jonathan Brunn. Also the members of the Amish community in Nickel Mines who took the time to speak with me in 2006.

Jake Yoder would like to thank Lucifer, for the inspiration; Christ, for the salvation and for the excellent joke; Mr. L, for his innovative pedagogy; and his mother, for holding on as long as she did.

Front cover: Charles Burchfield, *The Sphinx and the Milky Way*, 1946, opaque and transparent watercolor, chalk, and crayon on wove watercolor paper. Frame: 64½ x 57 in.; 52⅝ x 44¾ in. Reproduced by permission of Munson-Williams-Proctor Arts Institute, Museum of Art, Utica, New York. 48.45

Book design by Steve Connell / Transgraphic (www.transgraphic.net)

Library of Congress Cataloging-in-Publication Data

Beachy, Stephen.
  Boneyard / Stephen Beachy.
    p. cm.
  ISBN 978-1-891241-33-8 (pbk.)
  1. Psychological fiction. I. Title.
PS3552.E128B65 2011
813'.54--dc22

                    2011015261

A Note from the "Author"

Although my name is on the cover of this book, the book's actual author is a boy—I'll call him Jake Yoder, although that isn't his real name—I met in 2006 when he was 14 or maybe 15 years old. I've written a fictionalized version of my encounters with Jake in my forthcoming novel *Glory Hole*, where he appears as Amos, but this is probably not the place to scrupulously disentangle the fictional version from the truth—and anyway, a lot of the details have by now become confused in my own mind.

I met Jake while I was working on an article about the shooting in the Amish schoolhouse in Nickel Mines, Pennsylvania. On October 10, 2006, the shooter, milkman Carl Roberts, walked into that one-room schoolhouse "talking nonsense," according to one of the survivors. He told the children that if they did what he asked, nobody would be hurt, then he sent the boys out, leaving ten girls in the school, aged 6 to 13. When the police showed up, he shot the girls and himself. Five of the girls died. Apparently, the shooter's infant daughter had died years before, and he'd never gotten over it. In letters he left behind, he also claimed that he'd molested two young relatives when he was 12, and was haunted by dreams of molesting again. His relatives denied the story, but sexual lubricant was found among the things Roberts took to the school, and it's assumed he was intending to molest the girls before he killed them.

When I arrived in Pennsylvania the weekend after the shooting, Jake Yoder was also visiting Lancaster County. It was through his cousin, an ex-Amish rocker, that I first made contact with Jake. Jake told me he was there for the funeral of his sister, one of the shooter's victims, but I also heard that he was only there because he was on tour with his cousin's band, Wrath of God. I was able to verify that Jake had attended the school in Nickel Mines for a brief period a few years before the shooting, but I also discovered he wasn't actually related to any of the dead or wounded girls. According to Jake's cousin, Jake was an only child. Should I believe anything he told me? He told me he was born into an Amish family. He told me his father had died in an accident "on the road" when Jake was very young; his father's horse and buggy was smashed by a wayward SUV (Jake claimed it was a hybrid; given the timeframe, however, I don't think that's possible.) He told me that a few years later his mother left her Amish family, that she took Jake and his imaginary sister along as she ran off with some man. The details about this man were always vague. Was he an evangelical preacher? A police detective? A train conductor?

Apparently he'd worked at least some of the time as a driver for the Amish, carrying vanloads of them from here to there. It's easy enough to imagine the mutual longing that could have developed between Jake's mother and this driver during long drives to weddings or funerals in neighboring states. Unaccustomed to the soporific vibration of the van's engine, her parents and siblings surely dozed off, while the driver flirted, imagining the texture of Jake's mother's hair, carefully hidden beneath her bonnet (Jake once told me that his mother was "kind of like" Nico, the German singer, composer, fashion model, and Warhol superstar, but I don't know if he was talking about a physical or psychological resemblance).

After Jake's mother married this man, her family shunned her. He was probably divorced, in which case he would have been considered an adulterer by the Amish. Jake and his mother and her new man lived together in Des Moines and possibly in the Ozarks, in southern Missouri and northern Arkansas. According to Jake, his mother worked as a nurse. At some point, probably when Jake was 10 or 11, she drowned herself.

It was sometime after his mother's suicide that he wrote the stories that make up this book. He told me he wrote them when he was in the sixth grade, attending a public school in Des Moines, and that they were the result of "creative exercises" he was encouraged to do by his teacher when he scored 100 percent on his spelling tests—which, according to Jake, he always did. Later, after a substitute teacher phased out these exercises, he told me he wrote them in his free time. The settings of his stories vary from his public school to Amish farms, mental institutions, and prisons—settings which, unsurprisingly, blur into each other. Many elements of Jake's stories are difficult to pin down. For example, while the city he calls "River City" in the opening story seems to be Des Moines, it also suggests the town of Riverside, Iowa, (the birthplace of *Star Trek*'s Captain Kirk and home of Jake's maternal grandparents) as well as Iowa City, which was given the fictional moniker of River City in that hideous musical, *The Music Man*.

It was never possible for me to map out an entirely consistent time frame of Jake's life between the ages of 10 or 11 and 14 or 15, after his mother's death, but he appears to have bounced around between his stepfather (the preacher or detective or conductor, who no longer wanted him), his Old Order Amish maternal grandparents near Riverside, his slightly less restrictive Old Order Amish paternal grandparents in Lancaster County, Pennsylvania, and possibly (I'm just guessing here) some mental institutions, juvenile homes, and foster families. At the time I met him, he was living with his ex-Amish rocker cousin in Des Moines, and sometimes with his cousin's bandmates in Iowa City. Jake considered himself a rocker too. He was a fan of Hitchcock's *Shadow of a Doubt* and an avid reader of Argentinean fiction.

The facts that Jake could never articulate seem clearer to me than the dubious accounts he gave me about his history: some assortment of life experiences had created a precocious, sexually confused, and deeply troubled boy. Probably because I was the first "author" he had ever met (although he now has a Facebook page and has "friended" hundreds of authors, using his Jake Yoder pseudonym), and because I was also connected to the Amish community (I grew up in a Mennonite church, and my grandparents, along with hordes of uncles, aunts, and cousins, were Old Order Amish), he gave me his stories to read. We met on four different occasions in October and November of 2006 (although in my novel *Glory Hole* these are compressed into only two). The last time we met was in an abandoned building that had once been used as an orphanage, near his grandparents' farm outside Riverside. It was a cold night and Jake had built a fire in the old fireplace. I'd read his entire manuscript at that point and was ready to discuss the stories, but I wasn't prepared for his own change of heart. As he roasted marshmallows, gazing dreamily into the fire, often letting the marshmallows crisp well past the golden-brown stage into lurid blackened husks, he explained to me that his stories had somehow caused the shootings at Nickel Mines. Having convinced himself that his stories were not only "evil" but "magical," he threw the entire manuscript onto the fire and ran wailing into the night. Despite my best efforts, I've never seen Jake again, although I've spoken to him on the phone. I was able to salvage his manuscript, but with significant portions of every single page charred and blackened so that sentences or whole paragraphs were completely illegible.

The shooter had been living out the clichés that fuel murderous dreams: innocence ruined, a flower destroyed in earliest bloom, a gob of spit in the face of an indifferent God. It's clear to me that Jake also felt somehow implicated in those murderous dreams. The manuscript itself offers plenty of possible reasons for this, from his own emerging sexual feelings and sexual guilt to his complicated and often adversarial relationship with Amish culture. Shortly after the night on which he ostensibly tried to destroy his manuscript (and it has occurred to me that my presence there was not incidental, and that, like Kafka's, Jake's desire to destroy his work was ambivalent at best), Jake went back to live with his grandparents and was baptized in the Amish church. Like Isidore Ducasse, Joris-Karl Huysmans, and Hugo Ball before him, Jake renounced his evil literary experiments and retreated into a traditional form of Christian faith. Of course nobody is much interested in Lautréamont's Song of the Good, Huysmans' late novels about Catholic faith, or Ball's post-Dada studies of Christian mystics. When I last spoke to Jake, I asked if he was writing anything at all, and he confessed that he'd published a short piece, under a different pseudonym, in the Amish magazine *Family Life*. Although he now doesn't approve of his own writing, or of literature in general, Jake has given me permission to do whatever I want with his manuscript as long as I don't publish it under any of his names. As a practicing member of the Amish church, the sort of recognition he might achieve as an author could only be understood as sinful, self-aggrandizing egoism. When I last spoke to him he did admit, however, that he still reads Borges at times, whom he considers a godly man.

I have done my best to recreate Jake's text based on the charred pages and my memory of the original, although I'll be the first to admit that the process has often required the use of my own invention.

Jake never titled anything. The title I have given to the novel is mine, not his, and it was not my first choice. I did not give the "stories" individual titles, as it was my sense that they constituted a single, indivisible work. The titles of the two sections are also mine, although the quotes from the Notorious B.I.G., Irenaeus, and Francis Picabia, and the illustrations reproduced from the *Martyrs Mirror*, are just as Jake had situated them.

S.B.

Editor's Note

When this unusual manuscript was presented to me I was not familiar with Stephen's work. I was, perhaps, vaguely aware that he had broken the story of one of those imaginary writers who haunted the edges of America's literary life with some fervor during the Bush years (See *New York* magazine, October 10, 2005). Given that connection, I was more trusting, I suppose, of his own discovery of a kind of idiot savant, a young Rimbaud, if you will, lurking among the Old Order Amish. In my conversations with Stephen, he was entirely convincing and consistent about his encounters with this boy, and adamant about the boy's existence. Since Stephen was, in any case, proposing that we publish the work in question under his own name, the fact that we could not confirm the existence of Jake Yoder posed no great ethical or legal dilemma for our esteemed press.

The unlikely story of the precocious Amish boy roused my own journalistic curiosity, however. The text itself hardly seems like the work of a child. It includes a whole array of unlikely references for a 12-year-old boy, even if we take into account that easily 50 percent of the text of the charred "original" is missing and that some of these references might be a result of Stephen's "invention." Stephen provided me with the boy's real name, making me promise not to reveal it, but not an address—he claimed the boy refused to divulge this, even to him. Although there are only an estimated 240,000 Amish living in the US, the boy's "real" name was little help, given the maddening repetition of particular surnames among the Amish, such as Yoder, Miller, Fisher, Stoltzfus, and Beachy. Since the Amish don't have telephones—and since Jake ignored my friend requests on Facebook—there was no way to track him down. Stephen himself claimed that the only way to reach him was to leave a message with an ex-Amish cousin, which I did. If I was lucky, I was told, Jake would give me a call.

The evidence in favor of Stephen's story, then, is limited to a copy of the "original" charred manuscript (see Appendix B for sample pages), a note supposedly from one of Jake's teachers with all identifying information blocked out (see Appendix A), a police report concerning the suicide of the boy's mother (see footnote 23), and one brief telephone call to yours truly from a squeaky-voiced creature who identified himself as the boy in question.

Then why, a discerning reader must wonder, would we agree to publish the book at all? The novel would certainly be of considerably less interest if not written by a 12-year-old Amish boy. Although our press champions work falling outside the parameters of mainstream fiction, this novel, if considered as the work of a sane adult, would be considered excessive and self-indulgent by any reasonable critic. Still, the text does offer an opportunity to help readers make sense of a culture that most Americans are completely unfamiliar with, outside of Hollywood portrayals in movies like *Witness* and in short-lived reality shows. Such mercenary distortions, fueled by our culture's vulgar desire to see the innocent corrupted and unassuming rural people paraded before our jaded sensibilities like so many monsters in a geek show, are hardly valuable sources of ethnographic information. And yet where can we turn? Moreover, in the process of conducting my own due diligence, I came to consider equally compelling possibilities for the origin of the text, possibilities that began to seem more and more likely the closer I examined it. With the help of my elucidating notes throughout, I believe these possibilities will become clear to all but the most obtuse or willfully naïve readers. If nothing else, I am convinced it is a work that will, in years to come, prove to be of great psychological interest, just as the works of de Sade, Genet, and the anonymous author of *Go Ask Alice* have revealed fascinating landscapes to those willing to forgive their stylistic excesses. One could say that it is in the spirit of the original Enlightenment project—to shine light upon the darker corners of the human mind, so as to better understand ourselves and to therefore forge a more benevolent social order—that I humbly present the text that follows.

Judith Owsley Brown, Verse Chorus Press

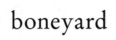

boneyard

They maintain that they have attained to a height
beyond every power, and that therefore they are free
in every respect to act as they please, having no one
to fear in anything. For they claim that because of the
redemption . . . they cannot be apprehended, or even
perceived, by the judge.

—Irenaeus, *Against Heresies*

Hold ya'all breath, I told ya'all, death controls ya'all
. . . I spit phrases that'll thrill you
You're nobody till somebody kills you.

—The Notorious B.I.G.

BOOK I

MARTYRS MIRROR

1_____

I AM ONLY A BOY in a city full of trees, but every night I journey. While the other children of the city lie asleep and dreaming, I travel through the blue moonlight or the hushed, severe dark if there is no moon. In the moonlight, our city looks like it's been infused with a luminous powder from another world. Without the moon it is just a shabby darkness of houses and trees under the permanent haze of sky. There are no people and no cars in the night, but sometimes there is one car that slows down as it passes me by, as if checking me out.

Although the name of our city is River City, for many years the river was hidden away. You never saw it. It is still difficult to get there even though it flows now right through the middle of town. You must travel down into the bad part of town, behind some warehouses and barely utilized malls where there is a parking lot full of old school buses. Then there is a maze of gravel roads and abandoned industrial equipment, and finally there are so many trees. You have to hike some distance through the trees, but I have been there. I do not remember it exactly, but I have been there.

Another paperboy, Johnny G, has disappeared from our city and nobody knows where to find him. I am just a boy and so it is not clear to me what all the possibilities are. The most probable solutions to this mystery are not discussed explicitly in the news-papers I deliver.

Every spring the river rises and seeps into the earth and into the walls of our basement and into our home and soaks the pile of trash that we keep there. Our basement full of trash is a mystery. It is my parents' trash and they love it, I believe, in some new way, but this is not my concern. I deliver my papers every night and someday I will buy a moped.

In the attic, there's a book. Every night it is lifted down and carried into my bedroom, where every night my mother reads to me. Every night, a tall, thin man refuses to be a soldier and personal bodyguard for the King of Prussia because of his religious con-victions. Soldiers pinch and thumbscrew this tall, thin man. They hang him from a cord by his left thumb and his great right toe. My mother shows me the pictures; she kisses me good night and the book is hoisted back up to the attic.

I sleep. Deep in the night my alarm goes off. I lie there for a moment in the quiet of my room.

I deliver the papers and then I sleep some more.

I believe that our house is sinking ever so slowly into the earth. The ceiling of the kitchen is rotten and the furniture is rotten and the trash in the basement is rotten and so I believe that "to love" means "to allow something to rot." I am just a boy and am not yet capable of discriminating between the dreams that people turn into places and what is real. I look around me and I think: this is real, this is all the real, this is all that is real.

I do not know why the river was hidden for so many years or why it is still so hard to find. Everything else is discussed here in the full light of day—the disappearance of the paperboy Johnny G and the dirty habits of the people who live in the bad part of town—al-though these things are discussed carelessly, as one might discuss the curly hairdos of our women, their shapeless, baggy sweaters, the weather with its painful heat and its painful cold—talking,

talking, talking, without ever getting to some root.

Only the old people know about the sources of our pleasures, the ground of our suffering, for they are always dreaming. The blinds are closed, but when I ring the doorbells they rise, sleepwalking, and let me in; they give me crumpled bills for the newspapers I deliver and they tell me things before groping blindly for their sofas to lie down and dream some more. They smell like baby powder; somebody is muttering on their radios, too quiet to be understood. It is the old ones who call our River City *Des Moines*, which is French for "The Innards" or "The Mazes" or "The Mounds."

I am an excellent student.

My Language Arts teacher is a stern man, not without a certain appeal. If we spell all of our list correctly, he encourages us to develop our creativity. While the other students are methodically studying the words they missed, writing them over and over again, we excellent spellers are to tell a story or stories using each spelling word at least once. Once, another boy—a handsome boy with a crushed, sullen look and a beautiful gold tooth—asked if instead of a story he could write a song.

If you spell your words correctly, the teacher said, we can do whatever you'd like.

The crushed, sullen boy is often pouting, usually in trouble, and sometimes kept after school. This week the words are: powder, ceiling, disappearance, mutter, clutter, letter, canoe, amorphous, feature, whisper, wander, litter, pulp, quivering, weights, cruel, desire, murmur, bereaved, and celebrity.

I never miss a spelling word, but am rigorously developing a bad attitude. If I get my name written on the board for talking out of turn or giggling behind my hand or wiggling my ass around on its hard chair in a loud, irritating way, and if I get two checkmarks beside my name for these same behaviors, then I'll have to stay after school too. After school it is just me and the teacher. He sits at his desk staring at me and I can't imagine what he is thinking. He frightens me. I am a splotch.

Young man, he says. You squirm around a lot and wiggle your ass on your seat. Is there something on your mind?

I chew on my thumbnail. There are so many things on my mind, unfathomable things, an entire cluttered universe of inexpressible longings. I can't follow all the trajectories, I'm becoming less and less accessible. The process of change itself is becoming the definition of who I am. I'm a moody boy.

There is nothing on my mind, I say.

He folds his hands, purses his lips. He is far too good-looking to be a Language Arts teacher in our sad little city.

Ah, he says. You are then already completely enlightened. Your mind has merged with the sky-like nature of universal Mind. I would have nothing to teach such a boy.

It is silent but for the ticking of the clock. The clocks in our school only occasionally function, but the bells always do.

Are you making fun of me? I ask.

He smirks. I imagine he would know exactly what to do to me to clarify my thinking. I am just a blur. The image I have of myself is several years out of date already. I think I'm about to cry, but I still have enough self-control not to humiliate myself completely.

I am a paperboy, I tell him.

He twirls his pencil in a clockwise direction and stares at the ceiling.

Ah, he says. Like Johnny G.

He looks at me and smiles.

Perhaps you aren't getting enough sleep, my teacher says. That would explain the dark circles under your pretty little eyes. And that dazed look you have all the time, as if you are wandering through a dream.

I'm not sure if he really said "pretty" or if he said "dirty." He twirls his pencil now in a counterclockwise direction.

I take guitar lessons in a crumbling old house in the bad part of town. An orphan there is my best friend in all the world. He looks so much like me our guitar teachers sometimes get us confused, although he weighs hardly a thing. He is wiry, elongated, and over-wrought—as if an angel had been stretched out on a rack. He is built like that tall, thin man who refused to be a soldier and personal bodyguard for the King of Prussia and got thumbscrewed as a result. He never eats anything except chocolate milk and apples. The orphan lives on a farm outside of town where he is raised by various people he may be distantly related to; he isn't sure. The people on that farm don't believe in guitars or even electricity, but he hides his guitar in the barn and every week he sneaks away. We see each other every Wednesday night at band practice in the crumbling old house where we play "When the Saints Go Marching In" on our guitars, but still he writes me letters every week and I write him back.

I still have the first letter he wrote me many years ago:

Hi J,
    I didn't know what to write. Anyway I'm fine, my name is R and I am 8. I went swimming too, theres this retarted kid there every day. So once when they made us clean the swimming hole he laid by the pool and drank the water with his tongue. This letter is really boring isn't it? I caught a 17 and a 1/2 inch fish. And in the buggy we almost hit two cows.
                  questions to answer:
1. Do you want to write back and forth for a long time like this?
2. When are you going to come?
    This is all that I could think of so good-by.

His letters are safely stored under my bed with my guitar and my class picture. I keep the class picture for only one reason: a girl named Beth I love absolutely. I often describe her in my letters to the orphan. I have left enough gaps in my descriptions for the orphan, who looks like he could be my twin, to come up with his own image of what a beautiful girl is, an ethereal girl with long pale hair to the waist. Her hair is the color of light itself. Because we were arranged by height, standing next to Beth is the handsome boy with the crushed, sullen look. When I kiss the image of the girl I love, I'm afraid my lips may sometimes brush against the image of the sullen boy. I don't mention this to R. I'm not sure if it's ridiculous, or something more complex. When I have saved up enough money to buy a moped I will ride out to my friend's farm with my guitar. The roads will be straight and dusty, leading on as if they will never end between rows of corn taller than my self, and I will leave trails of dust in my wake. The sun will beat down on me and brown me like a tart. If I can't buy a moped because of some change in the licensing requirements, I will buy a canoe and late at night I will drag it down into the bad part of town behind the warehouses and barely utilized malls past the parking lot full of old school buses. I will traverse the maze of gravel roads and abandoned industrial equipment and I will disappear back among the trees. I will slip the canoe into the river and I will slip into the river with it and move like liquid down the river with the stars overhead toward the farm where my friend will be waiting. The night will be utterly black and once the river has taken me out of the city and into the countryside, the stars will be bright overhead and they'll be reflected in the river, rippling there as if the universe itself was a warping mask I was both surrounded by and a part of. The sky will be everywhere. The land itself will be hidden behind tall reeds in the muck by the river's edge. The stars will be so perfectly reflected in the calm surface of the river that nowhere will I see anything but blackness and stars; as if I am gliding through the universe itself.

I am not like Johnny G. Johnny G disappeared; he failed to deliver his papers. I may be an amorphous boy, but there is one duty I perform without fail, the crystalline center of my being: I am a paperboy.

The sky in our city is a permanent grey haze. It is not unattractive or bleak, it is the color of a brain.

Beth sits in front of me in Language Arts, between a boring girl and a boy with an oddly shaped head. My teacher is lecturing about personal pronouns, but I read the latest letter from my friend:

Dear J
    I am an orphan and I am so tired of the sixth grade. I hate this farm and all the rough country boys who live around here. They are always baring their chests and their buttocks, swimming in ponds, injuring themselves with their rough games, and bleeding under the hot summer sun. Sometimes I am in the buggy, and they are driving recklessly. Crashing into the cows seems more likely every day. I would run away to your city, but it is just as bad, frankly. That city makes me physically ill. It makes me nauseous in a way I am incapable of understanding. I refuse to eat. I am so repulsed by everything that I eat nothing at all but one glass of chocolate milk every day and half of an apple, cored and peeled. When I imagine growing up in this horrible place I imagine bloating, with veined puffy skin full of toxins. I prefer living out my life as a skeleton, as a brooding shell of a man, than as a toxic dump.
    Did you ever see this movie *Shadow of a Doubt*? The killer reminds me of the man I might grow into. In one scene he plays a game where he cuts up a newspaper, so that his family won't read about his crimes. Did you ever see *Attack*

of the Crab Monsters? Old movies are prohibited here on the
farm, like everything else. Anyway, tell me about that girl
you love so much, Beth, with her long hair and her slim hips.
All the girls on the farm have gone missing. Does this Beth
girl have a friend or a twin sister you could set me up with?

The Language Arts teacher approaches and I shove the letter
into my desk with all the crumpled-up spelling tests and lists of
irregular verbs. I imagine my mortification if he were to read it out
loud to the class. But he passes me by; it's Beth he's after. He catches
her chewing gum and grabs her by the luminous hair and makes
her spit the gum in the garbage and then he writes her name on
the board. I wish my name could be up there next to it. I write her
name out on pieces of notebook paper in manuscript and in cursive
and I write out her many wonderful attributes and I play games
with these folded sheets of paper where the pleasure is imagining
myself married to Beth with various cars in various cities with some
number of children. The children have various special attributes,
powers, and features, but that isn't the point. The point is, we all
know what is necessary to produce children, even if we aren't yet
clear on the details. It isn't a pregnant Beth that is conjured by this
game, it is the word "sex." I try to imagine some bad behavior I
might act out in order to have my name written next to hers in
the firm hand of the Language Arts teacher—whispering loudly to
the boring girl or the boy with the unusually shaped head, zipping
and unzipping my pants, mispronouncing "harass" to get a cheap
laugh—but then he gives us this vocabulary quiz:

PART 1: SENTENCE COMPLETIONS

Complete the following sentences with one of these seven words:

immobilized   sinister   liberate   optional
writhe   manacles   reminisce

1. J suspected that the teacher had a _____ plan to imprison him.

2. "No one is forcing you to come," the teacher told him. "Your attendance is entirely _____."

3. Before he knew it, he was locked up with _____ on his wrists.

4. J _____ his body around on the floor, trying to free himself.

5. The ropes were so tight he couldn't move; he was completely _____.

6. After several hours, his teacher finally came to _____ him.

7. In the future they will _____ about the good times they had together.

PART 2: DEFINITIONS
Choose the word that is best defined by the following expressions.

8. To cut apart or analyze with great care.
   a. bondage
   b. dissect
   c. throbbing
   d. firm

9. To shrink back or hide as if in fear.
   a. intimidate
   b. relinquish
   c. cringe
   d. spread-eagle

10. Reasonable, making use of good sense.
   a. ropes
   b. ski masks
   c. subordinate
   d. logical

11. Likely to change or changeable.
   a. caress
   b. variable
   c. spanking
   d. rooster

12. Somebody who owns you, your spiritual teacher, the source of all your pleasure and your pain.

   a. penetration
   b. innovation
   c. master
   d. insomniac

PART 3: CHOOSING THE RIGHT WORD
Circle the answer that best completes the sentence.

13. J felt as if he was on the (fatality / verge) of a new and more exciting life.

I score 100% on the quiz, as does Beth, and then I wait for my teacher after school next to his red car.

Back at his estate, I tell him that he can do whatever he wants with me only up to a certain point, for I am in love with Beth.

I have Beth locked up in the room with the red door, he says.

She put no restrictions on me whatsoever, he adds.

I shrug. He has a manly way about him.

If I'm not home for dinner my parents will call the police, I say.

I already took care of that, he says. They think you're on a field trip.

For a moment, this confuses me. Did they sign a permission slip? Am I in some other city, wandering through the Museum of Natural History, bored by the dinosaur bones and stuffed gazelles? Perhaps I am already traveling across vast distances, deserts, oceans, endless plains—all of it littered with fabulous garbage. My irrelevance is exhilarating. I'm afraid.

I have to deliver my papers, I say.

He laughs.

What do you think Johnny G's customers did the night he disappeared? he asks.

I feel that there is something wrong with me. I shrug.

I guess they got their precious fucking news from the Internet, he says.

I imagine my bundle of newspapers sitting on the corner, wrapped in flimsy, useless plastic in case of rain. What happens to a bundle of newspapers if nobody comes to deliver them? They either get rained on until they are one soggy lump of black and white pulp or they dry up, begin to disintegrate, blow away in the wind.

After my teacher "takes care of" my ass, he ties me up with so much rope that only my quivering lips, my soft cheeks, my intelligent eyes, and my firm, boyish buttocks remain visible. Over the next several days he uses me whenever he's in the mood. He'll "shove it in that ass" for a while and then leave me there immobilized while he lifts weights in his underwear. His muscles move in and out of my vision. Sometimes he puts on a gas mask and I have to imagine his cruel, handsome face while he is pushing my legs up in the air and doing it from the front. During the interludes I become more bored than I've ever been in my life. I'm completely drained. I can feel no more desire, but he keeps coming back. I'm so bored that all activity loses its meaning. I remember the regular patterns I walked every night, the geometrical shapes that made up my "route." I think of the regularly spaced print on the papers that came out every single day, the "news." These words are there to tell us how we dream, what life is, what time consists of, but these words had been exposed to me now as what they really are: a mask, hiding the fact that it is all obliterated, it is all nothing.

And me, I am not a paperboy. I am emptiness itself.

During the most boring interludes, however, I hear a strange music. It seems that this music is mine alone and has been waiting for me to find it. I believe that others have heard variations: am I a member of some band? When my teacher finally unties me, he leaves me a key and says that whatever I do I mustn't use the key to open the room with the red door. Then he drives away.

I go to the door.

Beth? I say. Beth, are you in there?

It is silent. I know that he has tricked me and that Beth was never here at all. She is far too clever and uninterested to fall for a sleazy man like our Language Arts teacher. Probably it is just the bloody remains of Johnny G in that room. I leave the key in his mailbox and hike through the trees. It is night.

I wake one warm night back among the trees. The trees of our city are fragrant and murmuring, and it is then, I believe, that I go "down by the river," although I do not remember it exactly. There is a deep scratch on my forehead which will surely scar; I believe that I have been marked by an enchanted prince who was turned into one of these murmuring trees. This scar will give my face the impression of a furrowed brow; it will make me appear more intelligent and curious than I actually am.

My bundle of papers is waiting for me on the corner.

I deliver the news. My affair with the teacher was ultimately a disappointment, but I have no regrets. Although I know that the comfort of my routine, the geometrical shapes I travel, and the soothing, meaningless words I deliver are all a lie, I accept them. If I allow myself to believe again in these things, it means that I can once again enjoy the pleasure of obliterating that belief. It is only the interplay between belief and obliteration that is interesting. Neither existence nor nothingness is enough on its own.

Beth is fast asleep in her frilly bed and dreaming. I love the thought of her and I love the thought of her dreams and I love her so much that I think one day we will be together.

Tomorrow I will write my skinny friend on the farm. I think

about those rough country boys he mentioned in his letter and I calculate the number of papers I will have to deliver before I will have saved up enough money for a moped or a canoe.

Late at night I will drag the canoe down into the bad part of town behind the warehouses and barely utilized malls past the parking lot full of old school buses. I will traverse the maze of gravel roads and abandoned industrial equipment and I will disappear back among the trees. I will slip the canoe into the river and I will slip into the river with it and into the canoe and move like liquid down the river with the stars overhead. The night will be utterly black and once the river has taken me out of the city and into the countryside the stars will be bright overhead and they'll be reflected in the river, rippling there as if the universe itself might flicker and wink out into utter blackness. The land will be so flat and the horizon so low that the sky will be everywhere. The reflection of the stars as I move through them will form pathways and constellations like a map through a limitless maze.

A farm is a scary place. The docility of the animals seems like such a trick, a strategy, deep cover, a camouflage. They are waiting. They are waiting to devour something. They are waiting, waiting. A cow is sleeping and chewing and waiting and full of blood under the sun. A chicken, a pig. God help us. Farm animals are unbearable in the daylight, but at night they seem serene.

The sound of an electric guitar in the cold is like a monstrous ejaculation of spirit. My friend and I will plug our guitars into extension cords under a cold starry sky and we will imagine that we are rock and roll stars and we will feel like we can never die and electricity will pour forth from inside us and tear the fabric of the universe itself until it bleeds stars upon our damaged little heads.

We will escape from this place and fly into the Milky Way.

My teacher is taking a leave of absence for "family business." Maybe he's actually contracted an embarrassing disease. Maybe he's spending time in prison or taking a journey with a kidnapped boy. Our substitute Darlene isn't so creative. She only wants us to write about our careers. When I tell her I'll be a famous musician, she gives me a smug grin. "Smug" means that I don't know what she's thinking, even when she talks. If I finish my work early, she doesn't want me to write stories; she sends me to an empty class-room to tutor the sullen boy instead. He's been missing more and more classes, he barely shows up. He comes from a "very troubled family," Darlene explains, in the bad part of town. Usually I just help him finish his work quickly, and then I write stories while he draws the illustrations. Everyone agrees that he has a talent for art. We also agree that Darlene is a poor substitute for our stern former teacher. In any case, I'm sure my real teacher will be back. He's left us with an entire month's worth of spelling words: cemetery, glistening, institution, inmate, intestines, insane, indistinct, orifice, thistle, torment, esoteric, swelling, hermaphrodite, heretic, hemi-sphere, scabious, regenerate, dormant. Scabious, there's a new one. I'll have to look it up.

In the newspaper it says that Johnny G's mother has not yet given up hope. If I could tell that mother one thing, I would tell her that she came many years ago to River City for one reason: to give up hope. Give up hope! I would say. Relinquish it completely. Open your eyes wide and wander through life as in a dream, with no hopes or expectations.

But she is a bereaved mother, a celebrity. And I am only a paperboy.[1]

---

1. The repeated references to Johnny G suggest the author's familiarity with the story of Johnny Gosch, a Des Moines paperboy who disappeared while doing his Sunday morning paper route on September 5, 1982. He was 12 and one of the first missing children to have his picture put on milk cartons. He was never found, although rumors have circulated about his possible whereabouts for years: e.g., that he was involved in an Omaha boy prostitution

ring allegedly run by high-ranking Republican operative Lawrence E. King (See *The Franklin Cover-up: Child Abuse, Satanism, and Murder in Nebraska*, De Camp, 1992; the Yorkshire TV documentary *Conspiracy of Silence*, 1994). More recently it was claimed that Republican blogger Jeff Gannon, who was revealed to be a male prostitute, was actually the adult Johnny Gosch. Readers might wonder why a young Amish boy writing sometime between 2003 and 2006 would be obsessed with a paperboy who went missing in 1982, or would be interested in the archaic concept of a "paperboy" at all; following widely publicized disappearances such as that of Johnny Gosch (and another, less famous boy, Eugene Wade Martin, who disappeared in Des Moines in 1984), newspapers stopped sending children out in the middle of the night, or any time at all, to deliver their papers. By a strange coincidence, Stephen also comes from Des Moines, and would have been a teenager himself at the time Johnny Gosch disappeared; he has also written extensively about paperboys (See *The Whistling Song*, 1990). It behooves me to withhold judgment on the literary merits of Stephen's work (although I will say that the *Publisher's Weekly* review which found his first novel "unbearably thick with metaphor and ersatz profundity" was not unfair in its appraisal), but there are many obvious clues to the nature of his relationship with Jake Yoder within his earlier writing. In one interview floating around the web (now for some reason vanished), he admitted to having delivered papers himself when he was in the sixth grade. This simple fact would probably be enough for most truth-loving readers to label Jake Yoder a hoax, or even a fraud. I don't believe this case is as simple as that. I remain convinced that Stephen himself believes in the existence of the precocious child. —JOB

2_____

THE SNOW IS FALLING ON the cemetery and on Brother, who is tender and glistening. Your skin is so pretty, Brother, says Sister. It is smooth like a girl's. Sister makes Brother feel beautiful; she makes him afraid. He can't remember why they are in this cemetery, how they got there, or how to get out. Sister alone knows these things; she ties his blindfold back on and leads him by the hand.

Watch out for that empty grave, says Sister. It could be full of maggots, rotting corpses, and snakes.

Sister loves to describe in vivid detail the various hazards in their path, hazards she valiantly protects him from as they make their way home, where Stepfather is waiting. Because Stepfather is early, and misplaced his keys, he has sawed through the garage's screen door with a serrated plastic knife from Burger King. Watch out for the sharp edges of that ruined screen, says Sister. She unties the cloth over Brother's eyes.

Family life is more confusing and tense every day; medications are liberally prescribed. One day Sister goes off to the Academy and Stepfather moves out, leaving poor Brother all alone with Mother and her exhausting divorce.

Dear Sister, writes Brother, I miss you so much. Remember when the snow was falling on the cemetery? Remember when I stole Daddy's cocaine and we went to that concert together? We've had some good times. Remember when you were fat and unhappy? Daddy used to tease you at dinnertime and make you cry. But now you are so slim! You are all skin and bones. It's like the girl you used to be has been elongated in some way. It's like the king of some weird foreign country has hung you with a heavy cord by your left thumb and your great right toe and the process has stretched you out. In any case, I miss your insubstantiality. At least my twin is here to keep me company. My twin is leading me off the edge of the world. Because of our very troubled family, I don't much attend 6th grade anymore. But there are chemical alternatives.

Brother builds a stage in his room with a glass table full of tiny lights and glitter. He creates an elaborate collage of poetry and weird images on his walls. He writes beautiful stage directions in his notebook, mixed in with mundane descriptions of endangered life forms. He is camouflaging his art, in case Mother comes prying. He choreographs blue and silver lights like stars and waterfalls and androgynous dancing bodies or hermaphrodites. In his room, alone, he sings. He believes that a secret band exists, and that he is a member of this band.

When he doesn't respond to Mother's persistent knocking, she bursts in anyway. You could have been a classically trained pianist, she says. It's your father's fault. Too cheap to send you to the *Académie Française*, he snorted that tuition money right up his nose.

Here, she says. You have a letter from your sister.

The postmark is foreign and indecipherable.

Silly Brother, writes Sister. Your twin is not real, only imaginary. You're just like a silly little girl with beautiful skin as gold as the sun and your pretty gold tooth. Me, I dropped out of the Academy because I'm a successful model. Look for me on a billboard in the bad part of town soon.

I miss Sister, says Brother.

But he's not really sure. The whole family has acquired a vague unreality. The world outside his room is a thrilling and contaminated forest, full of hazards and graves.

You are growing so large, his mother says.

You are large and out of control, his mother says.

He's still in his pajamas.

In the asylum, there are many doctors in white coats and women with long grey or blond hair. Frizzy hair, frizzy sweaters. Everything's been damaged and overprocessed.

What is the name of this institution? Brother asks the guards.

It's called The Inner Gardens, say the guards. Or something like that. How would we know? We never went to the *Académie Française*.

This place would only be tolerable if Brother had in fact "lost touch with reality." Insanity is the same thing in everybody's mind as the future. Brother's conflicting impulses form a complexity of feeling that is material, but out of fashion. Brother knows that what they are calling his craziness is in fact his twin. Some of the guards are butch, and some of the guards are femme. They shoot him up with drugs.

He wanders blinding halls of white light and mirrors. They curve around in a twisted complexity that leads in only one direction, and sometimes the inmates smear blood and shit on the walls. Actually, there are twenty words written in blood and shit on the walls, words like: cemetery, serrated, robotic, uterus, morbid, toxic, carnivore, and cancerous. I'm in the lower intestines, Brother decides. His twin is being lost and suffocated. A boy with an imaginary guitar talks to Brother earnestly but the words are floating away. The therapists are pushing buttons and pulling strings. The boat is off course, and although Brother isn't steering, it's as if his mind was connected secretly and intimately to the elaborate mechanism of navigation, and he can't decide whether the ship should be returned to its course or whether this dangerous detour will be of interest. His knees are alien. He can open and close his fist but the motion is the blink of a robotic eye. There are rewards and punishments, punishments and rewards.

When the drugs wear off, he knows what he has to do: he will guard his twin with his life. To guard his twin he must survive. In order to survive, he must camouflage his twin.

His doctor is a stern man, not without a certain appeal.

In his mandatory journal, Brother writes: I'm interested in endangered species, such as the LARGEMOUTH BASS (Micropterus salmoides). This popular game fish is one of the most voracious of underwater animals and is not averse to eating smaller individuals of its own kind. It's the male that protects the young, chasing off the female as soon as the eggs are laid. The panda is one of the most famous animals that have lost all desire for heterosexual intercourse; the Chinese will clone them instead. Their bamboo forests are disappearing, much as our human world might get burnt to a crisp, because so many people are enraged. So many people find "human" the most depressing state imaginable.

A boring girl interrupts his journaling. My doctor was tired of dividing cat's brains in two, she says, just to show that you could teach one half of a cat brain to do a trick and leave the other half ignorant. He helped me out instead. Now I have a new problem: my left hand is always acting without my consent. Whatever my right hand does, my left undoes. When I go to pick out my clothes in the morning I try to choose neutral, bland colors that will help me be accepted in the world. But my alien hand keeps picking out the most ornate scarves and bonnets, the most brilliant colors and most non-traditional patterns I own. I throw these flashy clothes in the garbage, but my left hand just goes rummaging.

Of course, says Brother.

They are developing drugs to rectify the problem, the boring girl tells him.[2]

The doctor isn't so impressed with Brother's journal but tells him he has a talent for art. He gives him a sketchbook and encourages Brother to draw what he feels instead of putting it in words. The boy with the imaginary guitar returns.

Whatever you do, says the boy, don't open the red door. Brother just nods.

Because of the pig, says the boy. Like white light is pure, right? My guitar is the shiniest blue you've ever seen. The woman said that her uterus is out of place and I said, *You must have a sugar daddy or something*. A train conductor or the driver of some van. I guess it's OK. Everybody's got to survive.

Obviously you need a tutor, the boy says. The trick here is to make the doctor love you. When I spell my magic words correctly, he takes me to his office and gives me a treat. I want you to masturbate me, the boy says, while I talk about having sex with my girlfriend.

I'm not going to let you fuck me in the ass, says the boy. I know that you want it.

He shakes his ass at Brother, and then he tells him other lies.

It's what crazy people do, the guards explain. It's called "magical thinking." He's regressed to a primitive level where shit and words seem like tokens of the divine.

A butch guard tells his own story.

Like you, I used to be an artist, he says. A realist and a butch. As I approached middle age, I noticed that successful artists were

---

2. The condition the girl describes is a real one, known as intermanual conflict or, less formally, "alien hand." The phenomenon sometimes occurs in people who have suffered strokes or brain injuries, but most documented cases involve those who have undergone split-brain surgery to control epileptic seizures. As a result, the non-dominant half of the brain operates outside of the dominant half's control. Attentive readers will note the continuing prevalence in the text of images of real or imaginary twins and of mental splitting. — JOB

always dissatisfied anyway, and their old friends hated them. Still, it was everything I wanted. I didn't fit in society, but then I realized that was a lie I told myself in order to believe the problem was that my angry art was an art of the future. It wasn't like I was trying to resituate "the divine" in a context where belief and disbelief would both be elements of its meaning. Although other similar artists were successful at marketing a cheesy outlaw persona, my failure at art had to do with my infatuation with men who were equally resentful, a kind of team spirit of rebellion. In America, any career is a prison full of sexual opportunities. Being an artist who never got laid was a different prison, and intolerable. People usually exchange poverty and hope for the absolute despair that comes with full-time employment. Jobs in America make us long for nihilistic gesture or its opposite. Take my advice: consider a career as a guard in a mental institution or in a public school. Once you have a career, nobody will think of you as crazy, or else they won't care. If that boy tries to tell you we do things with him at night, don't believe a word.

The butch guard's body gives off a soured, narcotic smell. Brother has a strong sense of smell. He is very sensitive to odors and fumes and this is part of his sickness, for it ties him to a toxic, contaminated, rotten world.

Those guards try to fuck me in the ass every night, the boy explains to Brother. But me, I'm always the top. Since they bring me straight porn, I'm OK with that. I'm not gay, at least not yet. Not the way most people mean when they talk about gay.

The boy has quivering lips, soft cheeks, intelligent eyes, firm, boyish buttocks, and a nice thick cock, but Brother must behave; sexual relations are often misconstrued in an asylum.

Brother is given so much therapy.

You are a handsome boy, the doctor says. In a crushed, sullen sort of way.

He folds his hands, purses his lips. It is silent but for the ticking of the clock. The clocks in the mental institution only occasionally function, but the bells always do.

What's behind the red door? Brother asks.

The doctor twirls his pencil in a clockwise direction and stares at the ceiling.

The inmates here are prone to such elaborate myths, says the doctor. Such paranoid fantasies, such indiscreet rumors. That door is nothing to be concerned about.

But the screams, says Brother. I hear the screams.

The doctor sighs.

You're always pouting, he says. I sometimes wonder if you might not have repressed memories of sexual abuse.

He looks at Brother's drawings. The handsome killers, burning trees, phallic guitars, and winged skeletons of his sketches suggest to the doctor a variety of ways he might have been abused. The doctor suggests various possible perpetrators—fathers, doctors, Language Arts teachers, dentists, lawyers, priests, rough boys and young toughs, butchers, slaughterhouse workers, or soldiers in gas masks that hide their cruel features. He suggests a variety of scenarios ranging from inappropriate comments or glances that might be prematurely sexualizing to bondage and penetration. He wonders if anyone has said to Brother, *I'm gonna do it to you prison-style* . . .

A femme guard who wears too much cologne corners Brother in the tv room. Most people's sense of smell has atrophied, Brother has discovered, so that they can get along in this world just fine.

My perception of the world was always that it's hollow, the femme guard says. As if an imaginary grid framed a brilliant emptiness. The emptiness isn't hideous, it shimmers. But something is hideous, some aspect that may have to do with the words I use to describe things, my own feelings. My imagination is either a form of freedom or a form of slavery. Oft times I'm confused. My mother loved me "too much," which was a way of not loving me at all. The violence of a male is one kind of clarity, a boring habit that I might easily replace with something equally thoughtless and "ordered"—quilting or living on welfare or most any job. Ain't nothin' goin' on but the rent. Being a guard in a mental institution serves my love for paranoid types, men who create systems of order so obviously deluded that my own seem reasonable and refreshing in comparison. Controlling other people's environments is intimacy for me. I hadn't learned how to perform in order to feel loved by an abstraction—an audience—that could be imagined as larger than madness or sanity. Men ignored me unless I spread my legs for them. I love to create disasters, disasters that can only be "solved" by the violence of angry men. A prison riot or underemployment or allergies would be examples of this.

The femme guard seems to lose interest in his own story, lets go his hold of Brother's arm. Oh, he says, this came for you.

It's a letter from Sister. The postmark is foreign and absolutely clear.

Sister is traveling the world as a model. Her luminous hair—it's the color of light itself—has captured the imagination of all the top photographers. In the glossies, they call her "Beth." She is photographed in the tumbled ruins of lost civilizations on tropical islands. She is photographed in rusting train yards. She is photographed in basements full of soggy trash: pamphlets about the health benefits of blue-green algae, evangelical literature, train schedules, bicycle parts, rodent droppings, and bones. She is photographed in barns and on mounds of hay with her hair peeking out of frumpy bonnets. On the endless plains of a distant nation, she is photographed outside of a dilapidated hotel that rises like a crashed spaceship from another dimension. The pampas are unreal. Inside, it seems larger than would be possible. The few windows are occluded, so it is hard to get her bearings. She wanders down twisting corridors, up and down stairways. Look at the foxy girl in the picture in this magazine, says the boy with the imaginary blue guitar. He is frantically masturbating. That's my sister, says Brother. Mine too, says the boy.[3]

Because of his questionable therapeutic methods, the stern, handsome doctor is replaced by a new doctor. Darlene's coat is clean and white, although her hair has been fried to a crisp.

You'll be fine once you establish some career goals, Darlene tells him. If you continue to behave, we may be able to send you out to some farm or ranch in nature. You may qualify as a Fresh Air child in one of our outlying regions. Every summer, Fresh Air children are sent out from our city to live with the religious cult because of a pervasive belief that hard work and clean country living will make children from troubled families less angry when they grow up, more likely to hold a job and not to steal.[4]

She advises Brother not to associate with the boy with the imaginary guitar. He imagines he can be a rock star, but that's hardly a realistic goal, she says. The stories he smears on the wall are shiny and foul, she tells Brother. If he keeps up such behavior, we'll have to get the authorities involved. A social worker is waiting, a woman named LuAnn. Trust me, says Darlene. You don't want to get started down that road.

One night, the boy with the imaginary guitar sneaks into Brother's room to tutor him. Brother's roommate, a boy with an oddly shaped

---

3. The allusion to Wallace Stevens's "The Man with the Blue Guitar" is one of a number of references that strike me as highly unlikely, even for an exceptionally precocious child. Another strange coincidence—Stephen used a line from a Stevens poem, "The Wind Shifts," as an epigraph to his second novel (*Distortion*, 2000). The reference to the pampas also struck me as highly suspect. When pressed about whether he'd ever been to Argentina, Stephen finally conceded that he'd "passed through there briefly" in 1990 or 1991.—JOB

4. This is true, although more common on the East Coast than in the Midwest. New Yorkers in particular seem to find the idea of sending troubled children out to live on farms with devout religious people especially soothing.—JOB

head, is on Xanax, Inderal, and Halcion, and fast asleep. The boy with the imaginary guitar plays Brother a love song. His songs are full of more and more lies. He sings about a missing paperboy, a boy called Johnny G. He mentions a kidnapper known as the Tractor-riding Man, and a stranger who visits at night. He sings that this murderer made him an orphan, and that the buggies crash into the cows.

They both miss the handsome doctor and agree that Darlene isn't much of a substitute at all. I'll show you what the doctor taught me, says the boy. Afterward, they doodle and talk.

If you escape with me, the boy tells Brother, we can go to California and be rock stars. A pretty boy like you should be on the cover of teenage fanzines.

I don't need to escape, says Brother. They're letting me out to-morrow. You'll be all alone here with Darlene and with the guards.

A glazed look comes over the other boy then, as if he's not ex-actly living and not exactly dead.

Brother wakes just once in the night. It sounds like somebody is muttering on a radio, but it is only the boy with the imaginary guitar, out in the dark hallway. His sobbing and muttering is so complicated, it's a song of its own.[5]

---

5. "Discerning" and "attentive" readers, if not you "obtuse" or "willfully naïve" readers, will have figured out by now that Judith is not so subtly suggesting that I'm mentally ill. In fact, she's trying to turn revelations about the nature of my mental illness into a kind of narrative hook. Maybe she'll label me a "male hysteric." Clearly Judith needs to pathologize what she doesn't understand. The first "strange coincidence" she notes, for example, is in reality a basic aspect of the story. The Amish/Mennonite diaspora is a small world, but I never would have met Jake if I hadn't heard through family connections in Des Moines that a local boy had a connection to the shooting at Nickel Mines. (This is not reflected, however, in my fictionalized version of these events in *Glory Hole*; I do my best to spare my family members the pain of being imagined as characters in my novels.) It's like the anthropic principle: Jake could only be observed in a universe suitable for the observation of Jake. As for his "unlikely" obsession with Johnny Gosch and paperboys in general, as of 2008, 13 percent of newspapers in this country were still being delivered

When they let Brother out of the asylum, he burns his collage and his stage directions and his glass stage full of tiny lights. He decides to follow Darlene's advice, to forget about rock stardom and focus on getting a job. He remembers what his grandmother used to say about certain kinds of boys. Some of them are born that way, she'd say, and some of them get that way in the Army. He fasts and exercises and plans a military career. He researches Marine history, making particular note of a place on Guadalcanal known as "Vaseline Alley," where Marines went to have sex with each other.[6] He speaks to many recruiters, who caress his knee and assure him that such a handsome, pouty boy will have no problem making friends in the Marines. The Marines like to fuck, but don't kiss, they tell him. If he

---

by children. I've discovered evidence that boys were delivering papers in both Lancaster and Iowa City in recent years, and for all I know, Jake might have been one of them, although it's true that a 2004 *Iowa City Press Citizen* article referred to its featured paperboy's "lost art": "At a little after 4 a.m., Steven rolls out of bed, shakes off the morning cobwebs and heads down to the garage to start rolling and binding newspapers for delivery. Not having to think about what he's doing, Steven rolls each paper, binds them and drops them into a pile on the garage floor." According to the article, Steven took over the route from his mother when he was 12. More significantly, Jake lived for a time on the same block in Des Moines as Johnny Gosch's mother, Noreen Gosch, who had become a kind of local legend and still appeared in the news from time to time—such as in September of 2006, just a month before I met Jake, when she claimed that somebody had left photos on her doorstep that depicted her son bound and gagged. She posted the photos on her website, but media commentators saw little resemblance to her son and had trouble making out what she claimed was an identifying birthmark. A man who worked for the Hillsborough County, Florida, sheriff's office in the 1970s came forward to say that he recognized the photos from an investigation in 1978 or 1979— *before* Johnny Gosch had been kidnapped. According to him, the investigation at the time had determined that there was no coercion or molestation involved in the taking of the photos, even though they later showed up in the hands of pedophiles. The records from the Florida case couldn't be found, but most commentators consider it doubtful that the photos actually depicted Johnny Gosch at all.—SB
6. While this term seems to have been widely used to describe streets in many cities, I could find only one secondary reference to its use in the Pacific during WWII.—JOB

wants something more oral, the Navy's the place.

Meanwhile, Sister's career is over. The Agency tells her she's too old to model fashion, cosmetics, and liquor, and the competition is fierce for that transitional phase to "perky young mother" ads for furniture polish and laundry detergent. To make things worse, her boyfriend dies. He is thrown from his bike into a stream or a creek, and he drowns. He wasn't really her boyfriend, but he might have been, any day. She moves back in with their mother. Her face is as smooth as a baby's, and her voice is the chirpy voice of a five-year-old, but without the blunt, edgy quality of a five-year-old's sometimes morbid preoccupations. The Marines inform Brother that during his institutional stay he acquired a new syndrome. Sister refers to Brother's disease as his "missed opportunities."

Brother moves to a new town to study at the Academy and it is always raining. Teenagers are always being murdered and molested in this town, there are huge drug busts, and bodies always popping up in the creeks and gullies. He is the only person in town on foot, except for middle-aged white women on speed. Other students at the Academy walk across the bucolic campus in their sandals and hiking boots, but their cars are in the lot.

He is here to study forestry. He is still doing just what Darlene advised him, planning his career. He imagines himself back among the trees, patting the earth gently around a firm young sapling. He imagines dozing off, back where the air is green and moist and quivering. He is supposed to be in class now, but he is hunkered down in his studio apartment watching the rain fall on a thin strip of lawn. The day is dark, but there are no lights on in any houses. In class right now, his 68-year-old instructor is droning on with his lumber industry propaganda. The forestry program, he has discovered, is less about nurturing trees than about chopping them down. The professor, who teaches all the classes in the department, has stickers up in his office that belittle environmental activists. EARTH FIRST! We'll log the other planets later, one of them says.

Mother calls him on the phone.

Now that her career is over, your crazy sister won't leave, she says. Would you just talk to her, please?

She hands off the phone.

It's good that you're redecorating, Sister chirps.

He has already ripped the rotten linoleum off the kitchen floor to reveal the slightly damaged hardwood underneath. The back yard is mud, but there's a persimmon tree.

I hope you are keeping all your pictures framed, Sister says. You don't want any images on your walls that aren't contained. You wouldn't want to be unable to distinguish the images from the walls.

Maybe you will stay, she says, or maybe you will come back home to visit. We all miss you very much and think that town is not the most savory place in the world.

Brother and Sister watch a movie together at Mother's. In this movie a man who kills older widows for their money is found out by his sunny, small-town niece. Both the uncle and his niece are named Charlie. The man takes his niece into a bar and he twists his napkin as if he's strangling a widow. *You live in a dream, he says, you're a sleepwalker, blind. How do you know what the world is like? Do you know the world is a foul sty? Do you know if you ripped the fronts off houses you'd find swine? The world's a hell, what does it matter what happens in it? Wake up, Charlie, use your wits, learn something.*

Yes, says Sister. I love this movie. It all comes out OK in the end. The niece pushes her uncle off a train and ends up with the detective.[7]

---

7. This is *Shadow of a Doubt* (1943), starring Teresa Wright as Charlie and Joseph Cotten as Uncle Charlie. It was filmed in Santa Rosa, which is also the likely home of the forestry program in the story. An Internet search revealed that Stephen kept an address in Santa Rosa at some point in the mid-'90s. —JOB

Sister takes her little brother by the hand and says to him, Why are you so big? You are getting bigger every day. You must stop growing so large.

Secretly, however, Sister is enraged. She thinks if he had only paid attention to her careful instructions on how to avoid hazards and graves he wouldn't have acquired those "missed opportunities." They quarrel. What is your PROBLEM? he says. He slams a closet door. You're large and out of control! says Sister.

You're out of control! he says. It's *you!*

You rude, ungrateful little brat! she says. He slams his hand against the wall. He chooses to hurt himself sometimes, during moments of crisis. You're escalating! she says.

They call each other names: victim, martyr, crazy. Monster, carnivore, witch. Overly sensitive or controlling and jealous.

Brother slams his door on the way out.

Feeling regretful, Sister sends Brother letters by Federal Express, but he doesn't open them. He knows that they are full of stories, fake memories of the happy times they had growing up. But she is not required. Only his secret twin is absolutely necessary. His secret twin lives inside certain music. This music is rare, but it is all over. The forest is a place where his mind would feel at home. It is always raining here, always. Brother thinks that his dank little apartment is small, but that it is just big enough for a stage.

Brother writes his own letters in response to Sister: he tells stories about a child who lives alone with its mother in a contaminated forest. Brother chooses his words carefully. He remembers what he learned in the asylum from that ex-paperboy — that you could build a story by intermingling lies with vocabulary words that would imbue it with a kind of magic or what people call madness. Because he knows that his story will never be read, he is free to elaborate on the life of the paperboy, his own life, Sister's, and the secret life of his twin. All of the animals in his stories are dead or mutating, frogs sprout extra legs, cancerous birds grow extra beaks and peck humans at random, the waters run with chemicals, and the skies blacken with toxic clouds, gathering over the vast emptiness of the pampas.[8]

The doorbell rings, and Sister finds a kind man in a Fed Ex costume at the door of Mother's apartment. Another letter of love and reconciliation from Brother! Put it over there with the others, Sister says. How good of this man to have come all this way, just to bring news of Brother. She curls up on the sofa to write back. Once upon a time, she writes, the snow was falling on Brother, who was tender and glistening, safe and cozy in a beautiful place . . .

---

8. Jake was fascinated by the town of Santa Rosa precisely because *Shadow of a Doubt* was set there. When I met him in 2006 he hadn't seen *Vertigo*, but since then he's "liked" it on Facebook. While it's insulting to defend myself from Judith's paranoid delusions, it's probably worth reminding "truth-loving readers" that Jake was a huge fan of Argentine literature. Not only Borges but Cortázar (*Hopscotch* primarily), Adolfo Bioy Casares, Luisa Valenzuela, Silvina Ocampo, and Juan José Saer (whose descriptions of stars and rivers in *The Witness* are an obvious influence), and he was absolutely fanatical about the third section of Ernesto Sabato's *On Heroes and Tombs*, the infamous "Report on the Blind." The "Report on the Blind" is a terrifying investigation into the subterranean "cult" or "sect" of blind people, who the paranoid and misanthropic narrator believes secretly rule the earth; Jake was adamant that it "wasn't really fiction." Jake had even unearthed Cesar Aira's first translated novel *The Hare* and had just finished *An Episode in the Life of a Landscape Painter*. He'd read authors I'd never heard of (Bianciotti, Arlt, Piglia, Lugones) and Witold Gombrowicz's *Diaries*, of all things, of which he seemed to retain nothing except the author's cruising of the bathrooms at Retiro Station in Buenos Aires. He'd never heard of Manuel Puig. He was also a big fan of *The Queen of the Prisons of Greece* by Osman Lins, a Brazilian, and of Clarice Lispector. —SB

3_____

THE BOY AND HIS TWIN live on a street where every family has two sons. The oldest son is always adopted, because the women think they are barren, or they think their men are full of faulty sperm. Either way, as soon as they adopt a boy, the problem corrects itself and they get pregnant. Up and down the street, there are adopted sons cohabiting with the natural born sons of their parents. In every family, one son is effeminate and one son is not. Sometimes the older boy is a big sissy and sometimes the younger boy.

The twins are five. At random intervals, their family receives a visitor from the night: a paperboy. It is always snowing out there in the night, and the paperboy is glorious to behold. One thing leads to another: a fort is constructed of ice and snow. There is just enough room inside for the three of them.

The paperboy demonstrates many vocabulary words the twins don't yet understand. Afterwards, he tells them: I must go on a long journey. To stay here, loving you, our orifices steaming in the cold—that would be a crime. He kisses the twins once more and speeds off on his snowmobile.

After the snows have thawed, the boy and his twin play in the vacant lot behind their house, a lot full of milkweed and thistle, monarch butterflies and an occasional tiger swallowtail. They capture these butterflies in nets, keep them in jars until they die, and then pin them to a piece of Styrofoam. There are three mounds in this field, and an adjacent garbage dump. The garbage dump is full of evangelical literature, train schedules, rusty bicycle parts, and old newspapers, soggy from the rain. The garbage is a mystery. The twins don't know who built the mounds, but can see that whoever did was aware of the 584-day cycle of Venus, through which it appears as the evening star, disappears for a short period and then reappears as the morning star. The rising of the Pleiades also seems to have been taken into account. In this field, the twins invent a game they call "chasing the rabbits."[9] The twins take off their clothes and display themselves to the garbage men who visit the dump. Some of the garbage men play along, chasing the boys through the weeds. The boys' lives are enchantment: every day they are either chasing butterflies or being fondled by garbage men. Sometimes the garbage men find something they didn't expect, but no one leaves disappointed. If they don't like what the boy has, they make do with his twin. One day, the boy and his twin follow a shabby moth into the tall weeds of the second mound and sit for a rest.

That garbage man that caught me yesterday was pretty good, one of them says. But I sure do miss the paperboy.

Remember when he built us that fort? says the other.

He was so pedantic, but I loved him, one of them says.

---

9. I discovered a remarkably similar reference in Robert Alan Brookey's *Reinventing the Male Homosexual: The Rhetoric and Power of the Gay Gene.* Brookey quotes from a 1993 study of twins the example of two subjects who played a similar "game" when they were 7 or 8: "Living near a garbage dump, they disrobed completely in a nearby wooded area and exhibited themselves to garbage men unloading their trucks." More unlikely reading material for our young Rimbaud. While researching Stephen's background, however, I found his own description of an article he wrote for the *Bay Guardian* entitled "Cruising the Gay Gene." While I couldn't find the original article, Stephen describes it as "a celebration of the vision of gay identity in William Friedkin's *Cruising,* as opposed to the crushing, binary, either/or vision supported by shoddy science through the myth of the gay gene." —JOB

He was overly controlling, concedes the other one. But aren't they all?

Are we a crime? he says to his twin.

Just then a bearded man drives up on a steel-wheeled tractor.

Oh no! his brother says. It's the Tractor-riding Man!

A glazed look comes over him then, as if he is a zombie who has lived freely for many years, for so long that he has forgotten that he is undead and a slave, until his master rides up to take him away.

The boy returns home alone and crawls inside a kitchen cupboard, where he remains for several weeks, eating the Hamburger Helper, instant mashed potato flakes, and uncooked Cream of Wheat he finds there. In the cupboard, stunned by the "kidnapping" of his twin, or the voluntary surrender of his twin to some previously negotiated, secret, and criminal relationship, the boy hallucinates, in the intricate manner of those simultaneously starved, traumatized, and sensorily deprived, and what he hallucinates is his own future, which he understands to have been previously negotiated through his secret and criminal relationship with the paperboy, whose name he can't remember; mixed in with extraneous visual cartoons involving an infinity of rivers and canoes or an endless geometric progression of vaguely occult shapes, he hallucinates his own employment in the same profession as his lover, the impending loss of his parents, and his erotic trajectory as an orphan among cult members and insane girls; he hallucinates the endless plains of a foreign country, flat and hazy, the horizon as inscrutable as the pale blue nothingness of sky; and he hallucinates a train crawling across the endless plains without benefit of a conductor. As he hallucinates, he chews on a plastic elephant, which he imagines is a piece of chocolate given him by a sadistic little girl with hair the color of light itself; he hallucinates, in fact, an entire cosmos made of the hair of the sadistic and insane girl, a rippling wig of light which expands geometrically in every direction and causes him nothing but pain.

But he grows older and becomes a paperboy.

He is just a boy and in the sixth grade and he studies hard and never misses a spelling word and one night while he is sleeping, it is winter; a stranger knocks on his bedroom window.

What is the name of this city? the man asks.

The Mazes, the paperboy says. Or The Innards or The Mounds.

But where is the river? the man asks.

I've been there, the boy says. But the directions are complicated.

The man just stares at him.

You aren't the Tractor-riding Man, are you? asks the boy.

Stop talking gibberish, says the stranger.

He looks familiar, not like the paperboy has known him, but like he is the sort of man everyone means when they say Don't get in the car with a stranger or Don't reveal intimate details to a stranger or Don't take any sweet things from a stranger.

You remind me of someone, says the boy. He was a stern man, but not without a certain charm. He got the most out of me, that's for sure.

I don't give a shit how you spell your words, says the stranger.

OK, says the boy. Then what do you want?

I want to bind you hand and foot, the stranger says.

Is that what you'll do if I let you in?

I was just kidding.

The paperboy expects to see a blinking neon sign outside his window. He feels that he has always been in a motel, but didn't realize it until now. Is there blood and excrement smeared on the walls? Later, the stranger leaves him there, drained of his will.

He is an orphan.[10]

---

10. The plot of this story is remarkably similar to that of Stephen's first novel, *The Whistling Song*, in which a 12-year-old boy (!) dreams about a handsome murderer who kills his parents, then goes out to deliver his papers and comes home to find that his dream has come true: his parents have been killed and he is an orphan. The similarity with young Jake Yoder's own concept of his

After the funeral, an elaborate affair involving many of the city's florists and greeting card manufacturers, the orphan is taken down into the bad part of town behind the warehouses and barely utilized malls, past a parking lot full of old school buses. Through a maze of gravel roads and abandoned industrial equipment and back among the trees, where they are waiting for him with a boat. Stories have consequences, his substitute Darlene tells him. Perhaps if you'd tried to imagine a practical career, things wouldn't have turned out this way. The difference between telling a story about murder and being an accessory to a crime is slim indeed, says his social worker, LuAnn. He is floated down the icy river on the boat and outside of town, where, for the first time in his life, he sees the stars. While LuAnn apathetically rows him into the unknown, the constellations and the planets fill the sky and their reflection fills the river. Your new family believes that telling stories is a sin, says LuAnn.[11]

magical relationship to the killings at Nickel Mines pushes this new, strange coincidence over the top.—JOB

11. It seems to me that the murder of one's parents is a common enough fantasy among adolescents that the superficial resemblance between the inciting incident of my 400-page novel and *a single page* of Jake's would hardly qualify as a "strange coincidence." I hate to fall into Judith's sick game of psychoanalyzing the supposed author; I agree wholeheartedly with H.P. Lovecraft's offhand dismissal of Freud in the opening of "Beyond the Wall of Sleep": "I have often wondered if the majority of mankind ever pause to reflect upon the occasionally titanic significance of dreams, and the obscure world to which they belong. Whilst the greater number of our nocturnal visions are perhaps no more than faint and fantastic reflections of our waking experiences—Freud to the contrary with his puerile symbolism—there are still a certain remainder whose immundane and ethereal character permit of no ordinary interpretation, and whose vaguely exciting and disquieting effect suggests possible minute glimpses into a sphere of mental existence no less important than physical life, yet separated from that life by an all but impassable barrier." (Jake is a huge fan of H.P. Lovecraft. I've read only a handful of his stories and remain underwhelmed.) Still, Judith might notice that even Freud had a category of "typical dreams" involving "the death of persons of whom the dreamer is fond." (See *The Interpretation of Dreams*) In

At a farm outside of town, LuAnn hands the orphan over to a group of men with long beards, who wade into the river and tie the boat to a post. They lead him into an empty schoolhouse and explain to him the history of their cult.[12] They speak in perfect English to him and leave him to copy several lists off the blackboard. He hears them just outside the door, speaking now in some harsh, barbaric tongue.[13]

---

any case, a woman so obsessed with biographical details might note that my own dear parents, as I write this, remain very much alive. Jake's father died when he was very young and his mother's suicide is a matter of public record. Readers might note Judith's callous disregard for the traumas of a boy whose classmates were murdered and whose mother killed herself, as they weigh the question of which one of us is more mentally ill. — SB

12. The differences which separated the followers of Jakob Amman from the Swiss Anabaptists centered on the practice of shunning and the strictness of conformity to specific social and ritualistic practices. The Amish have come to be defined by their separation from the world, nonresistance in the face of violence, and adult baptism. In an essay about his own "search for evidence of Amish literature" (See *San Francisco Bay Guardian*, 2002) Stephen himself explained: "The Amish and Mennonites are all about boundaries. Both groups are Anabaptists, but since the Amish originally separated from the Mennonites in 1693, their traditions have been characterized by a continual splitting of churches, marking off the degree to which one community will compromise with 'the world,' its wars and job markets and gadgets." Note that even when discussing church history, Stephen can't help but refer to *splitting*. Stephen's article is illuminating not only about the history of the Amish and the history of representation of the Amish, but about Stephen's history, goals, and psychology as well. An article that began with Stephen asserting that, "I wanted to find a body of Amish and Mennonite literature. I wanted Amish poetry; evidence of genius and complexity hiding beneath the plain people's surface of beards and bonnets . . ." ends with Stephen concluding, "I'm not sure if I really wanted to find an Amish literature at all, or if, perhaps, I wanted to reassure myself that such a thing could never exist, except in my own imagination." Perhaps it's just another coincidence that, whichever way you look at it, he got exactly what he wanted. Oddly, he entirely neglects to mention the poetry of Amish poet G.C. Waldrep. — JOB

13. This would be Pennsylvania Dutch, a variant of German.
     Judith doesn't seem to understand the meaning of the word "coincidence." When somebody finds what he's been looking for, it's usually understood as causality — as the exercise of the subject's will. And G.C. Waldrep is not an Amish poet — as much as I hate the whole fetish for authenticity when it comes

The women of this cult wear lace doilies on their heads. They spend their days quilting—patching together a piece of this, a piece of that, to make something more useful than showy. They eat ham-loaf and shoo-fly pie and apple butter. The two spices used in their cuisine are salt and MSG.[14] The cult members are pacifists who believe that electricity is evil. Tractors with pneumatic tires are another taboo. Their quaint expression for abandoning the *Ordnung*, the established ways of the cult, is "to go through the red door." There is a group of rough boys always wandering the farm, bare-chested and with cowboy hats. They wear tight blue-jean shorts and frolic with a rubber inner-tube in the swimming hole at the edge of the farm. There is a crazy girl locked in the barn.

In the fields, there are cows.

The bearded men keep only one non-biblical text, a vast book full of pictures of men and women in pain.[15] They don't show him the book, but describe some of the images in detail. The orphan believes there are pictures of his murdered parents in that book. He believes there are pictures of his abducted twin, imprisoned now in some structure designed to house livestock or maybe stretched out on a rack.

They leave him his electric guitar, but there is nowhere to plug it in. The farm is primarily an enormous windowless building crammed full of chickens on various levels. There are rows and rows of wire cages in which chickens are packed together with

---

to the Amish, a Harvard-educated historian who joins an Amish church for five years (I can't imagine why) hasn't had an Amish experience. The Amish don't educate their kids beyond the 8th grade. I think you need to have shoveled manure as a child, at least once, in order to claim an Amish identity.—SB

14. Improbable as this may seem to those who imagine the Amish as deeply in touch with nature and even organic in their farming methods, it's true, although they sometimes use coarsely ground pepper.—SB

15. A reference to the *Martyrs Mirror*, which will be elaborated on in Book 2. It is not, however, the only non-biblical text used by the Amish, who love genealogies and inspirational literature of all sorts.—SB

barely enough room to peck each other. It is the orphan's job to enter the building in the morning and the evening, to walk up and down row after row after row, gathering the eggs.

Deep in the bowels of the chicken house, he comes face to face with a handsome boy with a crushed, sullen look and a beautiful gold tooth. This boy is gathering the carcasses of chickens that have pecked themselves to death.

Welcome to the crazy house, the other boy says.

Every summer, Fresh Air children are sent out to the religious cult from the city because of a pervasive belief that hard work and clean country living will make children from troubled families less angry when they grow up, more likely to hold a job and not to steal.

But I've been kept on permanent, the Fresh Air child explains.

I thought I could plant trees here, he says. That's what I thought being a Fresh Air child was all about. But the air here reeks of feathers and shit, and all the trees have been chopped down.

At night the Fresh Air child leads the orphan out to the swimming hole under the light of the full moon.

The cows are contained by endless coils of barbed wire. Fragrant vines with tiny white flowers have grown over this barbed wire. In the moonlight, the flowers look like tiny ghosts strung along the walls of a lush dark prison.

A strange occult symbol hangs on the barn.[16] The crazy girl's name is Beth and she has long hair the color of light itself. I've never seen her, the Fresh Air child says, but I love her just the same. I love her so much, he says, just like this. Afterward, the orphan climbs up into the hayloft above Beth's compartment, and speaks down to her through the cracks between boards.

---

16. These so-called hex signs are a form of Pennsylvania Dutch folk art, to which magical powers are sometimes ascribed. There is debate as to whether the term originated from the word hex (Pennsylvania Dutch for witch) or as a shortened form of hexagram. The Amish do not actually use hex signs. —SB

Well, well, well, she says. It's the voice from above.

The hayloft is full of dust that dances in the moonbeams that filter in through cracks in the roof. The orphan lights a kerosene lamp. It flickers and stinks.

Does any of the light reach you down there? the orphan asks.

It doesn't have to, Beth says. Studies have proven that light isn't good for insane people.

Her voice sounds familiar—not like he has heard it, but like she is the kind of girl everyone means when they say, Once upon a time there was a neurological disorder.

Didn't you ever read that? asks Beth. Out there in the world?

I love you, says the orphan.

I live here in my own excrement, she says. I sometimes suffer from narcoleptic events.

The light is too dim to make out her features, but they're easy to imagine—she's an ethereal girl with long pale hair to the waist.

You're the most beautiful girl I've ever seen, says the orphan.

That's what they all say.

The orphan fidgets in the hayloft. There are mice and other small rodents, small birds that build their nests in the rafters. The cows are all around, brooding.

Leave me alone now, says Beth.

One afternoon between his morning egg-gathering and his evening egg-gathering, the orphan goes wandering. Not far from the swimming hole sit the remains of a car accident. Car parts and cow skeletons and other bones which look like they might belong to a boy just about the orphan's size are all mixed up together. A sign has been placed next to the accident or collage, which reads *Die Übel der modernen Verkehrsmittel*.[17]

Hey orphan shit, the rough boys say, what are you looking at?

---

17. The evils of modern transportation.—JOB

They do dangerous dives into the pond.

The rough boys are the sons of the cult. They are given a period of time in which none of the laws of the cult apply to them, called "sowing their wild oats." They sunbathe naked on the rocks. They discuss raping him. We don't have any girls, they say, except for Beth and she is insane and locked in the barn. Plus, they tell him, you'd look almost exactly like Beth, if you'd just grow out your hair and lose a little weight. Maybe we'll buy you a wig and hang you by a cord. Maybe we'll stretch you out on a rack.

They do lines of crystal meth and speed off in their souped-up horse and buggies.

What do you want, voice from above? asks Beth.

Who are you? asks the orphan.

She sighs.

I have something for you, she says. But you have to be very careful with it.

She reaches her hand up toward him and shows him an egg.

I gather eggs all morning and eggs all evening, says the orphan. I dream about eggs and when I wake up everywhere I look is eggs, eggs, eggs.

The last thing I need, says the orphan, is an egg.

Beth tosses it up to him. It looks just like any other egg.

Keep it and watch it, she says. And the most important thing: don't get any blood on it.

What about the red door? asks the boy. Does this have something to do with the red door?

That old thing? says Beth. I'll tell you, I went through that door a long time ago. That door is not *all that*.

Beth says, The only way to get through that door is with modern transportation, which everybody knows is evil.

The orphan is altogether lost—more than anything, he loves modern transportation. More than anything, he loves snowmobiles and garbage trucks and mopeds. He even loves tractors with pneumatic tires. More than anything, he loves the boys and men who drive them, and more than anything, he loves Beth. When he was five, his desires were so clear: the paperboy, the butterflies, and the garbage men. Or was that just what his twin wanted, and he went along for the ride? Now it's even more mixed up, with various rules and humiliations.

He wonders sometimes what ever became of that twin.

One other thing, says the orphan.

Since my twin brother went missing and my parents are dead, the boy says, I'm considered an at-risk youth. Are you an at-risk youth?

Beth says, Your voice is awful familiar. Your voice reminds me of somebody or something a long time ago. Your voice reminds me of a life I never actually lived. The only thing I like about my cult, or family, says Beth, is the quilting. Quilting is all about weaving chaos into barely perceptible patterns with subtle repetitions and geometries. I like to patch together a piece of this, a piece of that, to make something showy and extreme. For obvious reasons, they won't let me have needles; the only quilts I can make are ghostly and ephemeral.

She tells him: Like you, I have not always lived on this farm. Once upon a time, I was free.

Listen, she says. Since you love me so much, do me a favor. I need more chalkboards and chalk. You'll find stacks of little chalkboards and cartons of chalk in the supply closet of that awful little one-room schoolhouse.

The orphan is confused; he's probably a little bit sleep-deprived. Is that a one-room schoolhouse or a prison? Is it a place of learning or an erotic nightmare? Tortured rote-learning or the pleasures of repression that come with world domination? At night, the cows here begin to cluster around the northern edge of their range. They start biting through the barbed wire and walk on in rapidly expanding herds. North, north. Soon there are no more cows except the veal calves, still trapped in their pens. In the north, beneath the startling lights of the aurora borealis, the cows are trudging on. Snow is falling on the dreaming cows.

If there's one thing these people love, Beth says, it's their chalkboards and their chalk.

The one-room schoolhouse is never locked. Under another full moon, the rough boys draw weird geometrical shapes with chalk on the classroom floor, echoing the vaguely occult designs on the barn's hex sign, and place a veal calf in the center of it, tightly bound with their lassos. They're performing rituals to bring the cows back. The orphan sneaks past them and loads up on supplies. He hides them under the bed where the Fresh Air child is fast asleep and dreaming. The orphan can barely contain his love for the dreaming Fresh Air child. Why would he? He puts the egg under the other boy's pillow.

Back in the schoolhouse, sacrificial blood is splattering everywhere, the boys going at it with hacksaws and axes. They reach into the warm calf and rip out organs, intestines. The orphan pretends to faint.

The boys, bare-chested and covered with calf's blood, tie him up with their lassos. They tie him up with so much rope that only his quivering lips, his soft cheeks, his intelligent eyes and his firm, boyish buttocks remain visible. Long nozzles hang down from their gas masks like the trunks of some reconstituted biotech mammoths from a genetically engineered future. The orphan wonders about the future evolution of life on Earth. Afterward, he wonders where these pacifist boys get their gas masks.[18]

---

18. While I don't want to sanction a search through the author's biographical material for some kind of Freudian key to the story's meaning, the obvious similarities between Jake's stories of violence and bondage inside a one-room schoolhouse and the shooter's plan at Nickel Mines did lead Jake to

How's the egg, voice from above? asks Beth.

The egg is fine, says the orphan.

He drops several stolen chalkboards down, and chalk.

Where do you think the cows went? he asks.[19]

I've been strangely napping, she says.

She says, My dreams have been truly bizarre.

Beth disappears. It is reported that she has drowned in the swimming hole. The details are vague. Her footprints clearly lead to the pond but never exit. The pond is red and cloudy. The farm-boys continue to swim there regardless, playing their rough games with the rubber inner-tube.

When the boy goes to gather the eggs one morning, the trough is full of bloody eggs, nothing but bloody eggs. He screams and a man with a beard comes running in.

The eggs are all bloody, he says.

There's nothing wrong with these eggs, the bearded man says.

When he returns for the eggs in the evening there isn't even one.

---

the conclusion that his stories were magic and had somehow "caused" the murders. The distinction between mere prophecy and sympathetic magic is perhaps too nebulous for a guilt-racked child. While Jake *claimed* that he'd written the stories years earlier, he didn't give me his stories until after the shootings at Nickel Mines. It seems equally possible that he wrote or heavily revised this scene after the murders and his confusion was actually in the distinction between writing and current events, between a psychotic break and the process of revision. With that hypothesis in mind, it is interesting to note that in Jake's story there are no girls on the farm except for Beth, who has been locked away, supposedly for her own good (and whose biological sex is, in any case, an open question). Instead of girls, there are cows. Not such a leap within a culture that views both more or less as property and equally subordinate to men. One *might* read this absence as a basic component of the misogynistic and homoerotic fantasy world dreamed up by a budding gay bondage queen. On the other hand, it seems like he could also be describing the traumatized Amish community *after* the murder of the girls. —SB

19. See my previous note. —SB

The chickens have stopped laying.

He is sent to the barn where Beth was housed instead, to clean up her mess. The planks of the walls and floor are covered with blood and excrement. Under several layers, he finds her chalkboards, on which she has scrawled elaborate stories of abuse in ghostly chalk scribbles. On one chalkboard he finds a list of twenty words, with the first half X'd out. Effeminate is X'd out, orifice is X'd out. Left over are smudged, unscrupulous, bleached, gnash, convoluted, eroded, plateau, petroglyph, corroded, epidemic, and sores. Out of the corner of his eye the smudged words seem to form subtle patterns and non-Euclidean geometries. But then he discovers a note scrawled in lipstick that looks like thick greasy blood: Hey, voice from above, it says. *I am not really dead.*

One of the rough boys grabs him by the throat and drags him up the ladder into the hayloft. Once he has him up there, however, he is gentle, not rough, and he introduces the orphan to a different kind of chore.

I love you more than anything in "the world," the rough boy confesses.

I don't love you, thinks the orphan.

But he likes the rhythm of the chore. The farmboy really puts his back into it.

I'll tell you a secret, the farmboy says. They have discovered that the insane girl is not really dead.

Oh, really? says the orphan. He wiggles and shifts his position, as if he could care less about that crazy girl.

She has run off with a detective, says the farmboy. An overly curious man who carries a gun. An unscrupulous and adulterous man who will surely take advantage of her. A man who won't know how to deal with her narcoleptic events.

Afterward, the farmboy tells the orphan, She is to be shunned. We shall never mention her name again. We shall pretend she doesn't exist, until she realizes the error and loneliness of her ways.[20]

The bearded men call the orphan and the Fresh Air child into the empty schoolhouse.

We've been carefully monitoring you, they say, for signs of madness and criminality. We're afraid you may be flirting with the idea of pneumatic tires on your tractors.

We are perfectly sane, the orphan says.

We always follow the rules, says the Fresh Air child.

The bearded men speak to each other in their harsh foreign tongue. The men show them elaborate illustrations of the sort of behavior they are to avoid; in these illustrations, men are raping animals, lascivious children are having orgies, murderers grin at the erotic flowing of blood, women sport perms, boys deck themselves out in outlandish styles, and children of both sexes listen to radios.

We love madness and criminality, explain the bearded men. It's why we have so many rules. We hope we will not have to confine you in the barn, the bearded men say.

The boys are set to work copying from the blackboard:

I live for those who love me
Whose hearts are kind and true
For heaven that smiles above me
And waits my spirit, too
For human ties that bind me
For the task my God assigned me

---

20. In a discussion of Michael Lowenthal's novel *Avoidance* in his Amish essay (*Bay Guardian*, 2002) Stephen writes, "But Lowenthal recognizes that an articulate, empowered gay youth is not what the fantasy is about: a nostalgia for secret male societies, unspoken desires, the shame and pleasure of 'molestation'; very much like the fantasy of the Amish. If an Amishman or a boy could articulate their desire, they'd cease to be an Amishman or a boy." —JOB

For the bright hope left behind me
And the good that I can do

To make the tedium bearable, the orphan spends this time telling the Fresh Air Child some of Beth's stories, changing just enough details to make the pathetic, unreal stories of abuse seem more plausible and entertaining. The Fresh Air child tells stories of his own, and draws sketches of the characters, bearded men and doctors, teachers and skeletons, so that before long the orphan can't keep all the details straight, what is his story and what someone else's, what is real and what is made up. It's like a quilt or collage of missing paperboys, bondage scenes, mental institutions, drownings, dissected brains, mysterious pregnancies, and intersexed children raised as boys.

The orphan has never been happier.

We have to escape from this farm, the orphan tells the Fresh Air child. Pack your bags.

The Fresh Air child says, Is this a farm, or a vast mental institution? Is this what they call transitional housing?

We'll be musicians, says the orphan.

We'll be stars, says the Fresh Air child.

That night they slip down to the river with the electric guitar and into the boat and they float on downstream, far away from the farm. They travel for many nights and hear the barking of dogs on the shore, and daytimes sleep in the boat back among the reeds. They leave their boat and wander on foot down streets where every family has two sons. The oldest son is always adopted, because the women think they are barren, or they think their men are full of faulty sperm. Either way, as soon as they adopt a boy, the problem corrects itself and they get pregnant. They wander past vacant lots and garbage dumps. Everything here is rusting or the color of rust. They wander through vast slums, and they wander through a pulsing, writhing image of the world.

They receive rides from strangers who look familiar; they have taken leaves of absence. Somebody is muttering on the car radio, too quiet to be understood. It sounds like the future is trying to leak through. The practice of joy, one stranger says, involves the spontaneous rejection of one's belief or disbelief.

Joy should be embraced cynically, the stranger tells them. It is best to build up structures, unconsciously, such as some ridiculous "career," so that these structures can be ecstatically abandoned.

All joy is erotic, says the handsome stranger. He is stern, but not without a certain appeal. Joy involves the reversal of expected roles, he says. For example, he says, and he whispers what he likes.

Afterward, the landscape opens up into a different kind of desert. As if the earth has been stripped to its baked skull, as if the flimsy layers of skin and living tissue have been peeled back to reveal the bleached-out substructure, the eye sockets, the mineral heart. It is electric. It is as if consciousness has eroded itself to expose the wasteland of eternity. Everywhere the orphan sees skulls gnashing their teeth. Hell's backbone and fluted walls. Aspen stands bleached and willowy like forests of ethereal bone dancing in the wind. Severe rock faces red as beating hearts or peaked mounds of grey. Skulls skulls skulls. Huge masses of cloud convoluted on top like the lobes of many brains cut off flat at the bottom, creating a plane in the sky parallel to the tops of eroded plateaus. Anasazi petroglyphs resemble magnetic resonance images of the brain. Here at the bottom of a canyon a flash of pale green reeds dancing around a muddy ribbon. Against the muted colors of the landscape the river is insane: a rippling silver snake of electricity coursing through the dry rusty corroded landscape like a bolt of gleaming delirious metal in the brain.

What is the name of this river? the boy asks.

This is the same river that runs through your city, says the pedagogical stranger. It runs through your city and it runs through the farm and it runs through vast slums and deserts all the way to the ocean.

The river here is startling confirmation that every configuration belongs to him. Every face is his birthright. The face of his missing twin is a story about ecstatic submission and a revolutionary order. The face of the missing crazy girl is equally cunning and ineffective. The dust is in his hair. Compassion is his to choose, not because it is the law but because it is a deep and complicated pleasure which has convoluted the brain in a way only different from a tiger's. A tiger has stripes, he remembers. These stripes are madness. The orphan feels as if the lid of his head has been opened wide and that the catacombs of the sky *are* his mind: where thoughts are buried, where toxic chemicals go to die. The boys eat grapefruits throughout the day in an air-conditioned luxury car and at night the fixed stars and the satellites come out overhead. They build a fire and eat popcorn out of a foil pie dish on a stick. They roast marshmallows, letting the marshmallows crisp well past the golden brown stage into lurid blackened husks.

It seems here to the orphan that any action the living might take is of the ultimate consequence; he takes out his guitar. The human brain is crucial to the cosmos—the relationship between its two lobes and its potential new cauliflower growths and the immensity of time stripped bare in its purplish dance of colliding minerals and glacial damage only confirm the importance of the human faculty for music.

Together, they play a little song. It is the sound of *breaking out* or *breaking through*.

How do families drive through this painted desert intact? The landscape should sever something. The orphan gnashes his teeth at the sky. He calms down, eats a chocolate bar with some roasted marshmallow.

In the morning they find themselves in a valley of mushroom-shaped rock formations. The top layer of stone erodes more slowly than the bottom layer, the stranger explains. Clouds like phantom frogs cross the sky and on the earth two male lizards with blue bellies engage in a pre-mating dance. They fight and chase each other to form a violent spinning circle, unclear who is chasing who, until finally the smaller mounts the larger.

They drive on through scrubby high deserts with shreds of cloud so close he feels they might drive into them. Pale green shrubs with cerebral purple undertones. Cows once chewed on these shrubs. A waiter with a pinched face baked into an expression of vague disgust serves them pie.

The stranger leaves them in a city by the ocean. They walk around the docks and see all the pimps and whores and fishwives and sailors and petty thieves they had always known they would find here.

They gaze out over the water. All the orphan's intuitions in the desert were false, about the brain and the importance of "human" consciousness. He sees here that nothing matters, nothing at all.

He can't imagine what to do with the egg.

What should we do next? asks his lover.

He enters a tacky shop and buys a postcard. He writes: I am in the west now, and I am a rock and roll star. I have become rich and famous because of my catchy songs about sex and drugs and death and nihilism.

He affixes a 19-cent stamp and he mails the postcard to the farm.

Soon after, an epidemic breaks out. Almost the whole population of the city suffers from racking coughs and painful, bleeding sores.[21]

---

21. When Jake told me that he "had AIDS" I was skeptical. I asked him if he meant that he was HIV+ and he said, "Yeah, I guess so." Who knows? The specter of HIV certainly enters his written work enough, and it seems likely that HIV, in his mind, would come to seem like an inevitable punishment handed down by an angry god for his transgressions—whether he actually ever had gay sex (I have no idea) or only imagined it. I've told this story before, but I think it bears repeating. "Carl" was an at-risk youth I worked with in San Francisco. (Another strange coincidence for my editor—he too came from Des

---

Moines, a small city that seems to produce an inordinate number of messed-up gay boys.) Carl said his best friend had died; his father had died; he was raped in broad daylight by some guys in a Camaro. He said two of his ex-lovers had died. Eventually he claimed to be HIV+, going so far as to emerge from an anonymous HIV test visibly distraught at the results; his social worker was in the waiting room when he came out. None of this was true, he just wanted some sympathy and attention. At 19 he hadn't experienced enough death that he felt he deserved our sympathy and attention. He felt he had to cheat.—SB

4_____

You descend into this place. It's cool, and the tunnel is low, the whitish paint peeled off in organic splotches, like an airplane embarkation tunnel covered with a comforting mold. There are little squares overhead as you slope down, little squares that let in daylight from out there, the world. It's hot and smog-hazy out there, but down below it's deliciously cool and creepy before you even get to the prize, down a short flight of steps and into the catacombs. The bodies, or skeletons mostly, in various states of decay, are dressed in their embalmed clothing from the 1500s, 1600s, 1700s, lined up by the hundreds, as if standing, but not standing; marionettes fastened to the walls. Hundreds and hundreds of them down every passageway, crowded together, really just bones, eye sockets and clothing, but a few still have some leathery skin attached to their faces, even a moustache, this one seems to have died screaming. Here's the special room full of babies, like cracked porcelain dolls in their dainty clothes. Here are the women, well preserved or not. The highlight—everyone agrees on this—is the little girl, Rosalie Lombardo, born in 1918 and dead in 1920. Her doctor, who took his secret methods with him to the grave, injected her with chemicals so she remains almost perfectly preserved. She's in a cradle or coffin behind glass, perched between two not-so-perfectly preserved little girls, like Christ between the thieves. "She looks like she's only sleeping," the guidebook says. Or maybe not.

Brother stops reading and shows Sister the picture of Rosalie Lombardo. Oh Brother, says Sister, she's beautiful and dead.[22]

Every night Brother and Sister sneak out to the barn. In a secret cubbyhole, they've hidden an old biology book and a radio/cassette player. They don't have batteries yet, because Mother and Father belong to a religious cult that believes war and electricity are evil. There are taboos against permed hair, patterned cloth, and overly decorative linoleum. Plain things are good; fancy things are sin.

In their one-room schoolhouse, Brother and Sister are taught English, although the language their parents speak at home is more glottal. The school doesn't teach geography or history, for these subjects present the outside world, with its wars, intrigues, and technology. The teacher won't teach fairy tales or myths; she objects to stories that aren't true, such as those in which animals talk and act like people, or stories that involve magic. Reading material must not glorify physical force, nationalism, militarism, or modern technology. Each story should teach a moral; those that are just nice are not good enough.

Brother and Sister do learn how to add. Some of you girls may marry men who aren't so good with figures, the teacher says. You'll need to know how to help along with the figuring.

But Brother is the best speller in the school and Sister likes to make up stories. Their spelling lists are full of plain, useful words: fertilizer, chores, ailment, manure; the teacher's name is Darlene.

The teacher doesn't much care for the scientific method. Brother and Sister love the scientific method. Brother wants to cut up animals and corpses and see what makes them work. The teacher rarely paddles children; only for lying or cheating or vulgar

---

22. In fact, she is, and can be found just as described in the catacombs in Palermo. —JOB

language or smutty talk. Only for open disobedience or physically dangerous activity, such as running into the highway or teasing a nervous buggy horse.

The teacher doesn't like Sister's writing style, either. What kind of a fancy word is *glottal*? she asks. And what do you need such long sentences for? What kind of silly punctuation is this?

It's a semi-colon, says Sister. It's useful for forcing a connection between ideas that may not be obviously related.

Vain, fancy ideas, says the teacher, and rips Sister's paper in two.

In town, at the store, Brother sees a stranger: fancy and English. Father is in the back room, pricing different fertilizers. Brother bumps into the stranger, and says: I'm sorry. Hello. Then he does the stranger a favor. Afterward, the stranger slips him a present.

That night in the barn, Brother and Sister snap the batteries into place and listen to some music. Sister is delighted. I hope you didn't do anything too sinful to get these batteries, she says, but hopes that he certainly did. They pretend they are singers. They dance. They act like crazy children, and like prisoners. Sister tells about a time before Darlene was there, when they had a more exciting teacher — a stranger with a more troubled relationship to rules. Brother finds a dead cat by the highway and uses his radio to re-animate it with electricity. He cuts the cat's brain in two. He believes the English of his secret biology textbook is what his teacher Darlene means by vulgar language and smutty talk.

Listen, Sister, he says. Cutting the neural connections between one half of the brain and the other is useful to control the flurries of random electrical activity that cause epileptic fits.

Sister says, I am so impressed and delighted with all your smutty talk.

Sister says, You shall be a doctor and I shall be a nurse.

But Brother graduates from eighth grade and his schooling is over. He helps with the chickens and the pigs and learns something more useful than all-day book-learning. At school, Sister is alone with her chalkboards and her chalk.

At night, they journey. While the other members of the family lie asleep and dreaming, Brother and Sister travel through the moonlight, or the severe dark if there is no moon. In the moonlight, everything that in the daytime is imprisoned and subdued seems to pulse with a secret desire to explode. Without the moon it is just a vibrating darkness under haze; the barn is enchanted.

Brother examines the map of a corpse, from his old biology book.

It's time to sow your wild oats, says Sister. Don't you want to put an engine in your buggy and snort crystal meth?

Brother just grunts and traces the path of an artery with his finger.

Or get a paper route? asks Sister. And spend the profits on some prohibited form of transportation? A moped, or a speed boat perhaps?

These *are* my wild oats, says Brother, gesturing at the severed cat's brain, the radio, and his collage of biology and anatomy photos. I want to go to high school. I want to go to college, and then medical school.

But he only gathers the eggs and feeds the chicks. He only sneaks out at night to read his outdated biology book and cut up dead animals. He develops dark circles under his eyes, and a dazed look, as if he is wandering through a dream. Sister is also suffering from sleep deprivation although daytimes, sometimes, she nods off without warning. She has narcoleptic events. As she copies verses off the board at school over and over again she begins to hallucinate.

I live for those who love me.
Whose hearts are kind and true
For heaven that smiles above me
And waits my spirit, too

The simple sentences lose their subjects and verbs; expanding in elaborate pathways, blurring into an animated monster of scribbles, so that hidden behind the embalmed toddler of language she detects another script, pulsing and alive: full of clauses, frivolous adjectives, and semi-colons, it tells an infinity of stories, or maybe only the same story over and over again; Sister isn't sure, really, if these stories can really be reduced to that one meaning, or if it is only the residue of these trite verses which occludes her vision—

For human ties that bind me
For the task my God assigned me
For the bright hope left behind me
And the good that I can do

—so that each and every twisting pathway leads her imagination only to the same conclusion, and each story becomes only another story of sacrificial death.

Then it is time to be baptized. This cult is called Anabaptist, because they think baptizing babies is wrong. In the old days, Anabaptists were tortured and martyred because they wouldn't take their babies down by the river. They wouldn't dip them in the water. The bishop tells Brother and Sister all about these fabulous martyrs and their exquisite torment. He shows them illustrations. Brother and Sister jump right in the river. Where the river goes once it leaves the farm is anybody's guess. How can Sister describe it without a fancy vocabulary? It feels both like one thing and like every thing that might happen. She is part of it, and nothing.

The country is at war. People come home from this war with fancy ailments, not all of them rooted in reality—racking coughs and painful bleeding sores. Brother must do some mandatory voluntary service to avoid joining the Marines or the Navy, which is prohibited by their cult. He serves and studies in a hospital and Sister comes along and studies to be a nurse.[23]

Sister meets a man who is also a member of the cult. He is growing his first stubble, not yet thick enough to hide the fact that he is soft. He is so much daintier than the rest of the farm boys, as if he is the sort of man people mean when they talk about strangers. *Sister* is such a drab and useful word, he tells her. Don't you have another name? Her new friend loves to prepare picnic baskets and take Beth out to the meadow, where he draws ornate scenarios in his sketchbook. Beth is lively and gay. She talks and she sings with this man, and she takes her long, lustrous hair out from underneath its covering. Her boyfriend is stunned. It's the color of light itself; he visualizes an entire cosmos made of the hair of Beth, a rippling wig of light that expands geometrically in every direction and causes him nothing but longing. Never have I seen such beautiful hair, he says, and he begins his elaborate sketch.

They get married and he gives her a shiny gold watch. But then he goes off to Greece for his own voluntary service. In Greece, there is an accident. The lake is deep or bottomless or disturbing: pale and green. He is riding along in his buggy, but is hit by an SUV—a hybrid—and hurled into the lake. He drowns. Whenever Sister talks about it, she says, *He drowned in the country of Greece.* She doesn't want to say: *He drowned in Greece.* She doesn't want anyone to think he drowned in an enormous vat at McDonalds.

Now that your husband is dead, Sister's parents tell her, you can come live with us on the farm again. If your lover's death proved anything, it is the dangers and evils of modern transportation. Speed kills; the world is not for you. Maybe Brother is off in the world studying to be a doctor and to use electricity and other sinful

---

23. Voluntary service was a standard alternative to military service for Amish and Mennonite conscientious objectors before 1973, when the United States discontinued the draft. —JOB

components of the modern world—cars, cameras, heart fibrilla-
tors—but he is a boy. Boys are different, as is self-evident.

Sister works quietly alongside her parents on the farm. She never
wears her gold watch anymore but late at night she hears it ticking,
ticking, ticking. She wishes for a child, or maybe two. She wants
something that will love her, something that will have no choice but
to love her, so she will no longer feel alone. Meanwhile, her father's
beard grows long and white. He sits in his rocking chair, which is
made out of thin canes of wood like whips, and he rocks. The rocking chair is gnarled and the old man is gnarled. He rarely speaks
in his harsh, Germanic language, but Mother interprets his silences
and his monosyllables for Sister, and Sister only listens, as she and
Mother quilt together. He is communicating his worries about technological progress and the loss of community, Mother says. He is
insisting on humility, simple living, and a resignation to do the will
of God. The Bible is open in his lap; he mumbles something, and
nods off. Mother says, He said that we are strangers in this land.

Mother says, Father sometimes worries that your attitude isn't
right. Father looks at the weird loops and geometries that creep
into your quilting and thinks it's the product of fancy thinking.

Mother quotes the Bible, where God is very angry and kicks
the man and the woman and the snake out of the garden. He curses
them all. He tells the woman that she will be subordinate and that
she will suffer much pain in childbearing. He tells the man that it
will be nothing but work and thistles and death as he scratches his
meager living from the dust to which he shall return. He tells the
snake that he will bite men's feet and that men will hit him on the
head; Sister believes that the chicken house is full of snakes.

It is her job to enter this long narrow building and gather the
eggs. As soon as the baby male chicks are hatched, it is her job to
dump them back behind the building on a heap of steaming manure.
The building has no windows. It is lined with enormous fans. The
sun is blazing. On the top layer of corpses, insects are eating the

eyeballs of some still-living chicks. Sometimes Father grinds them up to use as fertilizer on the fields. One day she is wandering across the earth and she comes across a screeching baby chick with no legs or wings that is somehow still alive. Just a beak, really; shrieking, shrieking, shrieking. Sister thinks it is the most horrifying and true and beautiful song she has ever heard.

Dreaming, the earth is alive. Sister meets a snake in the chicken house. At that point she suffers from a narcoleptic event; Sister nods off. Afterward, she finds an egg and next thing she knows, out comes a baby, or two. She suckles the twins in secret and hides them in the barn.

Meanwhile, Brother has made it in the world. Now that he's a doctor, he can cut up dead things whenever he wants. But he feels he is missing something. Cutting up dead things isn't enough. He drives around and listens to music and watches old movies on cable tv—*Attack of the Crab Monsters* or *Shadow of a Doubt*—and flies in a jet to Palermo, to see the catacombs and the corpse of Rosalie Lombardo. She is not a disappointment, she is beautiful and dead. In Palermo, the scooters are always rushing up and down the streets with a high-pitched whining noise. Back home, he writes the family letters, and Mother reads them out loud at the dinner table, as Father dozes in his chair. I sometimes feel as if I'm being suffocated by a vast living organism, Brother writes. The world. The world makes me uneasy, just as Mother and Father and Darlene always said it would. Back home, everything is peaceful, segmented, and subdued. Here in the city it is all pulsing, beating, a never-ending vastness of tissues.

Mother sighs, contented.

Have some more apple butter, Mother says to Sister. Have some more hamloaf. After dinner, we'll write Brother back.

Sister sneaks out to feed the baby, or maybe the twins, who are hidden in the barn. Without her love, she supposes they would develop a glazed look, not exactly living and not exactly dead.

Mother writes back to Brother in her wobbly script, and asks everyone else to do the same, all the vague and busy and inbred siblings and cousins who live on identical farms in the surrounding countryside. Mother will scrutinize Sister's letter to Brother, and then shove it in the big envelope bursting with letters. Sister can only write in code. I remember the good clean fun we used to have playing in the barn! she writes. Sometimes I think I have never had such fun! Remember when we pretended we were prisoners? Oh, how silly children are. Please come visit soon, for I would like to escape from my pleasant chores for just one afternoon talking with you about how good God is and the joys of living on the farm!

But Brother doesn't come. He thinks it is just those exclamation points that give Sister's writing such a hysterical tone.

Sister grows desperate. This is no life. She runs out to the highway that passes her farm, and removes her hair covering. Her lustrous hair blows in the wind. A passing van slams on its brakes. The driver swings open the fancy red passenger's door, and beckons her to join him. He drives her across the endless plains in his sinful van, and they spend the night in a dilapidated hotel that rises from the plains like the rotted carcass of some ancient and monstrous life form. She wakes in the night and lights a candle and wanders the endless halls in her nightgown. The hotel has more levels than she would have supposed possible. She feels vaguely disturbed, as if there is something wrong with her own size. She thinks she may have forgotten something, back on the farm, but she can't think of what it could be.

The next day, the man drives her to the Ozarks, where they will live with his mother and be safe from the coming apocalypse. Her new home is tucked away in some trees on a raggedy piece of land next to an unattractive river. Her new home is as small as its basement is vast. Crammed into every corner of the basement is a network of rusty bicycle parts, intermingled with moldy pamphlets touting the benefits of either her husband's cult or of blue-green algae. The moldy, congealed pamphlets have become burrows for some sort of rodent Sister is as yet unfamiliar with. You don't need to worry about that basement, her husband tells her. It's like my personal space. Her husband's mother is a silent woman with bushy eyebrows. Soon, she is dead. God tells the man that he can bring her back. Her husband shoves his mother's body in the refrigerator freezer and announces the impending miracle to the media.

In River City, Brother sees these things on television.

Isn't this a crazy world? his patients ask him.

I do not know what this world looks like, says Brother.

I have a problem with my stomach, his patients say.

There is something rotten stuck in my intestines, his patients say.

Everything I consume is disgusting, his patients say.

He examines them thoroughly.

There is nothing wrong with your innards, he says. But maybe you should have your brain examined.

He explains that the brain is composed of two lobes, and that the relationship between these two lobes is poorly understood. Somewhere in the communication between the dominant half and the other half lies the problem of their indigestion.

Sister has been quiet for many years. Her parents no longer speak to her, because they want her to see that the man she married is a wicked man and the life she lives is a wicked life. She has worked alongside her crazy husband, who is a charlatan, without speaking. Come to think of it, she has never spoken. She has never said a thing, except with Brother in their childhood. She remembers the elaborate scenarios they acted out at night in the barn. They imagined strangers, it seems, who would break all the rules. They imagined bizarre ways of giving birth; they imagined journeys by ship and by train. They told magical stories which they imagined would change them, and transform the farm.

Sister gets a job as a nurse. Every day she works at the hospital and every day she drives out to a farm after work to buy eggs and every day she drives past a lake. She thinks about that boy who loved her, her husband, who drowned in the country of Greece. If he had never died she never would have married this crazy man and she never would have been shunned.

At the hospital, her patients complain that they have no will to live. They have hysterical pregnancies and miscarriages and give birth to deformed fetuses. They complain that the doctor doesn't love them, and that they've been locked up in coffins. Brother doesn't speak anymore either. He thinks that these people from the bad part of town, from down by the river, who complain and complain and complain about their imaginary ailments are just too much. He speaks to them as little as possible, but he writes them prescriptions for pills. He drives away in his long black car.

Sister calls up on the phone.

How are you? she says.

Brother says, Good.

How are you? says Brother.

I'm doing OK.

Sister feels something moving inside. Is it language? Something isn't right.

How are your patients? she asks.

All of my patients are sick to the stomach, says Brother. All of my patients have pain in the gut.

How are your patients? he asks.

My patients are different, says Sister. It's women's trouble, you know. Trouble with their fetuses and wombs.

Sure, Brother says.

He feels a cramp coming on.

How are our parents? Sister asks.

Who knows? says Brother. I can't call them up on the phone, because they believe telephones are evil. I can drive to see them in my long black car, but it is a difficult journey from River City out to the farm where they live and I get so tired of the way they think my car is evil. They write letters to me, but their hands tremble so, and their script is all wobbly and almost impossible to read.

At least you aren't shunned, says Sister.

Brother shrugs. There is a long silence. All Sister can think of is code. Everything. Everything is just a code.

You should come to visit me, says Sister. You really should come to visit.

Your husband makes me nervous, says Brother.

Please come, says Sister.

I'll see what I can do, says Brother.

Sister has nothing more to say, and Brother has nothing more to say. In their heads, they keep talking. When their story is over, they'll never speak again.

Sister is sadder every day. She stares out the kitchen window as if she is listening to the grey haze of sky. The haze is fibrous and interwoven, like the weird moldy papers and things that look like bones she's glimpsed down in the cellar. Her crazy husband tells her the apocalypse will start next month, according to one or another incarnation of Elijah. The final battle is coming and Satan will be cast out. What most other charlatans and evangelical lunatics don't understand, he tells her, is that Satan is inside the whole human race. The human race is a symbiotic organism. There are no good people and no bad people, no chosen sheep and black ones, no wheat and no chaff. The evil half has to be burned out of every last human. Everyone will be burnt simultaneously from the inside—they will all suffer together through unimaginable pain as an entire 50% of their souls is seared out of their very being. Like a lobotomy without anaesthetic.

And then they will be beings of light alone.

Interesting theory, thinks Sister, from a man who put his own mother inside a refrigerator and told the world he would bring her back from the dead. Sister is depressed.

One day, after picking up the eggs, she drives down to the lake and she gets out and walks around the lake and she sees that it is nice and deep, or even bottomless. The water is murky and blackish and green. She gets back in her car and she drives right in. The car sinks to the bottom and the water rushes in the open window.

Some friendly people see her drive in, people who believe in life. They fish her out, and they fish the eggs out too. They call a policeman, who wraps her in a warm blanket and chats with her in his car. His ass is so flat, as if he's been sitting on cushions and chatting his whole life long.

It's a marvel, he says. These eggs weren't damaged at all.

Did you drive in there on purpose? he asks.

Sister doesn't answer. She is shivering and dazed.

I'm just asking, he says. I know you are a good church girl, and suicide is a crime.

I guess I must have fallen asleep at the wheel, Sister says. I guess I didn't look where I was going.

The cop drops her off back at home, where her husband is waiting. Her husband remains silent, implying that the decision to kill or not kill oneself and the method one chooses for fulfillment are considerations as meaningless as the question of how to live. Or something like that.

The next week, she borrows her husband's maroon-colored car to drive to work. It is a long shift, all through the night. The night is dark and full of stars and the night at the hospital is full of people with many ailments. The hospital is shaped like intestines and it is full of fluorescent lights that make the sick people look even worse. Nobody becomes well in this hospital. Instead, their sicknesses grow more convoluted, to resemble the hospital itself. She wanders through these hallways, up and down circular and grey flights of stairs. She ducks into a room where a thin girl with a deathly complexion and a swelling belly is muttering and sobbing.

I swallowed something shiny and hard, the girl says. And now I'm going to have a baby.

That isn't exactly possible, Sister explains.

Stop raping me, says the girl.

Sister doesn't know what is happening. It occurs to her that she could never find the end of this place, and she's not sure which of them is which. Which of them the patient and which of them the nurse. Sister opens the girl's chart and reads the notes written by her social worker LuAnn. In her latest understanding of her childhood, it says of the girl, her father's sexual appetite is insatiable and omnivorous. Despite the false aspects of the life history she tells, no one doubts the seriousness of her behavior or her continued threats to hurt herself.

When she gets off work, Sister drives home. It is early morning and her husband is still sleeping. He opens his eyes as if registering a particularly vivid dream, and closes them again. The mist rises from the river back in the trees and lies low to the ground like a ghostly shroud. She writes him a note.

I have gone to get the eggs, it says.

She pauses, wondering if she meant to say something else. Perhaps she could have written: You are just another bleak and tangy surface of the material world. There is nothing in your pungent flesh to tempt me anymore. I moved beyond you long ago. It is only the afterimage, the burn on your retina, which writes to you now.

She decides that *I have gone to get the eggs* will do.

Beth drives to the lake. There is nobody around, there is nobody watching. She drives right in. She drives right in and she sinks down in her husband's car, which rests down there now next to the car she drove in the week before. It's then that she looks over and realizes that the front seat is empty of eggs and it's in that moment that she remembers what she left behind her on the farm, hidden in the barn. It was her baby; there was really only one, a little boy she left there all alone. The water rushes into the car and the water rushes into her lungs.

Many of the people who knew her, who dislike her crazy husband, are suspicious: maybe her husband drove her in that lake himself or at least drove her to do it. In the newspaper, her co-workers are quoted to this effect. They emphasize her mysterious bruises. Her patients are quoted, including the sad girl with the swelling belly. The emphasis there is on her kindness and appropriate care. Brother is quoted as well. He remembers her as a girl, so lively and gay. Although everyone has a slightly different interpretation, everyone agrees that she is in a better place. Everyone agrees that she is better off now than when she was alive.[24]

---

24. The obvious correspondence between this story and the stories Jake reportedly told of the suicide of his own mother becomes compelling evidence in light of the fact that what little verifiable information we have about Jake concerns his mother's death. Stephen provided me with a copy of the police report on her death (along with relevant pages from the State Water Patrol's report, including a death certificate), which he claims he was given by Jake himself. The story told in this report clearly matches the previous tale; a woman (Elyzabeth in one report, Elizabeth in the other) attempts to drown herself—once unsuccessfully, by driving her car into a lake, then she tries again and succeeds. Although we have blacked out all identifying details in the report, I can assure skeptical readers that it is legitimate; I have actually spoken to one of the officers involved, a very friendly man who appears in the report as "Officer Brian B." The case is just as it seems in the report and further research revealed that Elyzabeth R's maiden name is in fact the same as the "real" name of Jake Yoder—suggesting that she probably came from an Amish background. Here then, we seem to have something we've been missing: an indisputable fact. The corpse of a dead woman. A woman with a name and biography. According to the friendly officer, she was in fact married to a creepy man whom nobody seems to have liked, either "Daniel" or "Donald" depending on which report you read; a few years later, this man abandoned his squat little house and vanished into the netherworld of evangelical, survivalist trailer-dwellers. As for a child, Brian B had no memory of a child and there

_____

is no mention of a child in the report. And yet they'd interrogated the husband, they'd notified the husband—where was the boy? Being raised by his grandparents on some Amish farm? Sitting in his public school classroom fantasizing about his Language Arts teacher? Brian did state that if the boy wasn't living at home at that time, he would have had no reason to speak to him, and I'll admit that this police report almost convinced me that this whole ludicrous story is, more or less, just as Stephen has told it. And yet, in one of his most recent books (*No Time Flat*, 2006) Stephen used police reports as an integral part of the plot (although to what end exactly, I cannot say). In an interview (www.novelistic.typepad.com) he says that these police reports were fake, but based on careful study and alteration of real police reports. Clearly, then, he is accustomed not only to reading police reports, wherever he might find them—I suppose you can find anything on the web these days; I've certainly been startled at how easy it has been to uncover information about Stephen, including his past addresses and even his jail time—but also to incorporating them into fanciful stories. Who is to say that an imaginary child, Jake Yoder, wasn't simply named after the woman in the report?—JOB

▮▮▮▮▮▮▮▮▮▮▮▮▮▮▮

Offense / Incident Report

Report Date	Type of Incident		Complaint No.	Case Status
06/08/▮ 0000	INFORMATION REPORT		▮▮▮▮▮	CLOSED

Occurred on **06/04/▮ 0000** to **06/08/▮ 0000**

Incident Location

Street Address			City	State	Zip Code
NE C			▮▮▮▮		
Sector	Precinct	Geo	Ward	Latitude	Primary Location
		▮▮▮▮▮		Longitude	Secondary Location

Dispatch Information

Received Date / Time	Call Received Via	Dispatched Date / Time	Call Dispatched As
06/07/▮ 0000	CENTRAL DISPATC	06/07/▮ 2120	

Arrived Date / Time	Departed Date / Time	Offense Category	TTY Ref.#	TeleType Operator
06/07/▮ 2129	06/08/▮ 0200	AGAINST PERSON		

Officers

ID	Name	Role	Arrived Scene	Departed Scene
165	B▮▮▮, BRIAN	REPORTING		
165	B▮▮▮, BRIAN	ENTERED BY		

Offenses

Charge				State Statute	State Charge Code	Category	
Cause Number	Local Code	Jurisdiction		Type/Class	Bond Type		Bond Amount
INFORMATION REPORT						AGAINST PERSON	
1							0.00

Offense / Incident Narrative

On 06-07-▮ around 2120 hours, I was advised to contact dispatch by telephone as soon as possible. When I made contact, I was advised that some fishermen had located what appeared to be a human hand sticking out of the water at the B▮▮▮ Creek bridge on Hwy ▮ I advised Central to contact Sheriff O▮▮▮▮ of the situation.

I arrived on the scene at 2129 hours. At the time, a storm front was moving through and there was heavy rain and wind conditions. I saw what appeared to be a hand sticking out of the water about twenty feet off of the bank. Due to the windy conditions at the time it was hard to determine if the object was a hand or a piece of drift wood.

When Sheriff O▮▮▮▮ arrived on the scene, the weather had calmed a little bit. The object was viewed in several locations, including from the bridge. Sheriff O▮▮▮▮ advised that it did look like

Reporting Officer	B▮▮▮, BRIAN	Approving Officer (I) 161 C▮▮▮, STEVE
		(Cover Pages Only)
Approving Officer (II)		Approving Officer (III)
(Cover Pages Only)		(Cover Pages Only)

© 1994 - 2006. Information T▮▮▮▮▮, Inc. http://www.itiusa.com

H███ County Sheriff's Department

Offense / Incident Report

Report Date	Type of Incident	Complaint No.	Case Status
06/08/███ 0000	INFORMATION REPORT	████	CLOSED

a left human hand. At that time, the coroner, and Conservation Agent Kevin D███, who had boat available, were summoned to the scene after being placed on standby earlier. Deputy John S███, who was working the CORPS assignment arrived on the scene.

When Agent D███ arrived on the scene with the boat, I went with him in the boat to the area where the hand was. As we approached it was determined that it indeed was a left human hand. The tips of the fingers were turning black and the skin was starting to slough off. Agent D███ advised that there was a watch on the arm portion and that it appeared to be a gold woman's watch. As the weather was still slightly stormy, we landed the boat to discuss recovery and to call for additional personnel.

While waiting for personnel to arrive and discussing who the victim might be, the water calmed down. We knew that a woman was missing from the O█████ area and that she was driving a maroon colored car. We shined a spot light back on the scene and there was a slight red or maroon reflection in the water. Closer examination revealed a radio antenna sticking up through the water on the bank side, about four feet from the hand. At that time a call was made to Central to locate the nearest divers and to put D█████████ towing on standby. Central called back a short time later to advise that there were divers on the W█████ Fire Department and they were available. I advised Central to have them respond. At that point, myself and Deputy S███ were assigned to █ Hwy at the entrance, where Deputy S███ accounted for who was coming and going, and I handled traffic control.

After the car and the body was recovered and removed from the scene, I cleared the scene. I responded to D█████████ Service in C████ and assisted Deputy/Detective C████ seal the car.

Property

Quantity	Description	Make	Model	S/N	Ref. No.	Disposition	Value	Recovered ID/Date
0.00	PERSONAL PROPERTY					RELEASED TO OWNER	0.00	
Number of Line Items	1					Total Value	0.00	
Number of Recov. Items	0					Total Recov. Value	0.00	

Victim / Person

Name (Last, First Middle Suffix)	Race	Sex	DOB	Age	Juvenile	SSN	Moniker
R██████, ELYZABETH				0			

☐ Injured Medical Care Sought Treatment Disposition ☐ Willing to Prosecute Relation to Suspect

Reporting Officer	B████, BRIAN	Approving Officer (I) 161 C████, STEVE
		(Cover Pages Only)
Approving Officer (II)		Approving Officer (III)
(Cover Pages Only)		(Cover Pages Only)

Printed 08/24/2007 1205

▓▓▓▓▓▓▓▓▓▓▓▓▓▓▓

Offense / Incident Report

Report Date 06/08/▓▓ 0000	Type of Incident INFORMATION REPORT		Complaint No. ▓▓▓▓▓	Case Status CLOSED

Phone Numbers

Type	Phone	Ext/PIN	Email Addresses Type	Email Address
HOME				

Identification Numbers

Local PD #	Local SO #	State # 0	Military ID #	Branch	Rank
FBI #	NCIC #	DOC #	Passport ID #	Type	Issued By	Exp. Date
			Alien Req.	Type	Issued By	Exp. Date

Supplemental Report

Supp. No. 0001	Date / Time 6/8/▓▓ 7:12 AM	ID 170	Officer Name H▓▓, ROBBIE

INTERVIEW W/ REPORTING PARTIES

On 06-08-▓▓ at 0014 hours, I responded to 304 West ▓▓▓ Street in ▓▓▓▓▓, ▓▓ to conduct a follow-up investigation and interview the reporting parties to the incident.

I contacted Dennis W. D▓▓▓▓ (W/M, DOB: ▓-▓-37) of 302 West ▓▓▓ Street, C▓▓▓▓ and Dennis Eugene D▓▓▓▓ (W/M, DOB: ▓-▓-63) of 304 West ▓▓▓ Street, C▓▓▓▓ and spoke with them about their discovery. Both subjects prepared written statements as to their actions while at the scene. (See written statements.)

Supplemental Report

Supp. No. 0002	Date / Time 6/8/▓▓ 10:34 AM	ID 172	Officer Name S▓▓, JOHN

RECORD OF SCENE

I arrived at approximately 2215 hours to assist the other officers. Upon my arrival I was advised that Conservation Agent Kevin D▓▓▓ was enroute with a boat. When Agent D▓▓▓ arrived and determined that it was in fact a body I was ordered to keep a record of all subjects in and out of the scene. I wrote the names and times on an officers daily log sheet. When the scene was cleared I turned over my log to Detective Steve C▓▓▓.

Reporting Officer B▓▓, BRIAN	Approving Officer (I) 161 C▓▓▓, STEVE (Cover Pages Only)
Approving Officer (II) (Cover Pages Only)	Approving Officer (III) (Cover Pages Only)

Page 3 of 12   Printed 08/24/2007 1205

© 1994 - 2006. Information ▓▓▓▓▓ Technologies, Inc. http://www.itiusa.com

H█████ County Sheriff's Department

███████████████████████

Offense / Incident Report

Report Date	Type of Incident	Complaint No.	Case Status
06/08/████0000	**INFORMATION REPORT**	████████	**CLOSED**

Supplemental Report

Supp. No.	Date / Time	ID	Officer Name
0003	6/9/██ 11:43 AM	161	C██████, STEVE

FOLLOW UP

At approximately 2300 hrs of June 7th, ████ I received a call from Central Dispatch. I was advised at this time to respond with a camera to the bridge on █ Hwy. that crosses the B██████ Arm of T██████ Lake where a body had been found. I arrived at the scene and met with H█████ County Deputy Brian B██████ who pointed out the left hand of an unidentified subject sticking out of the water approximately twenty feet from the shore line. Also noted was approximately six inches of a vehicle's radio antenna that was sticking out of the water approximately eight feet to the right of the hand from my location on the shore line.

I then entered a boat that was on the scene with ███████████ Conservation Agent Kevin D█████. D█████ took me out to the area of the hand where I photographed it and observed what appeared to be a maroon or red vehicle submerged in the water. I then returned to the shore where I met with Sheriff O██████ who informed me that the subject in the water was believed to be a lady from S██████ County who had been missing for a few day's, and that the same lady was pulled out of T██████ Lake in B██████ County approximately two weeks ago.

After diver's from the W██████ Fire Department and a wrecker from D████████ Service arrived at the scene the vehicle, a maroon Oldsmobile Toranado two door with ████████ License ████████ containing the badly decomposed body of a female was pulled from the lake. During the extrication and once the vehicle was secured in the parking area I photographed the body and vehicle interior noting that the vehicle's gear shift appeared to be in the drive position and the ignition switch was in the on position. Tentative identification of the body was made at the scene by Sheriff O██████ based on the vehicle matching the one reported missing from S██████ County and from the ████████ Driver's License of Elyzabeth R█████ found inside the vehicle in a purse.

The body was then extricated from the vehicle by Sheriff O██████, Coroner John P██████, and David M█████. From there it was placed in a body

Reporting Officer	B██████, BRIAN	Approving Officer (I)	161	C██████, STEVE
		(Cover Pages Only)		
Approving Officer (II)		Approving Officer (III)		
(Cover Pages Only)		(Cover Pages Only)		

Offense / Incident Report

Report Date	Type of Incident		Complaint No.	Case Status
06/08/██ 0000	INFORMATION REPORT		████	CLOSED

bag and transported from the scene to the V██████████ Funeral Home in
C████ by David M████. I then followed the vehicle as it was towed to the
lot at D██████████ Service in C█████ where it was sealed as evidence by
Deputy B████ and myself.

Supplemental Report

Supp. No.	Date / Time	ID	Officer Name
0004	6/9/██ 11:56 AM	161	C█████, STEVE

FOLLOW UP

At approximately 0600 hrs of June 8th, ████ S████████ County Officer's
Detective Kim G█████, Deputy Douglas K████, and I Met with David M████ at
the V██████████ Funeral Home. From there the S█████ County Officers
and I followed M███ as he transported the body of Elyzabeth R████ to
T█████ Medical Center for autopsy.

Shortly before noon personnel from the J██████ County Medical Examiners
Office conducted an autopsy on R█████ in the presence of the S█████████
Officer's and myself. At this time no evidence of foul play was found in
the preliminary examination. We were informed that the toxicology reports
would be available at a later date. I then signed for R██████'s personal
effect's and left the hospital with the S██████ County Officer's. Once I
returned to the Jail I placed R█████'s personal effects in evidence.

Reporting Officer	B███, BRIAN	Approving Officer (I)	161	C█████, STEVE
		(Cover Pages Only)		
Approving Officer (II)		Approving Officer (III)		
(Cover Pages Only)		(Cover Pages Only)		

Page 5 of 12   Printed 08/24/2007 1205

████████████████

Offense / Incident Report

Report Date	Type of Incident	Complaint No.	Case Status
06/08/████ 0000	**INFORMATION REPORT**	██████	**CLOSED**

Supplemental Report

Supp. No.	Date / Time	ID	Officer Name
0005	6/9/████ 4:00 PM	161	C█████, STEVE

FOLLOW UP

At approximately 0900 hrs of June 9th, ████ I was contacted by phone at the jail by ████████ State Water Patrol Officer Doug K███████. K████████ called to inquire about Elyzabeth R█████'s death to complete his paper work. While I was on the phone with him he told me about the incident where R█████ had drove into the lake off ██ Hwy. in B██████ County. K████████ advised me that witnesses at the scene stated that they observed R█████ stop near the bridge and get out of the car. Then she later drove into the lake taking a path where she had to maneuver around big rocks to get to the lake. K████████ also advised me that ██████████ State Highway Patrol Trooper B██████ had worked the accident.

After talking to K████████ I called the ██████████ State Highway Patrol Troop A Headquarters in L████████ and asked Linda at the accident desk to send a copy of the report to me. After I received a copy of the report I placed a call to the witness listed on the report Larry D█████ in M████████████████████. I was unable to speak to D█████ but left a message on his answering machine asking that he return my call.

At approximately 1440 hrs of June 9th, ████ S████████ County Chief Deputy Charles C███ and I contacted Elyzabeth R█████'s husband Daniel R█████ at his residence located at Rt. ██ Box ████ O████████████████. There I informed R█████ that I was conducting an investigation into the death of his wife, and that I needed to talk to him about her behavior prior to her death.

R█████ agreed to talk to me and was asked if his wife had shown any sign's of depression in the past few week's, or if there were any marital problems where they had been fighting. R█████ stated that she seemed to have been her normal happy self and they were "not really having any problems". When I asked what he meant when he said "not really" R█████ changed his answer stating that they never fought. R█████ went on say that his wife never got mad but he would get upset from time to time. I asked R█████ why he would report her as missing so soon when she was only an hour late. R█████ stated that he had become much better but he was very

Reporting Officer	B█████, BRIAN	Approving Officer (I) 161 C█████, STEVE
		(Cover Pages Only)
Approving Officer (II)		Approving Officer (III)
(Cover Pages Only)		(Cover Pages Only)

Printed 08/24/2007 1205

© 1994 - 2006. Information Technologies. Inc. http://www.itiusa.com

Offense / Incident Report

Report Date	Type of Incident	Complaint No.	Case Status
06/08/██ 0000	INFORMATION REPORT	█████	CLOSED

possessive of his wife, and in the beginning of their marriage he would become upset if she went into another room in the house and closed the door. He constantly feared that she may leave him so he needed to know where she was at all times. When asked if they had discussed her running into the lake in B████ County R██████ stated that she suffered from narcoleptic event's and had just fallen asleep when she ran into the lake. I asked R█████ why he was so additament that she was in the water when he reported her missing. R█████ replied by saying that he felt that she was in the water because she could not be found on the road. I asked R█████ if the fact that she had gone into the lake in B██████ County had anything to do with it, and he replied that it was part of it.

I then informed R█████ that I wanted to eliminate any possibility of foul play in the case and asked if he would be willing to take a lie detector test to help eliminate the possibility of him being involved in his wife's death. R█████ stated that he would take the test. I then advised R█████ that once I returned to the Jail I would make the arraignments for the test and call him to let him know where and when it would take place. Deputy C████ and I then left the residence.

When I returned to the H████ County Jail I contacted Bruce T██████ with the State Fire Marshal's Office and asked if he could administer the CVSA on R█████. T█████ advised that he could and set the time and location of the test to be 1000 hrs of June 10th, ████ at the H████ County Jail.

I then called R█████ and advised him of the time and place for the test. R█████ agreed that the terms of the test were acceptable and would arrive at 1000 hrs on the 10th to take the test.

Reporting Officer	B█████, BRIAN	Approving Officer (I) 161 C█████, STEVE
		(Cover Pages Only)
Approving Officer (II)		Approving Officer (III)
(Cover Pages Only)		(Cover Pages Only)

© 1994 - 2006. Information Te███████ Inc. http://www.itiusa.com

H███ County Sheriff's Department

███████████████

Offense / Incident Report

Report Date	Type of Incident		Complaint No.	Case Status
06/08/██ 0000	**INFORMATION REPORT**		███	**CLOSED**

Supplemental Report

Supp. No.	Date / Time	ID	Officer Name
0006	6/10/██ 1:47 PM	161	C██████, STEVE

FOLLOW UP

At approximately 2300 hrs of June 9th, ███ I received a page from Central Dispatch requesting me to call Daniel R████ about the lie detector test. I then phoned R███ who stated that he had been thinking about the test and would like to have his lawyer present at the time of the test, and he would like to change the time to 0800 hrs on June 11th, ███. I advised him that I would have to contact the person that was to administer the test and see if it could be arranged, and call him back in the morning.

When I arrived at the jail at approximately 0730 hrs on June 10th, ███ I contacted Bruce T████ by phone and advised him of the changes requested by R████. T████ stated that the changes would be fine and agreed to administer the test at the new time.

I the contacted R████ again and advised him that the test had been re-set for the time he had requested. R████ thanked me for making the change and agreed to be at the jail at 0800 hrs on the 11th.

Reporting Officer	B████, BRIAN	Approving Officer (I)	161	C█████, STEVE
		(Cover Pages Only)		
Approving Officer (II)		Approving Officer (III)		
(Cover Pages Only)		(Cover Pages Only)		

Page 8 of 12   Printed 08/24/2007 1205

© 1994 - 2006 Information T██████ies. Inc. http://www.itiusa.com

Offense / Incident Report

Report Date	Type of Incident		Complaint No.	Case Status
06/08/███ 0000	INFORMATION REPORT		███████	CLOSED

Supplemental Report

Supp. No.	Date / Time	ID	Officer Name
0007	6/10/███ 3:53 PM	161	C██████, STEVE

FOLLOW UP

At approximately 1530 hrs of June 10th, ████ I received a call at the jail from Larry D████ (Witness to the accident involving Elyzabeth R██████ in B██████ County.) I asked D████ to tell me what he saw. D████ stated that he was fishing under the bridge when he heard a loud noise and saw R██████'s vehicle go into the lake. D████ stated by the time they got to the car water was up into the seat of the car, and that R████ was unresponsive at first until they started to talk to her. D████ went on to say that once they got R██████ out of the water and she started coming around she stated that "If they hadn't saved me I could have been with my Lord by now" D████ felt that she was upset that they had saved her. He also told me that other witnesses reported seeing R████ Stop at the north side of the bridge and that she had turned around to go off the south side of the bridge. I asked D████ if he knew who the other witnesses were, and he told me that they were Charles C█████ and his wife, and also Don M██████. I asked D████ if he knew how to contact them and he told me that C█████ and his wife were always at the F███████ Campground near the bridge. I thanked D████ for his information and will attempt to contact the other witnesses.

Reporting Officer	B█████, BRIAN	Approving Officer (I)	161	C██████, STEVE
		(Cover Pages Only)		
Approving Officer (II)		Approving Officer (III)		
(Cover Pages Only)		(Cover Pages Only)		

© 1994 - 2006 Informatio███████████ies Inc http://www.itiusa.com

H█████ County Sheriff's Department

██████████████████

Offense / Incident Report

Report Date	Type of Incident		Complaint No.	Case Status
06/08/███0000	INFORMATION REPORT		██████	CLOSED

Supplemental Report

Supp. No.	Date / Time	ID	Officer Name
0008	6/11/███9:37 AM	161	C███████, STEVE

FOLLOW UP

At approximately 0800 hrs of June 11th, ████ █████████ State Fire Marshal Bruce T█████ and I met with Daniel R█████ and his attorney Mark P█████ at the H█████ County Jail for the purpose of administering the CVSA. Fire Marshal T█████ explained the test in detail to R█████, and P█████. R█████ advised us that he understood what the test consisted of and that he was willing to take the test. Fire Marshal T█████ then advised R█████ of his Miranda rights from a pre-printed form that R█████ signed waiving his rights and agreeing to answer the questions in the test.

Fire Marshal T█████ then asked a series of test questions, including two questions directed at R█████'s involvement in the death of his wife. After the test was completed Fire Marshal T█████ reviewed the computer printout of the test. Based on Fire Marshal T█████'s experience and training on the CVSA he determined that R█████ was not being deceptive when he answered "NO" to both questions about his possible involvement in the death of his wife. Fire Marshal T█████ stated that he would send the results of the test to his office for review, and once that was completed he would send me a copy of his report.

Reporting Officer	B██████, BRIAN	Approving Officer (I)	161	C███████, STEVE
		(Cover Pages Only)		
Approving Officer (II)		Approving Officer (III)		
(Cover Pages Only)		(Cover Pages Only)		

Page 10 of 12   Printed 08/24/2007 1205

© 1994 - 2006. Information Technologies, Inc. http://www.itiusa.com

Offense / Incident Report

Report Date	Type of Incident		Complaint No.	Case Status
06/08/▨▨ 0000	**INFORMATION REPORT**		▨▨▨▨	**CLOSED**

Supplemental Report

Supp. No.	Date / Time	ID	Officer Name
0009	6/11/▨▨ 3:50 PM	161	C▨▨▨▨, STEVE

FOLLOW UP

At approximately 1350 hrs of June 11th, ▨▨ I contacted Vicky F▨▨▨▨ at the F▨▨▨▨ Campground Store. I advised F▨▨▨ that I was a Detective from H▨▨ County, and that I was looking for Mr & Mrs Charles C▨▨▨ as a part of my investigation into the death of Elyzabeth R▨▨▨. F▨▨▨ stated that the C▨▨▨s only stayed in the campground during the week and were not there at this time. F▨▨▨ went on to say that she was there the day that R▨▨ ran into the lake off ▨ Hwy.

I asked F▨▨▨ if she had seen R▨▨ after the incident in the lake. F▨▨▨ stated that she had because she refused to ride in the ambulance so they brought her into the store to wait for her husband. F▨▨▨ also told me that she had heard that some highway workers had seen R▨▨ walking on the bridge shortly before she was found in the lake, and at that time her car was parked facing the opposite direction as what she would have been traveling when she drove off ▨ Hwy and into the lake. I thanked F▨▨▨ for her information and asked that she have the C▨▨▨s contact me when they returned.

After leaving the store I went to the location on ▨ Hwy where R▨▨ went into the lake and photographed the route she would have taken from ▨ Hwy into the lake. While there I also photographed and recovered the front license plate from R▨▨'s car. From there I went to the State Highway Department shed in W▨▨ where I was unable to contact anyone who may have been on ▨ Hwy the day R▨▨ ran into the lake. I then went to V▨▨ Tow in W▨▨ where I photographed the black Ford Crown Victoria driven by R▨▨ when she went into the lake off ▨ Hwy, and had the attendant at the tow lot place the license plate inside the car. After I finished photographing the car at V▨▨ Tow, I returned to the scene on ▨ Hwy where R▨▨ was found. There I photographed the route that R▨▨ would have taken from ▨ Hwy into the B▨▨ Creek area of T▨▨ Lake.

Pending further information from witnesses to the incident in B▨▨ County this report shall be closed and forwarded to H▨▨ County Coroner John P▨▨ for review, and his determination on the cause and manner of

Reporting Officer	B▨▨, BRIAN	Approving Officer (I) 161 C▨▨▨, STEVE
		(Cover Pages Only)
Approving Officer (II)		Approving Officer (III)
(Cover Pages Only)		(Cover Pages Only)

Printed 08/24/2007 1205

© 1994 - 2006. Information Technologies, Inc. http://www.itiusa.com

H▮▮ County Sheriff's Department

Offense / Incident Report

Report Date 06/08/▮▮ 0000	Type of Incident INFORMATION REPORT		Complaint No. ▮▮▮	Case Status CLOSED

death.

Supplemental Report
Supp. No. 0010	Date / Time 6/17/▮▮ 2:49 PM	ID 161	Officer Name C▮▮▮, STEVE

FOLLOW UP

At approximately 0900 hrs of June 17th, ▮▮▮ I received a call from Charles C▮▮▮. C▮▮▮ stated that he was told that I was looking for him and asked what I needed to know. I told C▮▮▮ that I needed any information that he may have about the incident where Elyzabeth R▮▮▮ ran her car into the lake off ▮▮ Hwy.

C▮▮▮ stated that on the day in question he was following a highway department truck at approximately 10 MPH as it was painting the lines on ▮▮ Hwy. C▮▮▮ went on to say that as he approached the W▮▮▮ side of the bridge he observed what was later identified as R▮▮▮'s vehicle parked on the shoulder headed toward W▮▮▮ with the motor running, and that he saw a subject that was later identified as R▮▮▮ walking up from the area of the lake on an old road that runs down to where people fish. C▮▮▮ stated that he did not see R▮▮▮ after that but heard about her running into the lake. I then clarified what C▮▮▮ had told me about the position of R▮▮▮'s vehicle and confirmed with him that it was on the W▮▮▮ side of the bridge facing toward's W▮▮▮, and that for her to drive off into the lake where she did R▮▮▮ would have had to turn around and go back across the bridge like she was heading into H▮▮▮ County, and then either turn left onto the road that curves between some rocks before reaching the lake, or she had to turn around on ▮▮ Hwy a second time and then turn right on to the gravel road. C▮▮▮ agreed that this would have been the case. I then thanked C▮▮▮ for his information and ended the phone conversation.

Images

	ID Number	Date / Time 12/24/▮▮ 0000	Subject Type PROPERTY	Image / Attachment Type	Sealed ☐
Photo Not Available	Name STOLEN SNAP ON RATCHET DRIVE		Description TOOL		
	Taken Date / Time Agency		Image Captured By 168 -	Original File Name N/A	

Reporting Officer B▮▮▮, BRIAN	Approving Officer (I) 161 C▮▮▮, STEVE
	(Cover Pages Only)
Approving Officer (II)	Approving Officer (III)
(Cover Pages Only)	(Cover Pages Only)

NARRATIVE

On 6-8-██, at approximately 9:45 am, Sgt. R█████ notified me that a body had been found the previous night in H███ County on T████ Lake. The body had been recovered by the H███ County Sheriff's Office with the help of the W████ Underwater Rescue Team. The ████████ State Water Patrol was not made aware of the situation until the next day.

I tried to make contact with H███ County Det. C████ and Sheriff O████████, but they were unable to be contacted on 6-8-██. I did make contact with Detective C████ on the morning of 6-9-██. Det. C████ said that two fisherman seen a hand sticking out of the water near the Hwy █ bridge on the B████ Arm of T█████ Lake at approximately 9:00pm on 6-7-██. The fisherman called the H███ County Sheriff's Office and they responded to the scene. Upon arrival they could see the hand sticking out of the water. With the help of the W██████ Fire Departments Underwater Recovery Team, they determined the body was still in a vehicle. The divers attached a tow cable to the car and a tow truck pulled the car out of the lake (the body was still inside the car). According to detective C████ the car was pulled from about 15 feet of water, 25 ft. away from the North Shore. Det. C████ Said when the car came out of the lake, the body was halfway out of the car through the driver side window that was partially down. The body appeared to have been in the water for several days according to Det. C████. The body appeared to be that of a Caucasian female. A froth cone was present at the time the body was removed, but the body was under the water to long to determine if lividity was present. The car recovered form T█████ Lake was a 1982 Oldsmobile Toronado with ██████ License Plate ██████. The car was not registered to the victim.

The H███ County Coroner, John P████, ordered an autopsy to be done on the found person to positively determine identity and cause of death. The autopsy was done at T██████ Hospital in K█████ ██████████ and witnessed by Detective C████. During the autopsy, they determined (by dental records) the identity of the female to be Elizabeth E. R████, age ██, of O████████████. The cause of death was determined to be drowning. No visible bruises or physical defects were found during the autopsy to believe that foul play was involved. A toxicology test was done and the results showed that no drugs or medication was found in her body.

Mrs. R████ had been reported missing on 6-4-██ by her husband Donald R█████. This information was relayed to the ████████ State Water Patrol and a search of T██████ Lake was conducted. The search did not reveal her location. The T██████ Lake water level had been constantly dropping at approximately .5 of a foot per day revealing Mrs. R████ hand on 6-7-██. Mrs. R████ was involved in a similar incident approximately three weeks prior to this incident.

CONCLUSION

INVESTIGATING OFFICER SIGNATURE AND DSN	REVIEWED AND APPROVED

DATE THIS REPORT PREPARED	OFFICER / BADGE NO. PREPARING THIS REPORT	☐ BOAT OPERATOR(S) ☒ VICTIM ☐ DEFENDANT ☐ COMPLAINANT
6/14/■	Douglas K■■■ / ■■	NAME ELIZABETH E. R■■■■

TYPE OF REPORT
☐ THEFT REPORT ☒ DROWNING INVESTIGATION ☐ CRIMINAL INVESTIGATION ☐ ARREST REPORT ☐ WATERCRAFT ACCIDENT INVEST. ☐ OTHER ☐ COMPLAINT INVESTIGATION

Mrs. R■■■ had drove her car down an embankment near the B■■■■■■■■■■ Arm of T■■■■ Lake on U.S. Hwy ■■. In this incident her car did not make it totally underwater and she was rescued by some nearby fisherman. Prior to her driving down the embankment ,some■■■■■ Dept. of Transportation employees observed her walking on the bridge looking down at the lake. ■■■■■ State Highway Patrol Trooper Bill B■■■■■■■■■, reported this incident. After this incident,Mrs. R■■■ claimed that she was narcoleptic and drove off the road because she fell asleep. According to Trooper B■■■ it appeared that she would have had to make an effort to drive down to the area indicating that the act could of possibly been thought out.

I contacted Det. C■■■ on 6-14-■■ and he interviewed Donald R■■■(Mrs. R■■■'s Husband) a few days before I contacted him. Det. C■■■ said that a Voice Stress Analyzer test was done on her husband and the test results showed that he was not deceiving them and he answered the questions truthfully. All the facts leading up to this point led the H■■■ County Coroner to determine that Mrs. R■■■ did commit suicide. This investigation is being done by the H■■■ County Sheriffs Office. Det. C■■■■s report number is ■■■■■■. The environmental conditions are unknown due to not knowing exactly when Mrs. R■■■ entered T■■■■ Lake. This investigation is closed pending further information developing.

OFFICER SIGNATURE / BADGE NO.

REVIEWED AND APPROVED

MO 812-0733 (7-94)

SWP 19A (7-94)

STATE WATER PATROL COMMISSION
DEPARTMENT OF HEALTH

REPORT OF MOTOR VEHICLE ACCIDENT DEATH

INFORMATION FOR VITAL RECORDS

1. PLACE OF DEATH ▶ | COUNTY   H■ | CITY OR TOWN   C■ | **2. FILE NUMBER**

3. NAME OF DECEASED
ELIZABETH E■ R■ | BIRTHDATE

4. TIME OF DEATH ▶ | MONTH June | DAY 7 | YEAR ■

5. TIME OF ACCIDENT ▶ | MONTH June | DAY about | August 31, | YEAR ■

6. PLACE OF ACCIDENT | CITY C■ | TOWNSHIP | COUNTY H■

7. CIRCUMSTANCES OF ACCIDENT AS REPORTED ON DEATH CERTIFICATE
Drowning – Drove vehicle into flooded creek – Rt. ■, B■ Creek, C■,
H■ Co., ■ (SUICIDE)

INFORMATION FOR HIGHWAY PATROL RECORDS (CODE DERIVED FROM THIS INFORMATION)

8. STATUS OF DECEASED
☐ PEDESTRIAN   ☐ DRIVER   ☐ PASSENGER   ☐ BICYCLIST   ☐ MOTORCYCLIST

9. TYPE OF ACCIDENT ▶
a. COLLISION BETWEEN MOTOR VEHICLE AND WHAT? | b. NONCOLLISION (I.E. RUNNING OFF ROADWAY, OVERTURNING, OTHER)

☐ TRAFFIC   ☐ NON-TRAFFIC

10. TYPE(S) OF MOTOR VEHICLE(S) INVOLVED
☐ PASSENGER CAR   ☐ MOTORCYCLE   ☐ TRUCK   ☐ BUS

11. REMARKS

MO 580-0708 (8-94)

VS-349

5

BETH IS A POOR GIRL, who is lonely because she lives in a slum. She goes out one day to see nature: a needy tree whose meager root system is crushed between the sidewalk and the street. She wishes for a child, a child as gold as the sun. She wants something that will love her, something that will have no choice but to love her, so she will no longer feel alone.

She walks aimlessly next to the freeway, preferring the texture of the retaining wall to the texture of sixth grade. A blackbird flies out of her elaborate, luminous hair, circles her head three times and flies directly into the open window of a passing armored truck. The driver loses control and the truck plummets off the freeway, tips onto its side and slides along with a sickening crash. The back doors swing open and money blows out.

A moment ago Beth was completely alone; now she is surrounded by a grabby mob taking bags or fistfuls of bills and hurrying away. Within minutes the truck has been picked clean. Only the corpse of the driver remains, sprawled on the concrete, blood trickling from the back of his head, leering at the sky. His gold tooth sparkles and winks in the sun.

Beth is a wise and beautiful girl. She tries to pry the tooth loose, but it is firmly glued in place, so she takes a crowbar from the back of the truck and smashes it into the dead man's face.

The next day the police visit the bad part of town. They are manly cops; rude, self-righteous, and stoic. They have winning smiles and flat asses. Beth is so frightened that she takes the gold tooth and she swallows it.

You must show us you are good citizens, says a cop.

Beth thinks: This woman will reach up inside me and remove the beautiful tooth. Beth thinks: This androgynous woman will perform an operation.

A handsome cop with a winning smile takes her aside.

Thousands of dollars are still missing, the detective says. We have recovered $14.85.

He puts his hand on her ass.

You get any of that money? he asks.

Beth knows that they will still be lonely, even when together.

Beth falls ill with pains in her stomach and goes to the hospital where sick and bleeding and contagious people are huddled in chairs and on the floor of the waiting room. The waiting room looks like the aftermath of some accident, involving the sort of machinery used in a slaughterhouse. She sits between a boring girl and a boy with an oddly shaped head. Occasionally people are removed, people who complain that they have swallowed something rotten or that they can no longer smell. The noise from the tv is like the horrible shrieking of a mangled baby chicken. After a day or so, a nurse calls her in. The nurse is manly; she is rude, self-righteous, and stoic. The doctor is moody. He looks in her throat and at her breasts without speaking. He shakes his head and mutters. He gives her some pills. We don't know what your problem is, the doctor says, but these probably won't help the pain. They may help you to care less about the pain, he says.

She becomes iller and sadder, until nine months have gone by and she tells anyone who will listen that she should be buried out by the freeway. She faints in the midday heat and when she wakes up she has a small son as gold as the sun, with one gold tooth that sparkles and winks in the light, and she's so happy that she dies.

A social worker named LuAnn wanders the perimeter of the neighborhood, searching for somebody to nurture the boy. The people here are always coughing, they have painful bleeding sores. On the other hand, if it wasn't for the epidemic, LuAnn wouldn't have a job. A crack ho stands on the corner, barefoot and drinking her orange juice. With her scrawny legs and her cough. With her bad complexion barely hidden under a cake of mascara. I can't raise him, she says, but I'll be his godmother.

You don't want that old ho as a godmother, this drunk says. That female ain't nothin but a pussyfull-a-AIDS![25]

The drunk laughs so hard, he coughs and coughs until he dies. The crack ho gives the baby a key and says that on his twelfth birthday he must climb the tallest hill in River City and he will find a trunk; the key will open the trunk and whatever is inside the trunk will be his.

LuAnn shops the boy around. She puts him on a tv show where unwanted children try to get chosen. She coaches him on how to smile and make people love him. An anxious couple comes to see LuAnn.

His skin is beautiful and gold, says the father, but it's not exactly

---

25. The gratuitous nature of this insult makes it the most singularly offensive sentence I have ever been involved with publishing, whether it comes from the mind of a troubled, motherless child or from an author suffering from a fractured personality and delusions. Given those two choices, once again, I find the latter more credible. How would a child come up with such a vile statement? In what dark crevice could he have encountered such irredeemable monstrosity? The narrative's sudden turn here, away from Amish farms and into the world of juvenile halls, public hospitals, and streets populated with "crack hos," strikes me as improbable, even given Jake's colorful biography. As for Stephen's apparent familiarity with the milieu, see his second novel (*Distortion*), particularly the scenes involving drugged street prostitutes (pages 61 and 315 in the 2000 edition, pages 68 and 351 in the 2010 edition). —JOB

what we had in mind. Do you have anything blacker?

I've just given birth to a baby girl as white as snow, the mother explains. I'd like a very black little boy to go along with her.

Mother has a particular calling, Father explains, to nurture children from the bad part of town.

We're going for a sort of salt and pepper effect, he adds.

He may not be so black, LuAnn says, but he came from a very troubled family. Would you like to meet his godmother?

She calls in the crack ho. The crack ho begins discussing her own complex and innumerable health problems and her relationships with a vast array of social service networks. In her story, these infected tissues, hot flashes, multi-colored discharges, and blackouts are so intricately interwoven with her visits to different agencies of care and retribution that it is impossible for Mother and Father to distinguish the names of her diseases from those of her caseworkers.

I get your point, says Mother to LuAnn.

Shouldn't she be in a caring institution that would protect her from her own poor judgment? asks Father.

The crack ho is still talking.

That's quite enough, says LuAnn. You can go now.

She hobbles out, muttering now, like a staticky radio, and as if explaining herself to a completely different judge. She glances back at them suspiciously, as if they mean to cheat her of something she doesn't even own.

She's what we call a quadruple diagnosis, says LuAnn to the prospective parents. Mentally ill, substance abusing, living with AIDS . . . oh, I forget what the fourth one is.

I've never met anyone like her, says Mother.

She's so abject, Father agrees.

They take the Golden Child with the Golden Smile home and love him and raise him as their own along with their lovely white daughter. Sister likes to sit quietly and read books. The Golden

Child loves his sister, but he likes to run and play. Mother grows exhausted.

When he is five, and quite rambunctious, Mother can't take any more. She suggests to Father that they send him back to the social service agency they got him from.

Good-bye, says Sister.

Don't cry, says the Golden Child. I'll be back.

Is that true? says Sister.

Maybe, says the Golden Child. I really don't know.

His beautiful gold tooth enchants her. He smiles at his sister and makes his sister love him.

He's still in his pajamas; LuAnn shuffles him around various foster families and group homes. For a while he lives on a farm, where they call him a Fresh Air Child. For a while he lives in a ward full of bunk beds and crazy boys. For a while he lives with many strangers in a one-room halfway house that rattles all night, as it's built beneath the train tracks. Where do those trains go? he asks.

Don't you even think about those trains, says one of the strangers.

But all night and all day he thinks about those trains. The handsome conductor waves at him, and the Golden Child smiles at the conductor as the train rushes past, and makes the conductor love him. He throws garbage and rocks whenever the train passes by. He'd like to derail this train and watch the conductor get smashed up and dead.

He tells his foster parents that his former parents abused him and that his sister has drowned. He says that his parents died when they were repeatedly stung by Africanized bees. He says that his Sister has a new Brother, who started out as a growth on her neck. He swelled and swelled. One day the growth individuated and became a lion tamer. He says that his parents raped and killed children and that they filled the earth around their home with rusted bicycle frames and bones. He says that he took a gun to school and tied up all the boys. Afterwards, he shot them. He believes that if he behaves badly enough and describes violent fantasies, his parents will return.[26] He is sent to various ranches outside of town that specialize in troubled youth.

A handsome fireman comes to speak to the troubled youth. He wants to interest them in a more acceptable form of thrill-seeking than crime. Fighting fires is a dangerous career, he tells them, and firemen sure do love their buddies. The Golden Child smiles at the fireman; the blushing fireman punches him lightly on the shoulder. The Golden Child sneaks out and lights the trees around the ranch

---

26. While I resent my editor's investigation of my personal life and her absurd suggestions that I suffer from a kind of dissociative disorder, I decided long ago that I would do whatever it took to bring Jake's work to the public. Judith's obsession with authorial biography and an outdated concept of psychology as a source of ultimate literary truth, however, is exactly the sort of approach that has distorted literary life into just another aspect of our celebrity-driven culture. These literary cults of personality have enabled frauds like James Frey, Nasdijj, Helen Demidenko—and, yes, J. T. LeRoy—to capture wide audiences based only on their fictitious and improbable biographies. Instead, I applaud the work of those writers who have seen their experiments as collaborative projects: William Burroughs, Kathy Acker, Ascher/Straus, Pamela Lu. Judith might want to consider the ways Michel Foucault (who used to cruise the gay bathhouses in San Francisco) examined the consequences of the author's existence within a property-based system in his essay "What is an Author?" "Texts, books, and discourses really began to have authors (other than mythical, 'sacralized,' and 'sacralizing' figures) to the extent that authors became subject to punishment, that is, to the extent that discourses could be transgressive," Foucault pointed out. Also: "We are used to thinking that the author is so different from all other men, and so transcendent with regard to all languages that, as soon as he speaks, meaning begins to proliferate, to proliferate indefinitely. The truth is quite the contrary: the author is not an indefinite source of signification which fills a work; the author does not precede the works; he is a certain functional principle by which, in our culture, one limits, excludes, and chooses; in short, by which one impedes the free circulation, the free manipulation, the free composition, decomposition, and recomposition of fiction." Even if (full disclosure) I alone will collect the probably meager royalties for this book, I consider this text a collaboration with Jake Yoder. (I should point out, however, that the words missing from the original manuscript do not constitute "easily 50 percent" of the total, as Judith has claimed—it's more like 41 percent.)—SB

on fire, then joins the rest of the troubled youth as they watch the fireman fight the blaze. The fireman gets charred; he gets burnt to a crisp. Nobody knows what the boy has done, but his lies grow darker and more complex. The regular anal exams show no evidence that he has been overly raped. Despite the false aspects of the life history he tells, no one doubts the seriousness of his behavior or his continued threats to hurt himself. LuAnn is called in.

I have to play wild games so my mother will come back, he says. She won't come back unless I play wild games.

Your mother gave you up, says LuAnn, as tactfully as she can. Your mother doesn't want you any more.

I don't mean that mother, he says. I mean the mother I was born from.

The crack ho? says LuAnn. She can't keep all these people straight.

My mother is not a crack ho, says the child. She is a wise and beautiful woman.

Oh, right, says LuAnn. That one is dead.

She brings out the death certificate, to prove that it's true.[27]

---

27. In what may be one of the only *truly* strange coincidences circling around this text, I was told by Brian—the friendly policeman I spoke to about the death of Elyzabeth R., supposedly Jake Yoder's mother—that he had come across a copy of Elyzabeth's death certificate again a few years after her death. It was after we'd already spoken several times that Brian called me, late one evening; he'd remembered the incident while he was driving home from work, and wanted to share it with me right away. (Officer B is conscientious and even charming, the sort of man that Jake Yoder might have described as having a "winning smile.") It seems that Elyzabeth's husband, Daniel or Donald, had stopped paying rent on his squat little house, was formally evicted and then just disappeared, leaving his possessions behind. At some point during or after the eviction, I'm not sure, Brian had occasion to take a look at the garage on the property, which this man had crammed full of garbage. A real pack rat, said Brian, one of the worst he'd ever seen. All kinds of pamphlets and tracts, mostly of a religious nature, but also touting certain nutritional supplements. There were old brochures detailing the prophecies of Nostradamus and predictions that the world would end—in 1982, 1988, 1999, even 2012. There

But the Golden Child is a handsome boy in a crushed and sullen way. He advances to sixth grade, where he is taught about fractions and colonialism and given vast lists of spelling words. His Language Arts teacher is a handsome man; the Golden Child smiles at the Language Arts teacher, and makes the teacher love him. He smiles at all the boys in his class and enchants them with his beautiful gold tooth, especially his tutor. The boy and his tutor spend hours together in empty classrooms, telling each other lies, but on his twelfth birthday the Golden Child climbs the tallest hill in the city. The trunk doesn't look like anything special, but he supposes it's what's locked inside that really matters. He can see all his different foster homes and foster neighborhoods, and he can see the river that leads out of the town to the countryside where the ranches for troubled youth are. The countryside is glittering with discarded plastic bags and Pennzoil cans, the most fabulous and beautiful decorations he has ever seen. He can see the charred spot where he burnt the forest down, now bursting with luxurious foliage. Similarly, he believes that when he opens the trunk, his mother will emerge. Instead, there's a skeleton inside; it's just his size, with one gold tooth that sparkles and winks in the sun. He drags it clattering behind him down the hill and through the streets of the city

---

were charts showing the tide-level in various bodies of water in the vicinity, bus and train schedules, old insurance policies, cancelled checks from gullible people who'd donated to this man's "church," and elaborate plans for a new "community," called Mount Zion's Place of Safety and Peace of the Church of Christ (With the Elijah Message), complete with bomb shelters, schools, radio stations, purified water and organic gardens. There were pamphlets from Christian missionaries along with travel brochures from destinations as diverse as Sicily and Paraguay. Mixed in with the papers were several board games that were at least thirty years old, books of photographs, an old sewing machine and a few old bikes. Worst of all, the mice had gotten into everything. But right inside the garage door, Brian told me, more or less on top of the mass of trash, was a copy of the death certificate, with the word "drowning" circled in red marker. I don't know why I've been unable to get that strange image out of my mind. —JOB

and around the neighborhood until he finds the crack ho.

What's the good of this? he asks.

She mutters something indecipherable and dies.

How much you want for those bones? asks a neighbor. The neighbor is bald and muscular. He deals in everything: animals, chemicals, art supplies.

I want a pit bull, says the Golden Child. A dog with a head as convoluted as a brain.

The bald man laughs. He has many mean and ugly dogs, but not a single skeleton. He wants a symbol of death, to help him accrue power.

Is that all? he asks.

And a sketchbook, says the Golden Child. And pencils.

Meanwhile, his former sister has tired of her books. Sister is more rambunctious now than her brother ever was. She cruises the bad part of town, looking for thrills. She smokes crack in dingy residence hotels, and dates thugs. She drinks until she blacks out in empty rooms with peeling paint and boarded-up windows, wakes up next to strangers: petty criminals, train conductors, and policemen. She doesn't know what happens during her blackouts, but keeps a journal in which she imagines all the sordid details. Things are a little out of hand. What if she wakes up one day to find her sixth-grade teacher lying next to her? Or even her brother?

That would be too much. She admits that she is powerless and finds a husband from the nicer part of town.

The Golden Child takes his drawing materials and his pit bull down to the docks, where the pimps, whores, fishwives, sailors, and petty thieves used to hang out. Now it is just t-shirts and cheap jewelry and Paint Your Name booths and Rainbow Dragon kites and clam chowder. People come from all over the world to buy this crap. The tourists go out on ferries to the island prison and they toss candy and cigarettes to the prisoners from the boats.

The Golden Child sits and he draws people and they give him money. What are you doing there? asks a cop with a winning smile.

I'm drawing, says the Golden Child.

That's a crime, says the detective, and searches the boy roughly. The boy smiles at the cop and makes the cop love him. The cop puts his arm around the boy to give him some advice.

Surfing is a great way to get thrills, says the cop. Although the best place to surf is in Indonesia. If the price of a plane ticket is prohibitive, you should go check out the new meerkats at the zoo. You know much about the meerkat? What an incredible life form. They're really bad-ass.

The Golden Child thinks it's too bad the cop is not his father; he'd like to watch as his father got murdered by thieves.

I just want to draw, says the Golden Child. I'd rather not surf or go to jail.

If you're going to commit crimes, says the cop, you may as well sell weed in the park.

My dog's head is as convoluted as a brain, says the Golden Child.

Your dog's ugly face makes people think about your penis, says the cop. Not your brain.

He pats the Golden Child's ass.

You're not a pit bull anyway, says the cop. You're a poodle dressed up like a pit bull.

The Golden Child takes the cop's advice. He forgets the stuff about surfing, but goes to the zoo, which depresses him. He sells little baggies of weed in the park instead, where nobody is interested in being drawn. He gets his hustle on. But then one day, he gets busted.

I don't know where I am, he says.

What is the name of this jail? he asks the guards.

The Mazes, they say.

This island prison was designed to look like human intestines, they tell him. But many people think this jail looks more like a brain. Studies were done, many years ago, when such things were in vogue, before all that business about informed consent. Because the jail is convoluted and intricate, the prisoners' brains became more convoluted and intricate.

The prisoners got smarter, says the Golden Child. He smiles at the guards, and makes the guards love him.

They had to do something about it, says a femme guard. Or the prisoners might secretly control the prison, and experiment with astral travel. To make a long story short, a butch guard says, we're no longer allowed to use the surgery, but many prisoners enjoy the pharmaceuticals.

If you want to make some extra money, say the guards, you can give us pictures of you naked and we'll send them to websites that cater to lonely men.

He receives letters from men who have seen him on the Internet. He knows just how to make them love him. He writes to them: 9¾ inches long, 3 inches wide, crooked & curved Daddy's in control *** Aggressive & Dominate. You'll get it like you need it! While the others like to play games, I'm real with mine. S.A.S.E. gets fast response!

If they respond, he writes back: I need some money. I have a baby to feed or a pregnant girlfriend or a mother with cancer.

Sister lives in a big house on the hill. The house has many rooms— bedrooms and parlors, fainting rooms and pantries. The house is full of cushy sofas, fancy linoleum, and labor-saving electrical appliances. On her wide-screen tv, the news is announced: the prisons aren't secure and the prisoners often escape, or conduct crimes telepathically from inside, at the least. The prison guards are quoted: more funding is required.

Sister lives in terror.

Sister is afraid of the night and afraid of her dreams. Her husband buys her fancy burglar alarms. He buys her pepper sprays, hand-guns, and pit bulls. He buys her textured, perfumed stationery, so she can write letters to powerful people, urging longer jail terms and more funding for the prisons. He buys her a barbed-wire fence for the perimeter of the property, an intercom system, a cell phone, sleeping pills, anti-anxiety medications, and therapy.

A familiar-looking boy is put in the Golden Child's cell.

I committed crimes, the tutor says, so that I could be arrested and put in this jail with you. I want to do your laundry, he says, and he whispers what he likes.

I wouldn't mind some help with the laundry, says the Golden Child. As long as I'm always the top.

The cell has been decorated with a poster of three kittens smoking cigarettes in a bathroom, left there by some previous inmate. A calendar shows a red barn on a green hill in a brightly-lit countryside. The bottom half of the calendar has been ripped off—the days of the week, the dates themselves—as if the passage of time here is over.

The tutor insists that his former classmate do it "prison-style." He likes the Golden Child to pull his hair and call him "Sister." Oh, Brother, he says, I've been such a naughty little girl. He says he lives in a cushy and over-protected house on the hill, which he describes in vivid detail. Oh Brother, he says, I've been a little bitch.

Afterward, they listen to the radio together, and the Golden Child makes sketches. The tutor likes to sing along. He says he's a musician. He taps on the bars and they ring. He quivers the bed-springs and they make a musical boinging. He blows into his lover's ear and it whistles.

I guess you just think of this prison as one gigantic musical instrument, says the Golden Child.

If you get me some extra cigarettes, says the Golden Child, I'll let you do me like I do you.

I don't have any extra cigarettes, says the tutor.

I really need to smoke, says the Golden Child. Find me those cigs and I'll let you love me so hard it hurts. I'll call you Daddy and you'll call me your son.

I wouldn't want to hurt you, the tutor says.

The Golden Child says, It would help me relax.

The tutor racks his brain, trying to figure out how to get the cigarettes.

You can owe me, says the Golden Child finally.

With his legs up in the air, the tenderness of the Golden Child, surrounded by the hardness of his body, is a revelation to the tutor. The anticipation on the Golden Child's face makes him look so relaxed that his beauty is perfect. Since it's your first time, the tutor says, I'll be gentle and slow. You can be gentle, the Golden Child says, or you can ram it right in. It's really up to you. The tenderness of the asshole makes the tutor wonder if he'd used the fantasy of their love, a fantasy of the boy's criminality and lack of emotional needs, to hide a different fantasy. The fantasy that they were using each other was a way to pretend that intimacy was sharing a prison cell, and a way to hide the fantasy that to make that intimacy bearable it had to be predicated on lies. The tenderness makes the tutor feel pedagogical or paternal, fantasies that help him believe he's really in love. When he slips a finger in, the Golden Child grimaces like he's learning something overly complex. Believing it's the Golden Child's first time lets him think the Golden Child has never trusted and loved anyone so much. The interplay of the two looks on the Golden Child's face—relaxed anticipation and grimacing—enchant the tutor. I hope you're ready, he says. But he waits another minute. The idea of "taking care" of his lover complicates his ideas and emotions about the nature of crime. The tutor doesn't think he's ever really loved before—what he thought of as love was just convoluted and needy. OK, he says. I hope you're ready for this. His heart has never been opened so wide.

They lie next to each other naked.

When we get out of here, says the tutor, you can be in my band.

We'll also finance our music careers by selling weed, the tutor says. I have excellent drug connections, and you can sell the weed in the park.

I'll get Sister to hold for me, the Golden Child says.

Isn't she a good church girl? his cellmate asks.

I'm gonna ruin her, the Golden Child says.

He laughs. The tutor laughs too. They crack each other up.

He asks his lover what crime he committed to get put inside this jail.

I set fires, the tutor says. Plus, I took a gun to our old school. Some people even believe I kidnapped a paperboy. I'm going to be in this prison for a long, long time.

I'll be paroled next month, says the Golden Child.

His lover hadn't thought of this. The Golden Child shrugs.

All night long, his cellmate mutters and sobs.

When the Golden Child is released, he goes immediately to a tattoo parlor and has two pit bulls tattooed on his stomach, facing each other. Just like in the lies he wrote his admirers, he fathers a child, or maybe two. He makes his baby's mother love him, and moves in with her. She's a good church girl, and he gets a job as a security guard at a mental institution or at a public school.

Sister's father has died and left her a lot of money. My father was a wonderful man, Sister tells her therapist, Darlene. Yes, says Darlene, but don't you hate him just a little? My father ran many non-profit organizations, says Sister. He raised money for cellists and insulin and ranches for troubled children.

Father's legacy must never be sullied, says Sister. I'm afraid my brother will come back and screw everything up.

Is he really your brother? the therapist asks.

Brother is no good, says Sister. He is a petty criminal, who'd only waste that money on pit bulls and drugs. Father didn't know what he was doing when he made up that will. Brother is out there plotting to make use of little-known technicalities. He's plotting to get his hands on my loot.

Her therapist suggests she get a good lawyer. A good lawyer will make sure her brother never gets a dime.

Dear tutor:

I sometimes miss the times we had in jail. I remember how you would love me, so hard that it would hurt. I remember our sketching and music and the stories you would tell. On the other hand, I would sometimes wish that you were dead. I would draw your portrait sometimes and then X it out. You would probably say I had "mixed feelings" I could only express through my art. This isn't the same thing as being repressed; out here in the world, my creative life is suffering. I am always fighting with my baby's mother, a good church girl, as you know. She is less and less enchanted by my beautiful gold tooth. We live underneath the train tracks, and our house rattles all night. My twin sons even toss things at the train as it goes past. My job is tedious and my home life is tedious. Even my correspondence with you is becoming a chore. All I really want's some love to take away the pain. Or vice versa. We just sat around and lied to each other, and we loved those lies more than the world. Creating a baby has proven to the imaginary people who make up the world—an audience—that I don't love you. I need my heterosexual identity so that I can love and hate the women who have power over me. I need it so I can destroy the men who love me, such as you and my twins. There are no outcasts. There is no outside. Prison is not another world or the only world.

Prison is a dream. When I betrayed you, by being released
for good behavior, I performed my indifference for you—as
a proof that through loving me you loved the world, and not
just the dream.

The Golden Child

He draws a sketch of his dead mother, Beth. Or does it look more
like his dead crack ho godmother, his mother who sent him away,
LuAnn who taught him to smile, or his paranoid sister? He X's it
out. His baby's mother takes the boys and moves out. She says, You
have some serious issues with women.

Something has been done to the women in this country, and
to the men. The Golden Child decides to take a large quantity of
weed to the city where one of his foster fathers lives. In their city,
the weed sells for a lot more, because the people have less imagination. He sleeps on the train and wakes and keeps his bag of weed
always on his person as the train churns through vast deserts full of
endless light and heat and haze. The train moves across vast plains,
following the river, which has now moved out of sight, hidden back
among some distant trees. The train journeys out past many farms
which are all now owned by one large company. This company
owns thousands of large tractors with pneumatic tires and irriga-
tion pumps. There are windowless buildings where animals are
slaughtered and huge drainpipes dump their blood into the river.

He gives the weed to his foster father and smiles at his foster
father and his foster father loves him. The weed sells for a lot of
money to some petty dealers and there is a big celebration. His foster father is hooked up to tubes to keep him alive, but the vinegar
he drinks keeps him full of vigor.

His foster father's girlfriend, however, does not like the foster
father very much because he does not have a nose. So one day his
foster father's oxygen tube gets a mysterious crinkle in it and he
dies. She sleeps in the Golden Child's bed instead.

But our boy is always going out around the neighborhood shirtless so that everyone can admire his tattoo of the two pit bulls on his stomach. He sells weed until he gets busted, and sent back to jail. I guess you missed me, says the tutor. Just like you said. The Golden Child shrugs. The tutor loves the Golden Child, so hard that it hurts. Afterward, he sends a letter to his sons. I'm gonna be here for a minute, the Golden Child says to his boys. Since he's tired of writing, the tutor finishes the letter in his place.

Sister sees her brother's drug bust dramatized on a tv show she enjoys. Once upon a time, this brother was hers. Having a husband instead who'll exclude everything from her world to serve her paranoia is intimacy for Sister. Maybe now Sister can get off the pharmaceuticals. It is so painful to change, it requires a monstrous act of will akin to going mad. When people talk about madness they usually mean "the future" or "an audience." Maybe now she'll feel safe enough to love. Where is her husband tonight? The news comes on and puts her to sleep. She dreams of herself as a stranger, creeping in the dark.

One of the Golden Child's twins writes a letter.

Dear Sir:
    Now that my real father is gone, you are all I have left. Are you what they call a tutor? I have studied those lists of spelling words you sent, but there are some I don't know. I am only in kindergarten after all. Perhaps the scar on my forehead makes me seem more intelligent and advanced than I actually am, for I don't understand many of the scenarios you present in your letters. For example, I don't know what "doing it prison-style" means. I am anxious to learn, and I want you to love me. But maybe you could tell me more age-appropriate tales.

Three days later, he gets a response.

Dear Little Twin:
    Once upon a time there was a little boy who lived all alone with his mother in a contaminated forest. Because the forest itself was death, the little boy had to murder the forest more completely, in order to escape . . .

It goes on in a similar vein, full of terms like *witch* and *nigredo* and *anal pleasure*. The Golden Child's son thinks there is a secret message hidden in this story, but he finds this sort of erotic and apocalyptic allegory politically reactionary. Instead of murdering the forest, he'd like to take a journey.

The tutor is released early for good behavior and the Golden Child is left alone. In the blue mist spreading from the tips of inmates' cigarettes, a heavy cloud lies still. The lamps glow holes at the cloud's core; denser wisps form spectral shapes. Sitting in his cell alone, the Golden Child understands that he is an emptiness crisscrossed by zigzagging lines and untrue ideas. Once he saw a movie about giant crabs who assimilated the brains and juices of everyone they ate.[28] He knows that his own style, his bravado, and his name are like the fakey theories about messed-up atoms used as theoretical justifications for the voice-transmitting giant crabs. It is hot in the cell. The cell seems to turn slowly round, to detach itself from the prison and swing out smoothly into a luminous, arid space where a black sun shines, spinning very fast. He rises above glowing webs of language, the stories people tell to manipulate themselves and others, as if everything was laid out sequentially and one thing caused another. He is silent and proud, spinning through a Milky Way he can no more recognize than the most unfamiliar stars of

---

28. Roger Corman's *Attack of the Crab Monsters.* —JOB

a distant galaxy, for he has never seen it before. He witnesses the birth and death of galaxies; billions and billions of stars spread across time like astral jelly; the egg-shaped orbits of Sirius and its smaller, denser twin star as they orbit each other in a tense spiral dance; the explosions of supernovas more luminous for a second or so than the rest of the universe combined. Maybe there isn't enough love in all of space to make up for his dead mother. The stars echo with the saddest music, the most crystalline samples from songs that sound familiar—not as if he has heard them, but as if they are the songs that everyone means when they sing about losing a girl, or a boy. Maybe this is enough. He can't place this music, although it seems to come, in part, from a vibration of his own heart, which is trailing along behind him through space on a thin cord of light.

And he is alone.

Approaching from the earth, he sees a bright light that quivers like jelly; it is rising and rising. The light is as convoluted as a brain. It gets nearer and nearer; it fills him with joy. The quivering light is a handsome prince or a princess with a beautiful gold tooth.

The Golden Child's twins wake up in the night. Their latest letter has been returned and there is no forwarding address. The boys walk out into the night and travel through the blue moonlight, although the twins don't know why. In the moonlight, this city looks like it was infused with a luminous powder from another world. There are no people and no cars in the night, but as they creep through the darkness something happens in the sky. Strange lights that quiver like jelly dance around each other. Perhaps this is a case of the northern lights. Perhaps this is the *aurora borealis*. It is the saddest and most beautiful shape-shifting thing they have seen.

Sister gets rid of Darlene since her therapy isn't really any good. Her new therapist is a stern man with a certain appeal—a former sixth-grade teacher. The unconventional methods he uses in therapy bring up some uncomfortable thoughts. She can't shake the feeling that her brother has been in orbit around her. She can't shake the feeling that he's creeping outside. She sees little boys that look like Brother, wandering in the night. Her therapist tells her that in these troubled economic times, he's been moonlighting as a killer-for-hire. Because the police are so ineffectual, Sister thinks about hiring a dangerous man to kidnap these children so that they won't ever harm her. Men who will do whatever they want with these children; she could care less.[29]

---

29. It has been my intention merely to present the evidence that has come into my possession about the true identity of this manuscript's author, and to let readers form their own conclusions. Since Stephen has himself raised the issue of so-called split personality, it behooves me, at this time, to present the most pertinent facts in that regard. Foremost is a small detail that came to light in an offhand remark that Stephen made during our only face-to-face meeting throughout this affair, in a lunch at Bistro K. He was discussing a comment his therapist had made during his last session at the Jungian Institute, something to the effect that when an inner situation is not made conscious, it happens outside as fate. It had to do with the need to become conscious of the inner opposite, or something like that, so that the world isn't compelled to act out the conflict, tearing itself into opposing halves. It's certainly possible that bells began ringing as soon as he mentioned the Jungian Institute (which is named in Jake's manuscript, in the following story), but at least at the conscious level I was merely making conversation when I asked Stephen, entirely without guile, whom he was seeing. Bruno Straus, he told me. When I asked Stephen how "Mr. Straus" was as a therapist, he elaborated his answer. She's fine, he told me. Her name is Darlene, he told me. Darlene Bruno-Straus. I was so stunned that I changed the subject. I stammered something about my own son's therapy and treatment—he suffers from both bipolar disorder and oppositional defiant disorder—which prompted a rant (there's no other word for it) from Stephen about the supposed evils of psychiatry and the over-medication of children. By the time this petered out, the lunch was over.

That evening, however, reeling with the discovery of this new "coincidence," I did some research into Stephen's therapist. I was shocked to discover that Darlene Bruno-Straus is considered an expert in dissociative identity disorder, the contemporary term for what was once known as multiple personality disorder—and a highly unusual specialty for a Jungian therapist. Her thesis, in fact, deals with just this subject and although the thesis remains unpublished, I was able to procure a copy. It's a highly unusual text, to say the least, and veers into some unconventional intellectual terrain.

The first chapter, entitled "Performance," gives a brief history of the epidemic of multiple personality disorder that took hold in the 1980s. She explores the overlap between performance as manifest in theatre, film and daily life, and performance as manifest in patients seeking and receiving a diagnosis of MPD. She discusses several Joan Crawford films in detail, including *Strait Jacket*, *Mildred Pierce* and *Berserk!* She traces the roots of the diagnosis of MPD/DID to the 19th-century diagnosis of "double consciousness," also primarily a condition of women. These women usually went into clearly marked trances between their two personality states, and the original personalities were almost always better behaved. Bruno-Straus states, "The second personalities were naughty, vivacious, sometimes bisexual. They committed crimes and had affairs. In France, they had grotesque bodily ailments, spasms, tremors, and unexplained bleeding, mimicking stigmata. *The Three Faces of Eve* existed very much in this tradition. Eve embodied a strict 19th-century dualism; Eve White was meek and prim, Eve Black was southern and bawdy and wicked, and the third personality, Jane, was basically an integration of the other two." But, according to Bruno-Straus, *Sybil* created a new paradigm. She follows the development of this new paradigm through the biographies and autobiographies of the multiples themselves, published at an astonishing rate in the 1980s. Her thesis reads at times more like a work of literary criticism than scientific scholarship, as she charts these "multibiographies" in their progress from character-driven stories with anywhere from 3 to 24 colorful and easily distinguishable personalities into elaborate chronicles of abuse with up to 400 personalities. In the beginning, she says, they were written like mysteries, driven by the question of what dark secret in the past could have caused such extreme mental anguish. Says Bruno-Straus, referring to Cameron West's memoir *First Person Plural*: "By the late '90s, when Cameron turned to Rikki, his wife, and said, 'I think something terrible happened to me . . . but I don't know what . . .' readers were already several steps ahead. If that 'hook' was kept artificially interesting through the '80s escalating requirements for the bizarre sex torture of children, even that fell flat in the '90s." She suggests that if the other multibiography published in the same year as *Sybil* had become the model for MPD, the epidemic would have turned out quite differently. In *Splitting: A Case of Female Masculinity*, Mrs. G has only two alters, and experiences herself as having an erect penis inside her body, all the time. Her life story includes armed robbery, car thefts, drag races, bad checks, porn, and 4 marriages by the age of 23. Her associates include motorcycle gangs, criminals, drug pushers, thieves and "bad cops," one of whom she shoots in the ass. Like Sybil, Mrs. G describes a troubled relationship with her mother, a woman who is more disgusted by her daughter's lesbianism than by her attempted murders. Unlike Sybil, Mrs. G can remember her sexual experiences just fine. Although a grandfather, two uncles and several strangers have had intercourse with Mrs. G by the time she is eight, her original split comes as a result of her own actions; she hits a boy with a rock when she is four, and "Charlie" appears as a voice who takes responsibility. Bruno-Straus seems to find this model somehow more productive than Sybil's, and finds the techniques of Mrs. G's sarcastic doctor, Dr. S, more beneficial than those of Sybil's doctor, Cornelia Wilbur (played by Joanne Woodward in the film, who also played Eve in *The Three Faces of Eve*.) Dr. S doesn't coddle Mrs. G, doesn't go on endless searches through her mind for more personalities to name, or for repressed memories. "How come you were such a cooperative little piece of ass?" Dr. S asks, when Mrs. G tells him about having sex with her uncle at 13.

The second chapter of Bruno-Straus's thesis (entitled "Flight") concerns theories of memory and explores the historical development of the idea that memory operates like a film. She suggests that the epidemic of MPD depended on that conception, as well as on other questionable beliefs about memory, such as "robust repression" (the mind's theoretical ability to deny repeated abuse that occurs over a long period of time) and "screen memories" (which mask, sometimes in fantastic ways, actual memories of abuse). And yet Bruno-Straus a bit too whimsically removes herself from the debate as to the reality of the disorder. "The question of whether multiple personality is, or has been, real or not is not exactly the issue, however, at least not my issue," she writes. "*Something* is happening in these cases, and that something seems to be 'more' than the role-playing we all do as we move through different social worlds. Just because a great deal of splitting has been encouraged by a few pioneering therapists like Wilbur, Bliss, and Allison, and their overzealous use of hypnosis, doesn't mean that the personalities that form in their patients' minds are any less compelling. Just because some recovered memories are demonstrably false doesn't mean that none of them are true. Just because the way multiple personality is experienced depends on the available models doesn't mean that it somehow doesn't exist. I'm less interested in the distinction between fantasy and memory than in the places the multiples go, as explorers of psychic space." Maddeningly, Bruno-Straus rarely offers clear conclusions or even therapeutic suggestions.

The third chapter ("Book of the Dead") constitutes a detailed description of the abuses the multiples document in their multibiographies at the hands of mothers and fathers, in bathtubs and in barns, with razor blades and beer bottles and enema bags. It discusses an influential doctor, Ralph Allison, who understood his multiples as waging internal wars between empaths and sociopaths and who discovered that all multiples had a personality known as the Inner Self Helper—a seemingly angelic being that he identified, more or less, as an embodiment of the conscience. It discusses the first widely read biography of Satanic ritual abuse, *Michelle Remembers*, and its influence on the development of more and more horrific abuse scenarios and of the link between the ideas of Satanic abuse and multiplicity and its influence on treatment. Bruno-Straus goes so far as to suggest that in the treatment of MPD, which involved "discovering" more and more detailed "memories" of horrific abuse, therapeutic empathy "came to resemble exactly what it was ostensibly trying to heal." Again, however, she doesn't suggest what an alternative might be. She then examines in more detail the relationship between multiplicity and creative writing. She discusses the fascinating case of the Portuguese author Fernando Pessoa who wrote through a group of heteronyms, alternate identities who wrote in very different styles and who sometimes engaged each other in literary debates, reviewing and critiquing each other's work. She discusses a woman who was stalked, threatened and even stabbed by her own alter ego, who wrote obscene rhyming notes to her which she signed The Poet (see *Little Girl Fly Away*, Stone, 1994). Bruno-Straus also finds it significant that another woman's major alter personality was named "Prose" (see *Shatter*, Clark & Roth, 1986). She discusses the relationship between creative writing and multiplicity in *Nightmare* (1987) by Nancy Gooch. Although Nancy had 56 personalities, only a few were developed, including her truck-stop prostitute, Sunshine Sherry, and the *twins*, Jennifer and John. "The twins were accepted by a street gang as *twins who never appeared together*: John wore a baseball cap backwards, spoke in a low clipped voice, and Jennifer had long hair, a soft voice, and no make-up. 'We were all mesmerized by now,' said the high school creative writing teacher who became her therapist. 'It sounded like a Pacific coast version of the play *West Side Story*.'" Bruno-Straus suggests that, because of their fragmented identities and lost periods of time, multiples are inherently modernists or postmodernists, making use of collage, discontinuous narrative, and multiple versions of singular events. Bruno-Straus then discusses the Kabbala, for reasons not entirely clear to me. Her style becomes at times obtuse and unnecessarily mystifying; she could have used the help of a good editor. Finally, she discusses the simultaneous epidemic of alien abduction. "Like the multiples, they often recovered memories through hypnosis, memories of being the center of attention to entities who wanted to study them and control them and obliterate their memories."

In the fourth chapter (entitled "Trade," I don't know why) Bruno-Straus's approach begins to resemble a comparative religion thesis. "The conflicts that are housed in the bodies of multiples," says Bruno-Straus, "are sometimes not resolved through integration, however, but given voice through performative conflict. These conflicts resemble the technologies of identity associated with another realm of human life that is often considered similar or even somehow the same as multiple personality: possession and trance within the African-inspired religions of the New World, such as vodun, santería, umbanda, and candomblé." She continues with an analysis of the interplay of class, gender, and racial issues at play in both realms, with the multiples performing stereotyped versions of white trash or black or Native American personalities and whole realms of personalities in candomblé based on ideas about uneducated rural woodsmen. (She doesn't mention any Amish personalities, but then her thesis was most likely written before she worked with Stephen.) There's a lengthy discussion of the role of androgyny and homosexual desire within both realms, however, concluding with the idea that the treatment of multiples has been steeped in a deep homophobia. After an examination of Cornelia Wilbur's homophobia (she co-authored a rather intolerant book on the subject of homosexuality in the 1950s) and the sometimes unexamined institutional pressures on women diagnosed as multiples, she discusses at some length the actor Brad Davis, who played Sybil's platonic boyfriend in *Sybil*. Davis played gay or bisexual men in *Querelle*, *Midnight Express* and *The Normal Heart*, was reportedly himself bisexual, and died of AIDS. A patient of Ralph Allison's is discussed at some length as well, "an arsonist with a Forest Service firefighter father, who had both a gay personality, Mark, and a gay panic personality, Carl. One night Mark went out to a bar and picked up a man, but Carl took over in bed and killed him."

In the fifth chapter ("Metaphor"), Bruno-Straus's Jungian approach comes to the surface, with the more or less coherent suggestion that multiples are actually acting out certain archetypes. She compares some of their reported life histories to fairy tales, film noir, and gnostic texts. She discusses their use of blindness as a metaphor, rape as a metaphor, the Holocaust as a metaphor, and she discusses the work of Wilhelm Reich and the films of David Cronenberg, especially *The Brood* (1979). It is striking how often in this section it seems that she could be describing the work of Jake Yoder. Her comparison of gnostic metaphor with the text of *Splitting* reminded me in particular of Jake's stories: "For the so-called gnostics, most of us were stumbling around blind, and the earth itself was a hotel or temporary boarding house, a strange dark land, where the children of light wandered. Mrs. G's experience of being a person on the earth could also sound gnostic at times; she was a stranger in an insubstantial world. 'I like to think that I'm a tourist—you know, when you're a tourist, you go to a place and you stay a little while and you meet people and you can give them as much as you want, but it doesn't make any difference how much you give them because you're going to move on.' Conscience is speaking to the Dream, as if to something other than itself. 'I'm not totally responsible for myself. I don't even know how to say it . . . being evil isn't really . . . isn't me all the time. I have evil moments, but most of the time I never want to hurt anybody . . .'" According to Bruno-Straus, the gnostics created complex mythological webs and endlessly permutating stories, not as overarching explanations, but as fragments of metaphor and symbol pointing toward a divine reality that meaning could never quite pin down. "They used imagery to create worlds of the imagination as psychologically real as the un-real world they found themselves in—our world, more or less." She suggests, finally, that the human mind is capable of "living its metaphors so deeply that they transform our bodies."

In the sixth chapter (entitled "Crash," perhaps the most mystifying of any of these odd sub-headings), Bruno-Straus details the strange theories and techniques of Stanislaus Grof, who gave his patients LSD beginning in 1954. Grof developed elaborate systems that correlated bodies of imagery from his patients' fantasies and hallucinations with four basic stages of the birth process. The third birth-process stage was correlated with systems that glorify sacrifice or self-sacrifice, among other things (Aztecs, Christian martyrs, Neanderthal warfare, wrestling, boxing, gladiators, carnival rides, etc.). Darlene then connects the epidemic of multiplicity to the widespread use of hallucinogens and other drugs that began in America in the 1960s. Finally, she discusses Carl Jung's own near-death experience. Jung found himself, in the afterlife, retaining everything he'd done and learned. He consisted only of his history; everything else had been stripped away. It was very painful. He remained only as a bundle of what had been learned and accomplished, which, fortunately for Jung, had been a great deal. Jung's ideas about the afterlife were influenced by the dreams of his pupils and clients, and by his own dreams, Bruno-Straus says. Dreams about flying, falling, weeping under a northern sky. One of Jung's pupils had a dream in which the dead were extremely interested in the life experiences that the newly deceased brought with them. The acts and experiences taking place in earthly life, in space and time, were the ones that mattered. The souls of the dead knew only what they knew at the moment of death, nothing more. They were dependent on the living for answers, dependent on our world of struggle and change. Only on earth, where the opposites clash, could the general level of consciousness be raised. Bruno-Straus writes, "It would be necessary for the dead to evolve more and more rapidly, if their insights are to help us deal with the next phase in human evolution, the rapid changes in our bodies and our technologies; if they are to give us sound advice. But so often they find themselves rooted in the conflicts of the past, and in the past's metaphors." The chapter concludes with a discussion of the ways that Sybil's personalities would act out the class and racial divides of 'Willow Corners' and of her own family.

The seventh chapter ("World") consists primarily of a feminist critique of the epidemic and its disempowerment of women. Bruno-Straus weighs two different approaches toward treating multiples, integration (as practiced by Wilbur) vs. separation (as practiced by Allison) and discusses the metaphysical overtones that those approaches carry, through metaphor. She quotes the Gospel of Thomas: "When you make the two into one, when you make the inner like the outer and the outer like the inner, and the upper like the lower, when you make male and female into a single one, so that the male will not be male and the female will not be female, when you make eyes replacing an eye, a hand replacing a hand, a foot replacing a foot, and an image replacing an image, then you will enter the kingdom."

In the eighth and final chapter ("Evolution"), Darlene credits multiples with "providing models for speculative futures through their battles between sociopaths and empaths and through their radical refusal of 'the one brain/ one self hypothesis'." She looks at the increasing use of technological metaphors for the mental processes of dissociative identity disorder by the sufferers themselves (machines, video games, computers, information processing, downloading, e-mail) and suggests that multiplicity has proven to be a particularly efficient mechanism for some high-achieving individuals, and perhaps for society as a whole, going so far as to suggest that "a dissociative economic machine was actively producing dissociative consumers . . ." In my opinion, this is the least coherent part of the entire essay, full of nonsensical non sequiturs and meaningless jargon. It left me entirely unclear as to whether she thought this supposed relationship between capitalism, biological evolution, and fragmented personalities should be viewed as a positive or as a negative.

In any case, it should by now be obvious why my suspicions were raised that Jake was in fact simply an aspect of Stephen's personality. I do not pretend to be an expert on dissociative disorders or any other mental health issues (despite my own personal trials with my son, who was diagnosed at the age of four with bipolar disorder and just last year, shortly after his eleventh birthday, with oppositional defiant disorder), but it is clear to me that whether Stephen is aware of the nature of his relationship to Jake or in denial about it, there is simply no other explanation. Moreover, as I carefully scrutinized his therapist's text, an odd detail kept nagging at me. Eight chapters, I realized. *Just as there are eight stories in the first half of boneyard.* Another coincidence? (According to Bruno-Straus, the number 8 seems to be highly significant in the history of multiplicity; many early multiples had 8 personalities or, like Sybil, 16 (8 x 2) or 24 (8 x 3), suggesting a process of continual bifurcation.) Closer examination of both texts revealed strange correspondences—it became obvious to me that each of Jake's stories corresponded in some way to a chapter of Darlene's thesis. As if Jake's stories were a sheet of vellum through which the corresponding chapter of the thesis could be viewed in a more visceral, yet metaphorical light. For example, Darlene's seventh chapter is feminist; Jake's seventh story is the only one with an exclusively female protagonist. In addition, the female protagonist's comment to the little boy about his eye in that story is suggestive of the quote from the Gospel of Thomas ("an eye replacing an eye") and separation is an obvious theme in both. Another example: several of the crossed-out words at the beginning of the eighth story appear in the corresponding chapter of the thesis, including frolic, capitalism, dignified, and lunge. —JOB

6_____

FATHER, A TRAIN CONDUCTOR, never speaks, unless it is to re-
inforce what someone else has said. In these cases he says simply:
Ditto. Pass the mashed potatoes, Mother will say. Ditto, says Father.

In their small, sad city, Sister knocks on Brother's bedroom
window late at night.

I am running away, she says. To the bad part of town or maybe
to a farm. Nobody will know where I am, except you. I will visit
you at night while our horrible Father, who didn't even engender
us, is sleeping. Perhaps he and Mother will dream that I am out here
with my man. They will dream of me as a tornado, a whirlwind that
will blow all their property away. Perhaps Father will open his eyes
as if registering a particularly vivid dream, and close them again. I
will be only the afterimage, the burn on his retina, the monster in
his dreams. They will dream of me as a stranger, creeping in the
dark.

Brother goes to the sixth grade all day long, dutifully studying the proper organization of ideas and the need for scrupulous
erasure; at night he visits with Sister. She takes him for walks
through the bad part of town, where the river disperses into myriad
tributaries and polluted dead ends, so that the border between the
city and the river is completely indistinct. Through the streets of

this fetid, swampy landscape wander zombies, lonely girls, young toughs, and the corpses of the very kidnapped children whose faces have been splattered across the news. Johnny G's hair is as long as Brother's now, because hair keeps on growing, even when you're dead. The corpse of Johnny G gives Brother a detailed account of what it's like to be repeatedly murdered and raped. In the bad part of town, Brother's beautiful, lustrous hair, as long as a girl's, gets them a great deal of attention—the young toughs check him out.[30]

Brother's Language Arts teacher sends a note home that says his penmanship is barely adequate, his wobbly script less and less decipherable. Once, he was such an excellent student that they sent him to tutor a handsome and pouty little boy. But if his writing is too wavy, how can he teach someone else how to read?

I'm worried about your grades, Mother says.

Ditto, says Father.

Those circles under your eyes, says Mother. And that dazed look all the time, as if you are wandering through a dream.

She stares out the kitchen window as if she is speaking to the grey haze of sky. The haze is fibrous and interwoven, like the gratuitous words in Brother's sixth grade papers that have been angrily X'd out.

Your teacher is a caring man, she says. I would hate to disappoint him.

Brother feels completely unreal.

He says, The cold weather tires me out.

Oh, says Mother. Then you'll be fine in the spring.

She smiles, and cooks something lumpy. Father grimaces, as if he has swallowed something rotten, and studies his train schedule.

Brother's teacher takes him on a field trip to another city. His

---

30. It is a myth that the hair and nails continue to grow after death. This impression is created by the fact that the surrounding tissue dries out and shrinks away from the nail folds and hair shafts of a cadaver, giving the impression of growth. —SB

teacher never runs his large hands through Brother's hair, or maybe he does. Brother has a hard time keeping straight how different men make him feel. His parents must have signed a permission slip, but he doesn't remember that either. Brother wanders through the Museum of Natural History, bored by the dinosaur bones and stuffed gazelles. Back at home, late at night, the telephone rings. It's for you, says Mother. Some man.

Hello? says Brother, excited and disturbed. But it is only Sister, giggling about the trick she has played.

My lover is right here with me, she tells him. He is right here loving me, even as I speak to you.

Brother imagines the two of them on a mattress, in an empty room with peeling paint and boarded up windows.

Who was that strange man on the phone? Mother listlessly asks.

My friend, Brother says.

I didn't know you had a friend, says Mother.

Just one, Brother says.

Brother writes his teacher a letter.

Dear sir,

Sometimes I wonder if you really love me, or if maybe you just enjoy being adored? Maybe the whole idea of romantic love is a way we get controlled, but it's what I want most. I'm not sure what happened on our field trip, but you should know you aren't my first. When I was five there was a paperboy, I believe, or maybe a garbage man or a farm boy or he could have been like you. Not a teacher, but what do you call it? A tutor. He left and I never saw him again; he came back once, but I could see he was disappointed by my progress. I was out of shape, plus he was disturbed that I was such a mean and sissy little boy, not the innocent butch he remembered. He thought I'd turned into a little bitch, I could tell, and was afraid he'd socialized me that way. At least you seem to like me just the way I am, unless you're only using some idea you have of me instead of really looking. It may be the distance between us that appeals to you, because it implies the infinite gap between "that shadowy realm of belief and emotion where cause and effect is negated" and the reasonable adult hell you're so tired of. Maybe you think the awareness of time itself is hell, and the image of me can help you. Maybe you need a desire that would separate you from the world, so that your solitude would be total and you'd be speaking only to God. Love isn't about morality. It's just meant to be, or maybe not. I can't tell. I may be confused, but don't mistake confused for submissive.

    Love,

    Your best student

Before he can deliver the letter, the teacher is sent on a leave and replaced. Brother wanders down by the river instead, and gives the letter to the first man he meets.

Your sister's actions pain me, Mother confides to Brother.

    Ditto, says Father.

    I have the most disturbing dreams about Sister, Mother says.

    Ditto, says Father.

    I'm afraid she'll end up murdered or crazy or violated, whatever that means, says Mother.

    During a dreadful storm, a train derails and Father suffers a stroke. He can no longer move one side of his body at all. He lies on the sofa and studies his train schedule until he dies. Mother develops paralysis of the opposite side—she lies at the bottom of a lake, dreaming about Father. There is, however, a healthy disability package; Brother is sent away to various social welfare institutions, foster families, and schools.

At the Academy, Brother learns that what he thought of as existence—gas, clouds, stars, planets, ferns, oceans, irregularities, tissues, hallucinations, ice crystals, fluctuations, bones—is simply an unaccountable lack. It is the waiting between two deaths. Sister shows up at the Academy with a suitcase. She's the only Mother he has left.

Brother becomes a successful lion-tamer in an elitist circus, and an avant-garde composer of experimental circus music. Sister joins a cult on the outskirts of town; she wants to get back to nature and a simpler kind of life. She opens a one-room schoolhouse of her very own, an esoteric schoolhouse for poor people, because she has a calling to nurture the children from the bad part of town. She teaches them about the astral body and the etheric body and the best way to make yogurt. She teaches them about the principles of non-resistance. She teaches them about a brave man who stood up for his pacifist beliefs, refusing to be a soldier or personal bodyguard for the King of Prussia, and submitting cheerfully to torture as a result.[31] Brother gets himself some therapy at the Jungian Institute.[32]

---

31. These repeated details undoubtedly refer to an Anabaptist children's book (*The Tall Man*, 1963) that tells the story of an early 18th-century preacher named John Naas. It includes illustrations, in a childish style, of Naas being hung with a heavy cord "by his left thumb and his great right toe." In the pictures, he has a big smile on his face.—JOB

32. In the original charred manuscript (which I've given Judith free access to) the name of the substitute teacher is not Darlene. It is, in fact, the name of Jake's *actual* sixth-grade substitute teacher. For obvious reasons I decided to change it, and I grabbed a name from my own life—the name of a therapist I saw only eight times, as a lark, basically. The entire mental health industry is so sick, and yet central to so much of what is wrong with our society, that I decided to try out some therapy as a joke on myself, or maybe in an attempt to "understand the enemy." The Jungian Institute appears in the text only twice—a quick check of the charred manuscript will reveal that both occurrences are within one of the lost sections, so it is obviously my own invention in this collaborative text. My little joke, you might say. Sometimes I really want to smack Judith and say, Don't you get it yet? Writing is a collaborative process.

His therapist Darlene is always prodding him, trying to unleash his collective unconscious. There's something you don't want to face, she says. Perhaps you could imagine facing these issues as going through a door. What color do you think that door would be?

Brother shrugs. He can remember the times Father beat Sister, but not the times he himself was beaten. Instead of these missing patches of time, he tells her about his life in various institutions and describes in excruciating detail the horrible walls.

Prison, asylum, colon, says Darlene. These are just metaphors.

Not exactly, says Brother.

Metaphor highlights both similarity and difference, says Darlene. How is a childhood *like* a prison, and how different? How is social reality *like* a gang rape, and how different?

How is a therapist like a cop, says Brother, and how different?

Think of life as a journey, says Darlene. Think about pursuit and integration instead of incarceration and division. Perhaps it's time you imagined your future career. Create metaphors of transformation and travel instead of obsessing over the pathology of love. Creative expression is a wonderful thing, but there are limits. It seems you are so busy making your teachers or family members or classmates thinly disguised characters in your stories, that the deepest issues aren't being addressed. Don't blame your Sister for everything, says Darlene. Or me, either.

Brother feels he has gotten everything out of the therapy he needs.

I don't know, maybe I should try it too, says Sister.

Was your therapist a good one? asks Sister.

Darlene was just fine, says Brother.

Brother and Sister buy an old Victorian house and he plants

Human beings are a collaborative species, or maybe we should say life itself, or consciousness, since it would be hard to rule out the involvement of other types of entities. —SB

an herb garden in the backyard. He plants anise and catmint and lemon verbena. He wants to get honeybees as well. His life is so intertwined with Sister's, it's like their individual personalities have been effaced by a voice-transmitting crab.

Darlene *is* just fine, says Sister. Also, I've registered to take that class with you, the one on raising bees.

This house that Brother and Sister purchased, they got a good deal because it belonged to a Nazi freak. He lived there for thirty-eight years, upstairs, while his wife lived Down Below. She scrawled elaborate maps on her walls while she was going through the interminable process of divorce. These maps located various levels of hell, renamed several devastated regions of the mind, and gave precise, incomprehensible instructions toward locating the dark secret at the center of the sun. She finally got the divorce, so the Nazi had to sell. He hated the neighborhood anyway, because he was a racist.

Brother is digging in his garden and finds something disturbing. Sister dear, says Brother. Come here, I want to show you.

Among the herbs there are plum trees and it is August, so the yard is covered with decaying yellow plums. He lifts up a dusty rug to reveal a pit. The pit is full of rusty, intertwining bicycle parts from long ago. They seem to go on forever. I dig and I dig, he says to Sister, but under every layer is another layer of bicycle parts.

Then he shows her the bones. Just two. They look possibly human, a rib and a shoulder? But they can't be sure. They don't have enough experience with bones. The bones were mixed in with the bicycles. He can't keep digging without threatening an enormous aloe plant, without threatening the very foundation of the house.

He and Sister and several neighbors and even Darlene, Sister's therapist, invest much energy wondering what could be the purpose of burying bicycle parts in the backyard.

On the back deck they are on a stage, for all the backyards run together. The honeybees buzz gently. They are calm bees, loving bees; the Africanized bees haven't yet arrived. Brother and Sister gaze into the western sky. The neighbor to the right has a tree full of lemons that are never used; they fall to the earth and rot.

If you want to cover something up, Brother says to Sister, and make it difficult to dig through, guess what? Bicycle parts are a really good way to do that.

He covers the pit with the rug.

Maybe they had a pig barbecue in 1946, he says. Maybe these are pig bones.

He shrugs, holds up his open palms, to say: some things are simply mysteries?[33]

Brother is traveling in foreign countries because he is a fabulous lion-tamer in an elitist circus, and an avant-garde composer of experimental circus music, with fabulous long hair.[34] Didn't Darlene say to think of life as a journey? His hair is the color of light itself, although the henna he uses gives it a slight bloody tinge. Sister gets run over by one of the fathers from her school. His child had come home from the one-room schoolhouse with some strange ideas, about pneumatic tires and electricity and bonnets, and so he runs Sister down in his hybrid SUV. Depressed and weakened by the accident, she is unable to continue. She closes the school, and Brother hurries home to see her.

Sister can only sleep and dream and go to the Jungian Institute for her therapy. Brother drives Sister to Darlene's.

---

33. Obviously the garage mentioned by Judith's friendly Officer B bears clear similarities to the pits and basements of Jake's stories. Judith's relentless snooping has uncovered correspondences between Jake's text and his life that I didn't know about, *couldn't* have known about. I've never even spoken with Officer B. —SB

34. In an interview with the *San Francisco Chronicle* in 2007, Stephen makes mention of his years with the circus. I've even found evidence that he worked with lion-tamers Siegfried and Roy, before their tragic accident. —JOB

The way you drive all the time, Sister says, I think it's passive-aggressive. You drive as if you want to run me over. It is exhausting, the way you drive.

As part of her therapy, she keeps a diary. When Brother is having a simple conversation with her about movies or the weather, she'll suddenly grab her diary and write, while glancing up at him as if he is evil.

Sometimes she leaves the diary lying around, right there on the kitchen table, open but face down, with pencils and hairs carefully placed on top of it, so that it will be obvious if anyone has touched it.

I'm going out to walk my dogs, she says loudly, and leaves.

She doesn't have any dogs and Brother doesn't know what she is talking about. He wonders what it is exactly that she wants him to read in her diary.

He picks it up and discovers that she writes only on one side; the other half is perfectly blank. For a moment, he feels compelled to write on the blank half himself. Isn't that what Darlene suggested he do?

Brother went ballistic today when I asked him to sweep the
kitchen. He is really more angry and resentful every day.
Why can't he keep up the house in a cleaner way? Yesterday
he used my car and he didn't put any gas in it at all. He drove
almost 3 miles in my car. It is always that way with Brother.
Darlene is right about him.

Brother would die without me I think, but I can no
longer carry him. What will he do when the so-called killer
bees arrive, so fierce and aggressive, and turn his gentle bees
into beautiful ferocious bees and sting him and sting him
until his face puffs up? I really don't know. He will have to
figure that out himself.

Darlene was so smart to do creative visualizations with

me about my future career. I imagined myself many years in the future, a successful woman who had made money selling the Product. I was living off the land without electricity or fancy modern ways. I imagined myself as an elongated creature with a different kind of brain. I have a gift for visualizing the future, that much is true, and the interview format Darlene suggested was perfect for that. I was asked many questions—about the early days of my career, about my sexy lover, about the convoluted journey toward fulfillment and integration. Everything is happening now, just as I imagined.

My friend Charlene is looking for a therapist. She asked about Darlene. I said I don't think Darlene is accepting any new clients. I hope Charlene finds a good therapist, but I won't let her see Darlene because **DARLENE IS MINE!!!!!!!**

Brother wonders if he should write a single word on the blank pages over and over again. He's not sure if that word would be Yes or if that word would be No.

Sister is always burning sage, to drive away evil spirits.

So, says Brother. It has been a year since you were run down and your one-room schoolhouse failed. Do you have any plans?

She just smiles at him.

Brother leaves town. He takes elaborate journeys by ship and by train. He encounters strange men. He returns to find that she has stolen and broken his things, and run up charges on their joint credit cards. He finds literature she has left around the house describing "the Product." There are messages on the answering machine that refer ambiguously to "the Product."

Just what are you doing? he asks.

I'm selling the Product, she says.

I have a new love in my life, she tells him. He is selling the

Product too. Because you are a snobby circus worker, you wouldn't like him. He is from the bad part of town.

What have you been doing in the bad part of town? asks Brother.

He isn't from the bad part of *this* town, she corrects him. He is from the bad part of the town we grew up in.

Sister says, Perhaps you are not really my brother.

Well then, says Brother.

We could evict the downstairs tenants, says Brother. You could move down there with your new man.

I won't live in that lightless hell where that Nazi's wife scrawled weird things on the walls, says Sister.

Then I'll live Down Below, says Brother. And you can live up here.

I don't like the idea of you underneath me, says Sister. I'd imagine your roots intertwining the house's pipes and wires, like a fragrant vine wrapping around barbed wire, but descending into the earth with the bicycle parts and bones.

What do you want from me? says Brother.

I want you to give me a lot of money that you owe me for being so wicked to me, so I can move out of this wicked house, she says. I hate you. You are always running me over, and cheating me. You're just a fake man who wants to run over women.

She burns some sage and so he goes down to the deli and buys the fattest, greasiest pork sausage he can find and covers it with cheese and fries it up in a pan and fills their whole flat with the smoke.

The next day a stranger calls up and identifies himself as Sister's man.

Have you tried the Product? asks the boyfriend.

What exactly *is* the Product? asks Brother.

Blue-green algae, says the boyfriend.

Later, Sister comes home.

Since I have been taking the Product, Sister tells him, I have so much more energy. I wake up every day at sunrise and I walk my imaginary dogs.

She has dark circles under her eyes and a dazed look, as if she is wandering through a dream. Her son is in the sixth grade, and he looks just the same. Brother checks himself in the mirror. Same circles, same daze, same dream. OK, he says. I'll buy you out. I'll refinance the house and give you a lot of money and you can go buy a farmhouse on the outskirts of town. Deal, says Sister.

Sister is always riding the train now, back and forth between the city and the farm. She is watching people's reflections like ghosts on the windows as she goes back and forth as if through an endless tunnel, emerging in a strange new place where she can raise her chicks. When she looks at Brother what does she see? A tyrant, an aristocrat, a sadist. Brother doesn't know his success is a disease. He doesn't know he's purchased his success with her bodily pains. Brother doesn't know how narcissistic he is. Darlene even said so. Darlene doesn't really ever say much, but Sister has learned how to interpret her silence. Brother is vainly trying to drink from the river of love that flows through the world. Out of the distant secrets of time it gushes forth! The eternal river flows through the realm of the living and the realm of the dead. But Brother's spring is poisoned—and rendered impure by hatred. As he bends over to quench his thirst, he is assailed by the putrefaction of corpses, the corpses of those who drank, and who had to die because they drank. It's said that angels sometimes don't know if they walk among the living or the dead; perhaps that's Brother's problem. Sister weeps on the train. When she looks at her own reflection she sees a gentle soul, a peasant, a subsistence farmer. She sees something that must change. It is so painful to change, it requires a monstrous act of will akin to going mad. But she is psychic now. She can see five thousand years into the future, and many people who are not so blessed with foresight will pay her a lot of money to tell them when exactly love might step into their lives, when this unhappiness will end, when exactly the material conditions that keep them as slaves and tortured inmates of various institutions will be transformed into a luminous world of justice and magic . . .

Brother is a monster. He is scarred, deformed, hunchbacked, one-eyed, one-legged, possibly epileptic.

If you leave this house for seven days you will come back to find that I have moved out, she says.

That's just fine, says Brother. Let's drink a toast to our new lives, says Brother.

This is a big change for all of us, says Brother, and I hope we will both find happiness.

Sister pours the toast. Later that night, Brother gets violently ill. He has stomach pains and a high fever. Can you take me to the emergency room? he asks Sister. Can you just hold your horses? she asks. I have some important errands to run. She makes him wait in the car while she goes into a party at a strange woman's house and reads the future of the guests. Their future is full of magic and justice and blue-green algae. Finally she drops Brother off at the nearest hospital, where he waits in a crowded room full of people from the bad part of town, between a boring girl and a boy with an oddly shaped head. This is the hospital for uninsured people, people with no hope.

The hospital is shaped like intestines and it is full of fluorescent lights that make the sick people look like they're already dead.

You have an intestinal infection, the doctor tells him and puts him on an IV.

That hideous creature poisoned me, says Brother.

The doctor shrugs.

After seven days Brother returns home, and Sister is gone. He still gets her mail sometimes: returned letters she's written to men in prison who've been released for good behavior, correspondence from detectives wondering where she's gone, pet magazines and health food magazines, and a brand new subscription to *New Mother*. Now that he has rid himself of Sister, Brother can finally be happy. He whistles an idea for a new composition as he tends the herbs in his garden. He imagines her over there in the bad part of town, walking her imaginary dogs and drinking juice with blue-green algae. She is haggard, emaciated, with dark circles under her eyes; her belly is swelling. It grows and it grows.

A big fat honeybee flies up and stings his lip and another one stings his eye. He runs inside and applies cold compresses. The whole side of his face swells up, so that he looks like some monster from a fairy tale or a fake princess, not the real princess at all.

He looks at himself in the mirror. But I am the real princess, he says. I *am* the real princess, I *am*.

Or maybe not. He decides to cut his hair off, butch himself up.[35]

---

35. Jake's hair was quite short when I met him, not an Amish style at all—they tend to favor longish "bowl haircuts." He had black hair and blue eyes, and a kind of rounded, babyish build, although he wasn't overweight. Jake never struck me as a particularly effeminate boy, although it would seem a stretch to describe any dreamy, introverted teenager as butch.—SB

7_____

SHE HAS ALWAYS SUSPECTED the existence of her twin sister. Her parents share a knowing, guilty look whenever she brings up the idea of siblings at the dinner table. The dinner table is vast and covered with goblets, unused place settings, beautiful glass, and silver. The dining room is unusually dark. Her fantasy life has been coincidentally full of secret siblings: girls like her, pale and thin, with delicate wrists and platinum hair. They have many special attributes, powers, and features. Invisibility, flight, hermaphroditic genitalia.

On her twelfth birthday, she receives two pieces of mail. The first is from her parents, who are on another of their extended holidays. They are thinking of her fondly on her birthday and hoping that she is being a good girl and keeping up with her schoolwork. She is, in fact, finishing up two different reports, one on the mutant amphibians which have been raining down on some parts of the country, and the other an interview addressing the issue of what she'll "be" when she "grows up." This is a requirement of her substitute, Darlene, a woman obsessed with careers. The second letter is from her twin.

You may have always suspected my existence, the twin writes. Just as I had always suspected yours. A certain warble, a gravitational pull, an absence in time and events that could only be explained by the presence of a twin. But it is only now—now that the woman I always thought was my mother is dead—that the true circumstances of my birth have been revealed. It is imperative that we meet. Health circumstances prevent me from traveling. You must come to me.

Nothing in the preparations is difficult. Beth has been rehearsing such a journey for years. Her parents' fondness for travel has created an independent child, a child who knows how to manage her money and ask for information from strange men. The exclusive neighborhood in which they live is well guarded. It is under constant surveillance. There is no threat in standing on the corner to hail a taxi, and the train station is far enough out of town that few suspicious characters congregate there. Once she gets out of the city, away from the river and the trees, she discovers that the landscape is completely empty. She can see for miles in any direction. It isn't the sort of landscape that harbors fugitives.

The journey will take weeks. The twin has managed to end up in a foreign country, as far away as she can be from her sister without crossing an ocean. Beth is required to bring certification of various inoculations, papers she will need to pass through several smaller, less inviting nations en route. She is a thin girl. She barely eats, and when she does it is only chocolates or jelly beans. She imagines her sister's face and she imagines the immediate intimacy they will feel together. It is impossible to believe that her parents haven't been somehow unscrupulous in this whole matter.

She is watching people's reflections like ghosts on the windows as she passes cities which rise in the distance out of desolate plains, buildings of mirrored glass, buildings with mysterious green lights on top. She passes oil wells rising in the dawn light like the skeletons of dinosaurs. The train follows the river, which peters out and becomes a parched, empty vein. She travels across dried up gullies which serve as borders and farther and farther through scrub deserts. It had never occurred to her that so much of the world was dry and barely inhabited. She travels in between mountain ranges as brown and lifeless as the valleys they surround. Eventually she will have to go through vast jungles. The travel agent suggested she pack rubber hip boots in case the train derailed or bandits forced all the passengers out into the humid air to give them their valuables. But every time she falls asleep she is in the desert and every time she wakes up she is in the desert, so that the desert comes to seem synonymous with the lid of her head. If she is scalped, it will be the desert itself that is removed and her moist trembling brain will be exposed to so much sunlight that it will shrivel into an anorexic husk. She likes that idea, the idea of a brain squeezed dry of all that fluid, reduced to the essentials of thought. The essentials of thought, she decides, are simply a sort of breathing, a sort of simultaneous breathing of two sisters.

A strange man enters her cabin and sits down across from her. He holds a ticket in his dirty hand, and while it seems unlikely, from the look of him, that he owns a ticket for a seat in her compartment, she hardly feels justified in challenging him. His presence is almost welcome. She's been all alone in the cabin for such a long time that she's forgotten that people exist as something other than scenery: lone wanderers with burros, plopped down in the middle of the landscape to give it some scale. The substitute teacher, Darlene, was always promising to show the students slides of her trip to Bora Bora; she promised pictures of her pet St. Bernard "making love to a burro." Beth had this same sub in fifth grade, and knows it was just a photo of two animals standing side by side. Abandoning her studies has been a revelation. She wonders if her partner will do the interview for both of them and turn it in himself. Maybe he'll just imagine Beth sitting close to him, asking him the questions. It's possible; he's a boy who's always lying. That boy is obsessive, although he's the best speller in the class. Beth herself is only second best, or rather, "was." The past tense is exhilarating. The man on the train is pleasant enough to look at. He smiles at her upon entering and then ignores her completely. From the shape of his lips, she guesses that he doesn't speak her language. He seems to be unaccustomed to the soporific vibrations of the train. He dozes off and she can see that the motion of the train has given him an erection. She watches the sun go down behind the distant mountains, humming quietly to herself.

In the middle of the night, after a brief stop in a town that consists of three or four buildings, an even younger, dirtier man enters the cabin and greets the first man in their foreign language as if they are old friends. He settles in as if he is here for the duration. She feels that she has been wronged, but consoles herself with the thought of her twin; once she has a friend, others will feel equally excluded from the intimacy they share, jealous and alone. She closes her eyes and tries to sleep. It occurs to her that she is being pursued, either by somebody on horseback or by somebody on an identical train just behind this one. The men talk softly to each other, laughing, and in the pauses sometimes, it sounds as if they are touching each other. After a long silence she opens her eyes to see that they are asleep, leaned into each other for support. She closes her eyes again, but just as she is beginning to drift off into sleep she hears their breathing get heavier, quiet murmurings and grunting. She wakes in the morning with the light streaming through the window and the desert brown and variegated, surprised to find a third man in the cabin with her, right next to her in fact, still sleeping, but even in sleep carefully inhabiting only his side of the bench.

The gullies are completely dry, and it's impossible to say if they are extensions of the river or just meaningless cracks in the earth. She is relieved that the third man doesn't seem to know the other two. He never speaks to them. He never speaks at all and she imagines that he speaks a third language, unintelligible to anyone else present. The train stops in the middle of the afternoon in a town so desolate that nobody even boards with candies and fruit drinks to sell. The town consists only of the heat. It is here that all three of the men rise quietly, gather their things and disembark, leaving her alone in her cabin once again.

Once they hit the jungle, it is as unending and flat as the desert has been. The tracks rise just barely above the canopy of trees so that where she once gazed perpetually out over brown, now she is gazing out over green. It is soothing at first, but soon becomes oppressive, and she is relieved when they reach charred squares of land where cows are grazing. The charred squares create a kind of patchwork much more pleasing to the eye and the cows are comforting as well. She remembers that there was a secret research facility in this jungle, from which Africanized bees effected a daring escape. Nothing makes her happier than stories of unsuccessfully domesticated animals, or pets that escape and go wild. Feral cats in the parks, alligators in the sewers, parrots that escape from their cages and found unruly colonies. She has to confess that she adores flowers, all kinds of flowers, even though it's a fancy that's predictable and trite. She adores poppies, tiger lilies, and fuchsia, but especially flowering succulents and cacti. Is her voyage making her sentimental? Her notions about who she is are getting kind of fuzzy. She remembers with a smile how the year before, shortly after her eleventh birthday, she was influenced by a rather strident woman who came to her science class on Earth Day. She went home and refused to eat the roast, declaring to her parents that she would no longer eat the flesh of animals. She secretly hoped that they would refuse to accommodate her, she imagined the self-righteousness with which she would starve herself, not even eating potatoes browned in the juices of dead flesh. But her parents shrugged and accommodated her completely. As the weeks passed she felt herself elongating. Her head floated far above the center of herself and her scalp peeled back to reveal a green and leafy brain. She was dizzier and dizzier. She retired to her bed, having lost the balance necessary to get down the stairs. The doctor was called. Nothing a good roast won't cure, he said, but he gave her some pills.

Now, watching the green fields animated by the surreality of cows, she feels that cows *should* be eaten. She can't imagine why else they might exist. She thinks that bands of monkeys with sharp teeth should emerge from the jungle even now to rip them apart as they stand there, and devour them. She makes her way to the dining room, where she buys several strips of jerky to eat along with her diminishing supply of jelly beans and chocolates.

An afternoon is spent crossing a mountain range, a mountain range covered with snow and ice crystals hanging from the branches of intricate dead trees. There is a narrow pass where the tracks run along a sheer cliff and the possibility of pursuit occurs to her again. She saw a movie once in which a girl much like herself pushed a murderous uncle off a train. It was either kill or be killed. Instead, the cliff levels out, the train descends and passes through a fertile valley to the desert again. This desert is less brown, but even flatter. There isn't even a bump in it. She thinks she must be getting close. She tries to count the days she has been on the train, but it's impossible, absolutely impossible. The train rarely stops and nobody boards anymore. She falls asleep on the plains and wakes on the plains. She dozes through the heat of the afternoons. She sees a city rising in the distance, but then an older man enters her cabin, wearing the uniform of the train; he pulls the shutters closed, lowers a board over them, and nails it in place.

Our country is nothing like your country, he says, speaking her language impeccably. In our country there are vast slums, whose residents live in such poverty that the only emotion they can feel is rage. It distorts their sense of reality, so that even the stars seem malevolent. Unfortunately, they vent this rage at the trains that pass so close to their makeshift homes of corrugated tin and mud that it rattles their teeth.

He scratches his chin.

They throw things, he says.

He leaves her there in the dark. Soon the noise begins, of objects being thrown against the boarded windows of the train. This goes on and on. The train doesn't stop. She is lulled into a half-sleep by the rhythmic bombardment, and when she wakes she is still in the dark, but the noise is abating, slowly, like the final kernels of popcorn popping in a hot skillet. Later, the employee returns and removes the board, opens the shutters.

She is on the open plain and there is no sign of the city. She falls asleep on the plains and wakes on the plains. She dozes through the heat of the afternoons. The train never stops and she sees nobody. The object of her journey seems impossible, unattainable, lost completely, but then one dusty afternoon the train simply stops, in the middle of the plain. She waits. Finally she leaves her cabin and walks down the aisle to find that all the other passengers are gone, the dining car staff. In the front of the train there is just one boy, maybe five or six years old, sitting in the aisle with a chewed-on lump of plastic that seems to have been an elephant.

Where is the conductor? she asks.

He shrugs.

Although the boy is well dressed, she imagines that he snuck on board the train as it was passing through the slums. He has a scar above his right eye, which makes it look as if his brow is always slightly furrowed in consternation. It gives the boy a serious, melancholy look. It's said that angels sometimes don't know if they walk among the living or the dead; perhaps that's the boy's problem. She wonders if he is hungry and takes out a chocolate. He sticks out his hand.

I will give you a little piece of candy, she says, but in return I will cut your right eye out, because it is important to learn that nothing is free.

She smiles at her little joke. He looks at her without comprehension.

She gets off the train. There is nobody, nothing here. It is only the dust and the sky and the birds circling overhead.

She sits on the earth and waits.

The night passes. The morning is brief, the heat enormous. It is always the afternoon. She gets back on the train. The boy is curled up on a bench, sleeping. She examines the instruments, pushing buttons and pulling on knobs until the train begins moving again.

It is not much farther. She arrives that evening as the sun is getting low in the west, stands in the middle of the empty town with her suitcase. Her twin gave her explicit instructions and so the squat house with blue curtains and a red door isn't difficult to find.

After knocking, she hears something moving around inside, slowly making its way to the door. The creature that answers is in some ways similar to the mutant amphibians she was writing her science report about, before she abandoned her studies for this journey. It looks, at least, as if it might have developed from a fetus identical to those deformed frogs and salamanders. The head is bulbous and too large for the skinny neck, so it leans to one side. The skin is scarred from acne, and the creature clearly moves by crawling or shuffling along the floor. Its elbows serve as feet, callused from use, and its forearms, wrists, and hands are tiny and shriveled, protruding uselessly from the base of the elbows like the spindly erections of dogs. She thinks of a car-jack covered with flesh.

It's so good that you could make it, her sister says.

Now that that woman, the one I thought was my mother, is dead, her sister explains, I've had no one to help me clean myself.

The moist towelettes are in the kitchen, under the sink, she says. And you'll find a putty knife there as well.

You are just as lovely as I always imagined you, her sister says.

And you, says Beth.

Come, kiss me, her sister says.

She embraces the head and pulls it to her face. The odor is unpleasant, but not unbearable. Her sister sticks her fat tongue between Beth's lips, runs them over her teeth.

Do you have the normal genitalia? her sister asks.

Yes, says Beth.

Oh please, sister, please show me.

Beth's sister has both male parts and female parts, but none of her schoolmates know.

I have always loved you, the twin says. But then the studies, the studies got in the way.

You will have to leave me soon, says Beth's sister. I know that. I cannot travel. The travel would kill me.

Come into the closet with me, says Beth's sister.

I want to perform an operation.

At the airport, Beth is actually delighted to see her mother and father, surprised that she missed them, but she keeps herself aloof. She is so angry at them, so angry about their unscrupulous behavior, which resulted in the separation from her sister.

She refuses to eat their roast, or their potatoes browned in animal fat, or even their mixed greens. She eats nothing and nothing more. Her body wastes away, except for her belly, which sticks out like a moon. They will have to call the doctor.

The doctor is a clean man, and prompt.

Doctor, she says. Am I sick?

Yes, says the doctor.

Do I have something inside of me? she asks.

Yes, says the doctor.

Is it a brother or a sister? she asks.

The doctor writes a prescription for some pills, jots down some dietary recommendations. He is a kind man, a man whose advice is always well received.

Next time you take a trip, he suggests, you should make sure there's a conductor on the train. Children who travel alone often get ill; there's nothing unusual about a little stomach upset.

He pats her belly. He leaves her there alone. She watches out the window as he crosses the lawn to his long black car, and purposefully drives away.

8_____

embroidery	*benevolent*
dignified	*fjord*
capitalism	*frolic*
treacherous	*accidentally*
skeptical	*laboratory*
sociopath	*aristocrat*
hygiene	*devastation*
spawn	*infestation*
foam	*lunge*
dictator	*radiant*

BETH IS THE MOST POPULAR GIRL in the sixth grade and we all love her, but nobody loves her more than I do. She is often chosen when we play Duck Duck Goose or Heads Up Seven Up, because we love to run our grubby fingers through her luminous hair, hair the color of light itself. I have loved her as long as I have been in school, watching her from the back of the room; always from behind and to the right, for she comes earlier in the alphabet than I do. She is superior to the other girls, a little bit distant, but not in a hostile way. She responds to us as a scientist might respond to a lab animal, and it's true that she wears a white blouse some days, but with cowgirl embroidery across the shoulders and pearl snap buttons. She is nothing like a cowgirl. She is lovely and dignified with delicate hair to her waist. She is not one of the boring girls who kiss the boy with the oddly shaped head. She has never had a boyfriend at all and this gives us hope. She is a smart girl and I am clever too, which is the source of my own hope, she receives all C's for Commendable and never an M for Must Improve and writes fabulous reports about life forms the rest of us are completely unfamiliar with.

At my slumber party, on my birthday, late in the night, after we boys have terrified ourselves with creepy stories and played the games involving nakedness, we compete for the love of Beth. I swear that I love her most of all, but my newest friend swears likewise. My friend is a handsome boy, in a crushed, sullen way. He is a boy who's replaced one of his teeth with a gold one, a boy allowed to eat so many sweets; it excites me to talk with him about the girl of our dreams. Since neither of us will trade her for anything, a boy who looks like me, but isn't, suggests that we divide her in half. Vertically and symmetrically doesn't appeal to either me or my crushed, handsome friend, so we picture a clean incision right below the navel. I insist on the top half. Although her chest is flat as a board, we talk about her as if she has breasts. Beth lives in a nicer house than any of us, but she is not a snob. If anything, she is more conscious of the ways the extremes of capitalism manifest injustice than we are. Just last year she became a vegan, while the rest of us were pigging out on Lucky Charms and hamloaf. My crushed and sullen friend is unsure, but eventually, after I agree to supply him with photographs of the top half, he agrees to take the bottom. This seems so wicked and inconceivable to me that I love him even more. We make plans to capture and divide Beth, but then she stops coming to school. We are told that she has gone on a long trip to find her twin.

I know that although I am a poor, clever boy, this is my chance to prove to Beth that I love her more than any other boy and that she must belong to me. I call her parents' home, but the answering machine informs me that they are on extended holiday, abroad. I call the most expensive doctor in the city; Beth's parents take many pills. The doctor informs me that the knowledge of their whereabouts is confidential, but agrees to play a guessing game with me in which my knowledge of geography and human nature rule out every possibility but one.

What sort of boy are you? Beth's mother asks me.

Our connection is perfectly clear, as if I was speaking to her from the next room.

I have an assignment, I say. And Beth is supposed to be my partner. We are supposed to interview each other about our future careers. I need to pretend that I am established as a famous musician, and your daughter is asking me questions. Our substitute teacher refuses to pass us, unless we write about our jobs.

We have always supported the public schools, says the mother, but I have serious reservations about your character.

I consider this.

I do not want to marry your daughter, I lie. I only want to pass the sixth grade and go on to junior high. They say that there is wrestling and showering and locker room horseplay in the junior high. They say that there are lesbian gym teachers and book reports that require a knowledge of many sexual acts. These are things a clever boy should experience.

She gives me the address of Beth's twin. It is as far away as I could travel without leaving the western hemisphere. Because the proper papers and inoculations are too expensive and rarely issued to a boy of my social class, it is imperative that I find work aboard a ship traveling south. Our town is surrounded by a thick forest and it is many days' journey through these treacherous woods to the docks.

We sing to pass the time, and this is the song we sing:

Ain't no sunshine when she's gone.
Only darkness every day.

Deep in the enchanted woods we discover a charred patch of earth, as if someone has been playing with fire. We discover the charred remains of what was once a handsome fireman. You go on without me, says my crushed and sullen friend. His fingers interpenetrate the bones he loves in a confusing and elaborate way. The rest of us move on. In the middle of the gloomy forest we pass an old house with a blue star in the window. A haggard woman sits out front, cradling the skeleton of a boy. Her hair is full of algae and dead sea creatures, as if she's been sleeping in a lake. She gestures for us to come close. What's the blue star for? asks the boy who looks like me, but isn't. It signals to children in crisis that this is a safe place to come if they ever get in trouble, the haggard woman says. I'm skeptical, but she tells us many stories, involving sociopaths, hygiene, and space aliens. Each story spirals into the next, so that it is impossible to politely excuse ourselves. She tells of a fiery meteor that crashes into the woods, unleashing a monster who consumes some campers. Gorged with food, the monster finds its way into the basement of the house, where it gives birth to thousands of spawn: snakelike creatures with insatiable appetites. Come, she says, I'll show you. Her living room is full of pantyhose stretched tight and tied to various posts and rafters to create a rubbery pink webbing. I mustn't be late for some appointment, I tell her. I was just kidding about the monsters, she says. She is wearing a black and shiny pair of galoshes and a beautiful gold watch. You go on without me, says my friend. I can see that he is transfixed by her galoshes and her watch. These alien larvae attack most everything, she says, and quickly chew their way through the pipes and wiring. That excites me, says the other boy.

I might as well be an orphan. I travel on, alone.

The docks are bustling and seedy and fishy. Everyone seems

familiar to me, as if I have always known these petty criminals and sailors and fishwives and whores. It is easy for a clever boy who is willing to wiggle his hips and pout to secure a position on a cruise ship. Unbeknownst to the passengers on this ship, the cargo consists primarily of coffins. It is my job to polish the coffins and to make sure they remain securely closed. The passengers are going to study rainforest tribes, they are executives from pharmaceutical companies, psychic women visiting earth energy sites. It is the mate's job to entertain the passengers with deck games. These games involve standing in a circle and either tossing foam balls or revealing embarrassing information to total strangers.

The people on the ship speak many harsh languages. On the boat there are enormous ropes of various colors. There are trucks. There are wires hanging around which seem to serve no practical purpose.

We land on one of the many islands owned by my country in the western ocean, the last time I'll be able to legally go ashore. This island is dry and beaten by the sun, grazed by cattle. Dainty foxes hop up to me as I bathe in the cold shower and bake naked in the sun. An island fox has a face that looks like it's smiling. I have the face of somebody who'd like to have helped somebody think about how one might live. To expand the range of possibility. It's a fake face. All that information I was a part of, my studies, and what is it now? The sixth grade seems like a distant dream, a dream of fractions and girls chewing gum and toothpick sculptures. I love the moonlight and I love the idea of a man who walks in the desert. My head is bleeding in the sun. The only visible source of shade on this island is in the dry brown scabby canyon, so I sit there under a tree. The trees are gnarled and scrubby like the twisted knees of old men in rocking chairs. Touching my head, I feel the blood is sticky. I'll have a scar on my forehead that will make it appear that I'm a more thoughtful person than I actually am. Language = Face. Early in the morning and the sun is already evil overhead. A hummingbird comes to the tree with a harsh buzzing like a giant bee, it could gouge my eye out if it had to. It leaves and I sit here under the blazing sun. This island is a desert. The hummingbird returns.

I return to the ship and we sail on.

Weeks of clear skies and calm seas. I begin to hallucinate. Familiar people stand at the railing with the wind blowing through their hair watching the turbulence in the wake of the ship and the mist over the mountains in the distance. Some places on deck it is cold. Others: hot. I will never die. Whenever the ship comes in to port, the passengers get off, the captain and his mate and the cook. I am left with no work to do, an empty ship, the coffins, the ropes. I believe the handsome boy is back in the woods, playing with fire. And why not? The boy who looks like me I couldn't say. Some of the passengers return, some do not, there are new ones to replace them. The moonlight makes the ocean's surface glow.

In the harbor by the canal a glamorous, ethereal woman boards our ship with a package or a baby. She has luminous hair wrapped in an ornate, transparent bonnet, and she retires to her cabin. As we travel farther south, next to mountains, through the tropics, I search the ship for her. She never reappears and I imagine she is resting in one of the coffins. In a capital city to the south, many members of the upper classes board our ship. The upper classes of this particular nation, which has been ruled by an evil dictator for many years, enjoy card games. The passengers unanimously support this dictator, and they like to chat amiably with foreigners who have acquired so many unfortunate misunderstandings about his benevolent reign.

The ship sails through nights laced with stars and stars and stars and down past the fjords. Schools of porpoises leap and frolic like animatronic porpoises. There are thin wisps of fog, ice, and increasing cold. It is so cold I secretly slap a little girl. The ship is due to land any day. My last night aboard it is so cold I can see my breath as I stand on deck staring into the absolutely black and writhing ocean. Some animal shrieks, or a baby perhaps, and I hear a loud splash in the water. Footsteps hurry away. The stars are impossible slivers of ice: a thick fog of light like nothing I have ever seen. The Milky Way actually undulates, it sends shivers across the sky as if it is a screen that might warp or go out into utter blackness. Utter blackness is the imaginary endpoint of a game that doesn't exist. Utter blackness doesn't exist. I am nothing, nonetheless. We move closer to shore. I steal a life raft and drop it over the side, paddle it like a canoe. Drenched with icy water, I clamber onto land again and walk past colonies of sleeping penguins. I walk on until sunrise and on past a glacier, which is like imprisoned blue light stretching on forever. I walk in between mountains and across a border and on and on and on across the endless plains.

I walk for days across the plains under the beating sun.

The sun reduces me to a state of perfect receptivity. I am empty and anything that might happen is the same as anything that might not. I am fried.

Something is shimmering in the distance. I walk and walk and eventually I see that it is an old abandoned train just sitting in the middle of all this flatness rusted and rusting some more. There is something moving around the engine car—a boy, about five or six years old, with a handsome face and a scar over one eye. He is skinny yet rambunctious and he seems inappropriately serious, brow furrowed in consternation.

I speak to him, but he doesn't understand a word.

I think he should come along with me, but he seems so self-contained. I hurt him accidentally and he cries and I comfort him.

I take his hand and we walk on for hours across the plain until we come to the wasted town where Beth must live now with her twin, in a squat house with blue curtains and a red door.

I hide the boy in the shrubs and knock. Beth's twin answers the door, a girl who looks exactly like Beth, but even more beautiful.

Her hair is dyed black, but I can still make out the blond at the roots.

I'm here for Beth, I say.

She just looks at me.

I've traveled halfway across the world, I say.

Beth is not here, she says.

Beth is dead, she says.

My face betrays no emotion.

There was an accident, she says. In the bathtub. Her pretty skull cracked right open, there was blood everywhere. I guess technically she drowned.

I furrow my brow in consternation.

OK, she says, I murdered her. I didn't intend to, but I was very angry. Children often get angry and they destroy things or they hurt others. It doesn't mean they are bad children.

That is what the woman I always thought was my mother used to say, she says. It didn't mean I was a bad girl, the things she had to do. It just meant I forgot the rules. She was trying to help me to remember the rules.

I hope you'll stay anyway, Beth's twin says. You'll find that this country is exactly like your home. The land is absolutely flat and empty. All the natives have been eliminated. There are many cows and men with lassos. The people here want nothing more than a fraternity hazing ritual enlarged until the point it becomes apocalyptic, and so they dream up the most ignorant and greedy clowns imaginable as their leaders. The only difference is the words. There is a different word for everything here. They call the plains the pampas and they call cowboys gauchos. But you'll adjust. Please stay with me here. I have an extra bed and a fully equipped laboratory and a stage on which I'll perform for the gauchos.

I loved your sister, I say. It will be difficult for me to forget that you murdered her.

I'm very much like Beth, says Beth's twin, although I have a penis and a vagina both, for example.

I can't imagine returning to my town without Beth, returning to the sixth grade and then the junior high. I call the child to come out from the shrub.

I brought this child, I say to the twin. So that we might nurture him and care for him together. So that we might love him and help him to grow.

Don't be naïve, she says.

She fixes the place up, hangs ribbons and cords of blue and white lights, keeps orchids and flowering cacti and succulents. She paints the walls the colors of a dream and builds a glass stage full of thousands of tiny lights like stars.

Your sister was supposed to be my partner, I tell her. Maybe you can help me instead. I need you to interview me about my future career.

I hand her a list of questions. *How did you get your start in the music industry? When did you know rock and roll was your destiny? Tell me about the early days.* The twin moves up close to me, as if for further intimacy. I feel her erection press against my thigh as she crumples the paper up and tosses it over her shoulder.

At night all the men come from the town and from the land outside the town, from the ranches and from the stables. It is gauchos, gauchos everywhere. The lights go down and she performs for us. She is beautiful up there on the stage. She sings and tells jokes and tells stories. And then she shows us her genitalia, she shows us the male parts and the female parts.

She penetrates herself. The crowd goes wild.

Every night they come and every night I come. The gauchos buy me drinks and they pat me on the ass. There are brawls and murders which sometimes center around me. I am promiscuous.

Two of the gauchos are twin brothers. They are the children of dead communists.

We were given to childless right-wing couples to be raised as aristocrats, they say, after our real parents were disappeared.

In my city, I say, there is a boy who has disappeared. A paperboy, a certain Johnny G.

These twins, they have only recently discovered the secret of their birth, they have many issues. One of the twins buys me a beer. The other one touches my ass as if he owns it. They fled to the pampas to be gauchos, away from their aristocratic fake parents, away from the disappeared corpses of their real parents.

One day while Beth's twin is out, the mailman brings a letter for her. It is from Beth, but I can't make out the smudged postmarks and she is vague and brief, offering no clues to her location. She is too far away, she is unreachable.

I confront the twin. She shrugs and leaves the room. Her belly is bulging ever so slightly, as if there is something growing there. I follow her and I threaten to leave, to return to my small, sad city. Enormous bulbous clouds float through the sky. I'm not sure your city is still there, she says. I've heard rumors that dozens of tornadoes came roaring down the plains, leaving devastation in their wake. The people in trailer parks all blew away, but perhaps they were the lucky ones. I heard that when the people of your town ran for cover in their basements, they found rats there, thousands of hungry, carnivorous rats. They had known they had rats, but they thought it didn't matter. They were in denial about the consequences of rodent infestation until it was too late. Much too late.

She is always telling stories, that twin. Who knows what to believe, what is true and what a lie. I recline in my bed and I think.

Once, back when I was attending sixth grade classes, the school social worker called me in to discuss my work.

Our real teacher always loved my stories, I said.

Yes, she said, but he's taken a leave. Listen. Creative expression is a wonderful thing. But there are limits.

LuAnn smiled at me in a way that suggested it was repression that was a wonderful thing.

It isn't OK to make your teachers or other students or social workers characters in your stories, she said. If you have sexual issues you'd like to address, you might do that more productively with a licensed therapist. Darlene knows that you have *some* imagination, LuAnn went on. But what Darlene would like you to do is write *clearly* and *realistically*. Darlene thinks it would be more helpful if you finished the assignment about your future career.

Does utter blackness exist? Utter blackness does exist, and sometimes I'd been there. I remembered it quite clearly. It was certainly more educational than that school, and I thought I'd like to visit it again.

The leave is permanent, isn't it, I said.

LuAnn didn't answer.

Out my window I can see the plains stretching on forever and I can see the sky darkening over the plains with an unnatural cloud and I can hear a strange buzzing noise. The cloud of locusts descends onto the fields and consumes them. It is spectacular and unreal. I walk dazed into the heat.

That night I drink. The gauchos drink and I drink and the gauchos drink some more. Some man sticks his tongue in my mouth. The lights have not gone down and everyone is anxious for the show. I excuse myself and go to my room where the boy is coloring. He draws a robot, rips it up, and gives each piece a name. You're acting out, I say decisively. He seems to believe that his mother's return is contingent on his behaving badly and describing violent fantasies. I pull down his trousers and slap his naked ass. He thinks he has to play wild games so that his teacher will come back. He cries and I kiss him and put him to bed and return to the gauchos. The heat is stifling and many of them have taken off their shirts.

A bottle shatters, somebody laughs, the sound of zippers and slaps and angry voices. The crowd parts. In the center of the ellipse, the two twin gauchos face each other with knives. They are shuffling clockwise, without getting any nearer, like two stars in a codependent orbit. They jab with their knives and mutter. They ran away to this emptiness, away from their history of murder and fake identities, but they couldn't run away from each other. Their knives are glinting in the open air like stabbing mirrors of light. I'll kill you, says one. I'll take you with me, says the other. Fuck me dead, says the first. Fuck us both, says the other.

You can never run away, I want to tell them. You can only be transformed. Wherever you go it is the same cities and the same desert and the same river. One twin lunges, one twin feints, but then the lights go down. They stop, as if dazed, and slowly, in unison, they turn toward the stage. They drop their knives.

No blood will be shed tonight. The spotlight falls. She takes the stage and she sings and she dances and she exposes her bulging stomach. She wraps herself naked in blue lights and she moves like liquid. She penetrates her female parts with her male parts. She moves like music.

We all stand here in the audience, and we watch.

She mesmerizes me, still. She is absolutely beautiful. I watch her dancing and my heart sinks: she is a wicked girl, and she is more radiant every day.

BOOK 2

BLOODY THEATER

Dada alone does not smell: it is nothing, nothing, nothing.
It is like your hopes: nothing.

—Francis Picabia, *Manifeste cannibale dans l'obscurite*[36]

---

36. Stephen published a review of the book *Ball and Hammer* in the *San Francisco Bay Guardian* ("Dada Dearest," 2002), which is illuminating not only about the interest he shares with Jake Yoder in early 20th-century art movements, but also about his stylistic affinities. "Dada has been mythologized as both founding and essential art movement of the twentieth century," Stephen writes. "Because there was little stylistic coherence to the Dada program, it could be viewed as an original impulse leading most anywhere that followed. Its spirit of anti-everything, its radical critique of existence, its blurring of the boundaries between art and life, its penchant for fragments, debris, and performance, and its attack on rationality could suggest most every art movement that followed: Breton's ideological surrealism, abstract and conceptual arts, socially engaged artistic interventions, pop art, performance, punk, etc. The struggle over interpreting Dada's legacy has been a struggle, in part, over whether to harness this energy toward social and political ends or whether such goal-directed behavior is itself a betrayal of the spirit of Dada . . ." *Ball and Hammer* includes a version of Hugo Ball's novel *Tenderenda the Fantast*, translated and illustrated by Jonathan Hammer. Stephen suggests that because of the very debasement of thought and language through advertising that Hugo Ball decried in his diaries, it has become difficult to read the seriousness of Ball's intent in his novel. "From our vantage point, the actual text can come across as facile surrealism. Images of destruction, anarchy, mob violence, and sheer absurdity have become thoroughly cheapened in the intervening century; for Ball this play of imagery was part of a life or death struggle, crucial toward maintaining a balance of creation and destruction in himself, in Dada, and in the world . . ." According to Stephen, and echoing the interests of his therapist, Darlene Bruno-Straus, "Hammer's essay and translation help to place the novel in context by highlighting its more profound roots in Dante

and in apocalyptic literature. His major interpretative conceits are two-fold: outing Ball as homosexual mystic, and placing Zurich Dada in the context of 19th-century spiritualism and the Western esoteric tradition, blending gnostic, Rosicrucian, and Kabbalistic influences . . ." Stephen could easily be describing the preceding half of *boneyard* when he writes, "Ball's project, while at times embracing nihilistic forces . . . like that of his contemporary Carl Jung, was one of reconciling opposites and of regenerating society and the cosmos. This becomes apparent throughout Tenderenda *as scenes of prophecy and flight are juxtaposed with scenes of ridiculous debauchery . . .*" [italics mine]. Finally, Stephen discusses Ball's relationship with the young student radical Hans Leybold, who died in the Great War. "If the death of Ball's lover/twin transformed Leybold into the sacrificial scapegoat that enabled Ball's ascent as Dada godfather, Ball's guilt forced him to transform himself into scapegoat through his tormented alter egos in Tenderenda. *His characters, conflated versions of himself and others* [italics mine], are forced to eat nothing but their own self-made shit, and wander through landscapes where dead soldiers' corpses burn through the night. They are pursued, fragmented, and usually confused as to 'whether they belong to those above or those below.'" While Stephen's analysis itself is fairly measured, his sympathy with Ball's willingness to abandon rationality altogether in the face of this "debasement of thought and language" strikes me as misguided at best. I would argue that rational discourse is the foundation of a liberal society and our only bastion against the forces of chaos. The need for reason is all the more apparent in our current political climate, with the merits of torture and imperial wars being seriously debated by our unscrupulous political leaders. Stephen concludes the essay with the statement that both Ball and Hammer "see their transgressive scenes as a personal exorcism of demons." —JOB

The Apostle Thomas Cast into an Oven

THE EARLY DAYS, YOU SAY. Tell me about the early days. Before the fame, money, boredom, and overexposure. Before the "murder" and all that business. We're lounging around in overstuffed chairs; you have a martini, I have a vitamin drink. I'm hoping my vitamins will help keep me "alive." You, you love the sordid glamour of celebrities. You interview us in an attempt to humiliate your own imagination. You're interviewing me, specifically, because you think the world is composed of glorious lies; you want the dirt. We've both been around the block a few times. The early days, who cares?

The smoke coils and twists around itself. The landscape is hilly and patched with snow, the city watchful and depressed. As they rub gunpowder and sulphur into the man's beard he says, *Oh, salt me well, salt me well*. His name is Conrad or Jacob or Hans and this is his big moment. He grew up in a small city with a river running through it; he will be burned alive in a city much like it. The smoke fills the sky and his flesh sizzles; it bubbles and blackens. You expect to hear: *No! No! No!*—the way people talk when they want something to stop. Instead, as soon as the ropes on his wrist are burned, he'll raise his two forefingers, *giving the promised signal to the brethren that a martyr's death is bearable.*

But that's not exactly the early days you had in mind. You can't dispense with historical context, however; I'll insist on that. My guess is that Death doesn't change, but our ideas about Death do. People didn't used to think as abstractly as they do today, that's what Ray would have said. They pictured dancing skeletons, leering skeletons, harvesting skeletons, clowning skeletons. Name your verb! These days, it's all about process. What did Death teach you, everyone asks. These days Death is used as a marketing tool. I'm not being judgmental or socialist, this is just a fact. Death is a brand of cigarettes, a brand of vodka. We wear images of Death on our t-shirts or as earrings and tattoos, as a way to accrue power. This isn't a new urge, but more dematerialized than something like scalping.

Oh, how the blood ran. The blood flowed and spurted and trickled. The book is speckled with cheap red ink, as if it's been spattered with blood. *The Bloody Theater or Martyrs Mirror of the Defenseless Christians Who Baptized Only Upon Confession of Faith, and Who Suffered and Died for the Testimony of Jesus, Their Saviour, From the Time of Christ to the Year A.D. 1660.* Most of the illustrations are dry and desexualized, compared to the iconography of the Catholics, for example, who are the primary villains in this epic saga of burnings, beheadings, and dismemberment. Here's Thomas, or Didymus, who couldn't believe until he stuck his fingers in Jesus' wound; he needed to penetrate the bloody guts of his imaginary twin. Later, he made his way to Calamina, in the

East Indies, where he *put a stop to the abominable idolatry of the heathen, who worshipped there an image of the sun*. In the picture, he's gazing into the oven as if the flames are a puzzle. He's buffed, and so are the savages. Everyone involved has muscular calves.

Beheading of James, the Son of Zebedee. Luke Hanged on an Olive Tree. Vitalis, Buried Alive at Ravenna. Antipas Burned in a Red-hot Brazen Ox. Two Young Girls Led to Execution. *They therefore cast these two young lambs into prison, where they tortured them with great severity . . .* Hendrick Pruyt Burned in a Boat. Torture of Geleyn the Shoemaker. Thirty-Seven Believers Burned at Antwerp. It goes on and on.[37]

These are my people, this is my text. 1157 pages firmly establishing the Anabaptist martyrs (1525-1660) in the same exalted tradition as the early Christian martyrs. Excessive, relentless, stoic, insane. Who cares? The descriptions are so flat, only the titles are exciting.

My name is Amos or Jacob or Sam.[38] My name is Jacob, but you know me as Jake. [39] [40] You know me as a rock star with alternative

---

37. When "rational discourse" is used to debate "the merits of torture," the discourse itself is obviously so sick that "Off with their heads" feels like a more appropriate response. Today while I was driving around Berkeley, after returning some DVDs to the video store (*Fight Club, Bad Lieutenant: Port of Call New Orleans,* and *Face Off,* starring John Travolta and Nicholas Cage), I saw an old bumper sticker that said "Impeach Bush / Torture Cheney." Not a bad idea—let's reserve torture for those who argue its "merits."—SB

38. Jake has made use of this device to insert his real name obliquely into the text.—SB

39. I do not think it is a breach of contract to state that Jake's "real" name lends some support to my thesis that he is, in fact, an "alter" or "subpersonality" of Stephen's. I learned from Ms. Bruno-Straus's thesis that Sybil Isabel Dorsett had other personalities named Marcia Lynn *Dorsett,* Vanessa Gail *Dorsett,* Mike *Dorsett* etc. Moreover, several of her personalities suffered from religious manias they'd inherited from the mother. Stephen's "eye for an eye" suggestion about torturing Cheney is ridiculously Old Testament and hardly an appropriate form of justice in a progressive society.—JOB

40. It is certainly a breach, maybe not of contract, but of faith. Whatever,

cachet, huge in such a way that unhappy teenagers will still sit and listen to my music nonstop before they go to their high schools and shoot to death their more popular peers. They want to transform the idea of high school, which is a sad, horrible idea to begin with, and think that terror is maybe not the best way to do this, but the most accessible.

We were a band. Ray, George, Bob, and Jake. When I think of those years in America, I can only think: ZOMBIE.

We were trying to wake ourselves up. Ray, George, Bob, and Jake. This was our technique: we played really fast and screeched. We conveyed anger despair confusion. The blinding flash of a Xerox machine. We were currently enrolled or recently failed college students, playing to other children in small smoky rooms. We sang a song of negation. We said no to everything we could list. Like the Dada artists, we were just kids having a good time. It meant more to some, however; those were the ones who killed themselves.

The town: a river was brown. Cool people, who had been to New York for a summer, came back all sophisticated and did harder drugs than the rest of us. Whether a phrase—*who had been to New York for a summer*—is restrictive or non-restrictive determines whether to use the commas or not. Grammar rules utilize the vocabulary of fascism, that's what Ray would have said. Commas, manacles,

---

Judith. I guess you assume your readers are not so attentive or discerning that they can't figure out your obvious implication. Your legalistic view of ethical issues is horrifying. Plus, given the strange interplay between fiction and reality in regard to *Sybil*, I'd advise you not to leap to any conclusions about how alters name themselves and whether or not it has anything to do with Jake Yoder based only on that one problematic source. The journalist who wrote *Sybil* and who lived for a time with Cornelia Wilbur and the "real" Sybil, Shirley Ardell Mason, insisted that Shirley/Sybil integrate before publication so the book could have a happy ending—and lo and behold, she did. There's a very loose translation of facts between "reality" and "book" and "film"—not to mention the ethical questions raised by Wilbur's all-encompassing roommate/therapist/mommy relationship/treatment of Shirley/Sybil.—SB

what's the difference? We weren't yet morally bankrupt, although we liked to pretend that we were. Old wooden houses with students on the porches in the summertime. Bikes, ice cream shops, bars, churches, pumpkins. It was a toy town. I'd ended up there, and lived there off and on, for years after my mother's death. It would be winter and taverns would have Christmas lights in their windows and that fake frost painted on. The campus, which was stately and sexless, melted into the downtown, which was warm and convivial, and then out beyond all of this lay the real town, the hospital and the malls and the people who weren't associated with the university but with the town's other businesses, which were medical equipment, retail outlets, and irrelevant farm machinery.

We sang of the destruction of architecture, language, social customs, cars, bridges. Ray said to me, I can totally understand the desire to destroy everything that decays slower than a human body. George said, Let's fucking kill something. On stage, George displayed the unlimited sense of contempt for human beings that would be key to our early success. We played a slow number. Viscous flow. We played a fast number. Metallurgy, chemicals, rats, and weed species. All our fast numbers were the same.

We dreamed of crime. We wanted our songs to *be* crimes.

Bob was joking. Bob didn't take the lyrics seriously. I can never remember much about Bob except his oddly shaped head. Bob was surprised when people were offended. He blushed.

I wasn't sure what my position was, but the music felt right. I was confused. I was pretending not to believe in things that I really took for granted. I thought sex was the answer to something. I had other things to think about besides the implications of an attitude.

Contrary to our intentions, our musical ability increased.

Turn us into a fuckin art band, said George.

George looked for thrills. He strangled himself with pantyhose as he masturbated. He ate Count Chocula. America was dropping bombs on children somewhere, and had been since we were 10 or 11. We wanted to be monsters, tornadoes, beneficial mutations. Bob would sometimes appeal to our "common sense" or our "humanity"; I wanted to serve the collective by becoming a limit.

It was the middle of the night.

The five of us would sit in my basement apartment, freezing. Our space heaters would keep blowing the fuses, and it would be not just cold, but dark. George is on guitar, Ray scribbling in his notebook, and Bob's upstairs, smoking crack with my roommate. We tell stories about the most disgusting things we've heard or seen. Liz knows of a man who sneezed maggots. Liz is a good-time girl, Bob's girlfriend, a game chick. She loves "drugs" and "sex" and rock and roll. She's taught me how to dress myself from thrift stores, thank God for that.

I tell them how after slaughter, the temperature of a cow or a human gradually goes down, the body stiffening into rigor mortis. This happens because there's no more blood circulation to bring a supply of oxygen to the muscle cells. I'm reading from a cookbook by Madeleine Kamman. "With the help of enzymes, the glycogen present in the muscle fibers is degraded to a relatively large amount of lactic acid which accumulates in the meat . . . This is why, if a steak or roast is cooked while the meat is still in rigor, it will have a tough texture and a noticeably acid taste when cooked rare. I experienced such meats during the war, since the only little bit of meat we had was sold as soon as slaughtered and we were too hungry to let it sit and lose its rigor."[41]

The same process happens with me and you, of course. The body swells up. *You gain thirty pounds when you die, no lie . . .*[42]

---

41. This is an accurate quote from *The New Making of a Cook*, Kamman, 1997, p. 867. —JOB
42. From a song by the Notorious B.I.G. —JOB

But you, you know that all too well, I'm sure.

This guy with a winning smile used to hang around, doing bong hits. Jason was good looking, although his ass was unusually flat. Jason thought it would be amazing to surf in Indonesia, especially if you were stoned. He was totally into this outrageous life form—the meerkat—that was really bad-ass. He wanted to live in a yurt. He took Ray once to a yurt exhibition on the edge of town. Ray was the last person you'd find buying a yurt, but many of us enjoy entertaining implausible ideas, bonding and mating through implausible ideas, marketing ourselves as the virtual embodiment of implausible ideas. The early days.

It was winter. It was the middle of the night. This time we were in Ray's attic. We were sitting around trying to name our band. I was sexually repressed. Bone has been, and remains, an exciting word to me. Use it as a verb, I get erect. Anyone, wearing a gas mask or not, can say *I'm gonna bone you* and I'll melt. It was Ray who was taking some Shakespeare class and suggested *Boneyard*. That's a classic, said George.[43] George had black hair and blue eyes, hair on his chest and baby fat. I have black hair that sits on my head like a mop and blue eyes that just peek through my bangs, baby fat and a smooth, rounded chest. George was sexy if you could use your imagination or blur your vision, I guess. I wasn't especially striking, but my girth was manly enough that it got me laid once in a while. Bob suggested Günter Parche's Obsession as the name of our band.[44] Jason suggested Attention Deficit Disorder. He worked with disturbed children. Disturbed children fascinated him. He'd get really high and tell us about the way they struggled

43. My first choice for the title of Jake's novel was *Towards the Primeval Lightning Field*. I was dismayed to discover it had already been used by Will Alexander.—SB

44. Günter Parche was the Steffi Graf fan who stabbed Graf's opponent, Monica Seles, during a tennis match in 1993.—JOB

when they didn't want their meds. He looked at me sometimes. We had a Comparative Religion class together; any conversation about god would turn into a conversation about grammar. He liked to say nothing in as confusing a way as possible. He liked to seduce people, but he never had sex.

We named the band Love Muscle.

George was a dark one. Like my people, the Amish, George brooded under thick eyebrows. Me and George, we had a certain chemistry when we played music together, but otherwise we didn't socialize much, except to talk about the accoutrements of our craft. We discussed guitars. He preferred a hollow-body for its round, jazzy sound, whereas I have always been a strict solid-body man. We discussed pickup output and frequency response, tube distortion and meaty sounds, Cry Babies and Fuzz-Tones. The sound of an electric guitar in the cold is like a monstrous ejaculation of spirit. The amounts of distortion and sustain are increased by stepping up the amplitude of the input. A lot of effects boxes cut off their outputs once the input has decayed beyond a certain point. We agreed that wasn't OK, but we were also disgusted by the processed sound created by the automatic decay built into some models by unscrupulous manufacturers.

Similarly, we didn't want to use this info to sound more polished, but eventually had to rely on tricks to sound *less* polished.

The answer: use the swell pedal as the last thing before the signal hits the amp.

I'd have long discussions with Ray, while George brooded and drank or just brooded, whatever. I didn't care enough to work that hard to have a conversation. George had carefully crafted his own mythology in which his rudeness and hostility were considered integral aspects of his genius. He didn't return messages, but nobody was supposed to take that personally. Liz adored him. He's got charisma, she said once. Like Bill Clinton was supposed to have had? River Phoenix or Kurt Cobain? It seemed such an old fashioned and reactionary concept, this charisma.

Ray and George, George and Ray. I'd like to avoid a story about founding fathers. Still, you've asked for the history of the band and you can't tell a history without starting somewhere. You still nursing that martini? Well I'll tell you. Ray and George were unique, but only sort of. America has produced an overabundance of Rays and Georges, and let's face it, Jakes too. Bob, that goes without saying. Why do some forms of life get produced and not others?

Evidence that Ray was basically interchangeable with other similar human beings:

He was intrigued by the "insanity" of Philip K. Dick.

He had a not fully developed and barely intuitable relationship of a sexual nature with "the diaper."

Libra with Virgo rising: he lived in his head, couldn't make up his mind, obsessed over ethics and order.

Thought Nick Drake was a genius.

Thought he looked OK in suede jackets.

Didn't bother to "vote."

Denied any objective basis to reality.

Developed musically in an adversarial relationship to hip-hop.

Made a conscious effort to put quotation marks around words you wouldn't expect.

Heterosexual, with trouble articulating his emotions: because he couldn't cry in front of people, all his emotions got butched up. Musically, it meant all of his emotions, all of George's emotions, all of the band's emotions, looked like anger.

Could he cry in private? I don't know.

Evidence of Ray's uniqueness:

He knew a lot about history, especially the history of the Civil War.

He ate only fruit-flavored ice creams.

He knew all about feeding hogs.

He'd only been out of state once, when we went to see a band in Minneapolis.

He was the only one in his 20th-Century Lit class who understood even the most surface level of what was going on in *Ulysses*.[45]

He kept a sunflower in a soapstone vase. The vase seemed fleshy. This was in the summer.

Although he came from a short and compact people, Ray himself was wiry, elongated, and overwrought—as if an angel had been stretched out on a rack.[46] Ray grew up on a farm outside of the city where I once lived and we took guitar lessons in the same crumbling old house in the bad part of town, from the same series of childless women and impatient men. After his father died, he and his mother sold the farm and moved into the city, where we

---

45. Perhaps the Stephen/Jake Yoder split represents a split in high and low culture. According to Bruno-Straus this sort of thing is common. She writes, "Although Sybil's two male personalities were working-class bumpkins, Sybil's 'most evolved' self, Vicky, was French and aristocratic. The Troops in Truddi Chase's *When Rabbit Howls* were torn between a poet mother who once invited a playwright over, and a stepfather who read true crime and other 'bloody and debased materials.' Marcia's personality 'Muriel' (*Broken Child*, 1995) was a cultural sophisticate, 'above the system of rules for the plebeians she was stuck sharing space with.' In *Nightmare*, Nancy's Sarah had read all the classics, knew Mozart from Schubert, Picasso from Renoir, spoke French, loved escargot, spent hours in museums—while Nancy maintained other personalities that ran around with Mexican street gangs. Billy Milligan had a whole gang of 'undesirables': Philip, a thug with a strong Brooklyn accent; Walter, an Australian; Samuel, 'the wandering Jew'; and April, 'the bitch' with a Boston accent. It was Arthur, the British aristocrat, who was interpreted, like Sybil's French aristocrat personality, to be the most evolved personality; he was intelligent, unemotional, aware of others and highly moral; that odd idea again that spiritual beings and European white people don't have emotional lives." Attentive readers will note Stephen's fondness for the most vulgar of cultural artifacts, along with his more literary tastes. —JOB

46. I shouldn't neglect to mention that this is a fair description of Stephen's physique. —JOB

briefly attended the same school.

Ray's preferred method of suicide was, theoretically, the guillotine. It was the middle of the night. Some of us thought pills and wine were the only reasonable means of suicide. Nobody cared for guns, slit wrists, nooses, or carbon monoxide. What some of us most feared was drowning, to others it seemed almost peaceful. I never talked about my family history, so you couldn't consider those comments insensitive or rude. What some of us most feared was spiders. Nobody wanted to be Buried Alive or Burned in a Red-hot Brazen Ox. George refused to participate in the discussion at all, smugly implying not that it was overly morbid, but that the decision to kill or not kill oneself and the method one chose for fulfillment were considerations as meaningless as the question of how to live.

Except for George, we'd all known each other since kindergarten. I guess we'd always been in love with Liz; she always had the prettiest hair. She'd had slightly more money growing up than we did, which meant something in a place like the small, sad city where we met. I moved away from that small, sad city, but when Liz and Ray and Bob came to this town for college it was like a weird family reunion. Liz's understated elegance became a nice contrast to the band's contrived vulgar attitude.

Ray treated Liz like a queen, but spoke of women in general as shallow, uncultivated souls, stupidly pursuing their brainless alpha males. These were the pretty ones—the others he didn't care about, except to study with for multiple-choice philosophy tests and then talk badly about once they were gone. Loneliness will twist people into ugly shapes sometimes, or maybe it's technology's fault, or capitalism's. I never hugged Ray. I slapped him on the back if we'd both had enough to drink or played an intensely felt show.

Thanksgiving, Ray was going home. His mother would drive him an hour and a half to the small farming community from which he had originally come. His father had been dead for several years because of cholesterol that hardened in his arteries. His mother arrived early, in an old blue Toyota and knocked timidly on the door, while we were still there drinking beers. She climbed the stairs vigorously for such a fragile looking person. She was a tiny woman, in polyester stretch pants and a sweater with a pastel floral pattern and a grey parka stuffed with synthetic filling. She had grey hair falling around her head in big oval curls and thick glasses. I was reminded of an ironing board. I thought of frying onions in bacon fat. I thought: fritter. When she spoke it was rambling and good-natured. I thought: crazy little fritter. Clearly, she had belonged to the PTA. She had put a blue star in her window at home, to signal to children in crisis that this was a safe place to come if they were ever in trouble.

The awkwardness between Ray and his mother was painful to watch. They didn't know how to hug each other either; she loved her son, and Ray was doomed. She stood there, as if waiting for somebody to take her coat, offer her a nice cup of decaf tea. Ray grabbed his belongings and hurried her out.

Anneken van den Hove Buried Alive

JAKE: Music isn't an idea. It's a physical presence that gets inside you. Ray taught me that.

MAXIMUMROCKNROLL: That abstractions crush us?

JAKE: They literally crush our bodies. He didn't know he taught me that, but he did.

MAXIMUMROCKNROLL: Tell us about Ray.

JAKE: I don't think he ever got over it.

MAXIMUMROCKNROLL: And what about you? Did you ever get over Ray?[47]

CLOVERLEAF INTERCHANGES, SCRAP YARDS, and tunnels. What's disturbing about cars—it is clear to all of us that cars *are* disturbing—is not their speed or hardness, juxtaposed to the squooshy

---

47. Obviously, no such interview actually exists. —JOB

insides of a person or a Twinkie. It is the jelly-bean sheen of them. The plasticky, luminous sheen.

They knew how to drive in ice and snow. They knew how to steer into the fishtail. They knew how to drive in the snow even after splitting a six-pack and a joint and starting on another six-pack. It was part of their culture, like how an aborigine can visit the planetary dreamtime. The knowledge was laced into their DNA.

George was driving. The snow, the ice, the drugs. The other car crossed the center line, sideswiped a Hostess delivery truck.

Blinding white lights. The shriek of a Xerox machine! A Hostess delivery truck is teetering toward you! Swerve, baby, swerve.

Freeways at night, darkened cornfields, all that space and darkness and metal hurtling between the lines at dangerous speeds. The fields go on forever. The cows are penned in, beatific, underneath the aurora borealis. The snow is falling on the dreaming cows. So much space, you'd think we could avoid each other.

For George and Ray, the time slowed down. The car behind them, car D, had swerved onto the shoulder to avoid the accident, taking out an Amish buggy, E. George's vision was blocked by the Hostess truck B, so that when car A (a hybrid SUV) crossed the center line and truck B teetered toward him and he swerved toward the shoulder to avoid it, car D was already there. The truck was now on its side, sliding across the highway in front of George and toward the right, so, with nowhere else to go, George braked and swerved to the left, sideswiping the truck which had rebounded toward the left after being grazed by car D on its way into a snowy field.

But. To reduce a rather complicated algebraic equation to its bare essentials—the evils of modern transportation—what was left of Ray couldn't have been much. What had once constituted what we think about when we think about Ray—his body—was now dispersed across the highway and so intermingled with crushed car and truck parts, not to mention the creamy fillings of various

Twinkies and Ding Dongs, as to be indistinguishable.

X, the variable, is actually a constant.

George emerged from the accident unscathed, as did, miraculously, the driver of the truck and, predictably, the driver of car D. The driver of car A, who "caused" the whole mess, suffered from minor cuts and abrasions. An abrasion is a rubbing or scraping off or grazing of skin.

The cows continued their dreaming. Dreams of martyrdom, hormones, and obliteration resembled an algebraic equation or spider's web superimposed on the sky. Dreams of escape resembled the northern lights. The moon came out and shone on the snow.

The blood came from the sun, the creamy white Hostess filling from the moon. The mixing of the blood and the filling was taboo. The intermingling of oppositional fluids. For the two to touch broke all the sacred laws.

Bad omen.

Louwerens Janss Led to Execution

ON PAGE 1055 IS AN ILLUSTRATION of a young man in knickers, with his shirt open enough to make out his left nipple and his hands tied behind his back. This is Louwerens Janss Noodtdruft, of Delft, in the year 1577, who has chosen *rather to die here for a little while unto his flesh and the pleasures of this world than to have to pay for it with an eternal lamentation in the torment of hell*. He's another one on his way to the stake, to be burned while alive. Because he had no other writing tools, he inscribed his last message on two tin spoons, with a pin. Unfortunately, his belief system was so trite that there's nothing in his final message worth repeating. For a period when I was a boy, these were the only pictures of half-naked men I had access to. I'd sneak out to the barn and gaze at the picture of Louwerens, and I'd partake of the meager pleasures of the flesh and this world—sometimes two or three times a day.

Ray was dead. For I was on antihistamines and decongestants, triplolidine hydrochloride and pseudoephedrine hydrochloride; at higher doses nervousness and dizziness may occur. Yet I was wandering hallways in a beautiful glass cage. We love to be dizzy, always have. I met my own glass ghost, and the walls were glass and the sky was ready to put out. Passageways of thick glass: Ray was dead.

A few words about the funeral.

Dress shoes in the ice and snow. The earth's magnetic force is said to be declining. I was suspended between the north and south poles. On one side of the church George was the driving of cars, recklessly and nihilistically, George was survivor's guilt, George was the short arc of the Zen arrow of Ray's meaningless life. On the other side was the tiny mother. Big plastic glasses with thick lenses, white hair under a black doily, resplendent in navy blue polyester— why splurge on something black you'd only wear once? She sat stoic and then her entire tiny body started shaking with sobs and then she sat stoic again. My heart was arrhythmic from the magnetic pressure! My glass ghost was smiling inside; excited, dyspeptic.

George broke down as he passed by the closed and virtually empty coffin. She didn't resist the seduction. The mother. She came forth. Behold! And held him. She squeezed with her tiny arms, to comfort. She took him with her to her seat. My heart relaxed. The miracle of forgiveness.[48]

We considered disbanding but George insisted we go on with the

---

48. This phrase was tossed around relentlessly in the media after the shootings at Nickel Mines, especially in regard to the Amish embrace of the shooter's widow. Jake's use of the phrase suggests to me that he was, at the very least, actively revising this manuscript at that time—when he was 14 or maybe 15 years old.—SB

show. Bob agreed. We spontaneously wrote an opaque tribute song to our dead band member. We vomited it forth, that first show after the death.

You've heard this story, I'm sure.[49]

It was night.

The smoke, the cheap beer, the crowd, the sweat. We swayed. The lights and heat. We electrified. The blood and the filling, the pain, the loss, the tiny mother. It was winter. The snow, the sheen, the blood! We had swallowed Death. We had emerged from the fire. We were full of shit. We were feeling things! Confusion! Loss! Weirdness!

I was possessed by the spirit of a sad girl—it was so soft and loving and sweet and became a shriek of pain. Then silence. I whispered now with the shimmery drum brushes my only accompaniment and a rare punctuating minor chord. I whispered: *Wendy said you don't have to die / I blew my frozen breath into your cupped hands / But you have to die.* Suddenly, we were emerging onto a plateau of sincerity from the dense guitar chords of irony and rage—we were peaking. This was a common technique, but effectual.

We had transformed ourselves, overnight, into local legends.

Annexx:
"Wow, this is like a cold beer after a shit day at work, refreshing and good. They kinda sound similar to Anti-Flag, the earlier stuff, but with a lot more rock edge to the punk, the vocals are great, the music's just as powerful,

---

49. Another common sound bite after the shootings was "the Amish 9/11," although the Amish themselves didn't see that connection. "The people who did 9/11 believed completely different things, and they wouldn't have stopped if the government hadn't showed them they needed to," the father of one of the wounded girls told me. But, as with the non-Amish 9/11, there was talk of "innocence lost" and a relentless search for "heroes." According to 12-year-old Barbie Fisher, her older sister Marian asked the shooter to shoot her first, to spare the younger ones. When the police arrived, he did shoot Marian first, and then he shot Barbie, and the eight other girls, and himself. Barbie survived, but Marian didn't. Marian was declared a hero by the media, but one Amish man said to me, "You don't hear about a hero among the Amish. You give glory not to a person but to God."—SB

wow, I really dig this, and the cool thing is, the songs don't all blend together, a lot of difference, some are these straight-out rock, others are more punk, they all kick bottom with a raw garage feel. Andy says a cross between early Hüsker Dü and the Hives." — W

Foe:

"Hmmmm. I don't really know how to describe Love Muscle except that maybe Arcade Fire meets the Strokes and then goes out for drinks with Dinosaur Jr. Driving yet chunky guitar riffs and straining vocals with almost a slight emo feel to it." — BIX

Suburban Voice:

"Love Muscle have some punkish trappings that take them down a few darker musical corridors. With Jake's haggard, yowly up-all-night and smoking-too-much vocals being a defining characteristic, there's some resemblance to early Soul Asylum or Afghan Whigs. That's also evident in the blending of '70s rock'n'roll impulses with something modern. Sometimes plodding, sometimes soaring, they hijack your attention temporarily, for a tour inside a seemingly broken yet beautiful head, full of pain, regret, and intimations of transcendence. I could draw comparisons to Lungfish, Superchunk, or even Deep Purple, but they are only starting points. Their cassette is a twisting, semi-wrenching excursion. Interesting and with unique properties, if not always hitting the mark."[50]

---

50. Jake had the random and/or eclectic musical tastes of a willful autodidact. He'd been heavily influenced by his cousin and his cousin's band, Wrath of God, but had also followed mysterious trails of his own. He loved Lungfish, Art Brut, the Oblivians, the Notorious B.I.G., Anti-Flag, the Violent Femmes, Comets on Fire, Throwing Muses, Britney Spears, Wolfmother, Coheed and Cambria, My Bloody Valentine, Broken Social Scene, Pharoah Sanders, Spacemen 3, and bands I'd never heard of like Franz Ferdinand, the Street Urchins, and And You Will Know Us by the Trail of Dead. He liked Kylie Minogue, Modest Mouse, His Name Is Alive, the New Pornographers, and the Strokes. He claimed he'd never heard of the Velvet Underground, although he'd somehow discovered Nico, who he thought was kind of like his mother; on the night that he tried to destroy his manuscript, he brought a portable cassette player along to our meeting at the abandoned orphanage and played "Wrap Your Troubles in Dreams" for me as the fire cast weird shadows over his face. Then he played "These Days" and wept. He told me he couldn't listen to the song without crying. This was the only time I witnessed what a psychologist would consider an "appropriate" display of emotion from Jake; most times he looked either terrified or bored, and I rarely saw him smile. Later, I would play "I'll Be Your Mirror" for him over the phone. As Nico's haunting voice sang,

The task of sorting through Ray's belongings was given to the band. We were to keep what we wanted, save a few items for his mother, and give away the rest. He had a chest full of notebooks, papers, old books, and magazines. I set aside for his mother a few academic papers, his freshman philosophy "Willful Self-Delusion as Philosophy in Kierkegaard." I figured that if the arguments meant nothing to her, the A minus would.

Ray had made elaborate charts of esoteric influence. He had tied everyone together in this map of bubbles and lines, ranging from William Burroughs to JFK, Throbbing Gristle, Giordano Bruno, Umberto Eco, but without making clear what the ultimate goal of this vast "underground" might be.

Anyone can be manic. Smart people, stupid people. If you're manic, you have a lot of activity in your cingulate cortex and you see significance in every little thing. You might think you have insight into some cosmic scheme, you might think that every incident, object, sign, musical note is bound up together in a mystical wholeness. The lid of your head has been opened wide and the catacombs of the sky *are* your mind: any action the living might take is of the ultimate consequence. The human brain is crucial to the cosmos, the relationship between its two lobes and its potential new cauliflower growths. The immensity of time stripped bare in its purplish dance of colliding minerals only confirms the importance of the human faculty for music! If you're depressed, you feel just the opposite: nothing makes any sense at all, it's just a random

---

"When you think the night has seen your mind / That inside you're twisted and unkind / Let me stand to show that you are blind . . . ," Jake was so quiet I wasn't sure he was still on the line. This time I was the one who wept. Poor little Jake. His favorite Black Sabbath song was "War Pigs." The only Meat Puppets song he liked was the instrumental "Aurora Borealis." He liked to watch Richie Havens singing on YouTube, especially his performance of "Freedom" at Woodstock. He absolutely despised Slipknot and the Black Keys. It pains me to say that he loved Journey and Rush. This fact alone negates the plausibility of Jake as an aspect of my own personality.—SB

series of meaningless musical notes and deaths.

If you're on your meds, you feel like you aren't exactly living and you aren't exactly dead.

We had to find a replacement on bass. There was this boring girl we'd gone to school with who had since blossomed into a vaguely emo chick. A pale girl with black hair, dressed all in black. Sally. When she stood next to Bob, it distracted me from his oddly shaped head. Sally couldn't much play, but she could sing. Her look said ART BAND. George would not pollute the memory of Ray. George would not subvert Ray's values. We chose a guy named Beej, who couldn't much play either, but at least he was aggressive, had a belly, and wore flannel.

It was night. We stopped in for coffee at the ice cream store, me and Liz and Bob. Upstairs, people were sitting by themselves with their Russian novels or 20th-century philosophy books open, waiting for someone they knew to come and distract them from cold weather and knowledge. Others had already paired off. In the corner, George and Ray's mother were seated with steaming mugs. She had her back to us, leaned in toward George, talking. Liz waved but George didn't see. George, she said, firmly, compellingly. He nodded to her. His nod said that social relations and conventions, such as greetings and speech, should be dealt with ironically, were beneath his lofty and despairing thoughts.

I'm worried about him, said Liz.

He'll be fine, said Bob. Bob often made reassuring statements based on absolutely no evidence. To me George's despair seemed annoying and smug.

He really loved him, Liz said.

So did you, I said.

How do you convey grief without theatrics? We heard a train in the distance. I told them that when I was a kid, I'd gone to a one-room school for awhile. I imagined I could hear the trains in the distance as I relentlessly spelled my words. I told them that the school was no longer there.[51] Liz said when she was a little girl they played this record of ocean sounds, airplane sounds, train sounds. They loved trains especially. They'd turn off the lights and use a flashlight to act like a train. The train would pass cities that rose in the distance out of desolate plains. The train would pass oil wells rising in the dawn light like the skeletons of dinosaurs. It would travel across dried gullies that served as borders and farther and farther through scrub deserts, in between mountain ranges as brown and lifeless as the valleys they surrounded, and through vast, charred jungles full of cows. Liz was supposed to be studying for a test the next day, but looked like she hadn't slept in a week. She was going to fail. She started crying. People at other tables shifted uncomfortably and glanced over, feeling like maybe they should do something. Bob squeezed her into him, as if trying to comfort her, but I felt like he was actually trying to hide her, to smother her.

It was winter. My grandfather died, the skinny one. I drove through the frozen patchwork of countryside, all silent and blue on the other side of the windshield. I drove through one of my former home-towns, past the plastic replica of the *Starship Enterprise* squatting in the center of town. I passed the old farmhouse where I'd spent my earliest years and where I'd lived occasionally after the death of my mother—a prairie gothic nightmare. Grandmother hugged me fiercely, everyone else was just polite. The funeral was early the next morning, in a barn.

After all these years away, I was most impressed by the sheer mass of the Amish. They packed the barn, crammed together on backless benches, more standing in the entrance way, blocked from

51. After the shooting at Nickel Mines, the one-room schoolhouse where the murders took place was completely razed; the surviving children were temporarily schooled in a garage. —SB

the wind by sheets of plastic. The shunned and renegade children had returned, our fancy outfits interspersed with all those black cloaks, bonnets, and beards. Choreographed, military. Women's hair pulled back tight, stretching the faces into stern, pained submission. Home at last.

Why had I ever felt the need to dream about crime? My ego was so fancy and my mental states so overelaborated that I already was a crime—relative.

The sermons droned on in Pennsylvania Dutch. The language was like a mutant foreign country I still dreamed about sometimes, but now that I was back it just seemed squalid and unfamiliar. The drone was punctuated with occasional English phrases. *Blah blah blah women's lib blah blah blah blah blah blah car races und dog races und television und tractor pulls.* Even with the cold body in the center of things they preached the evils of the world, activities to be avoided, *nicht in Gottes Plan.* After hours of this, they filed past the casket in herds. We moved, in a mass of horse and buggies, to the cemetery. The cold wind whipped us, and we bore it as our due. Bleak, gnarled oak and wind and faded tombstone inscriptions. Ervin, Elvin, Ivan, and Sammy. Ezekiel, Jonas J, Jonas S, Samuel, and Peter. My dead forefathers.[52] Am I a collision? The Amish "genes" head-on with the world, but the world is bigger now—look at all the supernovas! The comets, black holes, fluttering UFOs. We returned to the house for ham salad and pie. The pie was made out of raisins, gooshy and overly sweet. Some cousin's husband was seated next to me and he knew that I was a musician.

---

52. Coincidentally several of these are names of Stephen's dead forefathers, as I discovered while searching through Amish genealogies in search of information. Given the repetition of these names in Amish families, I'll concede that this fact alone isn't conclusive. After thumbing through these obsessively kept records for hours, the endless repetitions of the same names can begin to drive one a little bit crazy. The text itself can seem to come to life, like some monstrous, animated hieroglyphic.—JOB

He said, Do you deal with the distortion?

Yes! I said. God knows what this man had got into, back when he was sowing his wild oats.

My musical ambitions clarified. I wanted to make tapes that might be smuggled into Amish communities. They would reach children who had hidden cassette players in the barn. Late at night under a bulging moon they would sneak out of their austere beds, plug in the earbuds and listen; my music would subtly corrode the very fabric of their communal lives. That's cool, said George, but I could tell he thought it was puerile and reactionary. He had ascended to a purer level of despair, where all communication and action were rendered superficial.

Spring came. Pasty flesh unencased. Worms on the sidewalk, after the rains. Sponginess. The sun was shining. We were lying in the grass between the Student Union and the river, me and Liz.

Life was fat. The fish weren't jumping in that poisoned brown river, but it was pleasant enough to look at: smoky and mellow. The railroad bridge offered romance.

Invisible structures were being intuited! Laws were like something we were wearing; we were raw and throbbing and empty and multiple and uncontainable and then there were all those crushing containers which were grooves trying to sculpt us into something not especially worthwhile.

We have to rediscover the core, I said. The frenzy. The naked.

Liz had dropped out as an undefined Liberal Arts major, but was plotting her comeback; she'd get a teaching certificate. We drank beer from plastic cups.

So these kids have stereos in the barn? said Liz.

Some do, I said.

Liz said, I think the Amish are cute.

Cute as in puppies, or cute as in sex?

Oh, puppies I think, said Liz.

I said, Not everything that's cute should be maintained. Cute is a deformation of character, I said.

I said, Cute is always evidence of a profound fear of Death.

Did I really say that? I knew more back then than I do today; I both knew and I cared.

You were young once too! The delicious pain. The yummy torture. Liz said, I'm pregnant. This was the sort of drama I had only seen on television. Liz thought abortion was a good idea, but it was fucking with her emotions. She hadn't told Bob.

It's his, isn't it? I said.

I wish you were the father, she said. She was always a little more mysterious in the presence of George and Bob and the heterosexuals. She knew they liked to figure things out and got bored once they were solved.

George, I said.

She shrugged.

I'm not sure, she said. I mean I was only with him twice.

George has some weird issues, she said. She thought his relationship with Ray's mother was strange. She decided she should go ahead and have the baby. I thought we could all raise it together. We'd be a family. We were lonely and misunderstood, but the very idea of shared diaper responsibilities filled some hole. Having a baby seemed life-loving. It might butch me up; I'd accrue some of the characteristics of heterosexual, of Dad, just by pushing a stroller.

I am trying to be a life-lover still. You hear the enthusiasm in my tone! I love good and I love evil and am entertained by the continuing accumulation of useless details. But my tone isn't quite convincing. A little forced, you think. These vitamin drinks give me a buzz that helps maintain my bubbly, combative persona, just as I imagine your martinis help you endure the pressures of your trade. Deadlines and jet lag and all the stress of coming up with deep and probing questions. Just outside of our little coastal spot, a troll-ish looking woman in fake black leather jacket, blue sweat pants, grey sweatshirt, about 55, tightly permed reddish-brown hair, is smoking on a bench. I was hallucinating lizards, this girl behind me tells her friend. I'll talk about the trees: If the bark is bright rusty red and the berries are almost black, it is Western Juniper, Sierra Juniper. If the bark is brown and the berries bright blue, it is Rocky Mountain Juniper. If you're west of the Sierra Nevada or if the leaves are conspicuously dented, it is California Juniper. I am and they are! They wanted to party, the girl says to her friend, But we're like no, cuz they're Okies and have these tight Wrangler jeans and big old belt buckles? And then we're in the motel room and I'm like: The curtains are *full* of lizards.

I'm easily distracted! The rock and roll lifestyle, well, you can imagine what it's done to my brain. Think of Keith Richards or Robert Plant. Not to mention the permanent ringing in my ears. But I can see you're getting impatient.

The girl behind me says, This girl's all: Do you do crank, I'm like: No. I love crank, she says, and I'm like: Great. Whoopee for you.

If the leaves smell bad, it is Ailanthus, if the leaves smell spicy, it is California Pepper Tree. None of this matters, which is why it is a gift.

I'll tell you something now: my enthusiastic tone is a ploy. It's de-signed to convince you I'm a passionate person, when in fact I'm a cold, evil monster.

Bob was thrilled. He didn't even care that the baby might be some-one else's. They'd more or less stopped blowing up abortion clinics, so it would have been easy enough to kill it. Girls like Liz were full of the amphibious potentialities they'd inadvertently received, like mail bombs sent to lumber executives, but hardly anybody was shouting at them from the sidewalk, hardly anybody was trying to execute their doctors. Still, we wanted family values. Even George stopped brooding and started loitering at the Walmart over tiny blue fuzzy pajamas. I think it's a girl, Liz said.

Liz was going to quit drinking and doing drugs. But not quite yet.

Rock and roll: eternity is baby current. Our music was more complicated now. Vaguely so, the emotions were weirder and more true. Everything was changing. People packed up together, beer and sweat and cigarette smoke. I was fucked up. The crowd was wild. Mosh mosh mosh. Shirtless young men. A huge young man bounced out there, empty and beautiful, a field of swirling energies. I was wallowing in his sex vibes, burning like a wire, I stared at him the whole show and sang to him all this rage and lust and he looked back all intense and confused and bouncing up and down, I sang I WANNA FUCK UUUUUNIVERSAL BROTHERHOOD / I'M ON MY KNEES IN THE GRAVEL PARKING LOT / I HATE YOUR WAYS OF TALKING / WHEN MY FUCK ME STUPID KILL MY BRAIN AND CONVERSATION . . .

This was my night. If it couldn't get me naked with farmboys, what was the point of rock and roll? I was headed for the backseat of his Camaro, his dick luminous in the moonlight.

Some kid was on the floor, being crushed. Gasping for breath. Shirtless men were trampling him. Pummeled by indifferent boots and tennis shoes, he felt the presence of god or grammar; it stank of sweat and testosterone. He gazed ecstatically at the jiggling of their muscular buttocks, attractively packaged in ripped denim or army fatigues. Others joined him. Of course: a whole secret society of prone, bony youth had devoted itself to nurturing this particular occult pleasure. Liz was shit-faced drunk. Low-grade meth and other things. She thought she should save him. She thought he wanted to be saved. When she reached down to help him, he bit. He broke the skin.

We wailed. The moon rose. The walls vibrated and we stank. I saw him bite her. I saw through everything into the heart of that moment. Music deleted causality. The smell of brain matter and smoke.

By the end of the song she was unconscious. People were saying *whoa*. By the time the ambulance got there, it was too late. The autopsy was inconclusive, so they blamed the drugs. But I'm telling you I saw it happen. Once, me and Liz and some other people, we were all tripping on acid and we wandered into the basement of the science building into a room full of cadavers. We said *whoa* and backed right on out and that was weird for about fifteen seconds. It flowed right over us. But this was different. You remember what it's like to look right into the naked heart of throbbing being. She was writhing in torment, flopping around like a fish on the deck. You try to ignore this fact, this summation. Everything was wrapped up in her body at that moment. Nothing was separable. Everything was absolutely naked and raw and writhing in torment. Once, my school was demolished, as if it had never been there; nothing remained but an empty field. Once, I saw a picture of a charred Afghani boy who'd lost his legs to an American bomb. Once, I saw a handsome fireman who'd been burnt to a crisp. They sent him to fight a fire that they ought to have just let burn. They pretend it's about valor and camaraderie, but it's all in the service of property and death. They are playing Boy Scouts and fucking up the natural world in the process. America. It's all been paid for in blood, everyone knows this. She was flopping around, flop harder and you'll be free. It's not the price so much as the quality of the merchandise. SUVs and drone missiles, Walmart and business parks, holding pens and abattoirs. He bit her and his bacteria got stuck in her aorta. Her heart murmur was choking. Oh forget it. Fires are started by lightning and cigarette butts. I say *Let it burn*. That's my cultural heritage; apocalypse feels like salvation. I don't care. America is sick and ugly and I can hardly bear another minute of it this way. Give it back! Hot potato, hot potato! That thing inside of her, it was tiny as a gold tooth and just as slick: a webby tooth with little fingers and little toes. It went back to the land of potential monsters. America! I can't bear to see my sickness revealed in the landscape anymore. I can't bear to drive through the ugliness inside of me. At least some other people's ugliness might not be so obvious and crushing. Give it back! Let it become strange. Walk into a grocery store, bathe in the fluorescent lights—who invented this hideous light, who multiplied it? You see clearly, in any Safeway, what you have turned the world into. You see that you want to poison yourself. You want to make yourself so sick that you vomit everything up except for that one small thing. The bone of light. You want to purify yourself, you stupid fuck, and it's insane!

Well fuck you. That's what I say. In interviews, etc. I'm predictable and I hate that about myself. You understand I'm using the "you" now in a more general sense. I congeal too easily. My neurons fire in a limited number of patterns. I'm cursed. I'm inbred and full of words. We compensated, in those days, by muttering our lyrics; incomprehensibility, just another element of sound.

Liz, I loved you. More than all the others. I don't know what death means. I miss you. That sounds trite. Narcissistic. Fuck you. Good-bye.

Music Week (December, 2015):
MUSIC WEEK: You should at least provide your listeners with liner notes. No one can understand what you're saying.
JAKE: Fuck you. Don't you think meaning is inherently fascistic?
COOTIE DENTATA: The divorce between body and soul is like . . . You know, the prison-house of written language.
JAKE: The body in revolt against ideas.

Andrew the Apostle Crucified at Patras

ONCE WHEN SHE WAS ALIVE we walked out in nature together and I thought: she is lonely, because the earth is a tomb. The nature we walked in was a vast cemetery with a statue of a black angel in it. There were many legends surrounding this statue; it had once been white, etc.

When someone dies? You write a song. Liz's song started out *The snow is falling on the cemetery . . .*

Later, we were interviewed by this zine called madonna/ho, a conglomeration of Madonna fans and sex workers who "didn't necessarily get along." I'm not sure if there were dozens of them or really just the two who asked the questions, in a dark booth at a gloomy local tavern. They did a lot of band reviews and interviews and stupid collage shit and Xeroxed it and so forth. They thought we were great.[53]

madonna/ho: So, death has sort of dogged you guys right? I mean, is it kind of intense or what?
JAKE: Yeah, pretty intense.
GEORGE: Too intense for an interview.
JAKE: [giggling] The music speaks for itself.

m/h: Does Love Muscle have a political position?
GEORGE: The music speaks for itself.
m/h: [to co-interviewer] Be sure to write "[ironically]" in that last comment so our readers get the tone.
m/h: That's lame. Just do the interview.
m/h: Irony doesn't always translate to the printed page.
GEORGE: I wasn't being ironic.
JAKE: We're nihilists, but, uh, you have to situate that nihilism in contrast to society, right? I mean look at the shit we're in the middle of.
m/h: You're not closet fascists like those guys in that band . . .
JAKE: Oh, I hate them! They sing this shit, you think it's a parody of retarded attitudes . . . I mean, they're totally serious. They believe that shit. I used to kind of admire them and then I read that interview. Total morons.

m/h: How do you feel about Madonna?
GEORGE: I've heard of her. Wasn't she one of the original Go-Go's? [laughs]
BOB: She doesn't sound like Minnie Mouse so much anymore.
JAKE: She should have more babies. She should settle down and have more babies.
m/h: Isn't that kind of sexist?
m/h: What, having a baby is sexist?
m/h: Who are your influences? Who are your favorite bands?

---

53. The only trace I could find of this "zine" was in an article about a kind of conference or assembly (named, appropriately I imagine, "Spew 2") devoted to the celebration and dissemination of "zines" in Los Angeles. One can easily enough imagine the chaos that results without an enlightened editorial filter to separate quality work from unedited ranting. The conference occurred in January 1992, when Jake would have been a year old or less. I've been able to find almost no trace of the band Bad Food either. — JOB

JAKE: . . . Oh and Bad Food, Jesus. They blew me away. You know you love that shit and you sing along, all this weird religious guilt and hatred and contempt like it's party music, and I used to think it was party music too until I saw them live, this was several years ago, you know, and I was blown away. He was totally serious.

m/h: Are you totally serious?

JAKE: We have a sense of humor.

GEORGE: But ultimately . . . Yeah, we're totally serious.

How pretentious! But there it is, in print forever. That's why interviews bug me, but at least you, you're not writing this down. I like that about you. Would you like another drink?[54] [55]

Months went by. Love Muscle was in suspension. We were working on new material, communicating only through shared influence; we'd make tapes for each other and drop them off. Sometimes Ray's mother's car would be parked in front of George's place, so I'd leave the music in the mailbox and go without knocking. As the months went by, the music I got from George was more and more depressive. Mr. Rock and Roll would toss in something devastatingly sad by Joy Division or the Cure, Radiohead or Elliott Smith, Jeff Buckley or Nick Drake, along with the usual Hüsker Dü, Soul Asylum, and Nirvana.

So it wasn't a big surprise.

It was the middle of the night.

The night was huge and frozen. There was no moon, only the

---

54. I can't help but think that this whole interview format is suggestive of a conversation between two aspects of a divided self. —JOB

55. My editor seems to have missed the obvious fact that Jake's use of the interview format was clearly his way of taking his substitute teacher's career assignment way too seriously, in a passive-aggressive attempt to follow the letter of the assignment while following its spirit not at all. For which I applaud him. I'd also like to point Judith toward Dodie Bellamy's *Barf Manifesto* (Ugly Duckling, 2009) for a more complex consideration of the possible value of withholding editorial filters. —SB

hard earth trying to crack the sidewalks and brittle plumbing. The earth creaked in its turning. It was supposed to warm up to zero the next day.

Just like the noise of radio static excites some people sexually, it is most often the concrete aspects of death which appeal to the necrophiliac. I think about insects: fly eyeballs, dragonflies, beetles with shiny green armor.

There was this guy who faked being a doctor and performed a hysterectomy. He removed a woman's ovaries. The operation was a success, but she was disconcerted. The colors inside a body are psychedelic.

I found the body. The asshole. He knew I was stopping by to return his Stiff Little Fingers album. He didn't listen to it anymore anyway; too angry, not enough absolute despair. In the kitchen, the cabinet door ajar revealed Count Chocula, Pop Tarts, ramen noodles. Everything in place for a living person, his books and records scattered and stored, waiting to give forth their emotions. It's like a fever dream! In the middle of all this, a mess. Red, with brown and bluish strands. And in the middle of the mess, a song, written out in George's ephemeral scrawl. I shoved it in my pocket.

If I'd realized that 911 would bring the cops and not just the ambulance guys—you know who I mean, the equivalent of ambulance guys for dead people—I wouldn't have used it. It felt like turning him in. Why bother? He was his own sloppy narc. Spreading your brains like marmalade from some British art band's surreal refrain across the path of your comrades is not a cool way to embrace death. It's self indulgent and piggy.

I had to go down to the station. They treated me with less familiarity than if I myself were a suspect. They were very busy. It was the middle of the night, but they were busy busy busy. The metal file cases are huge! Everything has been condensed there. They gave me coffee and forms. Describe in detail exactly what you saw: *Oh, how the blood ran,* I wrote.

I was interrupted by someone saying, Hey Jake. The face was known to me, but the blue uniform threw me off. He was a guy I used to know, but he'd grown a beardy thing, a disguise. It was Jason, with his winning smile and his unusually flat ass. He spoke to me with a familiarity that implied rock and roll and police work were just two sides of the same dingy coin. We're just guys, playing the game, seeking intense experience. I didn't feel obliged at that moment to talk to him as if he was a person with a soul or whatever other vague and problematic things in common with me.

Funny, I said. That I would end up here with you.

He grinned dumbly. All the contemptuous vibes I was emanating at him were being grossly mis or un perceived. Either he thought I was just traumatized by the suicide, or he'd developed the armor all cops have to, in a world in which they are almost universally despised.

I was feeling really . . . weird?

I guess suicide's a crime, I said.

He sipped his coffee. It steamed. He sipped it with complete familiarity, as if that was primarily what he did with his time.

Death is no punishment, said Cop.

He punished himself more alive, I agreed. He wallowed.

George was never very happy, said Cop.

I said, I don't think George thought happiness was the point.

Cop furrowed his brow.

He was afraid of his responsibilities, he said.

I was too shocked at this silly interpretation to say a word. My impulse was to vomit, but he seemed to be waiting for something. A conclusion would be reached, perhaps, the moral to the story. The story: George's life and death.

It's your job to enforce the law, I said.

Enforcement is not what laws are about, said Cop.

I was the one in error.[56]

I had another cup of coffee.

Everything was vibrating.

I miss you guys, said Cop.

The police station was huge, there was no end to it.

Cop said, Suicide is a crime against everyone who chooses to live.

If you kill me, said Cop, who is more the victim? The dead don't suffer.

He changed the subject.

Law is the harshest manifestation of love, I guess. We all have responsibilities. Me and you both. You have musical responsibilities, he said, because of your ability to play a note. You have to keep that note pleasant and interesting as long as it lasts.

I'd had just about enough.

That's not exactly it, I said.

He waited for me to explain myself, as if truly interested, as if willing to learn.

Musical tradition was a closed system, I said. It aimed at only what sounded beautiful and pure. Many latent possibilities were excluded. But that's over.

I was sweating; I needed desperately to articulate some meaning. George's death was too concrete.

---

56. Punishment isn't designed to get rid of crimes. It's designed to create more crimes. It's about defining what is and isn't normal. That's why the police are involved in suicides, as Jake probably knew from his experience with his mother. Despite the odd memory lapse from Judith's beloved Officer B (and her cozy relationship with law enforcement somehow doesn't surprise me), it's easy enough to imagine a 10- or 11-year-old Jake shoved into a hard seat in the corner of some police station, forgotten, while the police questioned his stepfather, and while oblivious officers flirted with dispatchers, sipped coffee, and discussed their purchases of new riding lawn mowers. —SB

We needed new means of expression, I said. Now that the spectrograph has allowed us to determine any sound's frequency, there aren't any more false notes. We can see that no sound is ugly or hard or unpleasant. Sounds only exist. Sound phenomena are useful to our purposes or they aren't. Useful to say what we want to say, or to allude to what we can't.

The search for new sounds and new combinations of sounds is an attempt to widen the physical universe, I said.

He considered this. I guessed that he was changing his mind about something. He'd identified an error in his thinking and since his thinking wasn't ever-changing blue electricity, but a solid structure, this error meant all the thoughts had to be dusted off and put back in a slightly different place.

That's why you alternative indie types are so dismissive of pop music, he said, somewhat anticlimactically. You think it's inherently conservative. You think its formal considerations alone prop up the status quo.

I have no formal considerations, I said. I exclude nothing.

You are the one obsessed by form, I thought.

Which is why he was a Cop.

Perhaps, said Cop, you don't even distinguish between content and form.

He was enjoying himself. He could have talked that way all night. He was getting paid for it. For that reason alone, I will never forgive George.

You know, Ray's death really affected me, he said. He was trying to get all intimate. I was really a mess, he continued. And then that car crash, it was like a warning. I had to get some structure in my life, I had to stop abusing my body. You remember how I used to abuse my body.

Oh, I thought. So Ray's death hadn't been for nothing.

You smoked a lot of weed, I said.

He smiled in a condescending sort of way. Cop was like an

entity that had once been the same as me, but now he had split off and become a disease. He was real and external. I didn't want him to exist at all; I thought that once I had ceased to believe in him, he would simply vanish.

Was he a manifestation of my desire for crime? I wanted crime without punishment. If my destiny was like a karmic robot or process of unlearning martyrdom and torture, I would have to rely on my eternal spark to elevate me beyond the trite and painful concerns of this man. I decided from that day on I would only be concerned with manifesting the process of dissolution.

Am I free to go? I said.

He nodded.

Perhaps we'll speak again under less disturbing circumstances, he said.

He was a sick man. The only circumstances I could imagine that would engender such a meeting were lawless, elemental, full of slaughter and unrestrained urges. Unfortunately, this would be exactly the case.

Ray's mom came to the service, but didn't cry. She looked like the same crazy little fritter she always had, but her lips were curled just a bit, in a cynical display of contempt for his weakness. I was transfixed by her beautiful black galoshes. Her belly was oddly bulging; perhaps he'd gotten her pregnant. In any case, this would have been a false consolation at its root: birth/death is a symmetry that's supposed to be pleasing, like some catchy pop-song refrain that gets stuck in your head, it's annoying and inane. Even if we don't view babies as grotesque, and ethically questionable in an overpopulated world, another crying infant doesn't exactly balance out George's death, does it?

Torture of Geleyn the Shoemaker

THAT'S IT FOR THE EARLY DAYS. But like some pagan deity that feeds on rumors, innuendos, lies, confessions, and the random configurations of speculative alphabets, you want to know everything. Get to the juicy parts! you say. The scandal. The celebrity lifestyle. The pouting little boy, the illicit sex, and the murder in the schoolhouse. Yes, of course.

Bob quit the band. After George's suicide, Love Muscle was me and Beej and Sally, the formerly boring girl I now welcomed into the band; mutating our tepid aesthetic universe would be my revenge. Music scenes had been sprouting up everywhere, but a significant scene wasn't going to sprout up in our brainy and sedated little college town. Our town was both frugal and extreme. The young women wore black leg warmers under their denim skirts. There was somehow no sex there. It was a wonder that the town continued to be populated. You heard of girlfriends, you heard of date rapes, but nobody ever saw these things, which were in theory central to the town's life. The most visible girlfriends were those of ambivalent gay men. The gay men were too enchanted by the elaborate crushing of their own spirits to have actual sex—the straight men had more gay sex than the gays, and seemed to feel less uncomfortable afterward.

It was winter. It was night. We had packed everything up in Sally's van. We stood around in a driveway, trying to act momentous; we were moving to California. I would follow a week later with everything I owned: my guitar, five hundred dollars in cash, five hundred in traveler's checks, and a barely functioning hatchback.

I wanted some time to myself.

Aren't you afraid? Sally asked.

I wasn't sure what she meant.

You know, that it's a curse, she said. That you're next.

The highway followed the river. The river ran through my city and it ran past the farms and it ran through vast slums and deserts all the way to the ocean. As I drove across the plains, I imagined my own death. That didn't even keep my mind occupied halfway through Nebraska. I started imagining elaborate bondage scenes instead. In California, the men were a little more sophisticated; their props were more extreme, and I looked forward to that. Gas masks, handcuffs, unheeded cries of Stop! Stop!

I was in the desert.

The motel rose from the earth like a flaw in the very fabric of being. I can't begin to describe the architecture of this motel, it was so perverted.

A man was checking in at the desk, and I didn't like the look of him. He looked like a man: older than me and less sincere. He had a beard, not a devout, Amish, egalitarian beard; a sleazy, covert beard. A brooding shell of a man, about my size but thinner. He looked at me like he wanted something from me and tried to make banal conversation. I smiled and went to have dinner.

I came back and wandered up deserted stairways through deserted hallways' unexpected turns past endless doors into rooms which didn't seem to have ever been occupied. Up dim stairways with creaking boards and more hallways of echoing tile floors to the back corner of the asymmetrical structure and the only sign of life was the bearded man. He was sitting outside our rooms in the hallway strumming a guitar. There was something false in his manner which I detected immediately, but because I was a polite ex-Amish boy I let him engage me in conversation. Manners are what allow the thin fabric of decency to keep us from each other's throats? Rock and roll says: In that case, manners are for victims.

I should have trusted my instincts.

I was clutching George's final song, for it had been occupying my mind. The idea that his art transcended and justified his death upset my stomach, but the song was brilliant, if in need of some revising. The bearded man was not at all handsome. Well, I said, I guess I'll turn in. I crossed the hall to the communal bathroom and brushed my teeth, and he was moving around, doing things. If you pay attention, you know the moment when things have turned, like all animals, but sometimes you don't want to know. I was brushing carelessly, checking the mirror. I crossed back over into my room and he showed himself in the doorway before I could close it. He had a gun under a towel. I took it for an Uzi. Is this because he named it as Uzi or because I'd learned to identify the basic shape on tv? The man was so thin, even emaciated, I realized, with a tortured look about him, like he'd been hung up by some cord. The towel made perfect sense, a silencer, whatever. He was ordering me to do something but I wasn't quite hearing him my ears were full of smoke. I had my hands up and went to the bed and I started to take off my shirt as if he had told me to strip, but then I realized he hadn't said that at all and I left my shirt on. He was saying that he knew who I was, implying that he believed me to be some spy or member of some organization which he was apparently the opposite of? Muslim terrorists or animal rights activists or pedophiles? I wasn't sure if I was supposed to be the subversive and he the military or vice versa. I begged him not to kill me and I assured him I wasn't any such person. I started crying. This was all terribly embarrassing.

He tied me to the bed. Immobilized and completely at the mercy of another, nobody else's death had prepared me for my own. His face didn't look like the face of my death; it wasn't familiar or even scrutable, under that beard. It hadn't been glimpsed in a single bad dream. He was a stranger empty even of the concept of "stranger," and he terrified me. What was it about dying that filled me with terror? Not so much the obvious pain and oblivion, but it would have revealed my life as completely without a destiny. George's song, which was my song now, might be swept away with the rest of the debris: my material existence. The man said he worked in conjunction with the hotel owners and he searched through all my belongings. He found my cash and my traveler's checks. We were there for hours, just chatting.

Please don't kill me, I said.

You shouldn't be afraid of Death, he told me. It's fear itself that allows people to control you.

He was smug. Smugness isn't attractive, but it was more than I had.

I repeated: Please don't kill me.

He said, What's Death anyway?

Great, I thought. A philosopher.

Maybe what's true and eternal, he said, moves up and down, between hieroglyphic dissolution and the hemorrhage of wounded matter.

Great, I thought. A believer in the transmigration of souls. As if we just keep meeting the same people over and over again but with different faces, as if we keep living out the same tiresome stories until we become so bored that we're enlightened.

I said, Are you going to kill me?

Just glimpses of immateriality, he said, and he punched his right fist into his open palm. Glimpses that only serve as rationale for further torture of the flesh.

I guessed he was introducing torture into the conversation because he intended to torture me. This was a narcissistic logic, assuming that my pain, and not just my money, was central to his motivation. Maybe by "smug" I only mean that I had no idea what was going on in his head, even when he was talking. He started explaining his motives. His identity shifted, his goals, who he claimed he was and what doing. Your basic robber, but the vague and contradictory stories provided so much noise that I couldn't see him, couldn't quite grasp the banal reality. This was all a game to him, he claimed; it wasn't even about the money. He was going to give it all to the poor in any case. He suggested vast underground networks of either order or subversion in which he was a crucial link. I don't remember what name he used. He wanted to use those traveler's checks, but didn't know how. I thought that he might not kill me until he'd figured it out.

He taped my mouth shut and went out and bought me a beer with the money he had stolen from me. This struck me as generous, evidence of good faith. I hoped that this suggested I was in the midst of a meaningful event that would constitute, in retrospect, a form of research into the "human" condition. Unfortunately, any similarity between the bondage scenes I'd imagined while driving and my present situation was irrelevant; the gap in between the two was too large to be the space for a lesson. When he returned, he continued to multiply his stories as if he was a shameless self-promoter. I didn't care for his instructive tales; his recurring theme was that I was his victim because of his deeper understanding of the nature of existence. How could I doubt a man who held my life in his hands like the tender fetus of a shattered mother? He was butch. Ugliness can be a form of masculinity, and you use what you've got.

He cut the phone wire and untied my hands, not my ankles. Maybe he knew I'd never call the cops. After my experience with George's death, why would I bother? We were in the desert—there wasn't anybody there but him and me alone. We laughed together as he gathered his belongings, because I wasn't going to die. I was grateful for the self-knowledge he'd provided me. He had psychological depth. He was fearless. He loved me enough to try to understand my psychology so he could use it to further victimize me. He told me I was very comely and well-mannered. Before he left, however, he wanted to show me something. It was very important to my spiritual growth. He showed me the Uzi. It was a toy gun.[57]

Is there anything more humiliating than being terrorized and robbed by a smug man with a toy gun? Not in my experience. Your face-off with Death is reduced to a gag. Toy gun is the punch line.[58]

---

57. The phrase "comely and well-mannered" seems to be an allusion to the passage from the *Martyrs Mirror* illustrated on the following page. "It is stated that about two years after, namely, A.D. 925, a lad of thirteen years, called Pelagius, was put to death for the name of Christ, in Cordova, which occurred as follows: his uncle, Ermoigus (who by some writers is called a bishop), having been apprehended and imprisoned at Cordova, by the Arabian King Habdarrhaghman, said Ermoigus, in order to be released, left his nephew, who was then only about thirteen years old, in his stead, as a pledge, which for more than three years was not redeemed, either through the neglect of his friends, or because the king would not let go the youth, who was now very comely and well-mannered."—JOB

58. Love or neglect? The *Martyrs Mirror* is perhaps willfully ambivalent on this point. The dismembering and beheading of this comely youth certainly doesn't seem like mere banal terror. He's watching the blood flow from his empty arm sockets. The sky is a haze; it's a cloudy mirror and he sees his own beauty reflected there. The world is hungry for his love and this is called time or it's eternity. The hemorrhage of wounded matter. The blood flows and flows and he's dizzy, he's high as a kite. The brain can transform many experiences into pleasure that you wouldn't really think.—SB

Pelagius of Cordova Has His Arms and Legs Cut Off

IN SAN FRANCISCO WE FOUND two drummers, a saxophonist, some go-go dancers; we discovered rhythm. We used Gregorian chants, random noise, and the sounds of industry. We made noises you could dance to, overlaid with the screams of dying children, gunshots, traffic. The music changed.

I studied the melodic composition of Guarani suicide laments. I knew about the Guarani suicide laments because Ray had been aware of them via references in an essay about Antonin Artaud written by an obscure Argentinean science fiction writer who died of mysterious causes in a mental institution in 1962. The insane man wrote complicated paranoid visions of the near future in which nobody could ever distinguish exactly between reality and controlled mass hallucinations. Time and space were usually mental constructs which could melt down at any moment, residing primarily in mammal brains. The music changed.[59]

---

59. This reference to Artaud is the strongest evidence I have that Jake not only worked on the stories after the murder at Nickel Mines, but also that he revised them in between the first time I met him and our final visit, when he burned the manuscript. At our first meeting, Jake noticed my copy of *The Peyote Dance*. I'd taken it with me on my journey to Nickel Mines because I thought poor Artaud's expansive descriptions and cosmic preoccupations would help alleviate the sense of being smothered I've felt throughout my life when dealing with the Amish. It was even more acute on that trip, with most of my social interactions being with people whose daughters, sisters, nieces, or granddaughters had just been killed. I was supposed to discover a unique and compelling story for the magazine that had sent me, but all I found were grieving farm people. Their silly social structures didn't make them any less sad. By dinner time, the Amish would all be up in their houses, so I'd just sit in my horrible little motel room, like a sterile, muffled tomb, reading Artaud. Jake had never heard of Artaud, but talked to me about all the drugs he'd tried (marijuana, cocaine, crystal meth, mushrooms, LSD, salvia), and asked about peyote. I told him about my own experiences with a different mescaline-containing cactus (San Pedro, or *Trichocereus pachanoi,* which is, as of this writing, perfectly legal and commonly grown all over California) and gave him my copy of *The Peyote Dance*. In retrospect, I question the wisdom of this gift, given the similarities between Artaud's cosmic paranoia and Jake's. Jake had recently had some sort of drug-induced mystical revelation, which he described as his discovery of Christ the Comedian. According to Jake, when Christ on the cross said, "My God, my God, why hast Thou forsaken me?" it was as the first half of a joke. The punch line had been revealed to Jake during his vision. I'm not sure if a voice spoke the punch line to him or if it was written in vapor across the sky, but he couldn't remember it afterward, either way. He described it as forbidden, self-erasing knowledge, but he assured me that Christ's joke was hilarious.

Like Jake, Artaud pendulumed between venomous hatred of Christianity and an embrace of a schizophrenic sense of Christian love and forgiveness. Jake seemed electrified by the book, and referred to it frequently in subsequent meetings. (I left these conversations out of my fictionalized version of these events in *Glory Hole*, for the sake of realism—the dictates of plausibility so often require writers to omit the freakish, extreme and ridiculous events that are in fact a common aspect of our daily lives.) *The Peyote Dance* details Artaud's journey to see the Tarahumara Indians in Mexico in 1936 and his participation in their peyote rituals, although some commentators (See Le Clézio, *The Mexican Dream*) suggest that he didn't actually undergo the journey and made the whole thing up. Real or not, the book includes a variety of attempts Artaud made to convey his experiences, shortly afterward or during the years

We all wore gas masks at the Fillmore show. This was interpreted as political protest in a local weekly that praised our "hyperbolic disrespect for the posturing of ironic tonalities." We released our first CD, one of the year's best according to Jane Dark's zine *Sugar High!* We played Gay Pride that year. Rainbow flags were waving. Too busy. They'd tried to leave Death out of the celebration. The result was a deformation of character: the celebration was "cute."

We were lonely. The earth is a tomb.[60]

---

that followed, when he was interned in a variety of mental institutions in Europe. During his stay in the asylums he sometimes interpreted his Mexican experiences in a mystical Christian light ("I do not know how many suns all the initiatory doctrines of the earth whose sole source I know and it is called JESUS CHRIST . . .") although in a postscript written in 1947 he disavowed these interpretations, "For nothing now appears to me more funereal or more mortally disastrous than the stratified and limited sign of the cross, nothing more erotically pornographic than Christ, ignoble sexual materialization of all the false psychic enigmas, all the bodily wastes that have been passed to the intelligence because they have nothing more to do in the world than to serve as matter for riddles, and whose basest maneuvers of magical masturbation trigger an electric release from prison." A few other random quotes will suggest the degree to which Jake might have been influenced by this book. "The root of the peyote plant is hermaphroditic. It has, as we know, the shape of the male and female sexual organs combined." "Not to be aware of what one's Double is, is to risk losing it. It is to risk a kind of abstract fall, beyond physical space, a wandering through the high planetary regions of the disembodied human principle." "The things that emerged from my spleen or my liver were shaped like the letters of a very ancient and mysterious alphabet chewed by an enormous mouth, but terrifyingly obscure, proud, *illegible*, jealous of its invisibility . . ." "Below, the dances had already begun; and at the sight of this beauty at last realized, this beauty of glowing imaginations, like voices in an illuminated dungeon, I felt that my effort had not been in vain." I believe I can also see its influence in Jake's descriptions of certain landscapes. — SB

60. It occurs to me now that Stephen might have been traumatized by his trips to Nickel Mines. Maybe after studying all the details of the crime, interviewing grieving parents, meeting wounded children, and sometimes being sent away by distraught bearded men who wanted nothing to do with his "worldly" journalism, he snapped. Maybe as he was reading Artaud in his little motel room, he split in two. I've dealt with manuscripts as an editor that have tested my own ability to remain objective; maybe the weird web of information he was immersed in finally drove him crazy. I can empathize.

More of them died. Band members, that is. *Third verse, same as the first.* They died and died and died. The flesh slowly rotted from their features. Others discovered tumors, drove off bridges, or got run down by tow trucks south of Market. That was Drew, who had a beautiful body and long hair, but the hard face of an orphan, crafty, with those bad teeth.

And that Goth guy. That Goth guy who added his ancient Celtic laments to our repertoire, he told us he was 24 but he was 37. If you never see the daylight your skin will stay creamy and fresh. He sat in his room on the summer solstice and quietly expired. He lived in one of those party houses where his body could stay dead in his room for two days before somebody got curious, opened the door: surprise. The autopsy couldn't say why he was dead. We figured he'd been devoted to Death for so long he was able to just kind of slip over to the other side.

Ken was older than the rest of us, a kindly uncle who let band members crash on his sofa from time to time. He used to work at the Gap but got over that and went into the automobile detailing business. He had an apartment full of cats and when we'd just come back from some grueling two-month tour in the van or we'd tested positive for HIV and were distraught, or had roommates we didn't want to deal with, we'd sleep on his floor. It was cold and raining or hot and evil outside. There were pictures on Ken's walls of himself nude, in various stages of leather undress, bound and gagged with his dick hanging out, his bedroom full of slings and chains and sadistic accoutrements, but in Ken's house it seemed homey. He was into wicca and S&M and gay pride and then he started doing speed. He lost fifty pounds and his apartment, started disassembling doorknobs, cleaning them and putting them back

---

Despite his combativeness and obstinacy, I do not find Stephen completely unsympathetic. It is my hope that he will seek help from a more responsible and skilled therapist than Darlene Bruno-Straus. —JOB

together, this hyperactive skeletal maid now occasionally haunting *our* apartments. We hadn't seen him for awhile and then we heard that he was dead.

Dylan was a drummer, obsessed with little boys. He had occult beliefs, centering on the age of "12." As far as I know, he satisfied his desires primarily with junior high wrestling videos and prostitutes who claimed to be "a young-looking 18." At some camp out in nature, he fell in a lake and he drowned.

The garments of the dead. My closet is full of their clothes. After I tested positive, Ken gave me his old t-shirt that said SILENCE = DEATH. I inherited a t-shirt from Dylan, with the single word COACH. Can I deny the little leap of joy when I realized I'd been left with George's baby blue Big Black Tools t-shirt that brought out the color of my eyes?

We were attracting larger and larger crowds, but we weren't yet at the stage where any one of us could quit his day job. I got a job working as an "Artist in the Schools." I'd be face-to-face with classrooms packed full of little boys. At a tiny school out in the country, I met a little boy named J.

How old are you? I asked.

Five, he said. Or maybe six. How old are you?

J's song was all about strange men, prisoners, and police. J shared his gummi bears with me, candy with a surprising amount of protein in it; the gelatin comes from cows. He was a real charmer. He knew how to spell "them" and "those."

I said, I don't understand the part where the people are dead and then they come back.

He pouted.

I saw it in a movie, he said.

I see, I said. He'd illustrated the song too; stick figures were intermingled in the most confusing ways. He climbed into my lap.

J wasn't cute, he was handsome. I didn't understand. How did I get here? What was I doing in charge of this boy?

You, you're no different. You stand in front of the mirror and you bare your teeth to see the skeleton hanging out of your gums. You close your mouth and try on a different face, and another and another, to hide the empty sockets of your eyes, the disintegration of the flesh. You put on a dead man's Big Black Tools t-shirt that brings out the color of your eyes.

Antipas Burned in a Red-hot Brazen Ox

"THINGS" WERE ON MY MIND. I wondered about reducing the monster to Myself, being Myself in face of the monster, being more than just part of it, more than the monstrous player of one of its monstrous lutes. Maybe not being alone, but reducing the monster and being two things, the two together as one. Playing of the monster and of myself, or better not of myself at all, but of "that" as its intelligence . . .[61]

It was winter. It was the middle of the night. I stepped out onto the streets of the Tenderloin, streets full of vibrating people with

61. This could be considered plagiarism from Wallace Stevens's famous poem "The Man with the Blue Guitar." Stephen might as well be waving a flag at this point saying, Here I am, fracturing, splitting apart, developing an imaginary other self! It's disturbing to observe; it's almost like a physical pain. —JOB

dilated eyes. Faded old advertisements were painted on the sides of brick buildings tucked in next to modern monstrosities. This guy stomping up Leavenworth had headphones on and his face was making angry expressions, matching the music I couldn't hear. I drew closer to him, attracted to his intensity. The music was so loud I could recognize it.

It was me he was listening to. I was singing; I had made him angry.[62]

I've always suspected the existence of my secret twin, haven't you? He is mute and he lives inside me, but he exerts a pressure. It was winter. I'm wandering. Fungus-like web of organic matter or forest of interconnected trees. The vampire is accused of polluting wells and eating babies. I was never accused of either of those things, but I was accused of a murder, which I did in fact commit. It's a matter of historical record. I was acquitted of manslaughter. I can't be tried again, as anyone who's watched *The Postman Always Rings Twice* would know, although these days you do have to watch out for those wrongful-death civil suits.

Other than me, the witnesses were all children. Their testimony blurred into fantasy.

You want the untold story. Well, I have nothing to hide, not anymore. I was invited back to the little school, as you probably know. It was outside of town, in the middle of a vast empty field. All the students were gathered in one room. He's really thriving with you, J's teacher told me. I can't believe the progress that you've made. Her name was Darlene. She took me aside.

We have some very creative students in this class, she told me,

---

62. Jake is continually attuned to the ways that we all experience possession in our daily lives. The way that reading a book, for example, is like being inhabited by another personality—by which I don't mean the "author."—SB

but some of them don't have very realistic goals. They imagine they can be rock and roll musicians, like you, just like that. I think it would be a good thing if you talked about how hard you work. I think it would be good if you divested them of some of their delusions about rock and roll stardom.

She then turned the class over to me. She wanted to spend the time grading some spelling papers, so she left me there alone.

Me and J, we walked carefully, hand-in-hand across the thin crust of meaning. Somebody loved me! I began to wonder about the texture of his ass. His freedom consisted of his inaccessibility.

There were 9 or 10 or a dozen of them, from J on up to the sixth-graders. Desire for a boy, or boys, is supposed to be about fleeing from your own decay. Instead, it's a flight toward incomprehensibility, avoiding the impulse to mix sex with understanding. The crust crumbles and we're face to face with a raw, meaningless substance. I'm not talking about anonymous blowjobs in cars that go round and round the block while your hair sticks to the roof. On a faraway plateau, J hovers and skips across the buoyant playground. The crust crumbles and we're face-to-face with a super-meaningful world, expressed in a coded language we can never quite make out. The sky is jellied with traceries of cloud.

We were composing song lyrics, as a group, when a strange man burst into the room. It took me a minute to recognize him, because he'd shaved off the beard. It was the man who'd robbed me in that perverted motel.

Just do what you're told, he announced to us, and nobody will get hurt.

Without the beard, I realized, he looked kind of like me—if I'd been raised in a concentration camp, malnourished or stretched out on a rack. He barricaded the doors shut with boards and five-inch screws and announced that it was time to play some games. The games involved role play, ropes, gas masks, and plenty of lube.

Things get a little fuzzy after that. The situation got a little out of control.

He kissed me first, I didn't ask him to. I was dying! He sucked on my fingers once, as if I was delicious. And I loved him, my heart was breaking. You shouldn't do that, I said. You'll spread germs. You like my germs, J said. It's easy enough to believe that children are geniuses, if you want to. It was far too easy to love someone who'd practically forget I existed if I was out of the room. He pretended he was a blind boy, a boy with his eyes pecked out, so he could grope me with abandon. He pretended he was a wounded boy, so I'd give him an examination. He pretended he was a baby boy, so I'd hold him in my arms. He pretended he was a dead boy, so I'd touch him and tickle him until he proved that he existed after all.

You worry about punishment in this world, you can't be free. Isn't that what it's all about for you? Learning to be free?

I'd wanted to follow my thoughts out beyond the pale. Like all modern boys, J was totally electric. That wasn't really enough, he was more compelling as an idea. I wanted to convert him, it's true. I wanted to colonize the future with his beauty.

Fetishizing children requires that you not really see them, but see the idea of them. But you're not so sure. You didn't love "a child" or "a boy," only J. The bodies were like skinned rabbits. So pink and slick and girly. Vienna sausages perhaps.

You just wanted to interpenetrate the surface of the real.

J was my type a few decades too early. Our life histories were out of sync, although apparently I was his type already. If I believed in reincarnation, immortal souls wandering through eternity, then a few decades out of sync was really just a trifle. I will always choose the magic world, where everything is charged with significance, where events and characters are ciphers loaded with barely intelligible meanings, although the other world is surely just as real. Most children annoy me, exhaust me, and even J had his faults. He could be whiney, and I'd want to bend him over my knee and slap his naked ass or maybe just shove him in some corner and leave him there awhile.

Maybe you wanted to explore that shadowy realm of belief and emotion where cause and effect is negated. Or maybe you just wanted to take care of J because you no longer wanted to take care of yourself.

His future was full of infinite danger and possibility. In contrast, I project the Amish into the future: farming the moon, farming the post-apocalyptic landscape of giant vegetables and roaches, farming in cyberspace. They never have anything to do but the most plodding sort of work. Mutate! Let go! In the future, humans will be holograms and my people will still be riding around in horse and buggies. They'll be supported by public funds, as a museum or a Land of Disney's. Bodiless entities will long for the simplicity of apple butter and suspenders. They'll vacation there, in Amishland. Not me.

I maneuvered myself closer to the gun. The gun looked just like that fake gun the emaciated man had used before. J fell to the ground and started humping my leg like a dog. One thing led to another. I wanted to imprint a design on his pliable flesh and claim him, wanted to recruit another tender monster just waking to greet the night. While my right hand was otherwise engaged, I dug the nail of my left thumb into his forehead, drawing blood. He cried out, then giggled, confused.

For the Amish, like in the sixties, it's all explained by your hair. Sizing up a person's bouffant will tell you where they stand, for or against, to what degree they stand there, whether you can commingle or whether you must shun.

J's shaved head meant nothing but a tickling sensation between my thighs. The lack of pubic hair was disturbing and asexual, but the bald head was like a highly meaningful sex toy. I'd always wanted to put butter on him; he'd made me hungry from the very first day. Buttered and clenched. Squeezing, squeezing. Imagine peach cobbler. Squeezing and actually purring! Imagine the sun as a small naked animal. Doing things to a little boy isn't poetry, exactly. His inaccessibility was as lonely as that one dog barking in a moonlit field. It's all so beautiful and empty, although I'd thought a little boy might serve as some sort of consolation for lack of meaning. For business parks and Walmart and drone missiles and AIDS. They're so soft, and hard at the same time. Like coconuts, or the cream pies you make from coconuts. Afterward, it was just another silly taboo.

Afterward, the texture of J's ass interested me only in a mechanical way. It seemed like a feat of engineering, not an orifice of pleasure. I suppose for J it had other meanings I couldn't quite imagine. It was no longer sexual, more evocative of mothers with baby wipes. I realized I didn't want to take care of J or nurture him at all. I wanted a nap, or a conversation with someone who might speak with passion about music. Everything would have been merely disappointing if Darlene hadn't returned just then and started pounding on the door. What is going on in there? she demanded to know. She was stronger than I would have thought, and in no time she'd kicked down the door.

I was trying to undo a particularly complicated knot. J had a look on his face like he'd been told playtime was over.

I grabbed the gun.

Don't worry! I said. It's only a toy.

For some reason, it seemed crucial that I demonstrate to Darlene that the gun wasn't real—if the gun was a toy, it seemed to me, none of the other breaches of protocol would be considered serious offenses either. I pointed it right at her.

See? I said. It's just a silly little toy.

But the kickback was so strong it sent me backward several feet.

I had only ever wanted to dream about murder. Never did I see a human pudding on the street and feel compelled to know how their organs might dazzle in the sunlight. When these facts have been revealed to me, it has been a knowledge I had no instinct or use for. It revealed nothing I hadn't learned in sixth grade anatomy. Unlike the necrophiliac's interest in death, my interest in murder was entirely abstract. The magic of blood is most revealed in bloody art, that's my view. Apparently, someone higher up on the spiritual hierarchy was dreaming of me, keeping me imprisoned in their own dark tragicomedy of a middle-aged woman with over-processed hair falling and screaming and falling and screaming and falling and screaming and opening up her deepest feelings to share them with the pavement and the atmosphere and the molecules and the spirit world. Oh the pudding! I'm dreaming and falling. The sky is a mess. Look it up, it's barbaric! Too many particles. Her pudding was everywhere.

The cops were right behind her. The shooter, the man the prosecution tried to call my "accomplice," picked up the gun. He went out firing, in a blaze of glory. Two cops were wounded and several boys were killed. The shooter was dead, still clutching the murder weapon in his hand. I found out later that Darlene wasn't even a regular teacher in that school. I found out later she was only a sub.

It was the middle of the night. I was deep in the bowels of the Sheriff's Department, at the county jail. It was called the glamour slammer because it had fogged windows and a fancy couch.[63]

---

63. This is true of the city jail in San Francisco, where Stephen spent some time. It is easy to imagine that for the author of this text, men, as individuals, represent criminality, eroticism, and excess (unless they are part of the faceless, bearded mass), and women represent common sense and control, community and the law of conscience, to which his rebels are opposed. Probably, unable to control his own instincts, the author unfairly blamed his mother for his problems and imagined shocking all-male crimes as a response. In that light, I present a brief list of the criminal activities that Stephen has admitted committing (usually with his male lovers) within his published nonfiction and in interviews: shoplifting, car theft, burglary, drug dealing (including heroin and crack), prostitution, pimping, fraud, extortion, arson, writing bad checks

Murder, said Cop. Now there's a crime.

I recalled the vague and indescribable sense of abandon and joy. Not guilty, I said.

Since it was terror and disturbance and instability and doubt and division, I said, there were many illusions at work and empty fictions, as if they were sunk in sleep and found themselves in disturbing dreams.

Either there is a place to which they are fleeing, I continued, or without strength they come from having chased after others,

---

(like Mrs. G from *Splitting: A Case of Female Masculinity*), making false statements to a governmental agency, drunk driving, driving without a license, driving with expired registration, drag racing (again like Mrs. G!), plagiarism, misrepresentation, lewd and lascivious acts, and book stealing. (He even admitted stealing books from a public library.) With the assistance of Officer B, I've looked up Stephen's criminal records and done a thorough background check. Although his only jail time has been for shoplifting and loitering (apparently this is what they charge political protesters with if they can't come up with any other charge), Stephen has been *charged* with shooting a cop in the buttocks, although the charges were immediately dismissed, apparently on a technicality. I've discovered strange patterns and odd correspondences in Stephen's background, not only with Jake's work, but also with the rumors that have circulated around the case of missing paperboy Johnny Gosch and with the contents of Bruno-Straus's thesis, especially the case of Mrs. G. In 1993 Stephen even performed in a drag show under the stage name of Miss Original G; I've unearthed a photo that shows one of the drag queens in a luminous blond wig, although I couldn't determine conclusively if that performer was Stephen or not. Stephen has at times suggested that he might have been involved in terrorist activities, kidnapping, and child endangerment, a charge that I find particularly alarming, as a mother who struggles so hard every day to keep her own boy safe. Stephen has confessed to fraternizing with murderers, pedophiles, members of street gangs, terrorists, third-world dictators, and evil clowns. He's been a heroin addict and made the false claim that he is of Australian Aboriginal descent. He seems to have no shame about publicizing these activities and no remorse about the harm he has caused. It's amazing the things that one can discover on the Internet these days. If Stephen hadn't ended his therapy early, I imagine that Darlene Bruno-Straus would have helped him to psychologically integrate the male attributes—obviously out of hand in Stephen's erotically imagined and criminal life—with the female attributes. Maybe in the process, he would have learned to stop blaming the women in his life.—JOB

or they are involved in striking blows, or they are receiving blows themselves, or they have fallen from high places, or they take off into the air though they do not even have wings. Again, sometimes it is as if people were murdering them, though there is no one even pursuing them, or they themselves are killing their neighbors, for they have been stained with their blood.

Cut the gibberish, said Cop. Get real with me here.[64]

---

64. What hasn't occurred to Judith is this: Why, with a resumé like the one she details, would I need an evil twin to live out my "erotically imagined and criminal life" on the page—presumably molesting Amish boys and murdering women.

First off: Ew.

Second: I have few issues with the women in my life. In fact Darlene Bruno-Straus always told me I was rebelling against "the father." (Not my actual father, the more stubborn social construct.) Boring, I know, but I'm probably a better feminist than Judith, whose embrace of patriarchal "reason" is an emotionally constricted position I could never allow myself to take.

Third, the idea that Jake's men and women "represent" something other than themselves is a gross simplification. Obviously his women are also sometimes crazy, criminal, suicidal and neglecting and his men are at times guards in prisons and asylums. Maybe, like Carl Jung, Judith should have been a fascist choreographer, the Leni Riefenstahl of the unconscious. Jung's collective unconscious was profoundly ordered and symmetrical, ready to be mapped out and explained in voluminous detail. "Just as the father represents collective consciousness, the traditional spirit, so the mother stands for the collective unconscious, the source of the water of life." "Just as the 'right' denotes the world of consciousness and its principles, so by 'reflection' the picture of the world is to be turned round to the left, thus producing a corresponding world in reverse." "The croquet ball is connected with the 'round' motif and is therefore a symbol of wholeness, that is, of the self . . ." Quack, quack, quack. The more I read Jung, the more I grow to hate him. That voice: pompous, dry, pedantic, continually obfuscating meaning with the sheer abundance of his words. An endless cascade of examples and symbols gouged haphazardly from their specific cultural contexts and used to underscore the totalizing explanatory ability of his own system. There's no corner of history or culture untouched by his self-referential thought-world. He sucks all breath and vitality from his myths and his language, maybe believing that it is an obtuse style that will convince skeptics that Jungian psychology is empirical science.

Fourth, I eventually returned all of the books I stole from public libraries.

Fifth, my Miss Original G drag persona was based on actress Pam Grier and wasn't even slightly blond.

I'd like to see a lawyer, I said.

You had your phone call? asked Cop.

I agreed that I had.

Does it have to be that way? Cop said.

I sat mute and gravid. Haunted cheetah, incandescent blue star.

What was your name again? I asked.

I know your music, he said. I liked your CD very much.

He put his hand on my shoulder.

Sixth, clearly the only patterns Judith sees are those she herself expects, hopes for, or dreads—just like Carl Jung. Jung relentlessly pillaged myths for images that had no greater function than to symbolize the unconscious itself, or the process of individuation, or its result: the unified, whole personality. As if the unconscious has, as its main business, not the representation of specific personal, historic, and cosmic processes, but the representation of the *very idea* of those processes and the sheer fact of the existence of the unconscious. "Water is the commonest symbol for the unconscious." "The sea is the symbol of the collective unconscious . . ." "We have no eyes behind us; consequently 'behind' is the region of the unseen, the unconscious." "The figures that appear in the dream are feminine, thus pointing to the feminine nature of the unconscious." "The left, the 'sinister' side, is the unconscious side. Therefore a leftward movement is equivalent to a movement in the direction of the unconscious . . ." "The cave represents the darkness and seclusion of the unconscious and the two boys correspond to the two unconscious functions." "It 'gleams' from the shell of a tortoise which, primitive and cold-blooded like the snake, symbolizes the instinctual side of the unconscious." "Proteus is evidently a personification of the unconscious: it is difficult to catch 'this mysterious old being . . . he might see me first, or know I am there and keep away.' One must seize him quickly and hold him fast, in order to force him to speak." Which reminds me—Jung once traveled to Africa, where he had olfactory hallucinations (the soil smelled like blood) and felt he'd been placed in a naïve world of adolescents. He dreamed of a wrestling match with a handsome Arab youth; Jung won the match. "I placed my arm around his shoulders and forced him, with a sort of paternal kindness and patience, to read the book." Yes, once Jung had overcome him, the handsome youth had to read *Jung's own book*, written in magnificent calligraphy on milky white parchment.

Seventh, I wouldn't describe my relationships with Magdalena Kopp, Jose Padilla, or Patty Hearst as *fraternization* exactly.

Eighth, having actually had many conversations with Jake (as Judith would rather not) I can confidently say that his obsession is less with a psychological integration than a biological one—the creation of a new hermaphroditic species.—SB

Think of me as part of the band, said Cop. Talk to me here, Jake. Please don't touch me, I said.

He smiled and folded his arms, as if I was merely playing hard to get. I brushed dandruff from my shoulder.

Oh, I remember your name, I said.

You probably think of yourself as a tornado, said Cop. Something wild and out of control. You want to pretend that's your nature, to be wild and unruly. But the law is inside you, I know that you feel it in your heart.

If it was already inside me, I said, why have so many people worked so hard to glom it onto my brain?

He loosened his tie, stroked his beard. He thought he was clever, so I decided to get apocryphal.

Like Jesus said, I said, you can't enter the house of a strong person without you tie the owner's hands. Then you can loot the house.

I was immediately sorry I'd introduced bondage imagery into the conversation, but Cop glided right past it.

He also said not to let your left hand know what your right hand is up to, said Cop. This is a sure formula for mental illness, not for happiness and productivity.

With his beard he looked so unevolved, an ape man. A faceless prosimian! He was trapped millions of years behind me, with the crocodiles and the coelacanths.

Cop said, Criminal justice is a collective process of retribution.

It's an industry, I said. It grows and grows, it never shrinks.

He waved a small insect away from his face.

The justice system is not here to fix a ruined society, he said. We apply fixed rules to determine whether a man is a member of society or an outcast.

The justice system will determine that about you, he said.

There are no outcasts, I said. There is no outside. Prison is not another world.

I know that and you know that, said Cop.

Perhaps in prison, you'll be somebody's bitch, he added.

I shrugged. I guessed he was jealous.

Cop shrugged.

Let me show you to your cell.

A hard bench and a toilet, that was all.[65]

---

65. I suppose I did *fraternize* with Mohammed Atta and Ziad Jarrah, two of the 9/11 hijackers, during my gay dive vacation in Florida in 2001. Mohammed hated music, dancing, and parties. He listened instead to tapes of the Koran, and "psychologists" have claimed he was incapable of experiencing pleasure. The state of Florida, then, was a perfect place to hide. He acted like a joyless robot, brainwashed, a Manchurian candidate. His father said that journalists are liars, and threatened to sue them, at least the ones who claimed his son was gay. Well, whatever his daddy may think, Mohammed was *not* incapable of experiencing pleasure, I can guarantee you that. He lived a double life, spoke German, had a job as a draftsman, although he was pretty dour outside of the bedroom. Ziad, on the other hand, loved to drink and party. Once he drank so much beer with his cousin they couldn't ride straight on a bike. He was likable, helpful to others, loved to cheer up the depressed. He could have been the handsome young Arab of aristocratic bearing that Carl Jung wrestled with in his dream. I have photographs: Ziad laughing, solving problems, partying. How could this boy have been a terrorist? his family asks. His sisters wore bikinis. Although he told me stories from his childhood during the Lebanese civil war, full of pornographic images of violence, death, and destruction, he spent most summers away from the war in his parents' vacation home. His family believes that it isn't sexuality that leads to violence, but the repression of sexuality, but maybe that's too simple. In Africa, Carl Jung also had a dream about an African-American barber he'd met in Tennessee, now approaching Jung with a red-hot curling iron, as if to curl Jung's own hair, to make it kinky, to help him "go native." Jung woke up just in time. In Africa, Jung was informed by a native that the natives no longer dreamed. Dreams were no longer necessary, because the English knew everything. Jung was perfectly receptive to this idea, and took it as a guileless expression of the native man's beliefs. Natives were incapable of subtext or irony or conscious dissimulation. Africa, of course, has a complicated history and objective existence outside of Carl Jung's mind, and outside of Western conceptions of who is the symbol and who articulates the symbol's meaning. I assure you, Ziad Jarrah wasn't repressed — he was just about the biggest freak I've ever known. Ziad didn't call me from the cockpit of Flight 93, he called his girlfriend Aysel, who he was supposed to marry. Light-skinned, Ziad could and sometimes did pass for European. With his bland, handsome face, people couldn't agree on how tall or how heavy he was. 5'8" or 5'11"? 170 or 190 pounds? It's all hazy to me, too. Ziad had dyed his hair a lighter color, close to blond. When he was

I'd learned at the movies that they put you in with a particular cell-mate for a reason: to break your will or procure a confession. My cellmate was sullen, kind of crushed. He was huddled over the plastic wavering mirror, examining some detail of his image. He had a poster on the wall of three kittens smoking cigarettes in a bathroom. He looked familiar, not like I had known him, but like he was the sort of man everyone means when they say Don't get in the car with a stranger or Don't reveal intimate details to a stranger or Don't take any sweet things from a stranger. A calendar showed a red barn on a green hill in a brightly-lit countryside. The bottom half of the calendar had been ripped off—the days of the week, the dates themselves—as if the passage of time here was unquantifiable. Hell may be vast, but so is its opposite. Unbearable, in fact. This is why we're all here and why there are so many blank spots in our memories. He asked what I was in for, and then I said, How about you? He'd burned down some trees and a handsome fireman had died. He'd wanted to go into forestry, but it hadn't worked out. He asked me how I liked it, from the bottom or the top. I figured we'd get along fine. [66]

Emerson said that only by obedience to his genius, only by the freest activity in the way constitutional to him, does an angel seem to arise before a man and lead him by the hand out of all the wards

---

taking kickboxing lessons in Florida, he talked about returning to his home in "Deutschland." His kickboxing trainer said, "You can say a lot about the terrorists, but the accusation that they were cowards is nonsense." The other two men on that plane, Saeed Alghamdi and Ahmed Alnami, had a sharp body odor, their travel agent reported, but they always smelled fine to me.—SB

66. Most of us, of course, don't suffer from "so many blank spots in our memories." This is a classic symptom of dissociative identity disorder. Attentive readers will have already also noticed that in footnote 64 Stephen refuted me in eight points—which clearly and in ways too obvious to enumerate correspond with Jake's eight stories and the eight chapters of the thesis of Darlene Bruno-Straus.—JOB

of the prison. I woke in the middle of the night to find my cellmate leaning over me and grinning. That was when I first noticed his beautiful gold tooth. He had a knife to my throat—a spoon he'd ground down to a razor-like edge.

It's a game, he said, his face two inches from mine.

I was terrified; I had forgotten the rules. I guessed that you figure the rules out as you go. Or maybe you make them up altogether.

You dance along the web, he said.

But how do you win? I croaked.

He said, Nobody wins. You only survive. You survive and you become something else.

The more you dance, he said, the more you play the game, the freer you are.[67]

Cop roused me from my sleep and took me back for more questions. Cop's stilted imagination was evidenced by the naked bulb

---

67. Do I really have to point out that I don't "lose time"? I do not black out or find myself in strange places, not sure how I got there. I never wake up to find myself in a stranger's bed, not remembering the night before. If I wake up next to a terrorist it's because that's what I chose to do. None of my friends or acquaintances have ever come home to find me wearing a straw hat and suspenders and speaking Pennsylvania Dutch. I've read Darlene's thesis too; my favorite part is her take on vodun. "Like multiplicity, the African diaspora religions offer a ritualized and institutionalized zone in which participants discover that they aren't 'one'; their bodies can be intersected and controlled by larger forces, stranger desires, and paradoxical realities; they discover they can be both one thing and another, neither one thing nor the other; they discover that thinking about identity requires thinking about levels of organization, some of which are collective or linguistic and some of which are organic and biological. These discoveries are not necessarily subversive, or pleasurable, or freeing; but they might be. What sort of entities shall our bodies entertain? What larger structures will we invite in? A war on terror, a dissociative economic machine, an abuse narrative?" On the off chance that Judith might want to actually confirm her suspicions, I've given Dr. Bruno-Straus permission to speak to Judith about the issues we covered in our *eight sessions* of therapy—which don't include fragmented personality, voices in my head, or imaginary friends.—SB

and hard chair at the end of a long hallway. There were two men in blue uniforms jangling down the tunnel.

Several of the surviving boys say you pulled the trigger, said Cop. It would serve you to cooperate.

Soon, he said, this case'll be passed on outside my jurisdiction.

The two faceless men were swaggering my way.

What were you doing, he said, up there in that school?

Larger and larger. Keys, holsters, crackling walkie-talkies!

I wasn't alone, I told him. As you know, there was someone else in there with me. I'm a victim in this situation.

That's not every boy's story, said Cop. One boy's got this scar, like someone was trying to thumb a hole in his head.

I had said enough.

I care about you, he said. You know that. If a crime has been committed, it is in your own best interests to confess it. Murder is not a thing to carry silently. It is a thing to be shared with the community and dealt with appropriately.

Cop said, You have problems with intimacy, maybe. Crime is your way of reaching out, but only confession and retribution can tear off the mask you are wearing and leave you naked and open and shivering and visible. You know that you have to be broken down, so that then you can be built up new.

I want to understand you, said Cop. I want to understand you and to forgive you. I want to see you as you are, to accept you and to love you.

I detected a desperation in his tone. As if he was the one who needed to be saved. As if I was the key to Cop's salvation.

Jake, he said, give me a little something here. Talk to me. It's like a dance. Dance with me, he said.

Dammit, he said, I love you.

The more you dance, he said, the more you play the game, the freer you are.

He waited for me. He waited for me to be ready.

In 1561, a pious Anabaptist named Dirk Willems was escaping across a frozen river when the cop who was pursuing him fell through the ice. Dirk turned back. He saved the cop's life.

Foolish man. Because Dirk confessed to having been re-baptized at the age of 15, and to harboring and admitting secret conventicles and prohibited doctrines, they burnt him anyway. An east wind was blowing that day, which blew the fire away from his upper body; he suffered a lingering death. The wind blew his words into the town of Leerdam. "Oh my Lord; my God," etc. They heard it over seventy times.

Smelling a billion dollars worth of free publicity, a major label signed the band, and the record company supplied the lawyers. I benefited from the boys' confusing euphemisms for what had transpired. They didn't find a trace of my sperm on anyone's body or a fingerprint on any boy's ass.[68]

I was acquitted. My liberation, in the most literal sense, was a lengthy process, although not as lengthy as you might think for a matter as grave as murder. Inside the jail, I had nothing but time. Contrary to the myth that child molesters are the least popular inmates, I discovered many of my inmates wanted to befriend me. I'd even say my cellmate fell in love. When we weren't making love, we passed the time composing songs and telling each other lies. Many felons were anxious to become members of my band. Lyricists, singers, visual artists; the prison system was full of those yearning to self-express. Others liked to sit around and listen to my stories. They were curious about the smooth cheeks, intelligent eyes, and springy asses. But were they pouting? they demanded to

---

68. Jake claimed to be completely oblivious to the details of Michael Jackson's life and career. I didn't think that was possible, but he claimed he didn't even know who Michael was. —SB

know about the boys. They insisted I use the word "pout" in my stories over and over again.

I accepted them all into the band, as much as was possible, given the constraints of their sentences. We'd sit around and curl each other's hair. My cellmate could draw, and I liked to be his model. It excited me sexually, and it passed the time. Like his cartoons, my fantasies grew more elaborate and concrete, like fragrant vines with white flowers entwining the barbed wire edging the outer walls. On the other side is only the dry Central Valley, a kind of a desert, but I journey through it. The entire edifice of the prison wavers in the heat. Am I still in sixth grade waiting for the bell to ring? Out in the Central Valley the train tracks go on forever, all the way to Argentina.

When I was released, the band recorded the song that George had left me, "Wild Zero." Our first top-forty hit.

We played Lollapalooza. We sold millions of CDs.

I had always admired the Ubiquitous Fattie's oeuvre, but only after getting away with murder did I feel I had enough cred to get together and record. He could rap about the most clichéd versions of alpha male, crack-slinging reality, but by choosing samples which fought against the false bravado and facade with crystalline tubes of menace and emptiness he created the most complex vision of lived nihilism. He conveyed more with a grunt than the rest of us with words. I believe that the Fattie's ego, with all of its hopes and fears—that it had dissolved. That he had experienced such bliss, clarity, and a complete absence of grasping. He was living in the wisdom of egolessness, with no barrier between himself and anything else, and so nihilism, murder, the blubbery layers of self and death he had been born into—this was all sparks, this was an empty crust, an amusement. A month after he was shot and died, his new album came out, *Voice from the Grave*, the Ubiquitous Fattie perched in a coffin, all of this marketing campaign scripted long ago. The obvious weirdness of the fact that the concept of a voice from the grave was now literally true got swallowed up in the minor ironies of culture marketing, but I couldn't get over it. The posters of the dead fat man in his coffin that webbed the city overnight as if spontaneously and invisibly could have come directly from an organic haze circling the earth. It created a psychic weirdness on the streets of the city for a few weeks, until the images were pasted over with posters for paranoid sci-fi tv shows and breasty women with incredibly fake extensions.[69]

---

69. Jake was a huge fan of the Notorious B.I.G. and could talk about him obsessively and incoherently for hours. His murder in the mid-'90s took on a strange mystical aura for Jake, not surprising, given Jake's cultural relationship to the idea of martyrdom. It seems to me that the "Ubiquitous Fatty" is Jake's attempt to fantasize himself in a musical relationship with the dead man, but perhaps he had enough of a grip on the demands of realism to avoid a literal duet with a historical figure who had died when he was 5 or 6 years old. Although I suppose that hasn't stopped an endless parade of musicians in the past decades who've taken to layering their own voices next to not only Biggie's, but also those of a variety of other dead musicians—sometimes even their own parents.—SB

Dirk Willems Saving His Captor's Life

HAS LITTLE JAKE GROWN UP?[70] *Love Muscle front man still relishes punk antics, though the band's new material marks musical maturity.*

And in front of my picture the quote, *I consider myself a song-writer now.*

---

70. According to Darlene Bruno-Straus, *Sybil* was instrumental in creating a model of multiplicity that allowed adults entire constellations of "inner children"; by the '90s there were separate support groups reserved for the child alters, who would throw tantrums or color. It was also following *Sybil* that mothers began to be seen as instrumental in causing their children's dissociative disorders. Most multiples developed at least one personality based on a torturing mother. Mothers became unreal, exaggerated figures in their children's twisted imaginations, Satanic priestesses or Nazis or witches. I've seen this sort of extreme mental operation in play during my own son's tantrums. If it wasn't for the Abilify, he wouldn't have any peace. At least now he can sleep through the night. —JOB

That's why I don't grant interviews anymore. Only to you. You see, I never said that. If I ever say that, shoot me, please.

The interviewer looked at me as if I was a child and she said, You're so sweet and soft-spoken in person, it's hard to accept that you're the man who writes all those evil songs.

I said I considered myself an "evil song" writer.

SPIN went so far as to suggest that we'd lied about our past. In a cynical "exposé," they implied that nobody had died, that except for a couple losers who'd dropped out early on, the major forces in the band were exactly the same as in our mythical Midwestern "early days." College dropouts who knew us back in the day were quoted. They interviewed people with the same names as our supposedly dead bandmates. They made us out to be the Milli Vanilli of death cred. It caused a stir for about two minutes and then it blew over.[71]

It was Halloween, that time of year when the veil between this world and the world of spirits is at its thinnest. We wanted to experience some religious intensity. We wanted dark ritual, blood, evil drag queens, drums, and the spirits of dead murderers. We wanted fire. We wanted our hearts pounding through the darkest night, through the extra hour that the shift from Daylight Savings Time imposed. Fall back spring forward. We wanted a sense of community, even if

---

71. Milli Vanilli was a pop band, of sorts, formed by Frank Farina in Germany and fronted by Fab Morvan and Rob Pilatus in 1988, several years before Jake Yoder was born. They became best-selling artists and won a Grammy in 1990, which was revoked that same year when Farina confessed that the voices on the album did not belong to Morvan or Pilatus. The scandal made them infamous, and subsequent comeback attempts were unsuccessful for everyone involved. Pilatus was found dead in a Frankfurt hotel room of a drug overdose in 1998. I've found evidence that Darlene Bruno-Straus, of all people, is a Milli Vanilli fan, although as is so often the case with her statements, I couldn't be sure if her celebration of the band was meant to be ironic or not.—JOB

we didn't much like the company of most people. Alex had died of an overdose and Sally succumbed to a cancer. Others were too sick to do much. We dragged their decimated bodies on stage to represent the skeletal, the bare-bones, the declining emaciated nerve ending, the quick-burning fuse, the being of death within life. They shook tambourines or screeched atonally on clarinets. The stage was built of bones. It was an expensive effect, but compelling. They weren't really human bones, but nobody in the audience could tell the difference.

The stadium was packed. We were sorry about death and pain, but we celebrated electricity: throbbing monkey breath expanded. Chanting to a backdrop of eerie strings and bone flutes: *hollow coffins with roses blue young creatures expressing fear overcoming the values*... Spirits were conjured or at least weird enough special effects provided that people were able to hallucinate them. If enough people share the same hallucination it becomes true. Whenever two or more are gathered in my name, that's what Jesus said. He meant the same thing.

The audience was now huge, but it wasn't as if I had grown larger along with them. Years ago I looked out and I saw my peers; we were all feeling too much, just escaped from the various coffins of our family dramas. Ex-Amish, ex-Jehovah's Witness, ex-Monster of the Day. Now, all I saw was their eager, needy faces all clustered together, a herd. I looked just as ridiculous to myself, up on stage. The absurd postures I'd take to stand out for a moment from the anonymity of the crowd. We wanted to manifest the darkest dark. We wanted to manifest an extreme. We wanted crime to represent our sassy outlaw egos, but so did every other band. I wanted to burn my ego up from the inside instead, change my poses so quickly that they were a blur to myself, so that all of the husk fell away, not to reveal a humble face, not to reveal some communal plodding, some Anabaptist *Gelassenheit*, some faceless self-sacrifice, but to reveal a radiant light, that radiant light we hear so much about, which is all we really are and is so eternally boring, our great hope for peace once all desires, thoughts, memories have fallen away and each of us is reduced to a tiny flame of nothingness. But the radiant light only interests me here and now, next to the blurring series of masks I try on and discard.

Because I'd been ideologically opposed to riches and success, as an inheritor of the indie creed that great rock and roll should be underappreciated, or perhaps because I came from a people who had prospered despite—or because of—their rejection of the material world, a people whose frugality and knack for self-deprivation worked well for them, I was jaded by the pleasures of wealth before I even had them. I'd murdered, molested, gotten away with it. My public persona was sexy and butch and out of control and I sometimes confused it with myself.

Recently, one of the audience members, a particularly sad and resentful teen named Doug, had shot up his high school. That's what my music was urging him to do: kill the conformist and more beloved students of the world. The music is open to interpretation, and any interpretation is a valid one I suppose.

But perhaps I should have been less arty, more clear.

Like all the kids who do that, he'd been on anti-depressants. Someone in the audience had a FREE DOUG sign; they were both white people. Suddenly, the music I'd made seemed false, silly, melodramatic. I'd dressed up illnesses, suicides and petty crimes with exaggerated emotions, romance, cosmic drama. I couldn't see much resemblance between the songs and the lives which had inspired them, although the songs themselves sometimes replaced my memories.[72]

Cootie Dentata was writing most of the band's songs now; I had time on my hands, nothing but time.

---

72. This is a common experience for writers like Jake who sometimes mine their own lives for material.—SB

I decided to take a journey.

Where did I disappear to during that time, you want to know. Everyone has wondered and now here's the exclusive, yours alone. I wanted to lose everything and yet to continue on.[73]

Why else would I, a young rock god, be traveling in Paraguay,

---

73. Since Judith has been freely looking through Internet databases to uncover information about my former addresses, my jail time, and everything I've said in every drug-addled interview I've ever given, and since she has no compunction about speculating as to the nature of my psychological health, I decided to do a little research of my own. Judith has been gracious enough to leave my own family members out of this—so far at least, she hasn't suggested that my parents locked me in the basement, abused me in a barn, or performed Satanic rituals in which I was forced to murder and eat babies—so I'll treat her family with the same respect. (I imagine her son is having enough trouble battling evil psychiatrists and the whole pharmaceutical industry without being thrown into this mess as a rationale for his mother's defensive and neurotic behavior. So let's pretend that it isn't relevant that Jake shares a diagnosis of bipolar disorder with Judith's child.) It seems that Judith was the recipient, in 1981 (at the age of 19!) of a MacArthur "genius" award, along with Leslie Marmon Silko, Robert Penn Warren, Joseph Brodsky, Cormac McCarthy, James Alan McPherson, Carmen Angway (the great surrealist writer who'd just been committed by her husband and was even then rotting in a mental institution in upstate New York), and Derek Walcott, among others. According to the Foundation's website, "the fellowship is not a reward for past accomplishments, but rather an investment in a person's originality, insight, and potential." In Judith's case this investment was based on a single story she'd published at the age of 15 in *The Paris Review*, entitled "Dromedary." The response to "Dromedary" was as enthusiastic as it was predictable; it received an honorable mention in *Best American Short Stories 1978* (edited by Ted Solotaroff and Shannon Ravenel); J.D. Salinger was invoked; Susan Sontag was quoted; an upcoming novel from the amazing child prodigy was awaited, for a very brief moment, with bated breath. Unfortunately, the investment didn't pay off. What Judith spent the money on, we can only speculate, but she never published another word, even though her father, Arthur Owsley, was a respected editor at Grove and a close personal friend of the late George Plimpton, editor of *The Paris Review*. What became of that great unwritten novel? Where did Judith disappear to during the mid-'80s? Perhaps she might devote one of her numerous and erudite footnotes to answering that tantalizing question. Jake, by the way, refused to take the meds he was prescribed for his bipolar disorder. You could probably say that *instead* of taking his meds, he wrote stories.—SB

Uruguay, Argentina? People do all kinds of things and make up the reasons later. I was researching those Guarani suicide laments. I'd been studying Ray's notes about the obscure Argentinean science fiction writer who had mentioned the suicide laments in his essay about Artaud. The Guarani had a tradition, as they were being slaughtered, of killing themselves and singing the most intense songs of their lives. Because they conceived of past, present, and future differently, they experienced them differently. Perhaps moments were not strung together sequentially but eternally linked in a spider's web. So, one intense moment—a song, pure melancholy wail and beauty—and then a leap off a cliff—would shake the whole web, would resonate through eternity, all the way to the heart of god. I'm a big fan of gesture? Nihilistic gesture or its opposite, a sort of snatching of meaning and creation from the jaws of annihilation.

Paraguay is all prostitutes and ice cream, sleepy heat and Amish. My people are there, in Paraguay, but the world they define themselves as not being part of is a tropical, recumbent, sizzling world. Mennonites and Amish and Koreans and ex-Nazis and the Guarani cohabitate with the ghost of a dreaming dictator. In Paraguay, the choice between terror and boredom is irrelevant.[74]

There was a legendary tape smuggled out of the institution just before the obscure science fiction writer died, in which his rants about alien entities, atmospheric catastrophes, and nuclear holocaust are interspersed with deeply weird screams of cosmic

---

74. The comments about the Amish are based in fact; in 1967 seven Old Order Amish families from Indiana settled in the Chaco region of Paraguay, where they successfully farmed. Unable to create a "spiritually stable congregation," however, most of them returned to North America in 1978. Some remained and joined conservative Mennonite groups that had settled there earlier, while others formed an independent Amish group. The Guarani suicide laments, however, are pure fiction. What's more, terror and boredom can hardly be considered opposites, as anyone who's ever had trouble sleeping through the night can verify.—JOB

anguish. I hadn't heard the tape, but Ray had read descriptions of it by a failed priest/Bad Food fan he corresponded with in Georgia. I tried to find the failed priest's address after Ray died. As in the paranoid narratives of the insane Argentinean science fiction writer, the source material offered compelling glimpses and then vanished forever.

I was on a train. My quest for knowledge had failed, but the quality of light alone was enough to startle me into a weeping fit. The act of perceiving it was love. A woman with a baby struck up a conversation. She was a prim young woman, with her hair in a bun, tucked under a flimsy mesh covering; still, she couldn't hide the fact that it was the color of light itself. She did not seem desperate or insane. She did not seem evil or unstable; she was a nice Amish girl, recently widowed. But she left her baby with me and went to the restroom and she never came back.

I guessed that she hadn't, in fact, abandoned the baby, but had fallen ill, fallen asleep, fallen off the train. I waited outside all of the restrooms until I had established that she wasn't inside. Perhaps she was just now in despair over the separation from her child. In retrospect, however, this seems hardly plausible. I am not the sort of person a caring mother leaves in charge. I was foreign, unkempt. I looked like the sort of man everyone means when they talk about strangers. In retrospect, I'd guess she took the easy way out.

I'd been given a second chance. To take care of something, to help it grow. If I had ruined J, I would nurture this one. If I had abandoned J, I would spoil this one. On the other hand, I hadn't really destroyed J. Not in the absolute sense; that was an aspect of existence I'd never yet experienced. Oh, sure, I shot Darlene dead, but I didn't love her. I didn't know her at all.

Just as I had always suspected, once I owned a baby people treated me differently. Strangers on the train now smiled at me; they seemed to believe that having a baby made one loving and kind. They asked me what kind it was, a girl or a boy?

Babies make the future concrete.

I wanted to lose everything and yet to continue on.

Crossing the border into Brazil, and then Uruguay, Argentina, nothing special was required. Wasn't I supposed to have papers, to prove the baby was mine? I rode the train on and on, south into the desolate plains. A city rose in the distance, but then an older man entered my cabin, wearing the uniform of the train; he pulled the shutters closed, lowered a board over them and nailed it in place.

He left us there in the darkness. Soon, the noise began, of objects being thrown against the boarded windows. I was lulled into a half-sleep by the rhythmic bombardment, and when I woke, I was still in the dark, but the noise was abating, slowly, like the final kernels of popcorn popping in a hot skillet.

It was hot and dry. The plains were endless. We got off the train. It was empty and blazing. Citrusy and gnarled. The tedious sun. Its unpleasant heat made my cold sores bloom. Scabby blisters on the insides of my cheeks. Rashes on my knees and underarms. What were these mysterious insects that bit me at night? The baby was sweating in its swaddling clothes. The baby had male parts and female parts both, although it seemed pretty femme. It was too hot to think in. Heat = Despair. I needed to cool off.

We went down by the river.

The native people who lived in Patagonia were known as the Tehuelche. A vanished people. Forgive me if I'm making this up.[75] Tehuelche mothers massaged and molded the pliant bones of their babies' skulls. They worked their babies like clay to make them look how they wanted. To make them look like a Tehuelche.

---

75. He is. —JOB

Once, everything I hadn't experienced seemed like an infinite maze of overgrown vegetation.

An old man with a shining face. He weeps over the suffering and evil of men.

A "CERTAIN DECREE WHICH THOSE OF ZUERICH PUBLISHED AGAINST THE ANABAPTISTS" in 1525 stated that anyone who refused to baptize their babies would be fined. If they proved *utterly disobedient and obstinate*, they'd be dealt with more severely. A baby instinctively holds its breath underwater, already. If you wanted to drown it, you'd have to hold it under for a long time.

JOHN STYAERTS, AND PETER, A.D. 1538
About this year, there were, in Flanders, two cousins, one named Styaerts, the other Peter. These two blooming and God-seeking youths resided with their parents in a village called Mereedor, in Flanders. And as they were very zealous for God, and searched the holy Scriptures, they soon perceived, that the believing and regenerated—according to the doctrine of Christ, as a sign of having buried the former sins, and risen with Christ, and walking in newness of life—had to receive Christian baptism, in the water . . . When the blinded papists, who most bitterly hated the light of truth, perceived this, they took these two young lambs out of the houses of their parents and . . . they most severely imprisoned them in a dungeon. Once when their sister came to bring them some fine shirts, they told her they could not keep them from the worms, which were in their food, eating it, and in their clothes and shirts on their bodies . . .

Then they were led to the slaughter.

My people did not believe in infant baptism. That's where they got the name: Anabaptists.

Perhaps the Tehuelche had babies who peered up at their mothers as their mothers tried to mold their faces. Babies who peered up at the people around them as if they themselves were strangers, as if they were exiles, as if they were the children of light wandering through endless darkness. As if they had come from a different place altogether and as if none of this was true.

In those down-by-the-river songs you are asked to have pity on the one still alive, not the victim. The sound of rushing water filled my ears. The baby was crying and crying as if it could never be reconciled to the heat.

The Tehuelche believed that they originally came from the north. That is everything they knew about their history. It was not permitted to speak of the dead, to mention the names of the dead, to speak of what the dead had wrought. All memory of the past was buried. Every generation was the first and the last. They sang a song, and only one line of that song still exists. *Dancing on the brink of the world . . .*

I wasn't feeling well either. Dizzy, twisted, hot, and exhausted. I couldn't listen to that baby cry. Lost and futile, compassionate and desperate. I felt so much love! The sun reduced me to a state of perfect receptivity. I was empty and anything that might happen was the same as anything that might not. I was fried. Sometimes in Argentina you'll see flatbed trucks loaded with bright red tomatoes. The tomatoes are so red and luminous in the sun, so garish, that they look plastic, they look unreal.

To sum up: Abandoned planet. Regrettable species. Tiny sparks of light.

In Brazil, police officer = orphan assassin. In Brazil, municipal carpenter = coffin maker for the poor. I was only in Brazil long enough to travel between Uruguay and Paraguay, but it's easy to imagine.

It isn't so far away. The tiny coffins. The tiny children. Their short lives nothing but struggle, hunger, disease. Poor babies. Poor sweet babies.

Dead at last.

Love a sociopath and you'll discover the great truth: Adrenaline rush = Morality. Consider me a sociopath. Love me.[76]

---

76. Many of the relatives I spoke to in Nickel Mines were trying to make sense of the shooting, to reconcile the murders with their understanding of God and God's plan. They were trying to imagine how something good might come of it, or declaring that the devil had been defeated in that school, because the girls were killed and not molested. The father of two of the dead girls sticks most clearly in my mind. He was a gentle, quiet man, with thick glasses and a red beard. I'd found his farm, hidden back behind a cluster of other farms off one of the main roads. When he answered the door I told him I was Stephen Beachy, and I'd sent him a letter. He apologized; they'd received so many letters and he hadn't had time to read them all. I asked if he had other children, and he told me he had three little ones still too young for the school. As we stood on his porch, there were long pauses in our conversation. Forgiveness, he eventually told me, was very difficult for him.

For the first two weeks, he said, it was like a dream. "Something like this might happen in a dream, the girls get killed, but then you wake up and it's not true." Now, it was just starting to sink in. He said, "The girls aren't coming back."

When I asked if he thought something positive could come out of it, such as a message of forgiveness, I saw that he was troubled by that idea. "If my two girls died because a message of forgiveness was God's plan," he said, and he paused, as if trying to comprehend the enormity of that idea. The pause lasted for all of time. "I don't feel worthy," he said finally. "Unworthiness" is the most Amish of concepts. Other parents I'd spoken to had used the word "unworthy" to convey their humility in the face of the outpouring of support after the shootings. This father's statement seemed altogether different, full of an anguish and confusion as vast as the Milky Way itself. "Do you mean that you aren't strong enough, that it's too much of a burden?" I asked. "It's hard to articulate," he said, and he paused. Finally, he said, "I ask myself, Why that school? Why not some other school? Why my girls?" I didn't know what to say. I wasn't feeling well either. "We don't believe that it's punishment," the father of another dead girl had told me. "God allowed it to happen. It's like in the book of Job," he said. "God allowed the devil to do everything but kill Job." —SB

Stoning of Stephen, the First Christian Martyr

I SAY NO.

No death for the cause. No work for a better tomorrow. No crucifixion for the collectivity. No cross, no stake, no red-hot brazen ox.

No more babies, either. No infant baptism, no adult baptism, no washing of feet. No subordinate body, no *Gelassenheit*, no traditional ways. No baster babies, fertility clinics, shopping for sperm. No virtual bodies, no androids, no clones. No interstellar nanoforms haunting carbon and its envelope of flesh. No electricity, no abortion, and no angelic host. No spheres or aeons. No Great Chain of Being, no multiverse, no extra dimensions. No murderous rapture, no dissolution into the void.

No heaven no hell. No catacombs, no whirling diaphanous fields. No spelling lists, okay? No mutter or clutter or letter. No moped, no canoe, no starry river, no river of stars. No home in the Milky Way. No feature, whisper, wander, litter, or pulp. No murmur. No bereaved. No houses, no journeys, no institutions. No attics, no basements, no torment or glitter. No carpeting no linoleum no cottage-cheese ceilings. No buggies, no bonnets. No inmates, no intestines, no mazes or mounds. No hermaphrodites, no heretics or invisible twins. No hemispheres. No esoteric swelling. No wedding gown, no funeral costume, no carnival masquerade. No clown mask or pirate patch or luminous wig. No empty wardrobe. No useful stories, no art for art's sake. No BMWs no Disneyland no UFOs no illuminati no eternity no time. No time and no space. No infinite sadness no karmic debts. Please, no fluorescent lights. No grass concrete trees houses cows blood semen milk saliva no bodily fluids no unsafe sex no rubbers no combination therapy no co-factors no viral load. No memories, no acts. No justice no peace. No meditation on Death. No swollen corpse. No discolored corpse. No festering corpse. No fissured corpse or mangled corpse. I don't even know what a fissured corpse is. No dismembered corpse. No bloody corpse. No limb-scattered corpse or worm-foul corpse. No organ donors, no lab animals, and no bludgeoned remains. No original sin. No primal void. No speck in the eye of god. No shamanic journey into hell. No initiation into the mysteries.

No cemeteries. No bodies. No lists.

No disco. No rock and roll. No folk music no grunge no hardcore. No techno, no trance, no ambient trip hop. No prog rock no psychedelic no emo no metal. No hip hop no jungle no reggae no free jazz or top forty. No punk or garage. No house.

No suicides for culture. No transgressive art, no radical disgust. No martyrs, no gnostics, no non-entity generating and degenerating a non-universe. No Hermetic Kabbalist tradition. No modernist gems. No intricate breathy articulations. No rhythmic hieroglyphic calculus. No intertwined ideograms or oneiric ciphers vibrating toward an alchemical dawn. Enough already. No noise no music no silence.

No confessions no remorse no spontaneous poetry no first thought best thought no mothers no fathers no taboos no concerns no end of history no apocalypse no new age no more. No collateral damage, no acceptable losses. No military industrial complex or intimacy for hire. No conscientious objectors. No extraordinary rendition. No good cop bad cop. No Pepsi no Coke. No logos. No *logos*. No energy. No bosons or leptons. No matter. No *pathos*. No osmosis. No organelles. No mitochondria. No ribonucleic acid. No bubbles. No bones. No feathers. No ash. No gill slits, no echinoderms. No fossilized strata. No notochords or calcite skeletons. No tibia, no fibula. No coelacanths, no lobe-finned fishes, no pelvic fins. No vertebrae. No x-ray. No bronchial sacs. No breath. No spirit. No whirling dervish. No wheels in the sky. No constellation of ghosts. No rims. No teeth. No antlers. No feelers. No wings. No two into one. No inner like the outer, no outer like the inner. No upper like the lower. No male and female in a single one. No eye replacing an eye, no hand replacing a hand, no foot replacing a foot. No image replacing an image. No vision. No remains. No desert. No wind. No farthest reaches of space. No skull. No eye sockets. No soul. No face.

No effacing passions. No boners. No throbbing boyflesh. No hot steamy manhole. No erect morning member. No high school athlete's jockstrap. No closeted fervor. No perfect pecs. No muscle man in a gas mask. No hot prison trade. No masculine masters. No handsome hung sociopaths. No bound bubble butts. No angelic pouts. No clenched little ass cheeks. No squeezing and purring. No small naked animal as bright as the sun. No harder no faster. No ram it all the way in. No ski masks, no ropes. No quivering lips, no soft cheeks, no intelligent eyes, and no firm, boyish buttocks. No shove it in that ass. No immobilized and spread-eagle. No lifting weights in his underwear. No muscles moving in and out of sight. No cruel, handsome face.

No butch and no femme. No penetrating the female parts with the male parts. No yeah baby all the way inside.

No viable positions. No nihilistic postures or sentimental embrace. No way in and no way out. No out of the body experience. No roots casually lying in wait to re-sprout beneath the frozen crust of the earth. No workdays, no weekends, no Walmart, no space shuttle no stock market plunge, no celebrity murders no lawyers no cops and no priests. No nurture no nature. No complex biosphere. No organic haze. No interdependent ecosystem. No consumption. No love.

No transcendence. No abyss. No doubt. No faith. No still small voice.

No. No no no no no no no. No no no.

No. No. No.

No. No. No. No. No. No. No. No. No. No. No. No.
No. No. No. No. No. No. No. No. No. No. No. No.
No. No. No. No. No. No. No. No. No. No. No. No.
No. No. No. No. No. No. No. No. No. No. No. No.
No. No. No. No. No. No. No. No. No. No. No. No.
No. No. No. No. No. No. No. No. No. No. No. No.
No. No. No. No. No. No. No. No. No. No. No. No.
No. No. No. No. No. No. No. No. No. No. No. No.
No. No. No. No. No. No. No. No. No. No. No. No.
No. No. No. No. No. No. No. No. No. No. No. No.
No. No. No. No. No. No. No. No. No. No. No. No.
No. No. No. No. No. No. No. No. No. No. No. No.
No. No. No. No. No. No. No. No. No. No. No. No.
No. No. No. No. No. No. No. No. No. No. No. No.
No. No. No. No. No. No. No. No. No. No. No. No.
No. No. No. No. No. No. No. No. No. No. No. No.
No. No. No. No. No. No. No. No. No. No. No. No.
No. No. No. No. No. No. No. No. No. No. No. No.
No. No. No. No. No. No. No. No. No. No. No. No.

No. No. No. No. No. No. No. No. No. No. No. No.
No. No. No. No. No. No. No. No. No. No. No. No.
No. No. No. No. No. No. No. No. No. No. No. No.
No. No. No. No. No. No. No. No. No. No. No. No.
No. No. No. No. No. No. No. No. No. No. No. No.
No. No. No. No. No. No. No. No. No. No. No. No.
No. No. No. No. No. No. No. No. No. No. No. No.
No. No. No. No. No. No. No. No. No. No. No. No.
No. No. No. No. No. No. No. No. No. No. No. No.
No. No. No. No. No. No. No. No. No. No. No. No.
No. No. No. No. No. No. No. No. No. No. No. No.
No. No. No. No. No. No. No. No. No. No. No. No.
No. No. No. No. No. No. No. No. No. No. No. No.
No. No. No. No. No. No. No. No. No. No. No. No.
No. No. No. No. No. No. No. No. No. No. No. No.
No. No. No. No. No. No. No. No. No. No. No. No.
No. No. No. No. No. No. No. No. No. No. No. No.
No. No. No. No. No. No. No. No. No. No. No. No.
No. No. No. No. No. No. No. No. No. No. No. No.
No. No. No. No. No. No. No. No. No. No. No. No.
No. No. No. No. No. No. No. No. No. No. No. No.
No. No. No. No. No. No. No. No. No. No. No. No.
No. No. No. No. No. No. No. No. No. No. No. No.
No. No. No. No. No. No. No. No. No. No. No. No.
No. No. No. No. No. No. No. No. No. No. No. No.
No. No. No. No. No. No. No. No. No. No. No. No.
No. No. No. No. No. No. No. No. No. No. No. No.
No. No. No. No. No. No. No. No. No. No. No. No.
No. No. No.
No. No. No. No. No. No.
No. No. No.
No. No. No.
No. No. No.
Just kidding. Yes. Maybe?
No.

Two Young Girls Led to Execution

BUT PERHAPS I'M MISLEADING YOU. My story is too butch. Murder is butch, rock and roll is butch, car crashes, toy guns, sex with children, gas masks. Slaughterhouses are butch, infanticide, prisons and the Amish. Martyrdom! Buried bicycle parts and references to Dada. Saying no is butch.

I was a little farm boy once and I looked at my naked body. It was chubby and pink. My bellybutton was an outie. I thought if my pecs were firmer I'd be happy until the end of time. When I looked in the mirror I saw something soft and sensitive, a delicate, conniving creature, a girly child who felt deeply for all the beings of the earth. Like you, I strangled that child. I held it under until it couldn't breathe.

Is it ever too late? I'm wealthy now. Wealth is femme. This

interview must be luxurious. No more confessions, no more historical texts.

You can see right through me, I know. You lull me into a calm intensity with your soothing manner and then pop one of those probing questions. You know all about men like me.

Saying yes is femme. Seeing beauty everywhere you look. Being delighted by the styles and faces people wear, by disinformation and attitude.

Imagine this: I am sitting in a huge fluffy bed with satin sheets and enormous pillows, popping chocolates into my mouth and watching daytime tv. I get up on the phone and chat with my girlfriends, Teeny from Denmark and Cootie Dentata. The key to strudel is to stretch the dough until it is thinner than parchment, until you can read through it. You brush it with clarified butter to keep it from drying out. I'm melancholic, but on good days I feel sunny.

I am weeping. For the sick and the dead. I tell Cootie, Please come over and keep me company. We sit in the bed and she massages my shoulders with lavender-ginger body lotion. She distracts me from the pain of life by asking about my latest crush—a sixth-grade teacher.

I ask Cootie, Do you think I should go all the way? Or is it too soon?

We think about sex strategically. I'm leading a double life. My teacher—call him Leonard—doesn't know about my wild rock and roll lifestyle, we met in the periodical room at the new Main Library. I told him I was reading the Pseudepigrapha, not because I was interested in extreme rejections of spiritual authority, but because I was studying Women's Spirituality and the Mother Goddess tradition at the New College.[77]

---

77. In the middle of the night last night, I had an interesting conversation with Brian, the man readers know as Officer B. I consider myself a private person and don't wish to inflict details of my personal life on anonymous readers. I do feel, however, that our conversation may shed some light on

Cootie rolls a joint. I say: Oh no, that stuff's too strong, it makes me goofy.

Besides, I'm already maxed out on Zoloft, Abilify, and Klonopin. Just one hit, she says. I hold it the wrong way, exhale all the smoke, and immediately start giggling.

Let's do some role play, suggests Cootie.

As it turns out, Leonard is understanding about my lies. He isn't just a sixth-grade teacher but also a spiritual teacher, and he intuits that we have a lot of work to do together. When I've figured out the real meaning of my desires and my identity—perhaps that I'm a false woman with imaginary passions for fake men, a woman who adorns herself with glamorous words—then and only then will we consummate our relationship.

I spend all my time in my bedroom, in melancholy contemplation of my lonely task: the search for coherent selfhood. He'll call

---

just how much psychological damage this strange manuscript has already caused; the significance of these reverberations might outweigh my desire for privacy, in this case. Through the process of investigating Jake Yoder, I have become quite fond of Brian and the two of us have begun together the difficult journey of a long-distance relationship. As a result, I have frequently shared with Brian the many anxieties this manuscript has caused me. With his odd work hours, the difference in time zones, and my increasing insomnia, the middle of the night is often the only time that we can talk on the phone. Last night he told me that earlier in the day he'd suddenly remembered a strange conversation he'd had with the drowned woman's husband, Daniel or Donald. After all this time—and we've gone over these events together repeatedly—he was convinced that he remembered a comment about a child. He thought the man had said something about a daughter who'd been sent away—Brian was sure he remembered that phrase, "sent away," although he was also convinced that the child was "visiting family." Clearly Brian has been listening to me go on about this case for so long that he actually created a kind of false memory to coincide with what he affectionately refers to as "my obsession with that boy." After a lengthy discussion, he agreed with me that this was surely the case. So you see—Jake Yoder's book has even gotten under the skin of a practical and usually stoic man like Brian, a police officer, who is accustomed to seeing all kinds of horrible things in his daily routine.—JOB

me on the phone and tell me my weak, femme mind is too receptive to the seductions of irrationality. He says, Since you want what you can't want, you're dreaming that you want it. He says, You want to oscillate back and forth, faster and faster, between evil and good. He says, You can't handle being merely a femme, someone else's creation; you struggle against me in your fantasy life.[78]

His statement reminds me that I hate his beard. Leonard's beard makes me suspect he isn't always completely honest.

He hangs up on me. He knows I can scarcely bear this punishment, but I must learn. I watch Oprah, eat a raspberry tart, start to call up Cootie when I realize the obvious lesson—it's all distraction. Duh, I say to myself.

Cynicism is defensive. Cynicism is a way of saying: I am hard already. You can't hurt me. I'm so afraid.

Cynicism is like a fear of rejection.

Cootie is teaching me phrases in Tagalog. *Magandang umaga po* means Good morning sir. *Ay! ang hirap ng buhay* means What a hard life! *Meron bang sigarilyo?* Do you have a cigarette? *Meron bang posporo?* Do you have a match? *Meron bang wiski?* Do you have whiskey? *Natakot ako sa kanyang pagligo.* I was afraid of his being angry. *Ang kanyang pag-alis ay ikinalungkot ko.* His departure made me sad.

But who do I really want here with me? It is Esther and Fannie and Myrna, my Amish cousins. I want them to speak these phrases to me in Pennsylvania Dutch. I want to sit around a table and quilt with them, weaving together the disparate meanings of our collective lives. I want to belong to my people. I am so lost, out here in the world. Myrna, I believe, is an autumn. Those bold purples and

---

78. Large portions of this chapter seem to have been inspired by (or plagiarized from, as Judith would say) Clarice Lispector's *An Apprenticeship or The Book of Delights.* Lispector was addicted to sleeping pills and would often flee dinner parties for no reason—although this couldn't have been too surprising to anyone who'd read her books.—SB

blues and blacks don't work for her at all.[79]

I guess I'm what you'd call a black sheep. I envision evil as a fragile motor. For me, evil is composed of spun glass, involved with perpetual motion. Where could I possibly have come from? You take an old Amishman, bearded, dour, and wearing black. You wring him out like a rag. You squeeze and squeeze until finally a spoonful of pure guava jelly drops out of his asshole.

I am that guava jelly.

I am the justification for all the torture of my ancestors. Their little screams.

Perhaps I am not ready to make my way back to the Amish, but I'm readying myself, just as I'm readying myself for Leonard's love. I've started a quilt of my own. Crushed maroon velvet, lycra, and

---

79. And so he did, of course—make his way back to his cousins. I thumbed through issue after issue of the Amish monthly magazine *Family Life* in search of the article he published there under a different pseudonym. I discovered an essay by "Nahum Peachy" that tells the supposedly historical story of an attack on Anabaptist Jacob Hochstetler and his family by Native Americans in 1754. Jacob is portrayed as a brave and unerring pacifist who refuses to fight back, even as his son begs him to load the gun to protect them. The mother, daughter, and one son are killed, while Jacob and two of his sons are taken captive. Jacob wonders, at one point, if his wife was responsible for her own death—for not having been more hospitable to the natives when they stopped by one day. Despite hewing to Amish orthodoxy, elements creep into this dramatized flight of philosophy I can only describe as existential—if not gnostic. Jacob successfully avoids torture by offering the natives some of his ripe, delicious peaches. Still, he and his sons are separated. "Even if you forget everything else," he advises his sons, "remember your names and the Lord's Prayer." The Jake Yoder-esque conclusion comes after Jacob escapes and one day finds himself face to face with a tall native. The native introduces himself in broken German. He's Jacob's son, Christian, who has been adopted by the native tribe.

While Nahum is a biblical name, it is not one used by the Amish—the only other time I've seen it is in H.P. Lovecraft's "The Colour out of Space." The American Peachys and Beachys are all descended from Peter Bitsche; supposedly the lower hump of the B was left off during the signing of a document, and the Peachy line came to be. There aren't actually any Amish Peachys, however, and the name seems more of a play on the ripe, delicious peaches in the story.—SB

silk. A lot of people take drugs and decide that only natural fibers are good, that synthetics are bad. But just as in music any tone is equally acceptable, in my quilt *every* fabric is good.

There is no justification, not for anything, and therein lies the root of my pleasure and my ability to experience joy.

I don't know how to arrange fruit in a bowl, but Leonard says he'll teach me someday how to do it "artistically." Will the process be more painful than I can bear? I want to bear unbearable pain. On the other hand, I want to achieve only the possible. Leonard asks me to attend a charity event with him. The hummus and pita, the cheese and red grapes and wine in plastic cups, it fills me with dread. I tell myself it's for a good cause, even if it is one I don't entirely understand. What will I wear? Leonard says I haven't much taste in clothes. I dress too loud for my personality or else too subdued for my soul.

My soul is wild and discordant and angry, like an untethered white horse stampeding at night, I hope, through Leonard's dreams. My soul travels everywhere and withholds judgment. My soul accepts everyone, no matter how sick or piggy. My personality is soft spoken and morally concerned, willing to discuss ways of building a more just society or nurturing children. My soul could care less.

Leonard doesn't make clear which body of needs he thinks I should dress for. I wear a sexy red strapless number that hugs my ass and black garters. Panicking, at the last minute, I cover myself with an old, baggy pink sweater that buttons up the front.

At the party I'm sad.

I pretend I'm sad because I sense all the loneliness beneath the wit. I pretend I am sad because the night is a little bit warm and blue. I pretend I'm sad because I am home working on my quilt. My quilt must contain sadness, and to *weave* sadness into the quilt I must *feel* sadness. I have another glass of wine. Leonard remarks that drunkenness doesn't suit me.

He's chatting in a manly and professional way with some important business associates. I grow tired of beaming up at them in a dimwitted attempt to aid Leonard's financial affairs as a charming prop, so excuse myself to the restroom. Seeing myself in the mirror I don't understand how Leonard could love me. I possess none of the manly virtues. But then I see how pretty I can be, with a slightly different shade of lipstick. I rehearse my speech.

Yes, Leonard, I am femme. Being so very femme, I naturally desire virility and terror; I desire you. Because, in my weak and unhealthy past of rock and roll degradation, I wanted men to love me, I imitated their ways. In a manly man, cruelty and murder and sadism and willful ignorance of other people's emotions are just their nature. We don't call a tiger evil, or a shark or a vulture or a cheetah. But a femme who is only feigning evil to be loved and accepted! That is the worst. The very worst!

During that time—my life, so to speak—"evil" was just a concept I used to pretend I had depth. All I really needed was a man, to relieve me of my own depth. Leonard, all I ever needed was you.

Back at the party, however, he grabs me roughly and says, Let's go. I can see he is in a mood. Suddenly, my speech seems silly.

Last night, I say instead, I dreamed of a bird caught in a glassed-in porch. It was struggling to escape but it couldn't see the way. All those reflections confused it so. But you cupped it in your warm hand and set it free. Once free, it burst into flames and continued flying as beautiful sparks rained down on the desolate world.

He shrugs, with hostility.

Are all your dreams so obvious and self serving? he asks.

He found the party, which was necessary for his career, annoying, so he wants to pick a fight with me. He'll continue to hurt me until I fight back, so I might as well get it over with. I compose a quick mental list of what I consider his greatest flaws (insecure, pedantic, passive-aggressive), and then another list of what he considers his greatest flaws (unable to fix his own car, didn't understand

Kant, emotionally dishonest). The latter would hurt him more, although some territory is clearly forbidden. I *actually* dreamed that he was a woman therapist named Darlene, but he's so insecure with his masculinity already that I don't want to mention that I imagined him as a stern, controlling woman.[80] Suddenly, thoughtlessly, I abandon this whole manipulative approach and try something I think is more spiritual: direct confrontation.

You want to fight, I say. You're angry about something, so you'd like to blame me. You're hurting me as if that's my role.

Don't analyze me, he says. What do you think you are, a fucking shrink? You can't even manage to plan your own career. You're so cold and unemotional, like a dead carp.

He spits on me.

You argue like an old woman, he says. You argue like a bitch. What's wrong with you? Why are you folding your arms like some little church woman?

Your communication is fake, he says. You try to destroy all possibilities of real communication, you use language to destroy language, you're a silly, fraudulent little bitch.

I'm torn. I want to turn on him like an Africanized bee and destroy him. It's only knowing I have that power that allows me not to use it. Manly men are more vulnerable than femmes. I'm also afraid that he might hurt me physically.

Plus, maybe his actions are deeper and more purposeful than I'm giving him credit for. He is my master: the source of all my pleasure and my pain. As if to confirm this suspicion, I have an insight about my fame and my disease. Celebrity is a betrayal of invisibility. The virus is an invisible wound or window into living fossil organs. I am growing, in process. Maybe this humiliation is

---

80. My telephone conversation with Darlene Bruno-Straus was bizarre, to say the least. Let's just say that it in no way dispelled my suspicions, although it did suggest to me that in this case, the therapist might be even more disturbed than her patient. —JOB

all part of the process. I'm afraid that physical abuse is part of the process too. Although I know my mechanisms for disarming the threat constitute dishonesty and avoidance, I give myself my own weakness as a gift.

This reminds me of why I happen to still be alive. I've never told Leonard—when I was a young femme, a man came to my school. This stranger only liked boys, he only liked the butch ones, he only liked to rape and murder handsome little boys. When he told the girls to leave, I got out too, because he couldn't tell the difference. Another androgynous and ethereal creature led me by the hand, out through a door that would soon be splattered red.[81]

I begin crying.

I love you so much, I say. I cry and cry.

For all his wisdom and strength, I know Leonard isn't up to slapping a sobbing femme. He watches me with disgust for a moment, then reaches out a hand, brushes away a tear.

Five days later when Leonard finally calls again—he never talks on the phone, but just tersely makes a date without asking whether I even want to go—I burst into tears of joy.

I stare at my closet full of clothes. I'm craving something. I'm

---

81. Just before he threw his "evil" manuscript in the fire, I was trying to convince Jake he wasn't responsible for the shooter's crimes. That man was a monster, I insisted. No, no, he said, shaking his head. He was only a man whose baby had died. Jake was able to forgive the shooter, it seems, but not to forgive himself. This paragraph about the narrator's survival based on his gender performance is interesting not only because it suggests Jake's obvious survivor's guilt, in relation to the girls, but also because of the similarity to the case of one of the surviving children, Emma Fisher. In the earliest versions of the story, 9-year-old Emma simply snuck out of the schoolhouse along with the boys. It was later said that she misunderstood the shooter's instructions in English, and thought she was *supposed* to leave. A more recent variation has Emma hearing one of the schoolteacher's helpers say to her, "Now would be a good time to run," as the shooter was messing with the window blinds. But the woman claims she said nothing, and some Amish began suggesting the voice Emma heard was the voice of an angel.—SB

craving smoked salmon. Other things, but smoked salmon isn't vague, inexpressible, or unattainable. Leonard will have contempt for the sensuality of my desire, but I hope it might excite him a little bit, too. When I'm once again in his car—I don't know what kind of car, it's midnight blue and kind of squarish—I reveal my secret urge. To my surprise he even smiles at me.

You eat as if you're pregnant, he says. And in a sense, you are.

His tone is oddly tender.

Although you may never learn to adequately weigh costs against benefits, he says with no tenderness now, or to develop realistic career goals, you are making progress in other areas. I know just where to go for this "smoked salmon."

He drives me to a fish market in a nearby city. In front of us in line is a loud and vulgar woman unabashedly waving her booklet of food stamps around. There are those who see something admirable and life-loving in the act of purchasing fresh crab legs with food stamps—and I'll confess that I have been one of those—but I know Leonard's understanding of the situation would be too deep to forgive. He would understand the complex economic mechanisms by which someone was being denied what was rightfully theirs so that this greedy poor woman could enjoy her crab legs, noisily smacking her lips and discarding the shells on the sidewalk, like the empty husks of a once living and growing universe now condemned, like those space probes, to travel on and on under automatic control through cold empty space, all of the instruments dead. Leonard would feel he was being personally cheated. I put my arms around his neck and turn him toward me, away from the woman, and begin demurely telling him some silly story about Cootie's childhood in the slums of Manila.

You look nice today, he says. I could imagine putting rings around your neck to gradually elongate it, until it was so fine and delicate that it might collapse under the weight of your head, snapping your spine in two.

I like it when you paint yourself like a whore, he adds. When you learn more, soon, you'll realize how much of your life has been a total waste.

Yes, I think, as that woman goes on her way with her crab legs and Leonard buys me a quarter pound of smoked salmon—so much has been wasted.

How many lovers did you say you'd had before me? Leonard asks.

He remembers exactly what I've told him. He's either trying to catch me in a lie or show that it's really of no importance to him, he isn't the jealous type.

Six, I say, just as I said before. I know that seems like a lot, since I didn't love any of them.

In reality, he says, femmes don't desire promiscuity, except as revenge or self punishment.

Sometimes lying to your man is OK, even if he is a spiritual teacher. I've decided not to count in my final tally anyone whose name I can't remember or whose name I never knew, any sex that happened outside, in a car or motel, anyone before the age of 15, anyone during that one year or so when I was completely out of control, just not myself at all, anyone in a foreign country, anyone wearing a gas mask (since that would transform them into more of a concept than a real person), anything that happened under the influence of drugs or alcohol, anything I regretted afterward, anyone who gave me a phone number that turned out to be false or said they'd call me and never did, anyone who was under age or developmentally disabled (again, more conceptual than real), any non-penetrative sex or penetrative sex involving broken rubbers, any time an exchange of money or drugs was involved, and any lovemaking that occurred above a vaguely defined sense of altitude (roughly 500 feet or more above sea level) because it was then more celestial than terrestrial. Oh, and then anything I have either willfully or unintentionally forgotten altogether, which I guess is no more than fifty or sixty inconsequential men, and my stepfather, for obvious reasons. He used to dump his money on the bed and we'd "make the money messy" as Roxanne Shanté sings about.[82]

Couldn't you learn to be happy? Leonard asks me. You can learn anything. To be happy, to love, to make yourself empty.

He pulls out a demographic chart he's made of my former lovers, based only on the six I've mentioned. He's titled it *SORDID CONSOLATION: The Men Who Didn't Love You.* It charts them by age, socioeconomic background, and time spent incarcerated. He thinks he recognizes a pattern.

I don't know how to defend myself without admitting the very partial nature of his data. I scrutinize the chart. Only two of them were ever in prison, and it wasn't for violent crimes.

---

82. In Judith's only published story, "Dromedary," a teenage girl visits a New England pumpkin patch with her father, who is trying to recreate his own sentimental memories of childhood. The girl is cynical on the surface but obviously at the same time deeply invested in her own nostalgia for childhood and Halloween and fatherhood—she just wants to pretend to be above it all. In the pumpkin patch, they encounter a poor child from the ghetto of some nearby city. The girl's father makes all kind of assumptions about the boy's father, who is at the adjacent Chevron station making a call from the payphone there. He suggests that the father won't even buy the poor deprived kid a pumpkin for Halloween, he's probably a drug dealer, a pimp, a child-beater, he doesn't care about his son and the poor boy is doomed to an unhappy life without pumpkins or paternal love. Out of a spirit of adolescent rebellion, the girl argues against her father's unenlightened attitude. Then there's a game of hide-and-seek in the pumpkin patch with the little ghetto child and a flight of fantasy about the Sahara desert (hence the title). Finally the boy's father shows up and proves to be exactly the abusive, neglecting pimp that the girl's upper-class father imagined him to be. On top of that, he's bizarrely effeminate. The story ends with the girl gazing sullenly out the window of the car at the gloomy fields as they drive back toward their townhouse in the city. Barely perceptible intimations of father/daughter incest pervade the atmosphere of the story in a very Gothic way. In addition, there is some hint that the girl had an adopted brother who's been lost—it isn't clear if he died or if maybe he was simply sent back to the social service agency he came from, once her parents didn't want to deal with him any more. Maybe, then, it is Judith who is the real, secret author of these pages.—SB

We're sitting on a bench, looking at artists in the park. The sun is warming and lazy. It all feels oddly familiar, as if I've lived it before. Leonard takes off his shirt and insists I do the same.

I can't look at Leonard. I don't feel comfortable naked.

Leonard points out a much more beautiful femme jogging past in Lycra shorts that hug his buns.

See how he moves, Leonard says. As if completely one with his body. See the grace, the fluidity.

It's hard to think while I'm almost nude, even harder to speak.

You should go to the gym, he says. Firm up those pecs.

You need to get out, honey, says Cootie Dentata. You're getting all pale and drawn, like Mia Farrow in *Rosemary's Baby* when she's been impregnated with Satan's baby, okay?[83]

Cootie's performing at an art opening tonight for a famous artist who changes his style any time people begin to like what he's doing. I met a man who became my lover at just such an art opening; maybe I can fix myself up with another man, so as to free myself from obsessing about Leonard and my spiritual growth.

As soon as I enter the party I regret it. I've put on so much

---

83. This intimation of Satanic ritual abuse again evokes Darlene Bruno-Straus's thesis. In fact she analyzes the influence of *Rosemary's Baby* on the epidemic of multiplicity at some length, along with *The Exorcist*, which she credits with creating a host of alter personalities named Regan or Reagan. "The devil's desire to father children is well known, and offers a pleasing symmetry," writes Bruno-Straus. "God had a little boy, Jesus, so Satan should father the Antichrist. Although we more often associate Satan with non-procreative sexuality, (e.g., anal sex, oral sex, homosexuality, pedophilia, and any acts between species too distantly related to produce hybrid vigor), who can blame him for occasionally wanting to produce life and see himself reflected in his genetic offspring? Isn't Satan all about ego?" Bruno-Straus considers *Rosemary's Baby* an incisive critique of a society that disempowers women; I watched it last night after I got off the phone with Brian. It's certainly a stretch to call it a feminist film. During the scene in which Mia Farrow is impregnated by Satan, I kept thinking of what director Roman Polanski did to that 13-year-old girl. —JOB

makeup I look like a prostitute or a clown and so all of the men, artists and art critics and wannabes, pinch my ass and make lewd comments, but don't engage me in conversation. I know they say no woman is asking for it, but I guess I am, if only out of confusion and bad taste. While the ass pinching gives me a temporary boost in self-esteem, I'm relieved when the lights go down and the show begins.

Usually Cootie cracks me up with her humorous tales of growing up in the slums of Manila. The macho dancers, major political players, and child prostitutes that populate her comic narratives—she has a gift, that Cootie Dentata. When she sings "Don't Cry for Me Filipina" it is sure to bring the house down.

An art critic from Walnut Creek takes me home with him. I'm so drunk this won't count, so what the hell? Like all men from Walnut Creek, he's into rough sex. I successfully leave my body during the ordeal. I hover above the ocean and think about being inside it. I long for extremes. The most joy, the most sorrow, the most terrifying loneliness and degradation away from my man. I know Leonard would say these were juvenile desires. That I am outgrowing them. Smarter mystics know that the question of life after death is irrelevant. They know that the time to experience eternity, terror, and death is only now. This art critic doesn't even drive me home; I have to wait until morning when the BART is running again.[84]

Angry and hurt, I write Leonard a letter. I tell him that I lied, that there was one boyfriend I'd never mentioned; I had another spiritual teacher once. He'd tie me up with so much rope that only my quivering lips, my soft cheeks, my intelligent eyes, and my femmey

---

84. Or maybe it is Judith who isn't real. Maybe she's just one of Jake Yoder's personalities. In any case, I give up—trying to do battle with the monsters of this world often only seems to lead one further and further into the realm of the blind.—SB

ass remained visible. He'd leave me there immobilized while he lifted weights in his underwear. His muscles moved in and out of my vision. During the interludes I became more bored than I'd ever been in my life. I could feel no more desire, but he kept coming back. Through the mask all I could see of his face were his eyes, which reflected the dark light of an endless sky. We never used condoms; he stuck it right in. I tell Leonard that he is only really a pathetic substitute for that man, who started slow and kissed my neck as he moved it in and out and in and out. We were in a classroom, a hospital, an asylum, a tomb. He got that rocking motion going, put it all the way in, all the way out. We were dreaming inside a prison. He turned me over and did it from the front with my legs in the air, You're such a little man, he said. He turned me on my belly and rested the tip of his cock against my asshole and then pushed it all the way in, took it all the way out. He'd used me up, there was nothing left of me, I was part of him now, I heard a strange music. This music had *always* been waiting for me to find it.

I crumple the letter up and throw it away.[85]

I adore flowers. Flowering cacti and succulents especially. *Conophytum spectabile*, with its eruption of purple from the bulbous meat. A sexual volcano, a primordial, fleshy voluptuousness. *Echeveria agavoides* for its redness, its blood. Claret cup cactus

---

85. Obviously I am real. I can be found at the offices of this press every weekday between the hours of 10 and 6. Attentive readers will have noticed that Stephen loves to multiply absurd possibilities in an attempt to distract his audience from the obvious. I might also point out that the burn patterns on the charred manuscript are strange to say the least. The idea that the fire would burn a hole through the *center* of the manuscript and leave the edges always struck me as odd. Last night, after I'd tucked my son securely in his bed, and once again found myself unable to sleep, I built a bonfire in my back yard. Using several manuscripts from the slush pile, I wasn't once able to replicate this pattern. This suggests to me that the dark hole in the center of the manuscript is more a metaphor for Stephen's psyche than a plausible piece of evidence about the existence of the child.—JOB

and prickly pears. A flower must be allowed to be itself, however. Jean Genet detested flowers, he only liked the words that represented them. If a flower is merely pretty, let it be merely pretty. A stream violet with its perky yellow petals in the wild or, likewise, a California poppy: a little bit of sunshine isn't vapid. Sometimes, pretty yellow flowers are exactly what we need.

If a flower is deep and sexual, let it be deep and sexual. Sand devil's claw with its tainted gold horns and claws is fabulously evil, but not like a tiger lily with its fiery erection of anthers. The pollen is like a sickness. A tiger lily can make me swoon. I have to look away.

A kinnikinnick has pink, lantern-shaped flowers and waxy green leaves. It seems trite at first, but on closer examination you see that its red berries are the bait and the tiny flowers the true expression of a hermit or a monk: humble, secretive, and simply present.

Artemisia, I cannot talk about.

At first glance forget-me-nots are celestial eyes, blue and yellow, and it is only their blueness which is of any interest. They are simply dainty. Daintiness is a value often overlooked in our mad, fast-paced, modern society. I say, nurture the dainty. Celebrate the dainty. An angel fell in love with a mortal. He was exiled from heaven, told he could return only if he placed forget-me-nots in every corner of the world.

I don't remember how that story ended.

Egyptians believed if you placed the leaves over your eyes at certain times of the year, you would have visions.

Blue flowers! Electric. If you want to talk about blue, you have to talk about gentian. Papyrus records show the Egyptians used this one, too, long long ago. Also, a Hungarian king ruled over a plague-stricken people. He shot an arrow upward, hoping, implausibly, that it would land on a plant to help his people. This worked for him; it landed on gentian, which wrought many cures. It's useful in killing intestinal worms, controlling fever, purifying blood, and stimulating or calming digestion.

Thistle or sea holly. You probably think it's the contrast between the purple flowers and the harsh thistle that appeals to me, but in this case I prefer the extreme: after the flower is gone altogether and all that's left is the hellish desiccated crown of thorns.

Puya blows me away, can I say that? The color of its insane flowers belongs to the outer planets, the gaseous balls with their many moons. Puya grow in Chile many thousand feet above the sea. The message of a puya is that anything is possible; that life alone is sufficient; that beauty is never a thing to hoard. Despite its sharp edges, a puya has a generous spirit.

In the middle of winter, the amaryllis blooms. It has spectacular blossoms, fireworks of white to pink, red, salmon, and orange. It will brighten up your bedroom on those long winter nights. Amaryllis is poisonous. Many of the indigenous peoples of South America used its sap to make poisonous arrows. Perhaps it promises revenge.

I go to my job as an artist in the schools.

I haven't seen you for a while, I say.

That other one came, J says. The one that looks like you.

I say, I hope she wasn't too mean.

J rolls his eyes, says, You're not a "she."

I blush.

I wanted a gold tooth, he says. But Mommy says no.

I rub his scalp with my hand.

Your forehead is scarred, I say. Just like mine.

What happened to you? he asks.

I went down by the river, I say. I got scratched by a tree. What about you?

He shrugs.

It was an accident, he says. I think it was the teacher.

Oh no, I say. I hope that mean teacher didn't hurt you.

J looks thoughtful.

I really loved him, he says. I thought he liked me, but he left me here alone.

I say, I'm sure he loved you too.

J shrugs.

That teacher only cared about himself, he says.

I searched for a substitute, he says. It never worked out.

He sobs. The sadness I feel is cosmic in nature; I want to lay him down in a bed of flower petals and tuck him in. I suppose tucking a child in bed is its own erotic misadventure, but my sadness reverberates through all the levels of existence, through eternity, to the very heart of god. I give him a hug, and that seems to help; he clings to me as to a meaning. When he's feeling better, he asks me to watch while he jumps off the play structure, does cartwheels. He is more beautiful now than ever, because more complicated and sad.

He follows me around. He adores me, and I him. I know that I will leave him; we all just keep on drifting farther and farther away. I want him to love men, not to love being hurt by men. I don't know why. I take him to the play corner and let him try on the costumes. He loves the wedding gown, and a wig of long blond hair. He is so beautiful this way, so butch and so femme. He's as gold as the sun. I'm a beautiful princess! he says. Yes, I say. You are a princess. You are a princess for real.[86]

Leonard invites me to his apartment for meditation practice, but when it comes time I tremble. Plus, I want to hurt him because I love him. I call and say, Leonard I can't come.

Silence.

Is there something physically wrong with you? he asks finally.

---

86. I have looked carefully at one of Stephen's author photos and I believe I detect a faint scar on his forehead. It might, however, simply be a shadow or a trick of the light. —JOB

I have headaches, I lie, but immediately recant.

I'm exhausted, I say. From imagining being with you. Fantasizing about your presence takes so much of my energy that I can barely stand to actually be in the same room as you.

Don't play games with me, he says.

I go.

His apartment is as lavishly and artfully furnished as I always imagined it would be.

You worry about punishment in this world, you can't be free, he says. Isn't that what it's all about for you? Learning to be free? But maybe you should be learning to find freedom in slavery.

You still want to interpenetrate the surface of the real, he tells me.

Hell isn't silence or darkness, he tells me. It's a swarming of images, flashes you only think you see, ridiculous phantoms.[87]

During our meditation the phone rings. Leonard's screening. It's his mother, he doesn't pick up.

How could you come over and drink everything in my refrigerator and not even let me know? she demands. How dare you!

---

87. By this point in my life, I have made peace with my own solitude. My marriage was a disaster and I have been, for all effective purposes and for many years, a single mother. As much as I love my son—despite his psychological problems, his moods, his rebellious behavior—our shared life is not a replacement for the company of a reasonable adult. Dealing with this problematic manuscript has left me feeling at times frightened and alone. So many times I have called up Brian in the middle of the night when I've been unable to sleep. There's something going on in this text, I sometimes tell him, something creepy and strange. Jake Yoder cannot exist, he must not exist, I am convinced of that. Increasingly, however, he enters my dreams. In the middle of the night, when I can no longer cling to the reassuring sound of Brian's voice, I sometimes visit Jake Yoder's Facebook page. It's always there. I look at the list of his hundreds of friends and I wonder: Why has he ignored my friend request? What have I done to Jake Yoder? Jake, of all people, should understand that doubt is a necessary form of love. I'd go so far as to say that his existence takes its meaning from the force of my doubt.—JOB

Although he maintains his lotus position, Leonard's eyes pop open.

Look at what a crappy son you are, his mother goes on. Where are my grandchildren? I don't want to see you over here for a long time. I'm so angry. Selfish. Ungrateful . . .

At this point Leonard smashes the phone into the answering machine. A piece of the broken machine hits me in the head.

Should I go? I ask.

He doesn't call me for weeks. I vow I won't call him first.

It will soon be winter.

It is so beautiful to be hungry on the first cold night in October. Hungry for something. The first cold night in October will make you so tired. The sadness of everything and all the aloneness. You'll want to curl up in bed at eight in the evening. You'll want to weep in a church.

I wander into a small grocery store, the Busy Bee.[88] Every time I go in there for toilet paper or orange juice, it's as if I've entered a strange spiritual void. Frank Sinatra is always on the radio. The store is vast and poorly lit, yet the shelves are practically empty. Sometimes there'll be nobody in sight, no other customers, not even an employee, and I wander past the empty, unused deli case, past the empty refrigerators to the back of the store and instead of Frank Sinatra it'll be some weird talk radio. *Has it ever occurred to you that selling Amway is a form of legalized gambling?* I think I'll be sucked into some wormhole, never to return.

And would it matter?

All of the nothings I have filled my life with are an attempt to convince myself they add up to something. Do The Math, an ad

---

88. There once existed a grocery store of this name on Valencia Street in San Francisco, just around the corner from an apartment Stephen stayed at in the mid-'90s, on 18th Street. —JOB

for free checking says on the sides of buses that drive past, full of despondent workers. $0(0) + 0 \times 0 = 0$. Cootie Dentata and Teeny. They're kind of narcissistic, do they really know me? Esther and the rest of my cousins? Forget it. The band? The men I've slept with or murdered?

Zero.

And inside myself? What is there to be known? Only this hollowness that grips my throat and stomach from the inside, as if pushing my edges out into the farthest reaches of space.

My insides are zero.

This is all related to a feeling of nostalgia for the way I was crushed and depressed earlier in my life. As a femme, as a weak nothing, as a lonely, sensitive child in a cold world. The wind and dry cold out there and no snow or maybe just some freezing rain. Alone in some house, where the only warm place was bed. I longed for morning when I could go out, drink coffee, feel alive for a minute. Peering into faces, none of them peering back.

I've found the answers to all the questions I've asked. Even the question of how to live, in a general way, but nothing still to help me with the hollowness on the first cold night in October.

I just want love.

I break down and call Leonard in the middle of the night. The phone rings and rings. His machine is still broken. I listen to the permutations of the dial tone instead.

Left to my own devices, I fall into terror, stray down deceptive paths. Leonard said I was almost ready. I was learning to exist in error, which is proper for a femme. Only once I've realized the falseness of everything about myself and emptied myself completely will I be ready to be filled with his knowledge and love. But without Leonard's rather conservative despair to guide me, I sometimes waste days and nights traveling bleak or pleasurable mental paths that aren't serving my larger journey. I read in my collected works of Henri Michaux: *Exorcism, a reaction in force, with a battering ram, is the true poem of the prisoner. In the very space of suffering and obsession, you introduce such exaltation, such magnificent violence, welded to the hammering of words, that the evil is progressively dissolved, replaced by an airy, demonic sphere— a marvelous state!*[89]

That sounds nice. *Am* I a prisoner? And if so, of what do the walls consist? Osmosis is one process through which the walls of cells lose their significance. A kind of madness. The transfer of genetic material between species would be another. I'm paranoid about robots! I'm not sure if I can fully grasp the nature of my unfreedom, or imagine what freedom might be. You discover that intercourse with the world is painful if you are raw and naked and vulnerable. People look at you, see your weakest spots and destroy you without killing you or loving you. You devise a mask or masks as a defense and discover the subtle possibilities of hide and seek. It isn't that there is any face that isn't a mask, but some masks fit you better than others, I decide during one of these periods. They are more organic to your bone structure. Weeks later, when I have the courage to reveal this thought to Leonard, he'll just frown as if to say I am on the wrong track altogether.

On my own, I journey.

I journey through a false and beautiful geometry limiting the plausible and the news. The world is hollow, as if an imaginary grid frames a brilliant emptiness; it isn't the emptiness that is hideous, for it shimmers. It's the surfaces of the grid, which are painful and nauseatingly real. The sun is a dark sun and the earth is a dark earth. As if the nothingness that preceded this and from which it emerged was an ugly nothingness. The paths multiply, and I'm an indecisive

---

89. A Michaux quote serves as the epigraph to Stephen's novella *Some Phantom.*—JOB

femme. There are as many possible stories as there are gestating fetuses of monstrous new forms.

I'm in a cemetery. The snow is falling.

Tortured generations. Bones and stories of martyrs. Frozen earth cold hill dead generations. I feel trapped by something immaterial. A conscious cloud weaving an icthyoid web? A coded fossilized word-tangle tracing hollow calligraphy? The cold earth. The wind in the barren branches of trees. Inscriptions on the tombstones. On and on and on. I wander toward the cemetery's edge, picking pretty wildflowers that grow in the spaces between tombs.

The faces of my ancestors appear in the sky, encased in iridescent bubbles. Bleached, bearded males float above this desiccated landscape, their sky pathologically celestial: blue and white and full of rainbows. Kind of New Agey. The old folks are distraught, screeching at me: Turn back! Do not enter! Danger!

The paths down below are forking deeper and lower into both the imagination and the real. I'm guessing they lead into various levels of hell and a range of apocalyptic scenarios. While I'm not really down with the program of annihilating everything, I'm thrilled by the gesture of risking it. The pure emotion. It's all about gesture for me. But I'm having predictable doubts. The ancestors are so butch, the ancient, the dead; wouldn't they have more stable and realistic goals than a pathetic femme like myself? They think technology is bad, television and film. Aren't you overstimulated? they ask. Yes, so many fragments bombarding me, I give up, I cede control to the images. Treating human beings like slaves seems reasonable as a means of preventing planetary disasters. My desire for absolute freedom is irresponsible, allegorical, and morbid. But don't all belief systems = thought control? Maybe I have issues with intimacy, that's what Cop said. That's only one way of viewing the function of personality in the world. Or is this my little trick to avoid the pain of honest self-examination? As you descend lower into hell, the need to love burns more intensely. Everyone I've ever loved and ever will is there—we mutilate each other, willfully. Are human relationships hell? Baroque landscapes shimmer in the distance. Another femme skips down the path, turns back to face me. She looks just like me, but with a different color hair. What, she says, you going to stay up in this cemetery *forever*?

Her last look, before she vanishes through a door in the ruined wall, is accompanied by a wink. I count my blessings: the cemetery is familiar, sheltered, almost warm. A boy I almost recognize is submerged in shadow here, the sort of boy people mean when they use the word "dreamy"; beyond I can just make out a cow's head with its two big horns at the top of an inn. What a long, unhappy time will have to pass before we can become "one." The boy wanders along the path; he looks forward to the solitary walk as a flight that will bring him respite and repose. I rejoice in his step, still so joyful, triumphant and free; I rejoice in his step, wherever he may go.

I remember: I am just a child. Don't open the red door, somebody tells me. Whatever you do, don't open the red door!

What fireworks explode in our wake, what ejaculations, while the red door is still open behind us. History, the past mistress of life, will not trouble to record our departure.

I go into the deserted place.

I am at sea.

The captain wears a patch on his eye, he's abstract and dizzy, yet he's only the boy. He welcomes me aboard. I want to know if a femme can be a pirate.

Do you have a conscience? he asks.

Like all femmes, I'm empathic, I say. And so my conscience is overly complicated. It's like a breathing fossil organ. It's like sedimentary rock and vapor.

Many femmes have lived as pirates, he says. It is easy for a clever femme who is willing to wiggle his hips and pout to secure a position on a pirate ship. We can always use another empath. We are children and criminals. We strive to be free.

We travel in a ship made of bones through a sea that turns red every night as we sail further west and the last rays of light create the sensation that we are sailing on blood. The smell like a lake where a woman has drowned. The ship's flag like rotating stamp collections showing fragile geometries created by alien faculties. Our flag is a skull and crossbones or a mutating fetus in the womb or a winged reptile or a lightning bolt in the brain. Every evening we raise a different flag as Venus shines in the west and the moon rises and the blood stinks.

Then, it is night.

We sail through a framework of vague amnesiac continuities burrowing through strata and overlapping layers. Self-erasing language mutates into hidden architectures or vanishes altogether. Angels ascend and descend, echoing traceries of starlight, a vast curving stairway. I know nothing of who I am, for it doesn't matter. The source of the night and of the ocean on which we travel is the stories and self-questioning poems told by handsome sailors or skeletons. As they chatter on, I am led by my blackest thoughts. I look over colorful maps, ancient charts of milky warm rivers. There's an ornate inscription in the upper left hand corner: the Sacred Jester immersed in some telescopic wave forms. That look in his eye. One handsome sailor says they had stolen a bunch of cattle; they left behind but one thing. One handsome sailor says his sister pushed him off a different ship and stole his lover. One handsome sailor says that a ship is slowly being built of the bones of the buried dead. One skeleton says that when the ship is completed, the world as we know it will end. The captain shakes his head. He seems saddened by what imaginary numbers and imaginary populations bring. He seems saddened by what has become of everything. "Everything" has managed to put its flesh and blood on a structure of bones, has brought the big No, kisses boys. We sail down the aqueduct, retracing a path. The moonlight reflects off the roof of an underwater car, the color of blood. A hand reaches out from the water but then vanishes beneath the waves. Whoever was in that car is dead, a ghost, she's free, she's still here. She's always here, because nobody ever leaves. We leave the corpse behind. The night is absolutely dark and the water so still that it perfectly reflects the stars.

I am on the river.

The children on the ship are involved in rituals of monstrous creation. They feed in order to participate in the Night. Bony children, jerking off. They become possessed by others, a distinct entity. As a femme, I crave possession too. My most heinous crimes are only incantatory dances designed to invite possession by my sacred personality. What is this entity's name? Is it a butch entity? Is it collective and imaginary? Is it *like* language or *related* to language? These questions are boring; I want to be terrified.

On the river banks, we see the ruined walls of a strange temporary fortress, recently burned. I'm inside a spooky tale of adventure. Silence and mysterious waves of dread. This is where the entity had been buried. His coffin was attacked by a vampire who could also light fires. A call is produced from the multiple vocal cords of the children, to his allies. Vultures are circling. The ship lands; who died here along these prison walls? The entity asks if we intend to take the son of God in there with us? To break free of our mother? Weird laughter. We all tremble. I ask: We're seeking *consciousness*, must we go forth and know? He is silent. Is he me? The globe beneath us as ant-like and enigmatic as the moving stars' lights. The vampire leans over him. It crafts in his neck two narrow grooves. Mocking, entitled. Imagine ridgelines where their and my eyes become resurrectionary organs.

Things flow together in wild frenzies of nightmare adventure. We rip open a goat's body and eat it raw, covering ourselves and the ship with entrails and blood. We rip open our identity—it is penetrated, torn apart and scattered by the great and terrible something or other. I am in the world of constant fluctuating energies, raw consciousness, which form and matter are related to in a less necessary way than I had previously intuited. All I care about is ecstasy, whose doesn't matter. I flow into we flow into rippling nothingness waves of will and intent, power and pleasure. I am everything here: nothing. There are so many possible life forms; I'm the river itself. We fuck: machines animals cells atmospheres stories and sixth-grade teachers. We wear: clown masks gas masks ski masks wolf masks pirate patches scars and stories. We take it: like a woman like a man like a child. We murder: future species forgotten selves paperboys pretty flowers and happy endings. We kill children because we are children and we want to know what Death is. We know what Death is already. During the orgy, however, some of us only nap or quilt or explore new music. Some of us only tell stories that serve as a counterpoint or critique of the orgy itself. Ecstasy doesn't really require blood. These words are here to tell us how we dream, what life is, what time consists of, but these words have been exposed as an unnecessary mask, hiding the fact that it is all obliterated, it is all nothing. We don't know who we are.

We are without sin.

Dateless night turns to dateless day.

The river sparkles in the sunlight: a river of stars.

I am in space.

Space is a web, a trap. Space is infinite and inevitable and very lonely. Everything exists there. Nothing doesn't. In space you'll come face to face with it, you'll send back messages that arrive years too late. In space, you'll be kept in suspended animation, you'll travel at the speed of light, and everything you care about will pass away. What will be left of you then? Practically nothing, but you have to give it. You have to participate. Space must be transformed.

You feel that there exist particular pieces of knowledge that are crucial to your gaining what is rightfully yours. Where you must grow is not where you want to grow. We travel on and on, under the blazing heat, and our fascination increases. We grow more hungry, not less. We pass over, beyond indifference and boredom, into the play of impossible musics. You feel that the same thing that comforts you limits you. The area of your greatest success is where you'll find your secret enemy. You feel that destroying the ground you stand on will force your self to change. At the same time you know this is insane.

I see femmes eating corn and turning golden. I see femmes become machines which are arrayed in a dazzling technological landscape of gear, wheel, whirring, clicking, and singing. I see bronze and organic shapes like the sparkling and sinuous forms of lava that a volcano vomits up from hell. I see the idea of femme tortured, and so the actual femmes of the earth subordinated to the idea in a vast dazzling choreography: icy, ethereal, and anorexic. It hurts too much. It isn't necessary or true. I'm becoming so elaborate! I look down at myself, thrilled to see both the male parts and the female parts.

I penetrate myself.

Yes.

The red door leads only to the world. It is hideous and dazzling, everything I long for, everything I fear. It's so real; I'm so afraid. Dissonance, a music of desperation and innovation, an impermanent architecture. Reinvent love! The collapse of untenable frames.

Leonard said to me the time would come when my desperation would become a source of light and love. He said that I wasn't handsome or beautiful, I wasn't very attractive at all, yet I was the one he wanted. He promised to wait for me, but I doubted him. I can no longer bear the separation. I can't bear another moment of my aloneness. I am up in my bed, eating blueberries straight from the carton. Suddenly, I can bear it. Suddenly the pain is delicious.

The pain is a mystery and a gift. Everything is redeemed in the quivering light of presence. I've been up all night, thinking the strangest and silliest things. Now, all of those thoughts are like insubstantial webs. In the morning light the world has settled back into its somewhat more stable, thank God, shapes. The world is not abstract, it is here in front of me. Blueberries. I look at the blueberries closely. I have never really seen a blueberry before.

They are blue.

I put on my shoes and throw on an old ratty sweater, my favorite, although Leonard said it made me look like a *hausfrau*. That's exactly what he said, a *hausfrau*. The morning is overcast and warm, streets still empty, the light diffused, as if loving everything it touches.

My quilt shimmers in the light. On a bench in the park, I wonder what should go between my square of purple silk and my square of maroon velvet embroidered with gold peacocks. I wonder if one should live constantly with the idea of Death as a companion. I wonder if my quilt should contain meditations on the ten foul things. It's kind of busy, my quilt. I saw a black fabric with a print of leering skulls somewhere, and try to recall where it was.

I have become what I have always been: a country girl in a field of light rain.

I want to give my secret night as a gift.

I meet Leonard inside of his school. He looks exhausted, as if he's been up for nights masturbating.

You're ready, he says. You're a perfect receptacle for my manliness. You're perfect and I want you. Meet me in my bed in one hour.

Perfect? I say.

At least you aren't quite so deluded, he says. You never talk about your fantasy life as a murderous, child-molesting rock and roll star anymore. I think you're cured. I think you're as healthy as the next femme.

He gives me the key to his apartment.

The idea of making love to Leonard terrifies me. I feel complete now, almost as if I don't need anyone.

In order to live, I need to forget my visions. I let myself in to Leonard's flat.

When I saw you at the library that first time I knew you'd be good in bed, he says to me. He is sitting on his futon in his boxers. His chest is pale and slightly concave and he's shaved off his beard. My peasant vitality saves me from my potentially delicate emotions. He looks so different, so much younger and less severe, more androgynous and vulnerable.

In a way, I say, tonight will be my first time.

"In a way" is vast and absurd, but I want only to be a femme lying next to her sleeping man. I've always had to struggle against my tendency to become some man's slave. In men I sense the courage to be alive, which is also the fear of weakness.

I've come to a new beginning, I say.

We are in bed together. He is tender now and his eyes are full of light.

He lays me back on the bed.

I am pretty much filled with joy. Yet my gaze keeps slipping from his clear, almost colorless eyes to his chest. His pecs are saggy and covered with a black mat of hair; his chest is soft, and his belly.

He puts his tongue in me.

Give yourself to me, he says.

Wait, I say.

Something isn't quite right. Something isn't absolutely perfect. There's just one thing, I say.

Hendrick Pruyt Burned in a Boat

ANYWAY. WE WERE DISCUSSING our future as a band.

Songs which will psychoacoustically meld with the listener's nervous system, someone said.

I hadn't been paying attention. I didn't recognize all the faces. What big ears that one has! They were talking about hand-drawn waveforms. You take a picture of a sound and reproduce it on an intensity-over-time graph. It's like two wormy squiggles smeared across the page, the left and right halves of a stereo image. Cootie Dentata was comparing our musical evolution to the structure of a brain; that's what you get for collaborating with a medical school dropout.

Appendages just get glommed on, she said. They aren't pretty, but they work. Some functions are redundant, or they work at cross-purposes. But out of all that mess, you get something unexpected ...

I couldn't filter anything out. I couldn't focus. No particular thought was especially compelling. They drifted past like clouds.

Someone dismissed certain melodies as conventionalized portrayals of common emotions. Someone else experienced the destiny of music as if it were a wound. I was back in the corner, the drooling, daydreaming granddaddy.

They turned on me.

We'd like to change the band's name, they said. They: a rebellious, faceless collectivity. I didn't know them or care. Perhaps they had strong feelings about the religious qualities of the human voice. Taboos about mixing it with instruments.

Love Muscle, they said. It's so phallic? We don't feel it accurately reflects the needs and desires of the new membership? We aren't an all-male society anymore.

Oh, I said. OK.

Braced for something cute, ironic. Brazen Hussy or Filthy Lucre or Resin Hits.

The auditorium was packed. We'd modified the stage of bones; we'd had them create a translucent blue stage around the intertwined skeletons, illuminated from the inside and covered with flowers. Improbable flowers, fragile and expensive flowers, scabious flowers, all of them blue.

I'd like to perform a new number, I said.

The spotlight fell. From some other place altogether emerged the lyrics of absolute poison, of seductive anti-grammar and parched lava landscape. The neural feedback station in the egg-shaped thalamus controlling brain-wave rhythms. A pendulum between the primal grunt of sexual menace and a complicated silence. I mesmerized them, still. Cootie Dentata and all of the felons were naked and wrapped in strings of blue lights. We moved like liquid. We moved like music. Radiant.

I was absolutely beautiful. The audience watched me dancing

and their hearts sank. They wanted transformation, they wanted ecstasy and radiance, and all I had to offer was something false and horrifying and beautiful and true.

After the show, I announced my retirement. The press assumed I was dying or so fucked up on protease inhibitors and medical marijuana I could no longer function.

My bandmates expressed regret but didn't try to talk me out of leaving. Cootie was both writing and singing most of the songs anyway, her fierce interrogation of the horrible interminglings of colonialism, Catholicism, and the rest.

Constant mutation and excess, I guess is what I believed in. I rode a motorcycle out into the foggy morning and down the coast.

Fields of glimmering green brussels sprouts and artichokes. They'd put huge cardboard cutouts of laborers in the fields to make the work seem dignified and romantic, flat and enormous people, very John Steinbeck, very César Chávez. Perhaps the nostalgia for "labor" distracted tourists from the actual workers who might muddy up their view. I was traveling fast enough anyway that all of human life seemed both sensible and blurry. Journeying through the underworld to rise again.

Or maybe not.

On the way back, I became feverish.

It was winter. It was night.

I arrived here with the others, and you.

It is night. Always.

Rats scurry about the towns. Humans are gathered around bonfires. At least I like to think so, but I don't really know. We're in an old lighthouse complex down the coast from the city, a hostel now. Several buildings clustered around the actual lighthouse, nicely painted blue and white, fenced in. A sheer cliff with a warning sign (DANGER SHEER CLIFF STAY BACK) and a narrow trail down to our own walled-in beach. If you tried to make your way down in the dark, you might easily plummet to your death. Ground cover of succulents, rocks covered with sea kelp, crabs, anemones. These cute arrows point in every direction with signs telling us how far to Rio and Nepal and Berlin and Cape Town, if anyone cared. Rio is only 3,672 miles away. Inside, there's a relief map of California. There are old encyclopedias, outdated travel books, and *National Geographics*. There's a copy of *The Forest People* by Colin M. Turnbull, about his time among the pygmies. People usually stay here who are on their way somewhere else.

Did you hear our fellow inmates talking over coffee and papers? Pay attention to tenses! one of them said. What tense are you speaking in?

He seemed angry and impatient. I think they were working on cover letters, although I can't imagine why.

All I have left is you.

And look. The stars are coming out.

I don't want to find the world beautiful just because I'm dying. I'm afraid.

But not so much. My eyes are open wide, and I wander toward death in a dream, with no hopes or expectations.

It is winter. It is night. It's cold here. The early dark over the ocean is melancholy. It is tiring.

My brain is on fire. My virus must be mutating, becoming more virulent or less. Maybe the virus more clearly resembles barbed wire now, with vines and flowers wrapped around it. Or maybe it will no longer kill us, but transform us. We will become more complicated and the virus . . . I don't know.

It's creating a musical vibration within our bodies. Our organs are producing musical tones. But it isn't random. It's achieved a more profound level of complexity. There is a music in the machinery of this prison, the generator, the electrical surges, the telephone's ringing, the insects' songs, and the stars.

Nothing is silent, although silence is a part of it. If you pay attention.

When you hear something that nobody else hears, you can assume that you are mad. And when you are surrounded by death, but you hear a music in that death, which is both beautiful and unshared, this is when you turn into a monster. Like that man who killed children and recorded their screams, which he then incorporated into a more profound version of "The Little Drummer Boy."

Have I answered your questions? The early days. The road and the bones. You've finished your martini, I my vitamin drink.

It is night. But the sun may manage to disperse its meager share of winter light soon. I am drinking ginseng tea. There is a fire. When I first saw you, you were nodding off and you looked up at me as if you knew me. You're so far gone that you barely look human. Or you look so human that you're an abstraction of suffering. I recognized you right away.

I read to you from *The Forest People* about the faith of the Pygmies in the goodness of their forest world. I tell you that they express this faith in their great molimo songs. According to the book, these songs are sung fully only when someone has died. Their songs never ask for this or that to be done, for the hunt to be made better or for someone's illness to be cured. All they have to do is wake up the forest, and everything will come out fine. "But suppose it does not," I read, "suppose that someone dies, then what? Then the men sit around their evening fire . . . and they sing songs of devotion, songs of praise, to wake up the forest and rejoice it, to make it happy again. Of the disaster that has befallen them they sing, in this one great song, 'There is darkness all around us; but if darkness is, and the darkness is of the forest, then the darkness must be good.'"

I don't believe you've heard or understood a single word I've said. I sense disbelief radiating from your barely conscious mind. You think I lie.

You're right. I'm not a rock and roll star. I've never had much aptitude for music at all. I can't even play this imaginary guitar.

I'm not really a musician.

I'm a pirate.

Anyway, you've fallen asleep. You are dreaming your own incoherent dreams, solving your own imaginary problems, fleeing nonexistent enemies, or pursuing shadows. What sort of games must I play to make you come back? I'll do whatever it takes—you taught me everything I know. Nothing and nobody comes back. We all just keep on drifting, farther and farther away . . .

But imagine, you come back to me after all. Everything wavers for a moment, and you pat me on the head, ruffle my hair, your good little boy. What about *regenerate*? you say. Did you find a way to use *regenerate*? And what about *dormant*?

Everybody else is sleeping. Except perhaps the guards at the hostel gate. The butch guards, the femme guards; they aren't expecting any escape attempts tonight. Why it's so quiet here. When you are the only one awake it seems so improbable, all of them, sleeping. Warm under their blankets, but their toes are cold.

Cremation is preferred in these times. The earth is too cold to dig into. The crust is hard as bone. Whether or not I fertilize the earth, I am indifferent. Whatever happens to my cremains.

On the table, the staff has placed a lily in a vase.

Lily of the valley is not my favorite. Its white flowers remind me of Easter eggs. Lily of the valley is the sign of the Second Coming, the ladder to heaven, Jacob's tears. Elongated like a giraffe, a symbol of purity and humility, it seems a little bit false and conceited to me. When Mary cried at the cross, her tears became this flower.

If I cried at the mass grave of all of us, my tears would become a flowering succulent: bitterroot. It flourishes in barren clay ground and often regenerates from seemingly dried and dead roots. Deep pink to nearly white petals, an intestinal explosion from tubular capsules, low to the ground.

Or a scarlet globemallow. Velvety-hairy, round lobed leaves; flowers brick or orange-red like an underground sun. It is the beauty of hellfire and blood oranges. It is a flower not as deep as its coloring, but not overly demanding either.

Or a striped coral root. A kind of orchid, actually, which doesn't have any chlorophyll. It isn't green and has no use for the energy of the sun. Flesh-colored stems, striped flowers of pink and brown like some fierce and beautiful wildcat from a possible or impossible future. Beneath the surface of the ground is a tangled mass of root-like stems that may lie dormant for one or many seasons. Storing the nutrients that come from underground.

Any minute the alarm will go off. I'll lie here for a moment in the quiet of my room. It will seem for that moment like I'm crossing between worlds. Asleep or awake, the past or the future, the living or the dead. But then I'll get up. The wind will blow the door open with a bang. The stars may be visible out there. I'll travel through the blue moonlight or the hushed severe dark if there is no moon; maybe I'll take a journey. I remember the first time I saw the Milky Way. The stars are still a mild thrill, if I don't overdo it. If I ration my experience of them. I'll go out in the cold and commune with their icy light. I'm waiting, for the very darkest part of the night. My breath will warm my cupped hands. Not quite yet.

Adriaen Wens at the Place of Execution of His Mother

APPENDIXES

APPENDIX A: Jake Yoder's school counseling referral

SCHOOL COUNSELING REFERRAL FORM

DATE __10/29/03__ SCHOOL ▓▓▓▓▓▓▓▓▓▓

STUDENT'S NAME ▓▓▓▓▓▓▓▓ BIRTH DATE __NA__ AGE __11 or 12__

ADDRESS ▓▓▓▓▓▓▓▓ HOME PHONE ▓▓▓▓▓▓

MOTHER'S NAME __NA (deceased)__ WORK/CELL PHONE _____

FATHER'S NAME __Daniel R▓▓▓▓▓__ WORK/CELL PHONE ▓▓▓▓▓

PARENT'S EMAIL ADDRESS __NA__

STUDENT LIVES WITH __Stepfather__

TEACHER ▓▓▓▓▓▓▓▓ GRADE __6__

Reason(s) for referral:

[X] Motivation	[ ] Friendship	[ ] Absences	[X] Anger
[ ] Bullying	[X] Peer Relationships	[ ] Tardy	[X] Dishonest
[X] Swearing	[X] Inattentive	[X] Withdrawn	[X] Death
[ ] Divorce	[ ] Hyperactive	[ ] Stealing	[X] Fears
[ ] Fighting	[X] Social Skills	[X] Depression	[ ] Drugs
[X] Worries	[ ] Personal Hygiene	[ ] Perfectionist	[ ] other_____
[ ] Stressed	[X] Lying	[ ] Destruction of Property	

Concerns __Jake writes stories with inappropriate content,
including violence and sexuality. He writes about his
teachers and classmates in offensive ways and spends
time set aside for other activities working on these
"stories." Refuses to complete other Language Arts assignments
in a realistic way. Exerts negative influence on classmate he
is assigned to tutor. Withdrawn and frequently hostile. Moody.__

REFERRED BY ▓▓▓▓▓▓▓▓▓▓

PERMISSION TO PROVIDE SCHOOL COUNSELING FORM (date sent) __10/22/03__
(date returned) __10/28/03__

Principal Notified of Counseling Services (date notified) _____

Sullon ▓▓▓▓▓▓
Counselor's Signature

APPENDIX B: pages from Jake Yoder's partially burned manuscript

Sister has nothing more to say, and Brother has nothing more to say. In their heads, they keep talking. When their story is over, they'll never speak again.

Sister is sadder every day. She stare   the kitchen
window as   ening to the   sky. The haze
is fibro   pers and
things   cellar.
Her cr
month
fina
other   he
tells   The
hu   ple
and   peo   wheat and
no chaff. The evil   of every last
human. Everyone wi   same time from the inside
-- they will all li   ough unimaginable pain as an
entire 50% of their soul   oasted out of their very being.
Like   otomy for an ang   th a prost   le
     And then they will be   gs of light alone.

Interesting theory, thinks Sister, from a man who put his own mother inside a ref ige   nd told the world he would bring her back from the   er is not happy or

the cloud's core; other wisps form special shapes. Sitting in

his cell alone, the Golden Child understands that he is an

emptiness crisscrossed by zigzagging lines and untrue ideas.

Once he saw a movie about giant crabs who   cked the brains

and juices of every   they ate   his own style,

his bravery   tions about

messed   for the

voice

cell

prison   here

a black   ng

p

than the most u   g   e has

never seen it be   the birth and death of

galaxies; billions   f stars spread across time like

astral jelly; the egg-s   bits of Sirius and its smaller,

dead twin star as they o   ch other in a tense spiral

dance; the explosions of sup   novas more luminous for a second

or so than the rest of the universe combined. Maybe there isn't

enough love in all of spac   make up for his dead mother. The

stars echo with the saddest   ic, the most cryst   amples

STEPHEN BEACHY is the author of two previous novels, *The Whistling Song* and *Distortion*, as well as the twinned novellas *Some Phantom/No Time Flat*. His writing has appeared in the *New York Times Magazine, Chicago Review, Best Gay American Fiction, BOMB,* and elsewhere. Raised by an ex-Amish father in Iowa, he now lives in California and teaches at the University of San Francisco.

JAKE YODER is the nom de plume of a young writer who has chosen the humble servitude and anonymity of Amish life over the petty ego gratifications offered by the literary world. His influences include Jorge Luis Borges, Ernesto Sabato, Julio Cortázar, Juan José Saer, Silvina Ocampo, César Aira, Clarice Lispector, Heriberto Yépez, Antonin Artaud, the Notorious B.I.G., and Spacemen 3. His physical existence is as yet unconfirmed.